DATE DUE

DEMCO, INC. 38-2931

ALONE IN THE VALLEY

ALONE
IN THE
VALLEY

Kenneth Waymon Baker

℘

THE PERMANENT PRESS
Sag Harbor, New York 11963

Library of Congress Cataloging-in-Publication Data

Baker, Kenneth Waymon.
   Alone in the valley / by Kenneth Waymon Baker.
     p.   cm.
   ISBN 1-877946-17-6 : $21.95
   1. Vietnamese Conflict, 1961-1975--Fiction.   I. Title.
  PS3552.A4314A78   1992
813' .54--dc20   91-42101
                                                     CIP

Manufactured in the United States of America

THE PERMANENT PRESS
Noyac Road
Sag Harbor, NY 11963

This book is dedicated to Olga Medina, MD, the VA psychiatrist who kept its author sane, and to all those who left home as children to grow up in the jungle with rifles in their hands.

ALONE IN THE VALLEY

November 26, 1965

The Boeing 707 sailed westward through the clear blue sky above the South China Sea. Now that their journey was near its end, the teenage passengers were quiet. Youthful bravado that masked their fear throughout the long flight across the Pacific ebbed, then ended, after the plane took off from Clark Air Base in the Philippines. During the final two hours of that longest journey, the only sound in the cabin was the soft, steady drone of the jet engines. For a few moments more, the passengers would remain boys, boys afraid of the unknown that lay before them. But soon the plane would land, and they would begin the process that would make them men.

Of the hundred boy soldiers, no two could call themselves friends. They were assembled from scattered Army training sites, leaving behind the friends with whom they faced the challenge of becoming soldiers. Unlike the heroes of earlier wars, these boys would fight as individuals. They would face their anxieties alone, without friends to share their thoughts, their excitement, or their fears. When they reached the war, the Army would scatter them throughout the country. They would join existing units as replacements for men who fell before them; they were to be the outsiders who must fill the slots vacated by men who were integral parts of their units. Each boy would face the war alone, shunned by those who came before him, shunning those who came after him. For these replacements, and those that followed, the great danger would be not only to their bodies, but also to their minds. Whatever emotions war wrought, they would be endured alone. Anxiety would build without a comrade to serve as a release, for these new soldiers were going to war alone, and alone they would remain, alone until the end, whenever and whatever that might be.

The hundred boy soldiers would live a hundred different dramas, each one a tale worth telling. Some of those dramas would end too soon, cut short by one of war's deadly events. Others would grow to manhood before their dreams abruptly ended. And some would live to take the long flight home, to face a world they would never understand. Only the Author of all life's stories knew the details of what would happen to whom.

Of all the boys on board that plane, Daniel Perdue looked least like a soldier. His was a choirboy's face behind Army issued eyeglasses. His five foot seven inch body was made lean and hard by five months of intensive training which culminated with three weeks in Airborne School at Fort Benning, Georgia, just one hundred miles south of his home Atlanta. As if to emphasize the surrealism of war, Daniel Perdue was not just a soldier, but a paratrooper, one of America's best. He had succeeded in a training regimen designed to weed him out, and in the process he acquired more than the skills of a soldier. Above all else, he learned what every paratrooper learned, that his body could and would do whatever he required of it. Daniel had the skill, the confidence, and the determination of a paratrooper, but all the training in the world could not change his appearance.

Nor could it change the fact that he knew nothing about war, for training and combat are divided by a chasm called death. Military training, when done right, prepared the body for the rigors of war, but the mind could not be taught to go beyond exhaustion. Only war could teach one to think and act quickly, rationally, to do the things that must be done without fear, for fear slowed reactions and created thoughts whereas only deeds saved lives.

Daniel stared through the window at the ocean below, that vast, empty expanse that reached from horizon to horizon. He looked for another atoll like the one he had seen in the Pacific, an unchartered, unspoiled ring of white sand in an endless blue sea.

In time the blue water yielded a thin white string on its western edge. Slowly the string grew thicker and became a sand beach. Behind it appeared a nameless assemblage of thatched-roof huts. Then rice paddies spread out below the plane in quilted patterns, an endless patchwork plain bordered here and there by more nameless, isolated villages, some like islands in a sea of rice.

Along some edges of the paddies, the jungle began. Daniel saw only the top of the dense tropical rainforest, that canopy of trees so thick that there seemed no ground beneath it.

The plane began its long descent. More rice paddies spread out below. A large dike formed a causeway through a vast field, and from it grew innumerable tiny dikes, each forming its own design within the quilt. The sun reflected off a few flooded paddies, little lakes held together by dikes so small that the water seemed to be its own barrier.

The first person Daniel saw was a farmer tending his paddy. He wore one of those round straw hats that have become a symbol of the Orient. Accustomed to jets and their noise, the farmer did not look up.

As the plane dropped lower, the land below raced by. Daniel saw the first signs of western civilization, and war, but only in fleeting glimpses of that strange new world which would be his home for the next year, should he live that long.

There! A small clearing surrounded by barbed wire! Tents! Cannon! Army trucks parked side by side. And there: a building of some sort, gone quickly. A tank! And another! And roll upon roll of barbed concertina wire.

Lower still. The plane passed over the airbase perimeter. The barren earth was scarred by more barbed wire, and, behind the wire, bunkers and guard towers, and a dirt road snaking along the rear. Big green tents were everywhere. Lower. Tin-roofed buildings. Trucks and cannon, and now helicopters, raced beneath the plane. Then came the airstrip itself: more buildings and tents, and more helicopters parked amid stacks of sandbags. A row of camouflaged jet fighter planes, each in its bunker, appeared and was gone. Large rubber bladders of jet fuel streaked by, each surrounded by sandbags. Everything was surrounded by sandbags. The tents, the buildings, everything.

The plane touched down. More buildings and bunkers rushed by outside. More tents and trucks and fighter planes and helicopters.

The plane slowed and stopped; a stewardess opened the door. Without orders, the young soldiers stood and started for the exit.

The quiet tension of moments before gave way to excitement. Fear of the unknown yielded to the mystique of war. The fear in all their hearts was subdued now by the nonchalance boys display when they think they are supposed to be brave. But without that display, without that self-deceit, frightened children could not easily endure those first, tense moments of war.

The waiting, the anticipation, was over. The adventure began.

When Daniel stepped through the door of the plane and onto the ramp, he was hit in the face by the overwhelming heat and humidity. It stopped him in his tracks. Even his native subtropical Georgia had not prepared him for Viet Nam's tropical steambath.

"What's the holdup?" asked the soldier behind Daniel.

All the way down the ramp Daniel reacted to the heat, and he was totally aware that his khaki uniform clung to his instantly sticky body before he reached the bottom step. So strong was the impact of heat and humidity that Daniel's first step onto the soil of Viet Nam passed unnoticed. In the coming months, many unique moments would go unnoticed.

The new soldiers were led a hundred yards to a building, where they were told to wait. It was but the first of many buildings Daniel would see that had no windows, or, at least, no glass windows. The upper half of every exterior wall was screened. There would never be any cold weather to keep out, but there would always be flying insects wanting to get in.

Daniel sat quietly with the others, but his manner betrayed his youth. His eyes revealed the excitement he felt, an excitement born of childish innocence and the naive belief that death was but a scene in a movie.

Daniel was enthralled by the activity around him. Soldier clerks walked about with clipboards and stacks of papers. Trucks came and went outside. Cargo in a thousand shapes and sizes waited to be carried away. Officers scurried by without being saluted. Amid the hustle and bustle of war, Daniel sat and waited, just one more piece of Army equipment to be hauled away.

A group of GIs came in laughing and joking. They were going home. One of them looked at the new arrivals and yelled, "Forty-three minutes and counting, cherries!"

As Daniel watched them pass, he was struck by the disparity of their dress. Some were in new jungle fatigues that still had the oddly placed creases that develop during shipment to point of use. Others wore dirty and ruffled fatigues that displayed for all to see the results of months out away from the niceties of base camps and permanent positions. All had on their heads soft caps, but few resembled the army issue baseball caps that were so common on army posts in the States. Most were crushed and wrinkled as though they had been rolled in a ball and sat on for a week; others were new, but an odd shade of green and a shape that gave them away as being local products. The soldiers looked little like the clean, crisp formations back home.

Those who were headed home looked, too, at those who were just arriving. Whereas Daniel's reaction to the veterans had been one of silence bordering on awe, the veterans' reactions to Daniel and his comrades were vocal and crude.

"God damn!" one veteran said loudly. "Did you ever see such shiny fuckin' boots?"

"Fuckin' A," agreed another.

Said a third, "So that's what cherry fuckin' boots look like. Look at the fuckers."

Daniel glanced at the old soldiers' boots, which were scuffed and worn, but he reacted more to the language used by the veterans. Daniel was not raised in a monastery, and he was not offended by profanity he heard occasionally in his youth, but he was not prepared for the casual, and repeated, use of what, in other places, would be considered filthy language. He recalled that soldiers in the States had not used profanity in the same casual manner, as if the words were no longer profane. He wondered what circumstances could change people so, for he could not imagine that so many soldiers had all arrived in the war zone with the habit of extreme profanity already so richly developed.

The shorttimers moved on and home. Daniel and the other cherries sat and waited for transportation in the opposite direction.

"Damn, it's hot!"

The soldier sitting beside Daniel spoke. He removed his cap and used it to fan his face. Seconds later, he continued.

"Don't the wind ever blow in this country?"

"I sure hope so," said Daniel, also suffering.

"I'd give ten dollars for a shower." He raised his voice in hopes that someone would hear and respond, "And when do we eat?"

When the question went unnoticed, Daniel offered a hand to shake and spoke, "I'm Daniel Perdue."

"I'm Griswald. From St. Louis."

"I'm from Atlanta."

The budding conversation was cut short by a young sergeant, "Listen up, cherries." The sergeant spoke loud enough to be heard over the din that filled the area, but his words lacked emotion, as though he had said them a hundred times. "Pick up your dufflebags and follow me. When we reach the trucks, you are to put the bags and yourselves on the trucks. Any questions? Move out."

The group followed the sergeant out of the building and around a corner to where two deuce-and-a-halves were parked.

Griswald spoke up, "Come on, Sarge. There ain't no way in Hell we'll all fit on those trucks."

The sergeant looked at him as a babysitter looks at a foolish child. "Unless you're the base transportation officer, cherry, your opinion ain't worth shit."

Griswald started to speak again, but the sergeant cut him off.

"Get on the fuckin' truck, private."

And Griswald got on the truck, packed in with the others as only the Army can pack. The trucks began to roll and Daniel looked back at the sergeant who stood shaking his head.

The ride to the processing area was not long, but to Daniel it was interesting. All along the way new and exciting visions of war appeared. Everywhere there was the beehive of activity that denoted a combat zone, and everything was surrounded by sandbags.

The cherries passed a truck loaded with soldiers armed to the teeth, a real combat platoon just in from an operation.

One oldtimer, perhaps only twenty years of age, yelled at the fresh troops, "Seventy-one days and counting, cherries!"

And another, "Lookie! Fuckin' civilians!"

Others just glanced up and shook their heads. Some paid no attention at all, too tired to have an interest in new soldiers who seemed very young, very inexperienced, and very, very clean.

Moments later the truck turned into an area of closely spaced tents and jerked abruptly to a stop.

Another young sergeant, no more than nineteen, walked up to the trucks, "Okay, cherries, this is it. Everybody off."

Daniel and the others jumped down from the cramped truck and began stretching.

"Fall in. Fall in," the young sergeant ordered. "You're still in the Army, you know."

The young men formed three ranks, then stood at rigid parade ground attention while the sergeant looked them over.

"Listen up," the sergeant ordered. "From here over," he pointed, dividing the group in half, "you bunk in that first tent. The rest of you are in the other one. After you stow your gear, I suggest you locate the nearest bunker. In a while you'll be called for chow, so hang around the area and don't get lost. Anybody who don't hear the call don't eat. Fall out."

The men moved into their assigned tents and chose bunks, then followed the sergeant's advice and found a bunker that was convenient.

Daniel returned from the bunker and was sitting on his bunk when Griswald walked in.

"Well, boys," he announced, "I found out where the EM club is. Anybody want to go grab a quick beer?"

Several men agreed and started for the door. Griswald stopped and looked at Daniel.

"Perdue? Right?"

Daniel nodded.

"You coming along?"

"I'll pass this time," Daniel answered.

"Suit yourself," Griswald said as he turned and walked out of the tent.

Daniel sighed. Fortunately, he had not had to admit that he did not drink beer. He had tried it only once and it had made him sick. He resolved that he would acquire a taste for beer before he left this country, or, at least, learn to tolerate it well enough to drink one socially. It was a resolution he would not keep.

Someone outside announced that it was chow time. Daniel and some others were up and out of the tent quickly, ready to follow blindly anyone who knew where the mess hall was.

The dinner was bland, even by army standards.

The sun was setting when chow was over and the men had returned to their tents.

They pased the evening in different ways. Two men left saying they would try to find the EM club. One sat down in the dim light to write home. Most sacked out, including Daniel. After a twenty-four hour plane ride, Daniel was content just to stretch out. Only a few minutes passed before he heard the snoring of one who fell asleep quickly.

Daniel lay on his cot and listened to the sounds outside. Somewhere in the distance a generator chugged noisily. A truck cranked up and drove away, the rumble of its diesel engine fading slowly. A faint, but distinct, explosion echoed across the compound. Daniel wondered if he was the only one who could not sleep.

Morning caught Daniel by surprize.

"On your feet, cherries," called some private. "Rise and shine. Rise and shine. Chow in the mess hall in fifteen minutes."

Griswald did not move.

The private kicked his bunk on the way out, "Rise and shine, cherry!"

Griswald rolled over and sat up, "I may rise, but I'll be damned if I'll shine."

Daniel was up and dressed quickly, eager to continue the adventure, and hungry enough to want to be near the front of the line at the mess hall.

Soon he was sitting on a bench at a table staring down at what he was told were scrambled eggs. They looked a lot like scrambled eggs, except that the color was not quite right. Daniel took a bite.

"Whatever these are," he said to himself, "they're definitely not eggs."

Griswald sat down beside him, "Top 'o the morning, Perdue. Lord, this looks good."

Without looking up, Daniel replied, "Looks can be deceiving. Try it."

Griswald took a big mouthful of the eggs and all but choked, "What in the Hell is this?" He shouted so loud that half the men in the mess hall looked around.

Daniel turned to Griswald, "The Army calls it 'eggs'."

" 'Eggs' my great Aunt Hildagard!" Griswald fumed, causing men all around the mess hall to break into laughter.

Some unknown person in the crowd called out, "They're powdered eggs, you dumb fuckin' cherry."

"Powdered?" Griswald asked rhetorically.

Daniel pushed his eggs around his tray with a fork, "They must have used talcum powder." He pushed the tray away, "All I really wanted was toast anyway."

Breakfast done, Perdue and Griswald walked back to the tent together and began to wait, for what and for how long, they did not know. Griswald went to sleep on his bunk.

Sometime in the midmorning, the young sergeant stuck his head in the tent, "Listen up, cherries! Your assignments have been made. Everybody out front with your gear at 1030 hours."

He ducked out. Moments later, Daniel heard him say the exact same words in the next tent.

Daniel commented to himself, but aloud, "NCOs are a creative lot, aren't they?"

At the appointed time, Perdue, Griswald and the other new men formed up in front of the orderly room. An overweight first sergeant emerged from the tent with a clipboard. Several men, including Daniel, came to attention even though no order was given.

"Stand at ease," the first sergeant ordered. "When you hear your name called, holler 'yo,' then form up with your gear over by those deuce-and-a-halves." He paused for a moment, then continued, "The following personnel are assigned to the First Cavalry Division. . . ."

He called a lot of names. He was still calling names for the First Air Cav long after Daniel heard his name and moved over to the trucks.

The young sergeant appeared and told Daniel and the others with him to load up. As they pulled out of the area, Daniel looked at Griswald and saw him wave goodbye.

Daniel waved back. He felt a pang of sorrow when he realized that Griswald and he would not be together. The loud and agressive Griswald had been the perfect antipode to the soft-spoken and passive Daniel, who realized only upon their parting that he would have enjoyed their becoming friends. As the trucks rumbled along, Daniel wondered when he would find the friend with whom he could share the excitement.

The trucks pulled up to a different part of the airstrip and the soldiers were told to dismount and form up. The roaring engines of a C130 Hercules cargo plane all but drowned out the young sergeant's order. When the ranks were formed, the young sergeant issued one last order. "On the plane, cherries. It's time to go to war."

The men marched onto the plane through the lowered rear ramp, which closed behind them.

After takeoff, the Air Force loadmaster volunteered information. "You rookies are headed to An Khe. That's up in the Central Highlands." He paused, then smiled. "That's where all the shit's been lately."

The first time Daniel flew in an airplane he jumped out of it. He was in the third week of Jump School at Fort Benning, Georgia, less than two weeks earlier, when he boarded a C130 for his first ride in an airplane. Forty-five minutes later, he made his first parachute jump. The circumstances then were such that he had not observed the inside of a C130; he remembered only the four rows of seats, one against each side of the plane facing in, the other two back to back in the middle facing out.

Now he was sitting on the floor of a C130. The plane had no seats. As he sat, he began to notice the plane around him.

The C130 Hercules was a remarkable aircraft. It could take off and land on almost any unimproved runway, carrying almost any cargo that would fit into the large, barren chamber that was the inside of the plane. The cargo bay was stripped, devoid of frills and modern conveniences. Metal supports dominated the interior, while mile upon mile of brightly colored wires snaked along the walls. There were no windows for sightseeing, no hostesses to serve in-flight meals. They could be loaded so full of soldiers that the huge cargo bay became a cramped and stifling cage, and when they flew at low altitudes, that cage bounced and bumped and the passengers were shaken unmercifully. The C130 was designed as a cargo plane, and there was little chance that Pan Am would ever use one for passenger service.

The flight seemed to last forever, but eventually, just when nausea was becoming the general condition, the plane began its descent. No seats meant no seatbelts, so Daniel and the others held on to whatever they could as the plane rumbled and shook its way towards touchdown.

Even though expected, the magnitude of the impact as the plane hit the runway surprised Daniel. Then, quite suddenly, the propeller blades were reversed and the passengers were thrown forward in a pile, like so many old rags.

The craft slowed down and the troopers righted themselves. When the C130 stopped and its ramp lowered, the men gladly abandoned the plane and formed up in the mud. Only minutes passed before an old staff sergeant began calling names and assigning the men to vehicles. As Daniel listened for his name, he watched a line of veterans walk from a nearby area to the plane he had just exited. Having brought new soldiers to war, the C130 would now take old soldiers home.

Soon Daniel and five other newcomers were loaded on a three-quarter ton truck, the army's version of a pickup, and proceeded along the muddy roads of Camp Radcliff, three months earlier a mass of jungle, now the home of the First Cavalry Division (Airmobile).

The truck passed the chopper pad and Daniel got his first good look at the craft which were the lifeblood of the division. Row after row of tactical helicopters, Hueys, were lined up in their stalls, each surrounded on three sides by sandbag walls. Big cargo helicopters, the Chinooks with their two rotors, were nearby in another neat row, each of them protected by sandbags.

A formation of four Hueys flew directly over the truck, blowing dirt and pebbles around like four small tornadoes. Daniel stared up at them, fascinated by the roaring engines and blowing wind. He wanted to shout! Isn't that incredible, he thought. But the noise was great, and the others in the truck, like Daniel, were unwilling to behave like boy scouts on a camping trip. But then, the oldest among them was no more than nineteen, and anywhere else in the world they would have been called children. Only here, only in the army, were they treated like men. Daniel, like the rest, wanted to be sure that whatever he might do, he would do it like an adult.

Away from the chopper pad, Daniel watched the camp through which he rode. There were no buildings anywhere, just tents and more tents. And everywhere mountains of supplies, equipment and munitions. They passed an area of uncleared jungle, an acre of primeval rainforest, a place not yet of need to a unit that was just settling in. In every direction could be seen a thousand facinating objects and activities, each one worthy of a few minutes observation.

But the truck turned off what was, for now, a main thoroughfare and moved noisily up a small hill. It followed the path down into a small hollow and across a temporary engineers' bridge over a rapidly flowing creek, grown large by the water that fell from the sky that day.

Up from the stream and around a turn the truck rolled to a stop in an area covered with GP medium tents arrayed in neat rows. In front of one tent was a hand painted sign that read: Headquarters, 2/8th Cavalry.

The driver instructed his passengers to dismount and wait, then he went into the tent. In a moment, a career sergeant, "lifers" they were called, came out with the everpresent clipboard. He looked at the clipboard, then at the six replacements.

"Welcome to the Second of the Eighth, troopers," he announced without emotion. Then he turned towards the tent. "Butler! Get out here."

A young airborne clerk appeared from the tent, followed by the driver.

"What's up, Sarge?" the clerk asked.

"Replacements."

"Ah, fresh meat for charlie."

"The first two go to A Company," the sergeant said, "the second two to B Company and the last two to C Company."

"Roger."

"Hand carry them so they won't get lost," the sergeant ordered, then turned and went back into the tent.

"Right away, Sarge," the clerk answered. "Follow me, cherries."

The small group started off, then the lifer reappeared and shouted, "Hurry back, Butler. I need that report by 1600."

Daniel followed the clerk, not knowing where his name appeared on the list and therefore not knowing to which company he would be assigned. When two men were dropped off at A Company and two more at B Company, he knew that his address for the next twelve months would be C Co, 2/8th. Butler led his squad of two across a small, makeshift footbridge that spanned the stream somewhat down from the engineers' bridge. The rain-swollen torrent battered the insubstantial structure to the point where Daniel feared that it might be washed away before they were across. But it held, and just up the bank from the raging creek they entered an open area surrounded by GP medium tents. The clerk brought them to a halt in the mud at a smaller tent that served as the orderly room for C Company.

"Wait here," he ordered before entering the tent.

Seconds later he came out, waved at the two soldiers standing in the mud, and walked back across the bridge.

The two privates waited.

Daniel pondered his situation. He wondered if the boy beside him would be the friend that he expected to find. He had already decided that war should not be faced alone. All the new and exciting things should be shared with a friend, preferably a life-long friend, someone whose perspective on events would be the same, someone who could understand the emotions and share the anxieties, the way it had been in those movies about World War II. Somehow, it just was not proper to arrive at war alone.

"Got a cigarette?" the boy asked.

"Sure," replied Daniel, reaching for the pack in his fatigue jacket pocket.

"I'm Terry Jenkins," the other soldier said, taking the cigarette and offering a hand to shake.

Daniel shook his hand, "Daniel Perdue."

"I've never seen so much mud," Jenkins said as he lit the cigarette.

Daniel agreed, "There's a lot of things here that I've never seen before."

Suddenly Jenkins pointed behind Daniel. With awe in his voice, he managed to say, "Look at that!"

Daniel turned, and what he saw made his mouth drop open.

At low altitude, heading towards the chopper pad, a Chinook roared through the sky. Below it hung a mangled Huey.

They were still watching the two helicopters when the First Sergeant called their names.

"Jenkins and Perdue?"

"Right, sergeant," Jenkins replied, still looking at the helicopters.

"Perdue, First Sergeant," Daniel answered as he came to attention.

"I'm First Sergeant Everett," he said in a voice as rough as his complexion.

Oliver Everett was a large man, more than six feet tall and well over two hundred pounds. His hair was cut short, and what there was of it was gray. He was forty-two years old and had been a paratrooper for twenty-four of them. His face was long and narrow, with a nose that dominated his appearance not by its size, but by its shape; it had been broken the first time during a barroom brawl in England in nineteen forty-four. The incident preventing him from participating in the airborne assault that was part of the Normandy invasion. For five years he complained about missing "the Big Drop," until another paratrooper, even bigger than he, finally tired of his complaints and broke the nose again. After that, Everett never mentioned the episode, for, in truth, his complaints had covered up his relief at not jumping at Normandy. His unit had suffered seventy-three percent casualties in his absence.

The broken nose added to his aura. He was mean and liked to show it, but had managed to use bluff to avoid any actual fist fights since the second break.

First Sergeant Everett looked at his two new men. He thought, "God, they get younger and younger." He turned towards the tent, "Wilkerson!"

A voice answered from inside the tent, "Right away, Top!"

Everett looked at the two cherries, "My company clerk will take you to your platoons. After you get squared away, report back to him and he'll get your paperwork taken care of."

"Yes, First Sergeant."

"Wilkerson!" the Top Sergeant screamed, "Get your fuckin' ass out here right fuckin' now!"

Wilkerson emerged from the tent. He was of medium build, but had the angular features of a natural athlete. He did not look like a clerk; instead, he had the appearance of the high school football hero, the star fullback who bulls his way to the goal line and the winning touchdown. He had, in fact, played football, but he had been a second string offensive guard. The army had toned his muscles and trimmed his weight.

Everett gave his clerk a nasty look, more for the benefit of the two cherries than anything else. The First Sergeant knew that Wilkerson was not intimidated. The boy was not the army's best company clerk, but then, Everett was not the best First Sergeant. Wilkerson kept his boss out of trouble by always having things done on time, if not always done right.

"Take care of the troopers," Everett ordered. "I'll be back in an hour."

Without another word, the First Sergeant turned and exited the company area across the footbridge.

"You guys relax for a few minutes," Wilkerson told the two new men. "I'll be with you in no time."

With that, Wilkerson ducked back into the tent and left Perdue and Jenkins alone.

Daniel smiled, "Top's a peach of a fellow, isn't he?"

"Yeah," Jenkins agreed, "but right now I need to find a bathroom. You'd think these people don't ever piss."

Jenkins wandered off in search of a latrine and Daniel was left alone in front of the orderly room. He sat down on a small rock and waited.

A young veteran walked by and glanced at him.

"Hello," Daniel said.

"Hello, cherry," the soldier replied without stopping.

"I sure wasn't expecting it to be like this," Daniel said to himself. "Here I sit all by myself. It sure wasn't like this in the movies."

No, Daniel had not expected things to be the way they were. His knowledge of war, like most Americans', was derived from countless Hollywood movies. In the movies the men always had friends to share things with, except maybe for the star, who inevitably was the strong, silent type. Daniel recalled the movie, but not its name, in which the soldiers had all come together in training; it was there that the friendships had developed and the plots and subplots had formed; only then did they all go off to war together. None of the people he met in training were with him now. He wondered what part he was playing in this adventure, what role would he play?

"Maybe," he thought, "just maybe I'm the star."

He laughed. No chance. He was neither strong nor particularly silent. He was just one scared little boy trying his damnedest not to look like a scared little boy.

In the First Cavalry Division one six man squad produced greater, and more sustainable, firepower than the larger squads before the arrival of the M16 rifle, as much firepower as a full company in the days of the single shot muskets.

Firepower was paramount in small unit jungle operations. Even in the daytime individual positions were barely able to support each other; at night, adjacent units were too far away to provide any emotional support, even if fire support was possible. Other units on the perimeter would hear the action, but it is doubtful they would see it. If a two-position squad could not stand alone, it likely would not stand at all. Because of the increased firepower of the six man squads, patrols and ambushes were conducted by units much smaller in number than the squads of World War II.

The overall fighting ability of the division was not impaired by the reduction in numbers of the men actually confronting the enemy. The addition of air mobility increased, effectively and in fact, the fighting capabilities of the unit over traditional divisions more conventionally organized. It can be fairly argued, if not proven, that the First Cavalry Division (Airmobile) was the finest fighting force America ever put in the field. It was, without argument, the most expensive.

Daniel waited for the company clerk with no thoughts of firepower or organization, nor did he anticipate the amount of information he would be forced to assimilate if he was to become a good soldier quickly. His training was behind him, but his-on-the-job training would be more important. Fortunately, like most of the sons America sends to war, Daniel was full of enthusiasm and afraid only of being a coward.

Wilkerson emerged from the tent as Jenkins returned from the latrine.

"Sorry for the delay," the clerk said amicably.

Perdue and Jenkins followed Wilkerson through the mud to the first platoon NCO tent, where Jenkins was left in the hands of his new platoon sergeant.

The clerk then led Daniel to the NCO tent for third platoon.

Occupying the tent were two career sergeants: Platoon Sergeant James Stovall was the acting platoon leader during the seemingly endless shortgage of second lieutenants; the other was Staff Sergeant Sylvester McDowd, acting platoon sergeant. They shared only sergeancy. Stovall was a poor black from Opelika, Alabama, with little formal education; McDowd was from Cleveland, Ohio, and had attended Ohio State University for a year in 1947–48.

Sergeant Stovall was thirty-five years old and had joined the army in 1949. The Korean War started during his enlistment and he made rank rapidly in the paratroopers. He achieved the rank of Staff Sergeant during the war and was promoted to platoon sergeant performing spit-and-polish stateside duty. He was underqualified for the rank he held and had no chance of ever making first sergeant, but the army was the first environment he had ever known in which he was treated as an equal, and he meant to stay in it as long as they would let him. Being sent to Viet Nam was something he had not counted on. His plan was to avoid dying.

Sergeant McDowd was older than Stovall and had been in the army longer. He was drafted in 1944, but he saw no action in World War II. Discharged in 1946, he spent two unsuccessful years as a civilian before reentering the army in 1948. He established himself as a good soldier during the Korean War, when he was wounded, decorated for bravery, and eventually promoted to first sergeant E8. McDowd was less successful, however, as a peacetime soldier. A series of minor incidents culminated with his going on a three day drunk on an overnight pass; he was busted to corporal. By 1959 he had regained the rank of platoon sergeant E7 and had married a German girl. She divorced him in 1961, the subsequent depression and drunken binge resulting in his hitting an officer. Busted all the way down to private E2, McDowd enjoyed two years without responsibilities. But he was too good a soldier to languish forever in the netherworld of the enlisted ranks, and he quickly gained rank for the third time. He made staff sergeant E6 when the First Cav was formed at full strength from the old 11th Airborne. More than anyone else in the company, McDowd looked like a paratrooper, an appearance even his balding head could not alter.

Daniel followed Wilkerson into the tent where Stovall and McDowd were "resting" from yesterday's arrival at the Brigade NCO club, housed temporarily in a tent, of twelve cases of Kentucky bourbon from the United States. Stovall had a hangover, but was awake; McDowd had not arisen for the day, having slept through breakfast and just now having missed lunch. Stovall fully expected to recover in time for the operation which began the next day, but he was not so sure about McDowd, who had outdrunk him three to one.

16

"Got a new man for you, Sarge," the clerk said to Stovall.

The sergeant slowly looked up, then said, "Take him over to Rose."

"Sure, Sarge," Wilkerson replied. "Top said that was some party at the NCO club."

Stovall ignored the comment and gently lowered himself back onto the cot. A soft, unintentional moan marked the sergeant's head reaching its resting place.

The clerk smiled. "Some party." He turned to Daniel and motioned for the cherry to follow him.

They exited the NCO tent and walked to the next tent over. The platoon tent was a GP medium. Eighteen folding cots filled its interior. Assorted trash littered the dirt floor, residue from the previous night's celebration. The first night back in base camp always was marked with a celebration of sorts. The NCOs enjoyed their bourbon while the enlisted men consumed beer at the tent being used as the enlisted men's club.

The first cot on the right as they entered the tent belonged to Sgt. William Aaron Rose. Bill Rose was a handsome young man, six feet tall. He possessed the trim, hard body so common among paratroopers. The changes that had occurred within him as he experienced war did not show on his freckled face, nor in his bright blue eyes. His short red hair curled down slightly at his forehead. His nose was barely larger than perfect and his thin lips formed an almost permanent smile.

Rose had acquired that smile as a teenager working in his father's butcher shop in Queens, New York. His father had demanded that he smile all the time, whatever the situation might be and however he might feel. The father's reasoning had always been directed at pleasing the customers; a smile put the customers at ease, and a frown might cause them to take their business to another of the shops within walking distance. Deep inside, however, the father was concerned with other things. He was preparing his only son to be Jewish in what the father perceived to be a gentile world. The elder Rose had grown to adulthood in Germany in the years preceeding World War II. He had watched his neighbors be carried off by the Nazis one at a time. The fear that gripped the Jews in his village became a part of the growing boy's personality, a form of paranoia that never left him. Just a boy, he could not understand the politics, nor the evil behind it. In his innocence he believed that if he could just smile at those people that somehow they would leave him alone. When the boy had the chance in 1938, he fled to France, and then, in 1939, to the United States. The elder Rose settled among the Jewish community in New York City and, through hard work and determina- tion, had achieved a modicum of prosperity. Through it all, from Ger- many to Queens, he believed that smiling had somehow made people like him and help him, and, although he never talked of the old country, he instilled in his son the defense he had learned there, the defense that had served him so well. Knowingly or not, the smile served Bill Rose well, too, causing all who met him to like him.

The one outstanding exception was Sergeant Stovall, who disliked all Jews equally, if not intensely, for reasons he never knew and made no effort to understand.

When Daniel Perdue saw Bill Rose for the first time, the squad leader was cleaning his M16.

Wilkerson spoke to Rose, "Sgt. Stovall said to give you this new man."

"Thanks, Wilkerson," Rose said as he put down the rifle. "I'm Bill Rose, your squad leader," he said as he stood and offered Daniel his hand. The clerk left the tent.

"Daniel Perdue," Daniel said as they shook. "Glad to meet you."

"Drop your bag on that third bunk," Rose said, pointing. "Did you get to eat lunch?"

"No," Daniel answered.

"You missed chow at the mess hall, but there's some Cs around."

"Cs are fine with me."

"Over here in the box," Rose said as he sat down. "Do you have a P38?"

"A what?" Daniel asked.

"A little can opener?"

"I guess not."

"I think I saw one in the bottom of the case, unless somebody's already got it."

Daniel walked back to Rose's bunk and knelt down at the opened case of C rations beside it. Only four meals remained from the twelve that came in the case. Daniel chose a box of boned chicken and moved the other boxes around looking for the can opener.

"I don't see a . . ." Daniel hesitated, "what did you call it?"

"A P38," Rose said. "There are one or two in every case. We'll get you one tomorrow. You can borrow mine."

The squad leader reached in his pocket and withdrew one of the small little can openers.

Daniel went at the can with enthusiasm, having eating little of the powdered eggs that morning and having passed lunch by more than an hour.

"Where are you from, Perdue?" he asked.

"Atlanta, Georgia," Daniel answered as he chewed.

"I went through Advanced Infantry Training and Jump School in Georgia," Rose remembered, "but I never got to Atlanta. Is it a nice town?"

"Okay, I guess," Daniel said between bites. He had, in fact, nothing to compare his hometown to. The army had provided his first extended travel. "Where are you from?"

"New York City. Queens, actually."

"I've heard of Queens."

"When you finish with your Cs, I'll take you to the supply sergeant and we'll get you your gear."

Rose returned to cleaning his rifle while Daniel ate.

But for a lone soldier asleep in the rear, Daniel and Sgt. Rose were alone in the tent.

"Where is everybody?" Daniel asked.

"In An Khe."

"What's An Khe?"

"The village just outside camp," Rose explained. "We came in from the field yesterday and they gave us today off."

"What's in An Khe?"

"Not much. Some bars and a few shacks of ill repute. And as much junk as you could possibly want."

Daniel continued to eat and Rose finished cleaning his rifle.

When Daniel scraped the last bit of chicken from the can, he said aloud, "Lord, that was good."

Rose smiled. Quite some time had passed since he had last heard C rations called "good." He saw Daniel looking for a place to throw his trash.

"Just toss it back in the box," he advised. "We'll have to clean up the whole tent tomorrow."

Daniel disposed of the empty can, then took a pack of cigarettes from his shirt pocket. He removed the last cigarette and crushed the empty pack.

"Where can I get some cigarettes?" the new man asked.

"C Rations," the sergeant answered.

Daniel had seen the small pack of four Kool cigarettes in his C ration box, but they were not his brand. He had learned in training that cigarettes came in Cs, but he did not yet know all the different brands that were provided, nor how often any one brand appeared.

"What's the chance of me swapping for Winstons?"

"Not good," the sergeant said. "Almost everybody smokes either Winston or Marlboro."

Daniel grimaced.

"Well, not everybody," the sergeant volunteered. "Some of the guys smoke menthol; they'll swap. But you'll likely end up like the rest of us: smoking whatever you can get." An idea occurred to Rose; it showed on his face. He reached into the C ration case at his feet and rummaged through the trash. He picked up two four-packs of Camels. "Unless you can smoke these," he said as he tossed them to Daniel. "Nobody, and I mean nobody, likes these things."

Daniel put the Camels in his pocket.

"If you're ready," Rose said, "let's go to the supply tent and get you some gear."

The two young soldiers walked together across the company area. The novice of age eighteen followed the veteran of two months' experience to the supply tent, which stood beside the orderly room tent.

Inside the GP medium was virtually every type of military equipment that the infantry could use. A cot was on either side of the door, and beyond was a mass of confusion negotiable only by the supply sergeant who had supervised it's creation. A slightly pudgy, forty-year-old sergeant sat on the bunk to the left.

"Hiya, Woody," Rose said. "Is Sgt. Canella around?"

Staff Sergeant Wendall Dunwoody was the company communications sergeant. He knew the workings of the PRC/25 radio as well as anyone in the division, and he was the only company level commo sergeant that could disassemble one of the things and repair it. Woody had been in the army since 1945 and had seen limited action in Korea. He appeared shorter than his five feet nine inches because of the spare tire he carried around his waist; his marriage after the Korean War had cost him his lean look, but he had carried the extra weight for so long that he was comfortable with it, and he could carry it as far and as fast as many of the younger, thinner paratroopers.

"Canella's in town," the commo sergeant said. "Can I help?"

"My new man needs gear."

"I can get it for you."

"Thanks, Woody," Rose said, "I appreciate it."

Woody put down the radio he was servicing and led the two younger men into the maze of materiel within the tent.

"What size pants do you wear?" he asked Daniel.

"28–29."

"I remember when my waist was twenty-eight inches," the older sergeant said.

"Grammar school?" Rose teased.

"Junior high," Woody laughed as he reached into a stack of jungle fatigue trousers and pulled out the correct size.

From an adjoining pile of jungle fatigue jackets he pulled a shirt and tossed both articles at Daniel.

"What size boots?" Woody asked.

"Eight."

Woody grabbed a pair of jungle boots and handed them to Daniel.

Daniel had seen jungle boots only in-country and had not had a chance to examine a pair closely. Only the toes and heels of the boots were leather. The upper parts were a synthetic canvas, which allowed the boots to dry more easily. Also toward that end, the boots had been designed with small holes on the instep; water in the boots squished out through the holes with each step. They were the second most functional piece of equipment that the army had developed for use in tropical climates.

Woody then handed Daniel the most functional piece of equipment he would receive: a poncho liner. It was made of a synthetic material that was soft and comfortable, but, more importantly, it had properties which were dear to every soldier in the jungle. First, it would dry out in fifteen minutes. Second, it was warmer wet than it was dry.

"Do you need a poncho, too?" Woody asked.

"Yes, sergeant."

Woody pulled a poncho from a stack nearby and handed it to Daniel. Then he led the two squad members through the rear flap of the supply tent. In back were two large metal conex containers. The big steel door of one was ajar, the other was locked. Woody pulled open the unlocked conex container and stepped inside. In a moment pieces of equipment began flying out the door.

By the time the sergeant stepped out, both Daniel and Rose had their arms full of the many packs, pouches, packets and straps that came together to form the infantryman's harness.

"That's it," Woody said as he closed the conex door. "If I missed anything, let me know."

"Thanks, Woody," Rose said.

"Thank you, sergeant," Daniel added.

Rose turned and walked back into the supply tent, followed by Daniel. Without stopping, the two passed through the tent and out the front. A few feet into the mud, Daniel spoke.

"Don't folks sign for things here?" he asked, remembering that throughout training everything he had received had been religiously recorded. "I spent half of basic training signing and initialing supply records."

"All you get here," Rose said, "is what you wear. If anybody needs to know what you've got, all they have to do is look at you."

Upon returning to the tent, Rose helped the new man put his harness together. Daniel took his suggestions like they were orders. In very few minutes, or so it seemed to Daniel, the harness was assembled.

"It will take some time before you get it adjusted comfortably," Rose advised. "It's got a different feel when you're loaded down."

"I feel like a character in a Sad Sack comic," Daniel said as he tried to look at himself decked out like a soldier. "I sure hope I don't look like one."

"Not as much as you did earlier," said Rose, "if that's any consolation."

Rose picked up Daniel's steel helmet and removed the plastic helmet liner. He handed the liner to Daniel.

"Can you adjust that? Or do you need help?"

"I learned how to adjust these things in basic," Perdue answered.

"I'll fix your pot," Rose said as he pulled an empty sandbag from beneath his bunk. "The thing shines like a beacon when it's wet, unless you cover it. They make a camouflage cover, but we didn't get enough for everybody. I have a sandbag on mine, too."

By late afternoon, Rose had transformed Daniel into a soldier. Daniel felt more a part of the unit just by putting on the jungle fatigues. He had felt, correctly, that his stateside fatigues had been a neon sign flashing "Cherry." He did not realize that his brand new jungle fatigues were a sign announcing the same thing, only slightly less brightly.

At last Sgt. Rose pronounced Daniel fit to be seen in public and the two of them sat down. Daniel lit a Camel and offered one to Rose. Rose declined.

"Now you're an official 'grunt'," Rose stated factually.

"What's a 'grunt'?" Daniel asked.

"A grunt," the sergeant explained, "is a rifleman in a rifle squad of a rifle company in an infantry battalion."

"Okay. But isn't something missing?"

"Sure," Rose replied, "but the charlies we ordered for your examination had to cancel out. But we're going back out tomorrow. You can get shot at then."

"Don't I get a rifle?"

Rose shook his head. "Brand new jungle fatigues. Brand new jungle boots. All this nice new equipment. There's just no satisfying a cherry."

"I figure with all those rifles you were talking about that I ought to have one."

"Tomorrow morning, Perdue. All the unassigned weapons are locked up, and Sgt. Canella has the key."

Suddenly, four very loud explosions shook the tent. Daniel dove for the floor, certain that this second day in Viet Nam would not be as peaceful as had been the first. His mind's eye saw mortar rounds landing everywhere and Viet Cong charging through the barbed wire perimeter.

Rose's laughter brought Daniel back to reality. Rose had fallen back on his bunk and nearly off of it and through the open side of the tent. He tried to speak, but could not. The sight of a cherry diving for cover was not as funny as Rose's reaction might suggest. The laughter had grabbed hold of Rose and for a few moments controlled everything, the way it can when the laughter itself becomes funnier than the event that caused it. Laughter was too rare among grunts, and was enjoyed to the fullest. Soon Daniel, too, was laughing uncontrollably, certain he had been wrong about the danger.

"I'm sorry, Perdue," Rose said as he regained his composure. "You're the first replacement we've had. It's been a long time since I've seen anyone duck outgoing."

"Outgoing?"

"As opposed to incoming," Rose explained. "Those were 155 howitzers firing from a battery not far away. You'll get used to it eventually. Before long you'll be able to distinguish the calibre of everything."

"I'll be happy just to tell outgoing from incoming. Does every new man make a fool of himself like this?"

"You're the first new man we've had. But you should have been here two months ago." He looked around to see if anyone might overhear him, then spoke softly. "In October, the whole damn division was cherry."

The relative quiet of an empty company area began to dissolve when the first of three two-and-a-half ton trucks loaded with troopers who had spent the day in the village of An Khe rumbled to a stop behind third platoon's tent. The behavior of the soldiers as they dismounted from the trucks varied from the loud and profane to the silent and sedate. The noisiest of the lot were those who had sought relief at the bottom of a beer bottle, but all contributed to the changing milieu. The calm disappeared not because of any orchestrated attempt to envelop the area with spirit, but as result of the increase in the numbers of persons present, much as a downtown area comes to life in the early morning when the city dwellers begin to appear on the streets in ever increasing numbers. There was no exact point at which an observer could declare the change to have occurred.

In one group the members of second squad entered the tent where Sgt. Rose and Daniel Perdue sat talking. Peter Paul Minniefield, a thin, almost feminine black man with glasses, led the way; he walked directly to his cot and began removing articles from his wallet and putting them into the new wallet he had bought in town. Immediately behind Minniefield came Benny Terwilliger, a lanky country boy with dirty blond hair; he, too, went straight to his bunk and began the changeover to a new wallet. Carlos Perez and Cedric Wilson entered together. Both were large men, but Wilson had the hard body of an athlete while Perez was soft, almost flabby. Both bordered on inebriation.

When Wilson saw Rose, he spoke in a loud voice, "Hey, Rose. You shoulda seen the ugly whore that Perez fucked. Ug-lee. Lord, she was ugly."

"No way, man," Perez countered. "You fucked the ugly bitch." He turned to Rose, "My senorita was el primo."

"El primo my black ass," Wilson laughed. "Ug-lee. The bitch didn' have no tits at all."

"You did not see her good," Perez argued, as if the privacy of the lady's chamber had somehow revealed secret charms.

"I didn' wanna see that ugly fucker," Wilson roared. "I was fuckin' a classy bitch."

Perez looked at Rose. "She was a peeg, that one."

"Fuck you, man," Wilson replied. "You're jus' pissed off cause my lady had some tits." Then he turned to Rose, "Big tits."

"Her ass was big, too," Perez said, demonstrating with his hands his judgement as to the width of her anatomy.

"You shoulda seen Perez' whore," Wilson declared in an effort to direct the conversation away from his brief companion and back towards that of Perez. Then to Perez, "You got bigger tits than she do." He reached out and tried to pinch Perez on the nipple.

Perez jerked backwards, "I cut you, fucker."

"Jump on up, motherfucker," Wilson challenged.

"At ease, you two," Rose ordered.

Rose knew that Wilson and Perez liked each other and that their playful rivalry usually ended in ominous threats. The squad leader had considered letting them go at each other just once, but they seemed to expect him to stop them. Once, when Rose had been paying no attention, the two had challenged their way to a confrontation; they had stood face to face with fists clinched and waited for Rose to put an end to it. Rose had ignored their noise, but the silence caught his attention. He watched a few seconds to see what, if anything, would happen; when he noticed that each of them had glanced in his direction, he assumed that they would stand there all day waiting on him, so he told them to quit.

Perdue had sat quietly and watched the two men exchange verbal assaults. He did not know that their exchanges were never physical; he had prepared his escape route through the side of the tent, just in case the two had come to blows.

When someone in the company area yelled "Chow time", Wilson and Perez immediately left the tent together and began running towards the mess hall. Both Minniefield and Terwilliger increased the pace of their activities noticeably.

"Come on, Perdue," Rose said. "I'll show you where the mess hall is."

Perdue stood up, relieved that whatever had occurred was over. "Lead on, Sarge."

The battalion mess hall was located across the footbridge from C Company in two GP medium tents. One tent was used as the kitchen and the other as a small dining hall. Makeshift benches surrounded the latter tent. Rose and Perdue moved through the service line with their mess kits, then found Wilson and Perez.

"I want you guys to meet our new man," Rose said to the two veterans. "His name's Perdue."

Perez waved his fork, but said nothing.

Through a mouthful of food, Wilson managed a greeting, "Hello, cherry."

Perez, at age twenty-two, was the oldest man in the squad, older than Rose by eleven months. He was just over six feet tall and had a slight bulge around his midsection. His jet black hair and dark complexion revealed his Mexican mestizo heritage, although he was born and raised in Southern California. Perez' mother spoke no English even after thirty years in America and he had learned the language in the heavily Hispanic public schools he had attended. He was easy-going, with a sense of humor more amusing to himself than to others, yet he retained a certain amount of bitterness derived from a childhood in the ghetto.

Perez was a Specialist Fourth Class (Spec4 or Sp4), a rank above Private First Class that the army had created to allow for promotions among enlisted personnel without granting Noncommissioned Officer status. Spec4 was the same pay grade as a corporal, but it did not excuse one from KP and other nasty duties that NCOs did not pull. Corporal had become a virtually unused rank, since the promotion above Spec4 was to buck sergeant; the only corporals around, and there were none in C company, were onetime sergeants who had been reduced in rank.

Sp4 Perez had been in the army longer than any man in the squad, he being the only one who was on his second enlistment. He had been drafted when he was nineteen and had re-enlisted when his two years were up.

"They gave me so much money," Perez said, "because the generals knew this war was coming and they knew they could not win it without me." He paused and the grin left his face. "But if I had known this war was coming," he added, "I would have told them to stick their gringo dollars up their fuckin' asses."

Perez was the squad's machinegunner.

Cedric Wilson was also a Spec4. He introduced himself.

"Wilson," he said. "From Motown."

Rose spoke, "Wilson's a drafted volunteer."

"A what?" Daniel asked.

"I was drafted by a judge," Wilson explained with a laugh. "He said I could join the army or go to jail. Ev'ry time the shit gets thick, I think, 'man, I coulda been in some nice, safe prison back in th' world.' " He laughed again. "And th' shit charlie thro's at us here is a whole fuckin' lot worse than the shit back on th' street. And man, my fuckin' street was bad." He filled his fork from the mess kit and then filled his mouth. As he chewed, he continued. "And th' fuckin' army don't pay worth a shit, either. They fucked me up, man. I went airborne for the extra fuckin' bread, you know, and they sent my fuckin' ass over here. I ain't had a goddamn break in years."

Wilson was the biggest man in the squad at six feet three inches and a lean two hundred and twenty pounds. He carried the squad radio and an M16.

Minniefield and Terwilliger sat down with the squad and began eating. The squad was all any of its members had in common, but the varying personalities and backgrounds, which would have precluded any relationships among them had fate brought any of them together in the peaceful United States, were subordinate to the dependency each had for the squad. They picked at each other, often without mercy, but rarely did any one of them separate himself from those with whom he must face the cabala of war, even at those times in base camp when other soldiers having similar peacetime lives were near at hand.

Rose involved the two new arrivals in the introductions.

"Minniefield. Benny. This is our new man."

Peter Paul Minniefield had the good manners of a Baptist preacher's son. He stood and offered a hand to shake.

Benny Terwilliger looked up and said, "Howdy," then continued eating.

Minniefield was eighteen years old. His narrow shoulders, and his high-pitched voice, made him appear smaller than his five feet eleven inches. He had grown up in back of the Baptist church where his father was minister. The church was small and poor, but the aging wood sanctuary in a Yazoo City, Mississippi, slum was all that Minniefield's father had ever wanted, his desires tempered by his lack of formal religious training. The Reverend Minniefield had given his son much responsibility in church affairs, and the boy had led the Baptist Youth Fellowship at the church. Peter Paul had been taught to play the piano and to sing in the choir, and one Sunday evening he had even given the sermon, but he had paid little attention to academic training. Out of the small town environment for the first time, Peter Paul had learned quickly of his intellectual shortcomings, and had decided while still in basic training that his GI Bill would be used to acquire a formal education before an ecclesiastical one. Although still intent on a career in religion, he was slowly, almost unconsciously, drifting away from the innocence produced by his childhood. He was, without doubt, the least infantry-looking of the citizen-soldiers.

Wilson jabbed Perez with an elbow and winked, then turned to Minniefield. "Tell the cherry how you got to be a paratrooper, Preacher."

Between mouthfuls of food, Minniefield told his story, "When I went to join up, they gave me all these tests, and I think th' only thing I got right was my name. Some big ol' white sargent kept yellin' for me to hurry up and finish, so I jus' gave him th' paper th' way it was. They wasn't gonna let me in th' army at all, cause of th' tests. I tol' that ol' sargent that my daddy was 'spectin' me to join. They jus' had to let me in. So he tol' me I could get in if I signed up for airborne. 'Sho', I said, thinkin' I was gonna be workin' on airplanes or somethin'.. Th' nex' thing I know, they's tellin' me to jump outta one of th' things." After a bite of food, he concluded his tale, "Scared me to deaf, I tell you. Scared me to deaf."

Minniefield carried an M16 and was, technically, assistant machinegunner, but in fact, he was not much of a soldier.

Soon after supper, the squad was settled into the tent. Rose and Perdue sat together on Rose's bunk. Minniefield worked on a letter he was writing while the other three squad members slept. Except for an occasional helicopter flying overhead in the dark, the company area was quiet.

"Any questions?" Rose asked.

"Does everybody here cuss like a sailor?" Perdue asked.

"It seems that way, doesn't it?"

"Except for you and the Preacher, there, yes," Daniel said.

"Benny doesn't curse much," Rose offered. "But then, Benny doesn't say much of anything."

"The strong, silent, Gary Cooper type?"

"Hardly," Rose laughed. "He's a strange case. Harmless, but strange."

"Strange how?"

Rose leaned back in his bunk and propped his head against one of the tent supports. Perdue lit a Camel, coughed, and settled back to listen.

"When Terwilliger was eighteen, he tried to join up but they wouldn't take him," Rose said. "He finished only the seventh grade and could just pass the test. Then a year later he was drafted. He took the same tests, but that time they let him in. He didn't complain about it, though; he was just glad to get in. He's from somewhere in the West Virginia backcountry and was glad just to have a job. I asked once why he went airborne, and he didn't even know how it happened, much less why. But he's a damn good soldier. He shoots his M79 like it was made with him in mind. I saw him drop a round in a hole that was a good three hundred meters away. He loves that M79; says it reminds him of his shotgun, the way it breaks open."

Three quick explosions rumbled through the tent. Daniel started to duck, but stopped himself. He looked at Rose and smiled.

"Outgoing, right?"

"Right, cherry," Rose agreed. "You're learning."

"For the life of me, I can't see how you can hear explosions that loud without jumping."

"Practice. Just practice. After you hear enough of them, you get used to it. Believe me, incoming sounds altogether different."

"If you say so, Sarge."

"We better turn in," Rose advised. "Tomorrow you get to go out on your first operation."

"What will we be doing?" Daniel asked as he stood.

"I don't know. They never tell us ahead of time."

"Security?"

"Naw. They just figure there's no reason to tell us until it's time." Rose kicked off his boots and laid back on his cot.

"Enjoy a full night's sleep, Perdue. It's the last one you'll get for a while."

Daniel returned to his own bunk and started taking off his boots. He noticed that every man in the tent had gone to sleep fully dressed. He decided to do the same, having no idea what might happen before dawn. He hooked his glasses across the tops of his boots and laid back on his bunk. The faint light of Minniefield's candle went out as he finished his letter and the tent was dark. Daniel lay awake and listened to the distant sounds of an army camp, hoping to hear the 155s fire again. After an indeterminate time, the artillery pieces began to fire; they fired long into the night. Daniel fell asleep trying to imagine how incoming might sound.

Daniel was awakened by the sound of rain beating on the canvas tent. He put on his boots quickly, then pushed aside the tent flap and looked at the sky. Thick clouds, varying from light to dark gray, rolled by overhead, reminding Daniel of the summer thunderstorms he had grown up with in Georgia; but these clouds held no lightning or thunder. The rain was heavy, but it fell almost softly, without the wind-blown sheets that had always accompanied the heavy rains that he had known. But here the rain fell straight down, even though the clouds moved rapidly across the sky; Daniel could not understand how rapidly moving clouds could release a rain that fell straight down. As the morning passed, the rain changed. For a time, the wind picked up and the rain fell even harder, harder than Daniel had imagined rain could fall, but then it slacked off and fell gently, like a soft spring shower. The sun peeked briefly through a hole in the clouds, but quickly the clouds closed ranks and the rain again poured down, straight down, smoothly, like a drizzle but with incredibly large drops.

After breakfast, Rose took Daniel to the orderly room to make arrangements for a rifle. While there, 1st Sgt. Everett told Rose to have Daniel ready by 1000hrs; the company was moving out before lunch.

In basic and advanced infantry training Daniel had used only the M14 rifle, a large, heavy weapon that was an improved version of the old M1 rifle of World War II fame. The first time he touched an M16 was when Rose handed him the one he would carry into the jungle that same day.

Rose and Perdue stood in the back of the supply tent, just inside the back flap, and waited for Supply Sergeant Dino Canella to return from a leisurely breakfast. Sgt. Canella was first generation Sicilian-American, lean and hard at five feet three inches. His jet black hair was a bit longer than any other man in the company and his nose was bigger. He had the dark complexion and rough face so common in the Mediterranean.

Sgt. Canella had, upon arriving in country, developed his own supply regulations. He had learned quickly that the tropics posed problems that the army had not anticipated. Everything mildewed in the humidity. Materiel that sat too long in any place, soon became useless; duffle bags holding the unused khaki and green uniforms became breeding grounds for mold, ruining whatever the soldiers were not wearing. Everything was written off as combat loss, since the situation did not allow for the men to keep and maintain the peacetime accouterments. Supply records for individual soldiers were pointless. The infantrymen were responsible only for what they wore, and as shirts and pants became unusable, the men were allowed to DX, Direct Exchange, articles that required replacement.

Sgt. Canella, therefore, was most concerned with insuring that the men in the field had everything they needed, and towards that end, developed creative bookkeeping techniques to satisfy division supply officers, whose interests were more administrative than military.

Sgt. Canella entered the tent and immediately demanded to know what Rose and Daniel wanted, "Whadaya need? Whadaya need?"

Rose hesitated one second too long, "I got a new . . ."

"Hurryitup. Hurryitup," Canella ordered in his rapidfire way, unaware, or not caring, that the two soldiers had waited for him for nearly thirty minutes. "The war won't wait. Hurryitup."

Rose spoke even before Canella stopped, "New man needs a rifle, Sarge."

"Rifles I got. Rifles I got. Bullets I got. Grenades I got." The sergeant stepped out into the rain and unlocked the conex container.

Rose asked, "How many magazines can you. . . ."

Canella interrupted, "Magazines I don't got. Gimme an hour." He gave the rifle to Daniel, "Grenades? I got grenades."

"Yes, Sarge."

Canella tossed to Rose two cardboard cans which held hand grenades. "Magazines I don't got. Gimme an hour. Gimme an hour. I'll get 'em somewhere. Gimme an hour."

"Thanks, Sarge," said Rose.

"Thank you, Sergeant," added Daniel.

"Wait!" Canella ordered, having found something in his mind, if not yet with his hands. "I got magazines. Not many, but I got magazines."

He led Rose and Daniel into the supply tent, where he began searching. "Here they are. Eight's all I got. Gimme an hour."

"Thanks, Sarge," Rose said again.

"Gimme an hour, I'll get more."

"We'll be back, Sarge," Rose told the supply sergeant.

Canella was lost in a search for something he had decided he needed to find and ignored Rose. Rose motioned to Perdue and the two of them left the tent and walked through the rain back to their tent.

"That supply sergeant's a character," Perdue observed.

"Yeah, a character," Rose mused, finding the description new, but exceedingly appropriate. "He is a character."

"Is he always like that?"

"Yeah. But he's a good man. You'll appreciate him more when we're out in the jungle."

"I appreciate him already," Daniel said as he followed Rose into the tent.

"Let me help you load your magazines," Rose offered after he had sat on his cot.

"Do you suppose you could show me how to take this thing apart," Perdue asked as he held out his rifle.

"You don't know?"

"This is the first time I've ever touched one of these."

"Really?"

"Yep. I was trained on an M14."

"I guess we all were. Here, let me show you." Rose took the M16 and proceeded to demonstrate how it came apart and went back together.

After a brief lesson on the workings of the M16 rifle, the two soldiers began loading bullets into the magazines.

"Consider yourself lucky," Rose said. "These things are more precious than gold. First chance you get, you need to scrounge around and try to find some more."

"Won't the supply sergeant get some more?" Daniel asked. "He said to give him an hour."

" 'Gimme an hour' is Canella's way of saying he's working on it. No body in the division has enough of these things."

"How many is enough?"

"How many can you carry?"

Perdue sat silently pondering the question.

Rose answered his own question, "You'll never have enough."

Rose opened one of the grenade containers and handed the grenade to Daniel.

"Be careful with these things," he warned. "Some fool in A company was playing John Wayne and blew himself up."

31

"It killed him?" Daniel asked like a cherry.

"Let me put it this way," Rose explained, "what they found of him was dead."

At 1000hrs the platoon sergeants were called to the orderly room and given the POOP by the company commander. They, in turn, passed the information along to the squad leaders, who gave it to the privates. As first and third squad leaders did the same, Rose called his men together at his bunk.

"We'll be moving out at 1130hrs," he announced. "The company will be on perimeter duty."

"All fuckin' right!" Wilson shouted.

"Skate time," Perez said with a grin.

"At ease, guys," Rose ordered. "It's not what you think."

The two talkers fell silent. They had learned that any duty can be dangerous and they were disappointed that whatever they would be doing, it apparently would not be sitting behind concertina wire on an easily defensible position. Perimeter duty was, as Perez had called it, el primo.

"First platoon has patrol duty," Rose announced. "Second platoon along with first squad from our platoon will be pulling garrison duty on Hong Kong Mountain. Us and third squad will be on the little mountain."

"Aw, shit," Wilson commented.

"It's gonna be colder than a fuckin' witch's titty up there in the rain," Perez moaned.

"Get your gear together; we're pulling out at 1130hrs," Rose announced. "We're going to fly up."

"All fuckin' right!" Wilson shouted again.

"Knock it off, Wilson," Rose ordered. "You and Perez get down to the supply tent and pick up our Cs."

"Can I go see if the supply sergeant got some more magazines, Sarge," Perdue asked.

"Sure, but he didn't."

The last second details necessary to prepare a cherry for the field made the squad late to the company formation. First Sergeant Everett had just called Sgt. Stovall to the front of the formation to ask the reason for the delay when Sgt. Rose and his men fell in to line.

The rain began to pour down, but Daniel was the only soldier that paid it any attention. He thought about breaking out his poncho and putting it on, then he decided that if no one else was doing it, perhaps he should not.

Daniel, accustomed to peacetime drill, had expected the first sergeant or the company commander, or someone, to yell "Forward Ho!" and lead the unit gloriously into the rain. Instead, the first sergeant went back into the orderly room tent and the company began moving out and across the footbridge without an order being given. Only when someone yelled to straighten up the ranks did Daniel know that the company was, theoretically at least, marching at Route Step. Apparently, Daniel thought, the army was not as sensitive about rigid marching formations in combat as it was in training.

The company marched the short distance to the brigade chopper pad, a natural clearing on a grassy knoll. The order was given to fall out and the squad began an indefinite wait for the helicopters. Daniel readjusted his harness, the short march having demonstrated that it was too tight in some places and too loose in others.

Daniel had never ridden in a helicopter, therefore he waited for the Hueys with greater anticipation than the other men. Of course, he made every effort to appear as disinterested as the veterans, but the choppers, the guns and the array of equipment were all new to him and exciting. No matter how serious the business of war might be, the little boy inside him was thrilled by the elaborate toys involved when grownups play soldier.

Daniel tried to be casual, but when he had finished with his harness, he was without busywork to use as camouflage. The other men all had ways to pass the time. Wilson ate C rations; Perez and Terwilliger dozed; Minniefield read his pocket Bible. Daniel was neither sleepy nor hungry, nor would his anxiety level have permitted reading even had he wanted to.

Rose noticed his new man's situation.

"Nervous, Perdue?"

"No," the cherry answered quickly. Rose smiled. "Well, maybe a little."

"We're all scared. It comes with the territory."

"They sure don't look scared."

"They are," Rose said. He puffed on a cigarette. "We all are, every time. After a while being scared don't show. You're in a hurry, that's all."

"I'm not in a hurry," Daniel said in defense. "I'm just tired of waiting."

The veteran knew. "We've only been here five minutes."

"It seemed longer," Daniel said sheepishly.

"You're in a hurry to find out what it's like out there. It's the not knowing that scares us all. Every time you go out, its new. You wonder if this time you'll . . ." He paused, then pointed at the squad. "They've been out there. They know what it's like."

"I guess my being new shows."

The squad leader took a last drag from his cigarette, then crushed it in the grass. "Being new shows on everybody," he said as he stood up.

Sergeant McDowd called out, "Saddle up, troopers."

Daniel rose to his feet and tugged at his harness. It felt better, but it still was not exactly the way it should be.

As the noise from the approaching choppers increased, Rose raised his voice, "Follow me and get on the chopper I get on."

Daniel stared through the rain at the roaring formation of Hueys as they came into the Landing Zone (LZ) in groups of fours. The noise and wind awed the cherry. The first four Hueys sat down as GIs from the other side of the LZ ran up and jumped on. Only brief seconds after touching down, the choppers were back in the air and pulling away. A second group came in and sat down. Again the noise and wind filled the senses; rainwater blown by the chopper blades beat against Daniel's face. In seconds, that group, too, was loaded and lifting off.

Rose pointed to the next group of Hueys and yelled to Daniel, "That's us. Stick with me."

The helicopters had not yet touched the ground when Rose started running towards them. Daniel stayed right behind him, fighting his way through the whirlwind and flying water. Just as the chopper touched down, Rose was at it and jumping on. The others in the squad mounted with no effort. Daniel jumped for the platform but fell short. Rose grabbed the cherry's harness and pulled him aboard. The chopper was off the ground and rising before Daniel had settled in.

Daniel looked at his squad leader and shrugged his shoulders, embarrassed that his first entry into airmobility had required help.

Rose shouted, "Don't worry about it." Then he tugged on his own harness and yelled, "Extra weight."

The first thing on the chopper that Daniel noticed was the doorgunner's M60 machinegun. The inside of a Huey was a platform six-foot-wide by four-foot-long. Behind the platform on either side was a doorgunner with his M60. In front of the platform was the cockpit, with the pilot and copilot in their flight helmets looking over a panel of dials and gauges.

Daniel watched the doorgunner shout something into the microphone in his helmet, apparently talking to the pilot. The roar of the jet engine made normal conversation impossible.

Then Daniel looked down.

Camp Radcliff spread out below him. He saw the tents and tiny men, and the equipment of war. The choppers flew over the company area and Daniel saw the nearby artillery battery that had scared him so. Off in the distance he saw the airfield with the few small spotter planes assigned there. Beside the airfield was the division chopper pad; Hueys and Chinooks were lined up there by the score.

The choppers passed over the division perimeter, a naked stretch of ground fortified by barbed wire.

Rose tapped on Daniel's shoulder and pointed at the huge mountain rising up just beyond the perimeter.

"Hong Kong Mountain," he shouted. He then pointed to a smaller mountain south of Hong Kong Mountain. "See that little one? We're going there."

Hong Kong Mountain rose up five hundred feet above the rolling hills around it. The mountain stood out like a tower in the ocean; it was, obviously, the most significant military position for many miles around. Camp Radcliff and the division had been located here because of the observation and communication advantages that the mountain afforded. Its summit commanded a view of every place within the perimeter. Every GI in camp knew of charlie's attacks upon it. The mountain, and its smaller companion, had been havens for the Viet Cong when the division had first arrived. Almost every night, charlie had fired mortar rounds and rockets at the airfield and chopper pad. Every day the infantry had swept the mountain's slopes and found nothing. On numerous occasions the VC had attacked the secured perimeter atop Hong Kong Mountain; once they even fought their way through the barbed wire before helicopter gunships had helped drive them off; eight troopers died that night. As the division settled in, the patrols around the mountain saw fewer and fewer signs of charlie. Well placed night am-

bushes made it more and more difficult for the VC to infiltrate men and
materiel in sufficient quantities to mount a ground attack; even mortar
and rocket attacks on the base camp were less frequent.

The summit of the big mountain was defended by a reinforced
platoon of infantry. A communications unit and a searchlight battery
were also stationed there.

Daniel never heard anyone call the smaller mountain by a name, it
being lost in the grandeur heaped upon its big brother.

No one in camp paid much attention to the little mountain, only half
as high as Hong Kong Mountain, although it too was a significant
military position. It was considered less important because observers on
the higher mountain could easily direct artillery fire at any attacking
force. Only twelve soldiers defended the summit of Hong Kong Mountain's nameless little brother.

Rose tapped on Daniel's shoulder, "When the chopper touches
down," he shouted, "get off fast!"

Daniel nodded that he understood.

Then their chopper went in. It was still several feet above the ground
when Rose yelled "Go!" and jumped. Perez and Minniefield were out of
the other side of the platform before the chopper touched the ground.
Daniel and Wilson followed Rose. Benny went out behind Minniefield.

As Daniel ducked under the blades and ran after Rose, the squad that
was being replaced ran past him onto the chopper. The back of Daniel's
neck began to sting, and he almost ran over Rose when the squad leader
stopped.

Suddenly the wind was gone and the noise from the chopper was
fading away. Daniel turned to watch the chopper fly off. As the Huey
swopped down below the level of their positions, he began rubbing his
neck.

Rose saw him. "I should have warned you that choppers blow dirt
like a sandblaster, and sometimes some damn big pebbles."

"Even when it's wet like this?" the cherry asked.

"Makes no difference," Rose explained, "but it is worse when it's dry
and dusty."

Having overheard the exchange, Wilson joined in.

"Just wait 'til you're attacked by a fuckin' shithook!"

Another chopper, carrying the third squad, swept into the small
perimeter. Having been pelted once, Daniel had learned the lesson. He
lowered his head against the blast and listened to the blowing grit
bounce off his helmet.

The four positions that covered the summit of the mountain were
divided between the two squads. Rose put Wilson, with the radio, and
Perdue at the position that faced east, the one that looked down upon

the base camp. He led Perez, Minniefield and Terwilliger around the crest to the position that faced south and put them there. The positions facing north and west were manned by the third squad.

Rose returned to the foxhole where Wilson and Perdue were dropping their gear and unbuckled and dropped his own harness.

Daniel stood near the hole and gazed down on base camp.

"You'd better start looking a bit closer," Rose warned.

"At what?" Daniel asked.

"At them fuckin' trees, you dumb fucker," Wilson answered.

"He's right, Perdue," Rose agreed. "You need to pay attention to what's happening up here and let the garritroopers down there take care of themselves. The only thing that should be of any interest to you is that treeline below the wire, and what might come from it."

The foxhole at the position was large enough for all three men assigned to it. Being a permanent position, each new group over the past two months had improved it. Sandbags lined the hole and formed a shield in front of it. A few yards behind the hole was a second hole, not as deep, but also lined with sandbags. It was there that the men not on guard would sleep. Two sticks to be used as tent supports were placed one at either end of the hole.

Beyond the foxhole, the ground sloped down to three rows of barbed concertina wire twenty yards below. Twenty yards farther down the slope was the treeline and the jungle.

"Perdue, break out your poncho and help Wilson put up the hooch," came the order from Rose.

Daniel helped, but mostly watched, the veteran combine two ponchos and string them over the stick supports. Rope appeared from somewhere, perhaps it, too, was part of the permanent position, and Wilson used it to tie down the sides of the newly created tent.

"Why do'n t they use a real tent for this?" Daniel asked.

"You ever tried to carry one o' them fuckers?" Wilson answered.

"No."

"And you never fuckin' will in this squad," Wilson said. "Them fuckers is heavy as shit."

So the poncho was for use as a tent, Daniel thought, rather than as raingear. It was not like this in training.

"Fuckin' nice hooch, huh, cherry?" Wilson said.

"It looks okay to me."

"Okay, the fuckin' cherry says," Wilson moaned. "Fucker, you don' know shit about shit."

Rose commented, "Compared to what you'll have out in the jungle, this is heaven."

Heaven, Daniel thought. If this is heaven, I wonder what Hell will be like.

The rain fell harder and the wind picked up.

Wilson pulled out a can of C rations and began opening it. Then he carefully balanced it on two small rocks. Between the rocks he placed a heat tablet, the odd smelling material used in the field to heat meals. Ignoring the rain, the veteran deftly lit a match and ignited the tab. Daniel followed the same procedure, but with less success. He was not yet able to negotiate matches in the rain, but he was never again quite so inept as he was that first time.

The afternoon passed uneventfully, but Daniel noticed a subtle change in the way the veterans treated him. In camp they had joked about his status as a cherry, but they had not ignored him. But now, outside the safety of base camp, they avoided him. Even Rose kept a polite distance. Daniel's attempts at friendly conversation were brushed aside, not meanly, but firmly. Finally, he forced Rose into a dialogue.

"What in the hell have I done?" Perdue asked.

"About what?" Rose replied.

"I must've done something stupid," the cherry surmised, "why else would everybody be avoiding me?"

"You're a cherry, Purdue. That's all."

"Do cherries have the plague or something?"

"In a way," Rose answered with a smile.

"What way?"

"The guys who have been here a while just don't trust a new man," Rose said. "Cherries are more likely to screw up."

"Anybody can make mistakes," Daniel argued.

"Mistakes aren't exactly what they're afraid of," Rose said, subconsciously omitting himself. "I can't explain it to you. You'll understand eventually."

"Eventually I won't be a cherry."

"Right," Rose agreed, then he turned and walked away.

Formal guard duty began at dusk. Rose assigned Wilson to the first watch; after an hour and a half, he would wake Perdue for the second shift; Perdue would pull guard for another hour and a half, then wake Rose; when Rose's time was up, he would wake Wilson and the cycle would repeat.

Wilson took up position in the foxhole and Rose and Perdue settled down in the hooch to sleep.

Perdue listened to the rain fall against the hooch. So many things filled his mind. He wondered if any charlies would attack their position; he wondered if he could actually kill a man if he had to. He wondered what real war would be like, if he could do the things that he had been trained to do without fear paralyzing him. He wondered if he would ever get to sleep.

The last thing he remembered before sleep surprised him was Rose putting a can of peanut butter and crackers in his helmet and wondering why anyone would possibly want to do that.

Daniel awoke when Wilson whispered his name.

"Perdue?"

"Yeah?"

"It's your guard," Wilson said softly. "Here's Rose's watch. Wake him at eleven."

Daniel crawled from the hooch and over and into the foxhole. Wilson took his place beside Rose.

The rain was still falling, but not as hard. Daniel looked out over his field of fire. He could not see anything; beyond the sandbags was nothing but empty darkness. His daylight perspective was lost in the blackness of night; he could not remember exactly where the treeline had been. The steady drone of the rain drowned out any other sounds. He sat with his M16 in his hand, his finger on the trigger and his thumb on the safety. He could do nothing but sit and look at the watch and listen, always listen.

Midway through his guard, Daniel decided he was hungry. He thought about the can of cookies he had saved from his evening C rations. He regretted not having brought it to the foxhole with him. In the darkness, he would have trouble finding it in his pack without disturbing Rose or Wilson. It dawned on him why Rose had put the peanut butter and crackers in his helmet; they would be handy when he woke for guard. Daniel decided that hunger was more important than embarrassment and crawled back to the hooch. He was rummaging through his pack when Rose spoke softly.

"What are you doing, Perdue?"

"Looking for cookies," Daniel answered.

"Do you suppose any charlies are coming through the wire while you're looking for cookies?"

"I . . . I don't know."

"Get back to the hole, Perdue," Rose ordered. "You can eat tomorrow."

Without moving at all, Wilson spoke, "Dumb fuckin' cherry."

Daniel returned to the foxhole without his cookies. He was still hungry, but he also felt very stupid, justifiably. He decided to light a cigarette.

As he crouched deep in the hole, he thought, "I won't screw this up. Nobody, and I mean nobody, will see me light this cigarette."

As if the rain knew Daniel was a cherry, it fell harder. Daniel pulled out a cigarette and a book of matches. Ten minutes later, the book of matches was used up and three soggy cigarettes had been thrown away, and Daniel had mumbled every curse word he knew.

Explosion in the distance! Two, three of them!

Instantly Daniel was up and straining his eyes to see if there was anything in the dark in front of the position. He listened for any sound that might be audible over the sounds of the rain. Explosions rolled up the hill and over the mountain again. Daniel decided that artillery must be firing from the camp below, but he still mentioned it to Rose when his guard ended.

Rose's comment was, "You'll learn, cherry. Eventually."

Back inside the hooch, Daniel thought about trying to find the cookies; but suddenly he was very tired. He was wet and cold more than he was hungry. He fell asleep trying to remember exactly where the cookies were.

Daniel slept soundly, without dreaming, but when Wilson called his name, he was instantly wide awake.

"Your guard again," Wilson said as he stepped back to let Daniel out. "You sure as fuck wake up easy."

"I always have," Daniel replied.

"I'm glad. I had to wake up Minniefield once and I thought the fucker was dead." Wilson crawled into the hooch and settled in. "That fucker sleeps like a fuckin' log."

Daniel moved the few yards to the foxhole and looked out over the sandbags and down the slope. The rain had stopped and the moon lit the clouds enough to give detail to the slope in front of him and the camp down below. The outline of Hong Kong Mountain rose ominously above him on the left. On his right he heard noises coming from the other position. Daniel listened to Perez call Minniefield's name several times, then something in Spanish. Perez then called Minniefield's name loudly twice. The sounds of movement followed, then Minniefield's silhouette appeared.

Daniel heard a single helicopter in the distance. He searched the night sky but could not find it. He saw a light moving below him; the chopper was flying lower than his level on the mountain. He followed it to the landing pad. When its engine shut down, the silence returned. A gentle breeze shook the trees; water fell noisily to the underbrush. It sounded like someone walking around out there.

In the darkest, quietest hours of early morning, Daniel sat wide awake.

In the emptiness, Daniel pondered this new experience. Never before had he sat anywhere with a loaded rifle in his hands. Never before had he waited to shoot anything, anyone, that might appear in front of him. Never before had there been people who wanted to shoot him just because he was, to them, on the wrong side of the barbed wire.

Perhaps there is within us still the hunting instincts of our primitive ancestors, instinct for survival experienced in peacetime only as fear. But in war, somehow, the instincts become a controlled intensity, an intensity that prepares the mind for instant reaction to danger. As if an unknown strength were suddenly found, Daniel had a feeling of self-worth, a new knowledge that he could survive in the most basic struggles of Nature.

The primitive instinct that made the earliest men the most efficient killers, but now lay buried deep in the subconscious of modern men, was being awakened in Daniel Perdue. And once awakened, it would never sleep again.

The squad stayed on the little mountain overlooking base camp for four days and three nights; on the third day, Daniel's nineteenth birthday passed without notice. The rain continued in the pattern of the monsoon in the Central Highlands: drizzle in the mornings, downpours in the afternoons, and little or no rain at night.

During this time Daniel began to learn some of the tricks infantry soldiers used to function effectively in the jungle. He stopped wearing underwear; neither shorts nor T-shirts ever dried out, and the retained moisture caused a strange rash known in its more severe stages as jungle rot. He learned the best way to carry C rations: the cans were carried in an extra sock that was tied to the harness. This solved a major problem that Daniel had encountered: In his pack, the C ration cans had joined forces with the rain to destroy the cardboard boxes that held his extra ammunition. Not only was the loose ammo a mess to carry, it would be extremely difficult to load into magazines rapidly during action. He was also convinced that Rose had been right about never having enough magazines; it took some time, but eventually all the M16 ammo he carried, 400 rounds/20 magazines, was in magazines.

On the morning of the fourth day on the mountain, Rose called the squad together.

"We'll move out today," he announced. "We're supposed to be relieved here at noon."

Wilson interrupted, "Are we goin' back to base camp?"

"Eventually," Rose answered, "but we have to run a patrol to get there."

"Aw, shit!" Perez said. "How fuckin' long are we going to be out?"

"Yeah, man," Wilson agreed. "They're fuckin' with us again."

Rose restored order with a curt "Cut the shit." Then he elaborated, "We're just going to patrol down the mountain and around the perimeter. We'll be in base camp before dark."

"All fuckin' right!" Wilson shouted.

"Start getting your gear together," the squad leader ordered. "And eat lunch early. We'll be on the move at twelve."

By eleven hundred hours the squad had struck the hooches and prepared their harnesses; they sat in the rain and ate chow while they waited on the choppers that would bring their replacements.

Just before twelve, two choppers approached the perimeter. Wilson's radio squawked.

"Roger. Out," he said into the handset. "That's the word, Sarge."

"Mount up, guys," Rose said. "Let's go."

With those few words, Daniel was about to enter the jungle for the first time. Seeing the other men do it, he pulled back the bolt on his rifle and made sure there was a round in the chamber.

Rose took the point himself and led the squad through the barbed wire and down the slope to the edge of the jungle. In no time they were engulfed by the heavy underbrush beneath the canopy and Daniel's world narrowed down to the few yards that were within his view.

The steep slope was thick with vines and bushes of shapes and sizes that would have been unknown to Daniel had he been able to take the time to consider them. The tree trunks rose up to form a solid canopy of limbs and leaves that hid the sky from the soldiers below. The rain created a steady drone above as it beat against the vegetation high in the trees; big drops of water fell in stages through the canopy, soaking the jungle floor.

Daniel slipped and slid down the hill, fighting his way through thistles and thorns. A thin vine covered with sharp, tiny thorns grabbed him and yanked him to a halt as it tore into his skin. He struggled in vain, for the vine would not let go.

"Damn," he muttered.

Terwilliger, the man behind Daniel, stopped to help.

"You done been caught by a wait-a-minute bush," he said.

In front of Daniel, Minniefield looked back and laughed.

Wilson, further ahead, called to Rose, "Better hol' up a second, Sarge. Th' fuckin' cherry done got himself caught."

Daniel struggled to free himself, but succeeded only when Terwilliger assisted him.

"Them fuckers is Hell, ain't they?" Benny said with a smile.

"You sho' gotta watch out for them things," Minniefield agreed.

Rose called back to the squad, "Keep it moving. Keep it moving. Let's go."

Some yards along the squad reached a patch of elephant grass. Daniel was struck by the length of it, in places more than six feet high.

As Rose created a path through it, he pushed it down into a flat, smooth surface. By the time Daniel reached it, a smooth, slick slide had been formed. The cherry's feet slid out from under him and he slid on his fanny towards Minniefield. To keep from crashing into the man in front, Daniel grabbed a handful of grass. He stopped himself, but the grass had extracted a price: his hand was cut in several places and was bleeding just slightly. The elephant grass was sharp as a razor.

Daniel was relieved when the grass patch ended and the vines and thorns returned. Although there was little pain, Daniel could not stop looking at his bleeding hands and arms. He assumed that the cuts were more evidence of his being a cherry, until he saw that Terwilliger had similar wounds.

Daniel felt like they had been traveling for hours when at last the slope of the mountain leveled out. A very few yards remained before the jungle ended and fields and rice paddies opened out for hundreds of yards. On the edge of the first paddy, Rose halted the squad for a rest.

The squad leader walked over and sat down beside Daniel, "How are you getting along, Perdue?"

Daniel was exhausted, dirty and still bleeding from a score of tiny cuts. "Okay, I guess," he lied.

"The first time you hump the boonies is always the worst," Rose consoled. "You'll get used to it."

Rose talked to Daniel without looking at him. The veteran's eyes continuously scanned the treelines in the distance. He lit a cigarette and leaned back. Everything rested but his eyes. Beyond a perimeter, breaks were for only the body, not the mind.

A few yards away, Wilson spoke to Perez, "You suppose the fuckin' cherry saw them punji stakes?"

"I doubt it," Perez replied. "He ain't seen nothing yet."

Wilson's eyes also watched the trees in the distance, "One o' these days I'm gonna stick my sef with one o' them fuckers just to get some fuckin' time off."

"Don't bullshit me. Go fuck the cherry."

"I ain't bulshitting, Perez. One o' these days. . . ."

Daniel did not see any punji stakes; then, of course, he did not know what punji stakes were. He was bothered that the veterans saw anything that he, too, should have seen. He was so distracted by the difficulty of the terrain that he paid little or no attention to war. He resolved to keep alert to the business at hand, regardless of whatever else he might be doing.

Being a cherry, Daniel thought, is dangerous.

Rose interrupted the cherry's thoughts, "You'll make it okay, Perdue. We've only got two clicks to cover this afternoon before we go in."

"What's a 'click'?"

Rose looked at his new man and shook his head, "A 'click' is a thousand meters."

"Right," Daniel acknowledged. He pulled out a cigarette and started to light it.

Rose whipped out a match and held it for Daniel to use in a move that totally ignored the rain.

Daniel asked, "Where were the punji stakes, Sarge?"

"There were a few just below the perimeter and some more in the elephant grass. Why?"

"I sure didn't see them."

"I'm not surprized. You were struggling pretty bad back in that bush."

"Sarge, I hate to sound stupid like this, but what in the Hell is a punji stake?"

Wilson and Perez broke out in laughter.

Rose's smile grew wider, but he managed not to laugh, "We'll probably run into some more along the way, I'll tell you about them when we do."

The afternoon downpour began.

Rose flipped away his cigarette and stood, "No sense in sitting here in the rain, guys. Let's move out."

After a few groans of complaint, the squad was up and moving through a dry rice paddy.

"Spread it out," the squad leader ordered. "There's no sense in letting one round kill us all. There'd be no one left to tell the officers how dumb we were."

"Yeah, cherry," Wilson laughed, "you spread out way the fuck over there."

After walking forty yards, the squad came to a large dike three feet high and six feet wide. They walked along the top of the dike on the well-worn path the locals used before the area became too active for farming. The trail led through a cluster of trees and out into more rice paddies. The squad followed the path as long as they could, then stepped down into a dry paddy. When they reached a series of flooded paddies that were still being cultivated, they traveled along the tops of the tiny dikes that separated the individual paddies.

As they entered another wooded area, Rose called out, for the cherry's sake, "Punji stakes. Keep your eyes open."

On either side of the trail, almost hidden in the grass, scores of punji stakes pointed at the squad. Rose called a break and the squad dropped to the ground to rest.

Rose sat beside Daniel, reached into the grass and pulled up one of the stakes, "This is a punji stake, Perdue."

Daniel took it in his hand and examined it, "Bamboo?"

"Yeah. Charlie cuts a tube of bamboo into these thin sticks, then sharpens them into points. They burn the tips to make them hard, then dip the points in human shit."

"Human shit?"

"It causes infection. You don't have to get stuck bad. It's the infection that keeps the victim in the hospital."

"I didn't know shit would do that."

"It's not something you run into every day in the world."

"How does charlie decide where to put the things?"

"Who knows? They'll stick a bunch of them on both sides of a trail," Rose pointed, "like this. Then one charlie will fire a round when some GIs come by. It made a Helluva ambush."

"How?"

"Back before we learned what was happening, the guys would dive for cover when they heard the shot. All kinds of guys got hurt. One lousy round from an AK47 and half a dozen men would be injured."

"That was a neat trick."

"You better remember it," Rose warned. "Anytime we get incoming, whether its small arms or what, always drop down right where you're standing. If there are guys in front of you, then you can lay out where they've been. If you're ever on the point be especially careful. Don't hit the ground at all; just squat down as low as you can. Charlie has a lot of tricks he uses to screw up a unit, so don't ever go diving for cover just to avoid getting hit. You could land on something a lot worse that a bullet."

"I'll remember."

And Daniel did. From that day forward, he never passed a punji stake without seeing it.

The squad continued the patrol in the wide arc two thousand meters out from the perimeter of base camp.

The steady march and the heavy equipment finally got the better of Daniel. When he stopped and threw up, Rose called an unscheduled reststop. Daniel was thoroughly embarrassed.

"Don't let it get you down, Perdue," Rose said. "I told you that humping the boonies would wear you out."

"I don't understand it," Daniel said as he regained his composure. "I just finished jump school. I can run forever."

"Humpin's different," Rose said. "It takes a different kind of being in shape. Everybody's out of shape when they first get to the boonies. You'll get used to it."

"He's right, Perdue," Minniefield agreed. "The same thing happened to me my first time out."

After five minutes of rest, the squad was on the move again. Four hundred meters down the trail, in a small clump of underbrush, Rose stopped the men and called for Daniel to come up.

"Look at this, Perdue," Rose said as he pointed to a small puddle.

Perdue stared at the water that filled a depression in the ground.

"It's one of charlie's old mortar positions," Rose said. He knelt and picked up a small piece of wire from among the many scattered around the puddle. "These things come off the mortar rounds before they're dropped down the tube." He handed the wire to Daniel. "Notice how the puddle is round?"

"Yes."

"This is where the base plate sat," Rose explained. "It made a round hole in the ground when it was fired. The deeper the hole, the more times it was fired."

So the enemy really is around here, Daniel thought. Or at least they had been not long ago.

Rose stood and spoke, "When the division was first setting up camp, charlie used to drop mortar rounds on us almost every night. But since we've been patrolling out here every day, we haven't been hit as often. And the ambushes we set up at night have been working. Hey, Perez. When did the ambush shoot up a bunch of charlies?"

"It's been a week or more."

"Fired up them fuckers good," Wilson announced.

"Anyway," Rose continued, "It wasn't too long before you got here. I'm surprised they have us coming in tonight. I expected us to be on an ambush."

The patrol continued through rice paddies and fields until just before dark. When the assigned area had been covered, Rose called a halt and sat down.

"I'm beat, Sarge," Daniel said. "How long are we going to rest here?"

"Til the chopper comes to get us," Rose answered.

"All fuckin' night!" Wilson shouted.

"Keep it down," Rose ordered.

"I figured we'd walk back," the cherry said.

"The area right in front of the perimeter doesn't need patrolling," Rose replied. "And besides, it's never safe to walk up on a perimeter, especially at twilight."

"How come?" Daniel asked.

"How come?" Wilson echoed. "That fuckin' cherry's stupider than shit."

"Perdue, what would you do if you were on a position and a bunch of armed men approached you after dark?" Rose asked.

"Challenge them," Daniel answered, "Like on guard."

Wilson and Perez laughed.

"Listen, cherry," Rose ordered, "If anything comes up on you after dark, do your damnedest to kill it. Understand?"

"I guess so."

"Perdue, you've got to stop guessing," Rose warned. "You either know or you don't know."

"The fucker don't know nothin'," Wilson stated factually.

"Let's have a little test, Perdue," Rose said. "First question: Do you ever walk up on a position after dark?"

"No, sergeant."

"Why not?"

"You could get killed."

"And what do you do if you're on a position and someone walks up on you?"

"Open fire."

"Remember that," Rose concluded.

The chopper came in to pick up the squad. Daniel was tired, wet and hungry. He was so happy that the walking was done that he took no particular interest in the ride to camp, even though it was just his second time in a helicopter. War was turning out to be a lot of hard work, hard enough so that an event which a week earlier would have been exciting was now taken in stride.

They landed at the brigade chopper pad and walked back to the company area. They had just dropped their gear on their bunks when Wilkerson, the company clerk, stepped in.

"They held the mess hall open for you," he announced, "but you better hurry on up. They won't wait forever."

"Let's move out, guys," Rose ordered. "We've getting special treatment, so let's take advantage of it."

The squad left their tent and walked through the muddy company area to the footbridge. The creek had risen even higher than when Daniel had first seen it. A rushing torrent lapped at the two-by-fours, and at one place actually appeared to come up from between the boards. Daniel turned to his squad leader.

"Where'd all this water come from?"

"The rain is all I know," Rose replied. "We didn't have creeks in Queens."

Wilson spoke up, "The fucker got so high once that we had to wade across it."

"True," Rose agreed.

Wilson continued, "Jus' be glad you can see the fucker, cherry. Wait'll it gets really fuckin' high."

They crossed the footbridge and made their way to the battalion mess hall. Hot chow seemed like a reward after twelve meals of C rations. The squad members enjoyed the semblance of civilization provided by the mess hall. The cooks knew they had just come in from the field and allowed them to linger a bit longer than usual before breaking up their party. Daniel was learning that the end of every operation outside the perimeter called for a celebration of some sort.

Throughout their meal, the rain continued to pour down. Rose had hoped it would ease up before they had to return to the company area, but the time had come and the rain had not abated. When they reached the footbridge, only the dim lights of the mess hall and a few flickering lights from the company lit the area.

Perez, leading the way, stopped dead in his tracks. The near end of the bridge was completely under water and the far end was barely out of it. The absence of handrails and the darkness, plus the force of the surging water, made crossing somewhat scary.

"Who wants to take the point?" Rose asked jokingly.

There were no volunteers.

"How about you, Perez?" Rose asked. "You want to give it a try?"

Perez shook his head.

"How about you, Benny? You want to try it?"

"Sure," he answered.

Terwilliger stepped slowly into the water. Had it not been for the far end of the bridge projecting out of the stream, it would have appeared like there was no bridge at all. Terwilliger inched across slowly, followed by Perez.

"Step on in there, Perdue," Rose ordered.

"You talking to me?"

"Right," Rose continued. "If you stay behind the man in front of you, you'll know where to step."

"Follow me, cherry," Wilson said as he stepped into the water.

"Here goes," Daniel said in a whisper. He followed Wilson's steps exactly.

Rose and Minniefield brought up the rear.

When Daniel was in the middle of the current, Rose spoke, "Hey, Wilson? When was it that that guy got washed away doing this?"

"Sometime last month, wasn't it?"

"Oh, fuck," Daniel said only half under his breath.

They all made it safely across the bridge, and other than a little teasing for Daniel's benefit, the veterans did not consider wading knee deep on a submerged bridge across a fast moving flood of water as anything out of the ordinary.

Back in the platoon tent there was not much conversation. It was good to have a bed to sleep in, even if it was only a sagging army cot. Daniel fell asleep quickly.

At daybreak the Charge of Quarters (CQ) went from tent to tent waking the company. Before his echo faded from the tent, Daniel was up and putting on his boots.

Immediately after breakfast, Daniel went to the latrine.

The company latrine had been improved since the early days after the company had arrived when it was a fragile structure astride a slit trench. It had been replaced by a permanent building with four seats, each directly above a half of a fifty-five-gallon drum. This improvement was lost on Daniel, who considered the facility to be most primitive.

Daniel had not been seated long when an officer entered and sat down. He was the first officer Daniel had seen in the company area.

"Good morning, Sir."

"Good morning, trooper," the lieutenant replied.

Daniel did not know who the officer was and was too embarrassed to ask. Since the officer did not initiate further conversation, Daniel kept quiet.

The officer pulled out a book and began reading. Out of curiosity, Daniel tried, discreetly, to see the title. When he finally was able to see it, he very nearly broke out laughing. He finished as quickly as he could and hurried outside. He was able to maintain control until he was well away from the latrine, then he began to giggle. He had found it amusing that anyone would sit in an open air latrine and read *Lord of the Flies*.

Back at the platoon tent Perez and Wilson argued over which of them would interact with the prettiest lady while in town.

"Are we going to town today?" Daniel asked.

Wilson answered, "Ain't nobody said so for sure, but we ain't got nothing else to do."

Perez chided Wilson, "You just want to fuck that peeg again."

"You jus' callin' her a pig because she had tits," Wilson responded. "That bitch you fucked didn't have no tits at all."

Minniefield entered the tent, saying "I jus' heard that there's gonna be water in th' showers this morning."

50

"Wilson sat up, "No shit?"

"That's what I heard."

"All fuckin' right," Wilson shouted.

Daniel could not understand the enthusiasm caused by the possibility of a cold shower. He had not been completely dry for any appreciable length of time since he arrived at Camp Radcliff. To Daniel, a chance to get really dry would have been better.

Sergeant McDowd stuck his head in the tent.

"I want you troopers to get down to the creek and clean up your gear."

Wilson spoke up, "Minniefield heard there'd be water in the showers this morning, Sarge."

"Roger. If it shows up you can break for showers. But I want your gear done before lunch. No excuses."

The squad walked in a group to the creek. The morning sun had burned away the clouds and had begun to beat down on the company area. Within minutes steam was coming out of the ground, puddles were shrinking and dry patches of ground had appeared. By midmorning all but the largest puddles would disappear in the tropical heat.

Washing equipment in the creek proved to be interesting. The raging torrent of the night before was subsiding rapidly. On three separate occasions Daniel moved down the bank because the stream had receded out of his reach. The footing was treacherous in the slippery mud that formed the banks, but only Minniefield was unfortunate enough to lose his grip and drunk a foot in the water up to his knee, although Wilson did have to chase a canteen carrier down stream.

Daniel never understood why they were required to wash their equipment in a muddy creek, but the action was accepted without question by the others in the squad so he did not seek an explanation.

Minniefield saw the water trailer arrive at the showers and the entire squad began a line that grew steadily behind them.

The battalion shower looked to have been built hurriedly, without much concern for appearances. Like all buildings in the country, it had a concrete floor upon which a frame of two-by-fours supported a corrugated tin roof; the walls were plywood up to four feet and from there up screens; a structure beside the shower provided a roof-level platform from which four fifty-five gallon drums sat; water for the showers had to be hand pumped up to the drums.

The shower water was clean, but ice cold, giving Daniel no reason to avoid the order to use as little as possible. He hurried more than the others in the squad because, being new, he had not yet learned to ignore the shouts and obscenities that came from the ever-lengthening line outside. Had he known how rare showers were for the infantry, even cold ones, he would have taken longer, used more water, and gotten a bit cleaner.

Returning to the platoon tent, the squad walked past the drum that was used to burn the company's trash. It burned most of the time the company was in camp and occasionally provided some excitement. Such was the case that morning.

A sound like a gunshot rang out and Daniel was not the only squad member to seek cover!

Wilkerson, the company clerk, stood outside the orderly room and watched the display.

"You fuckers hiding from peanut butter cans?" he shouted.

A big grin crossed Wilson's face as he stood.

"The little fucker fooled me good," he laughed.

Daniel turned to Minniefield, who was rising to his feet.

"What're they talking about?" he asked.

"They ain't 'sposed to, but sometimes men throw C ration cans in the garbage. When they heats up, they explodes."

"It sure sounded like a gun to me," Daniel said.

Wilson's sheepish grin continued as he spoke, "Close enough to fool the fuck outta me."

Just then another can exploded in the burning drum. Daniel saw it happen and watched a small amount of ash and trash fly up and over the rim of the drum.

"Tricky, isn't it?" Daniel asked Minniefield.

"Yessir," Minniefield replied. "Tricky."

Sergeant Stovall came out of the orderly room with some other sergeants and called to Rose to assemble the squad in the platoon tent.

"I bet we're gonna get to go to town," Wilson said with the enthusiasm of a child at Christmas.

When second squad had joined Sergeant Stovall in the platoon tent, he looked at Rose and frowned.

"Where the fuck is everybody," he asked sternly.

Rose answered, "Still in the showers, Sarge."

"Shit!" Stovall thought a moment, for him a significant undertaking, then began talking in a monologue. "The company's going on highway duty starting this afternoon."

Wilson interrupted, "Ain't we gonna get to go to town?"

"No, Wilson, you're not," Stovall replied. "Now listen up. Second and third squads will ride shotgun on a convoy to Pleiku, then join the rest of us on positions along Highway 19."

Wilson mumbled, "I thought we was going the fuck to town."

"Shut the fuck up, Wilson," Stovall roared. "You don't get fuckin' paid to think!"

Perez chided Wilson, "Put you down, fucker."

"All of you be at ease or you'll all end up on KP!" Stovall had lost what little patience he began with. "Next fuckin' sound outta anybody and you're all up shit creek."

Rose motioned for Wilson and Perez behave.

"You people will spend tonight at the MACV compound," Stovall continued, "Sgt. McDowd will be in charge. Rose, you pass the word along to third squad when they get here."

"Roger, Sarge," Rose replied.

"How long will we be out, Sarge?" Minniefield asked.

"Two weeks. We're supposed to be back in camp before Christmas. Now get you're gear together; we move out when the truck gets here."

"Roger, Sarge," Rose agreed. "Let's get it together, guys."

The squad waited in the platoon tent until noon, when Rose asked for and received permission for the men to go to the mess hall for chow. A truck was waiting when they returned to the company area.

Second and third squads rode through base camp to the main gate, where they dismounted and waited for the convoy to pick them up on its way out. The convoy was small, consisting of only six trucks escorted by two recon jeeps mounting M60s. Two men were assigned to each truck: third squad took the first three trucks and second squad took the last three. Perdue and Terwilliger were put on the fourth truck; Rose kept Wilson and the radio on the fifth truck with him; Perez and Minniefield were assigned the last truck. One recon jeep led the convoy out through the gate and the other fell in at the rear.

The quarter mile long drive that led to the highway was empty near the perimeter; the rice paddies were overgrown and pitted with shell craters. Nearer the highway, activity picked up. Shops appeared beside the road offering native clothing and an assortment of trinkets. A motorscooter was parked in front of one shop, and two GIs in a jeep sat in front of another. Vietnamese were everywhere, but there were no civilian vehicles on the road.

When the truck reached Highway 19, Benny spoke, "An Khe is down that way about half a mile." He pointed to the left. "Off on the right side of the road you can see the Special Forces camp."

Daniel saw some low buildings surrounded by concertina wire.

"I went there once with Sgt. McDowd," Benny continued. "We picked up some beer back before the EM club opened up." He shook his head. "Them fuckers got it made. They got fridgerators, radios and everything, but even them Green Berets run outta sodas once in a while."

As Daniel looked left, the convoy turned right and headed west towards Pleiku. The adult Vietnamese paid no attention to the convoy, but every child smiled and waved when the trucks went by.

"Watch this," Benny told Daniel.

He opened his C ration sock and pulled out a can of Ham and Eggs, Chopped, then retied the sock to his harness. When the truck next passed a group of children, Bunny threw the can over the side. The can bounced once, then landed in a roadside ditch. All of the kids chased after it.

"Ain't that somethin'?" Terwilliger asked.

Daniel was not amused by the display. He did not understand it, but he was saddened by his first lesson in Third World poverty. How tragic to be a child in such a place; how fortunate to be born in America, where even the poor are wealthy when compared to the subsistence economies of Third World countries.

The huts and people near the base camp thinned out into seemingly endless rice paddies with only a hut or two scattered among them. Daniel watched the land with fascination; it was so different from his native Georgia. He did not realize that the well tended paddies were far more productive than the neglected red clay fields of the Georgia piedmont.

Benny called to Daniel, "Look at that!"

Coming at them was a three wheeled motorscooter packed with people. Young men hung from the sides and held on to the top.

Benny spoke again, "There must be twenty of them fuckers on that thing."

Daniel watched it pass by them, then commented, "I've seen fewer people on a crowded bus. Isn't that dangerous?"

"I suppose, cherry," Benny answered. The dangers of riding on an overcrowded scooter seemed small to an infantry veteran. "I guess it's about time for us to start watching for charlie."

Terwilliger broke open his M79 and checked the grenade in the chamber. Daniel had not noticed when, still at the main gate. Benny had loaded his weapon. Daniel pulled back the bolt on his rifle and chambered a round.

The cool wind counteracted the hot sun as Daniel settled into a comfortable position among the truck's cargo to watch the countryside roll by. In the distance he saw an old man plodding along atop a primitive irrigation rig, slowly lifting small quantities of water into a rice paddy. Later he passed a bombed out hut and a burned out civilian truck.

When Daniel noticed the trucks ahead slowing down and turning to the left down an embankment, Daniel wondered what was going on. Then he saw the lead jeep and the first truck rising out and returning to the road. The truck ahead of him turned to the left and Daniel saw the reason for the detour: the highway bridge was out.

Daniel watched the bridge as his truck turned left along a dirt road down into a small valley. As the truck crossed an engineer bridge over a small river, Daniel looked up, and down, at the highway bridge. Only the first of its four spans was still in place; the second span had fallen at the middle support and was lying at an angle from the surviving span down to the third span, which had fallen at both ends and sat flat in the river. The last span was down on the end by the third span and angled up to the road. Infantry soldiers manned positions on the road at each end of the damaged bridge that looked out over, and guarded, the engineer bridge. The GIs waved at the passing trucks.

Daniel had never seen a bridge that had been blown up. He could not take his eyes off it. Seeing how neatly the job was done, and how little actual damage there was, Daniel realized that the Viet Cong were very good at their work. They had not tried to destroy the concrete spans, that was probably impossible; they had, instead, rearranged the spans so that they served no useful purpose.

As the convoy traveled on, Daniel saw that every bridge on Highway 19 between An Khe and Pleiku had been similarly disrupted. At each one, the convoy made the detour down the side, across an engineer bridge, and back up the other side. Each engineer bridge was guarded by two infantry positions manned by what Daniel assumed were hardened combat veterans.

But Daniel had seen veterans; he had not seen downed bridges. At each site, his eyes were drawn to the fallen spans, those massive slabs of concrete, virtually undamaged as they lay in disorder. Daniel imagined that a giant crane could come along and lift the spans into place. But there were no such cranes, and the fallen bridges remained monuments to the difficulty of construction and the ease of destruction.

By midafternoon the day's rain arrived. As if to counterbalance the hot morning, the wet afternoon turned cold. At thirty miles an hour, the wind cut through the thin jungle fatigues; the blowing rain covered Daniel's glasses and made it impossible for him to look in the direction the truck was traveling. Only by turning away from the wind could Daniel hope to keep his glasses clear. The pleasant ride became a torture test for a cherry not expecting ever to be cold in the tropics. He completely lost interest in the repetitious rice paddies and thatched roof huts. Even Benny disappeared from sight under his poncho.

Suddenly, the distinct sound of an explosion pierced the truck's highway noise. Daniel looked ahead and saw a dark gray cloud rising from the ground near the front of the convoy. Benny reappeared quickly and searched the horizon with an intensity that Daniel had not seen in him before.

Another explosion! Only two trucks ahead. Daniel watched the dark gray cloud disperse as his truck roared by it.

I think this is war, Daniel thought to himself.

Benny vocalized his thoughts, "Hey, driver! Them fuckers is shootin' at us! Can't this here truck go no faster?!"

Suddenly Daniel's ears filled with the roar of an explosion that seemed within his head. The truck swerved to the right, kicking up gravel along the side of the road. A mortar round had detonated in the air almost directly beside the truck. On Terwilliger's side, the two outer tires were shredded, but they had protected the inner tires, although the driver would have kept going even if he had had to run on bare rims. A section of the wood railing near Benny was ripped away. Benny's helmet lay at Daniel's feet.

Daniel reached across the truckbed to the grenadier.

"Are you alright?" he shouted.

Benny looked at Daniel without expression, then shook his head to clear his senses.

"Yep. I think so. Do you see any blood anywhere?"

Daniel scanned Benny for visible injuries and found none.

"I don't see any. Does it hurt anywhere?"

"My ears are ringing real bad, but I guess that's all."

"My ears ring, too. God, you were lucky. That coulda killed you."

"It blew my helmet right off'n my head."

Daniel reached down and picked up the helmet. The cover was torn and a deep scratch showed shiny metal.

"God, you were lucky," Daniel repeated. "Look at that!"

"I wonder if'n they'll let me keep it?"

"You damned near got your head blown off and all you can think about is a souvenir?" Daniel was amazed. "Don't you realize how fuckin' lucky you were?"

"You were lucky, too. Look at your rifle."

Daniel reached for the M16 he had left lying against the railing. The hand guard had a chip in it the size of a half dollar. Daniel opened his mouth, but no sound came out. He was, for the first time in his life, quite literally, speechless.

"It don't get much closer'n that."

Daniel stared at the rifle. Benny leaned forward.

"You okay, driver?" he shouted.

The driver was intent on pushing the big deuce-and-a-half as fast as it would go and only nodded to Benny that he was unhurt.

At the next gathering of huts, the convoy halted. The lead recon jeep, which also carried Sgt. McDowd, turned around and sped down the length of the small convoy. When it pulled up beside the damaged truck, the sergeant driving asked if anyone was hurt.

"No," the truckdriver answered.

"Nope," Benny agreed.

The sergeant looked at the shredded tires and spoke to the driver, "Can she make it?"

"She fuckin' better make it," the driver replied. "I ain't gonna sit here, that's for fuckin' sure!"

"Okay," the recon sergeant said. "You people stay alert. A truck yesterday got sniper fire along this next stretch."

The recon jeep moved to the rear and turned around. It paused for a moment at the rear jeep, then returned to the front of the convoy. As the jeep passed Daniel's truck, Sgt. McDowd waved proudly at his two men.

The trucks rolled forward into a harder rain that all but drowned out the sound of the shredded tires flapping in the wind. As they wound their way through smaller and smaller groups of rice paddies, the last vestiges of civilization faded behind them.

At the next, and last, fallen bridge, the GIs on duty there pointed at the truck on which Daniel and Benny rode.

Daniel thought, I'll bet those men don't know I'm a cherry.

The minutes and miles passed. Rice paddies were no longer visible from the road. The jungle crept closer and closer to the shoulder of the road. The convoy started up a long and winding hill and diesel engines roared trying to maintain their speed. Daniel wondered why there were no infantry positions anywhere along this stretch of road; it seemed perfect for an ambush. The young soldier kept his eyes focused on the edge of the jungle. For the first time since he arrived in-country, he paid no attention at all to the rain.

When the trucks reached the top of the long hill, Daniel got his first glimpse of the South Vietnamese Army. Two dozen or more ARVNs (arvins) lounged around an unsightly small perimeter adjacent to the right shoulder of the road. Their unkempt appearance was not at all reassuring to a cherry just recently shot at.

The convoy picked up speed on the downward slope of the hill, reducing Daniel's worry about an ambush. The jungle near the edge of the road slowly fell back, but any signs of civilization awaited the trucks at the bottom of the long grade.

Benny pointed and called out, "Mountainyards!"

A family of *Montgnards* walked along the side of the road. They were primitive people who lived in the more remote areas in the mountainous central highlands; their crude animal traps were a constant source of danger to GIs operating in their habitat.

The group was led by an older man wearing a loincloth and carrying a spear, followed by two younger men similarly clad and armed. Next came an older woman and a teenage girl, both topless, and three naked children. Daniel had never seen aboriginals in their natural state, but he did not notice more detail because of the speed at which the truck was traveling, and because he was looking at the teenage girl.

Near the bottom of the long hill the first rice paddy gave notice that the land was changing back to productive use. As the road leveled out, the jungle gradually gave way to cultivated fields. The random hut became the occasional group of houses, then scattered villages, and finally the Vietnamese version of suburbs.

The convoy slowed when it entered the hustle and bustle of Pleiku. Civilian traffic filled the street: Some trucks, but mostly scooters, motorcycles and bicycles. The rain stopped and the sun peeked through the clouds, casting shadows from the palm trees that lined the broad avenues and filled the courtyards between the houses. Throngs of people crowded around the shops and markets. Daniel had seen nothing so normal since he had arrived in-country. For a moment he forgot why he was there and felt like a tourist.

The convoy turned off the main street and onto a road that led to the MACV compound. The Military Advisory Command, Vietnam, had compounds throughout the country; they were the command centers from which the U.S. Army's assistance to South Vietnamese forces was controlled.

The sun was low on the horizon when the convoy reached the gate of the compound. A sergeant stationed there ordered the men on each truck to "clear all weapons" as they passed by him. The perimeter of the compact little base was designed more to keep out curious civilians than to repel armed attack. Two ten foot high wire fences contained three rolls of concertina wire; the bunkers and gun positions were well constructed and protected by sandbags, but their fields of fire were woefully small because civilian structures had been built much too close to the fence. Within the compound, every building was sandbagged up to the level of the screens. Everything was neat, orderly and clean. It was very GI.

The trucks halted in an area in the middle of the compound that was used as a small parade ground and as a temporary parking lot for the numerous convoys which passed through Pleiku. The infantry dismounted and gathered around the one damaged truck.

As usual, Wilson made the first comment.

"Tore that fucker up, didn't it?"

"Too fuckin' close, eh, Benny?" Perez asked, using Benny's first name because he had difficulty pronouncing "Terwilliger."

"Knocked my helmet off, sure'ern shit," Benny said as he handed his steel pot to Perez.

Perez rubbed his finger along the deep gash in the metal then spoke reverently, "Mother of Jesus."

Sgt. McDowd took his first good look at the truck.

"Musta been an aerial blast ten feet above the ground." the old warrior surmised. "Couldn't have gone off more than ten fuckin' feet from you troopers."

Benny declared, "I don't never want one no closer."

Perez handed Benny's helmet to Minniefield.

"Look at that fucker," he said with awe.

Minniefield shook his head, then spoke softly, "The good Lord sho' looked after you two."

Rose addressed Daniel, "How does it feel to get shot at, cherry?"

"It happened so fast," Danield ansered, "I didn't have time to feel anything."

Wilson laughed, "I bet th' fucker was scared to death."

"The' fucker better been scared," Perez insisted. "Don't hafta been no cherry to get the shit scared outta you."

"Scared you, too, didn't it, Benny?" Wilson asked.

"Damn right, it scared me," Benny agreed. "That's the closest I done come yet to gettin' my ass kilt."

Wilson turned to Minniefield and spoke with authority, "I was watching when it happened. The fucker went off right beside 'em."

"The Lord looked after 'em," Minniefield repeated.

"I thought they was fuckin' goners for fuckin' sure," Wilson insisted.

"How'd the' cherry act, Benny?" Perez asked. "Froze up, didn't he?

"Nope," Benny replied. "He handled hisself right good. He was on top 'o me afore my head stopped shakin'."

Wilson was not impressed, "Aw, the fucker was prob'ly divin' for fuckin' cover an' jus' bumped into you."

"Nope," Benny insisted, "I don' care if'n he is a cherry, he shore kep' his shit together."

Rose took Benny's helmet from Minniefield and examined the gash in the metal.

"Damn, you were a lucky fucker, Benny," he said forcefully.

"Perdue was lucky, too," Benny replied. "Did ja see his gun?"

Daniel held up his rifle so the squad could see the hole in the handguard.

"Shrapnel did that," Benny informed them.

"Le' me see it," Wilson ordered.

Daniel, a well-trained soldier, cleared again his already empty rifle before handing it to Wilson. A sizable hole in the black plastic handguard was the focal point for several lengthy cracks.

Wilson examined the weapon thoroughly, then handed it back to Daniel, "You musta had it sitting somewhere, huh, cherry?"

"It was in my hands," Daniel   stated flatly.

"You hombres were fuckin' lucky," Perez said softly.

"Th' good Lord looked after 'em," Minniefield repeated. "He sho' did look after 'em."

As the infantry talked, the soldiers assigned to the compound watched from a respectable distance. Although they were curious, they were somewhat in awe of men who worked beyond the safety of a perimeter. The infantry had opinions of them, as well, considering all soldiers stationed inside a perimeter to be garrison troopers, garritroopers, the paratroopers called them.

A sergeant from the compound approached Sergeant McDowd, "You men just missed chow. Once you're settled in for the night, I'll send some C rations over."

"That'll be fine," McDowd replied. "Where do we bed down?"

"I'll show you," the sergeant said.

McDowd turned to Rose, "I'll be back in a minute."

The men continued their discussion around the damaged truck while McDowd located their sleeping quarters. The infantry was assigned to a barracks just inside the barbed wire, a building that was not regularly used by the men in the compound because it was virtually adjacent to the perimeter.

When McDowd returned to his men, he was greeted by a question from Wilson.

"When do we eat, Sarge?"

"You'll get some Cs once you've settled in for the evening."

"Aw, shit!" Wilson said, disappointed. The permanance of the compound led him to believe that the mess hall would be like a restaurant. "You'd think these fuckers could come up with enought fuckin' chow for two fuckin' squads."

"These men work regular shifts," McDowd explained. "They eat on schedule."

"Fuckin' garritroopers," Perez declared.

"Don't get pissed," McDowd ordered. "You get to sleep in a building tonight."

Wilson looked at Perez.

"Yeah, fucker. You're always bitchin' bout something'."

"Fuck you," Perez replied.

"Knock it off," McDowd ordered. "Grab your gear and follow me."

The sergeant led his men to their barracks. When the last of them entered the building, he asked for quiet.

"Listen up, troopers. I want everybody to stay in the barracks. These garritroopers can't handle a bunch of rowdies."

"Ain't the fuckers got no EM club?" Wilson asked.

"They got one," McDowd answered, "but it's off limits."

Wilson threw down his harness, "Aw, shit!"

"Give us a fuckin' break, Sarge," Perez pleaded.

"Knock it off!" McDowd barked. "I don't want any of you fuckers causing any trouble. Rose, I'm leaving you in charge."

"Sure, Sarge," Rose said.

McDowd turned and walked out of the tent, almost knocking down a garritrooper who carried a case of C rations. The soldier dropped the box inside the door, and, with a curt "Enjoy," left.

"Hey, Sarge?" Wilson called to Rose. "You 'spose you could sneak around and find us some beer?"

"No," the squad leader answered. "But I will try to find some sodas for you guys."

The NCO club in the MACV compound was small because of the limited number of soldiers assigned there. It was housed in a typical army building, but time and use had granted it a degree of personality. A variety of military paraphenalia, pictures and unit patches hung from the studs that supported the screens. On the wall behind the bar, a Chinese-made AK47 automatic rifle hung on commo wire. A captured Viet Cong flag decorated the area above the entrance. The bar was handmade, functional rather than aesthetic. The bartender was tall and skinny, almost sickly looking. He was clean shaven, but his black stubble gave the appearance of a five o'clock shadow. Simple tables with straight black chairs lined the walls. The naked light bulbs cast hard shadows on the concrete floor. Making one of those shadows in a corner was Sylvester McDowd.

When Rose entered the club, McDowd was drinking from the second of four opened beer cans that sat on the table in front of him. He called to the young squad leader.

"Rose! Over here."

"Hello, Sarge," Rose said as he approached McDowd's table.

"What are you doing in here?"

"Gettin' some sodas for my guys."

"That can wait. Sit down and have a beer."

"Sure, Sarge."

As Rose sat down, McDowd pushed an untouched beer toward him.

"Kinda hairy out there today, wasn't it?"

"Coulda been worse, a lot worse."

"I bet the cherry shit in his pants."

"No, Perdue seemed to take it in stride."

"Makes you wonder."

"About what?"

"Luck. It's all just fuckin' luck."

"That's true."

"Five feet closer and both those fuckers woulda been down the tubes, sure as shit."

"Another fifty feet and I woulda been down the tube."

"That's what I mean about luck. It don't make a shit what you do. If the fucker's got your name on it, it's just rotten fuckin' luck. Duckin' don't help. Praying don't help. If the shit's meant for you, it don't matter a fuck whether you're a cherry or not. You coulda been born in a fuckin' foxhole and been dodging bullets all your life and still get it. It's all fuckin' luck."

"Sometimes I wonder if God keeps a list that has everybody's name and the date and time they're gonna get it."

"Yeah. Fate."

"Something like that."

"It wouldn't bother me so much if we stayed in the boonies. It's fuckin' around camps that gets me." McDowd sipped his beer. "It's the fuckin' sittin' around that gives you the time to think about it."

"I know what you mean, Sarge."

"I guess that's why I drink this shit." McDowd raised his beer. "It keeps me from thinking about gettin' killed."

"Alcohol has given men courage since biblical times."

"Yeah. I guess they had war back then, too."

Rose turned up his beer and finished it.

"I gotta get back to my squad, Sarge. Thanks for the beer."

"Pleasure was mine." Rose stood. "You know, Rose. You're not a bad fellow, for a Jew."

"And you're not a bad fellow, either, Sarge. For a lifer."

Rose walked to the bar and ordered six soft drinks.

"Don't the infantry drink beer?" the bartender asked.

"Gotta go to work in the morning," Rose replied.

"Yeah," the barkeep laughed. "I imagine you do."

"Damn. These things are ice cold."

"They always are," the bartender bragged. "We've got our own ice machine."

"It must be nice."

"We like it."

"I'll bet you draw combat pay, too."

Rose turned and headed toward the door with the sodas. As he passed close to McDowd, the platoon sergeant called out.

"Tell the men that we'll be pulling out at first light."

"Roger, Sarge." Rose took one more step toward the door, then he stopped and looked back at McDowd. "Good luck."

"Thanks. You, too."

Rose passed out the drinks when he returned to the barracks. A quiet party began and lasted as long as the drinks. The anticipation of an uninterrupted night's sleep under a roof was sufficient to put every man in the sack early.

When everything was at last quiet, Daniel walked over to Rose and sat down.

"Not sleepy, cherry?" Rose asked.

"No."

"You've got a right to be uptight."

"It's hard to get it out of my mind."

"I know the feeling."

"I think the boys are treating me better because of it."

"The guys are friendlier because we're inside the wire. You aren't as dangerous here."

"I was hoping that maybe they'll go easier on me."

"Don't rush it. The guys aren't going to ever trust you completely. Gettin' shot at once doesn't mean you know all you need to know."

"I guess not."

"What did I tell you about guessing?"

"I'm sorry, Sarge."

"Cheer up. You're less of a cherry every day."

"I'll sure be glad when they get around to making friends."

"Don't count on that ever happening."

Daniel was puzzled, and hurt.

"Why not?"

"It's like the guy said in the movie: Friends you come with, you're stuck with, but you don't make new friends."

"Why not?"

"It hurts more when a friend gets it. One day you'll realize that the less you care about people, the less you'll suffer if and when they get killed."

"Somehow that doesn't seem fair."

"You'll understand. . . ."

"I know," Daniel interrupted. "Eventually."

Rose's smile became a grin, "Right."

Daniel stood.

"Good night, Sarge."

"Good night, cherry."

Daniel returned to his cot and sat down. He took off his boots and stretched out on his back. When his eyes closed, his mind replayed the events of the day. He watched Benny's helmet fly off and land at his feet. As the compound fell quiet for the night, he heard the ringing in his ears for the first time. Again his mind's eye pictured Benny's helmet flying off.

Somewhere in the compound, a gasoline generator cranked up. As Daniel listened to it, the ringing in his ears was less distracting. But over and over, he saw Benny's helmet coming off and landing at his feet.

A cold chill caused him to shiver, but it was not a product of the unforgiving climate.

Daniel Perdue, for the first time, realized how close he came to being killed, and it scared him.

On quiet nights, he would feel that chill again, and that fear. It had become a part of his subconscious, and would remain a part of it for as long as he lived.

viii

The MACV compound was dark and quiet when a private entered the barracks and announced that morning had arrived. Second and third squads finished breakfast and were waiting in the barracks when first light appeared. As the compound came to life, Sgt. McDowd ordered his men on a deuce-and-a-half and they headed out towards Pleiku and Highway 19.

Daniel was more anxious about the return trip than he had been about the adventure the day before. Having been directly involved in an attack along the highway, he now had some idea of what to expect. He was particularly worried about the long, steep hill that led to the ARVN position; that stretch of road, with the jungle so close to the shoulder, was perfect for an ambush, and Daniel had no faith in the Vietnamese soldiers who guarded the area.

The bright sun shining through fluffy clouds provided a warm, restful setting for those on the truck. While Daniel watched for trouble, others slept. Wilson was asleep before the truck left the compound and all of the third squad dozed. Of the few who stayed awake, only Daniel did not appreciate riding, for he had not yet spent significant time afoot.

When the truck began the long, slow ascent, Daniel was so intent on watching for an ambush that he did not notice when Rose nudged McDowd and Perez and advised both that they had reached the most dangerous part of the journey. And after they passed the ARVN position, Daniel did not see all three settle back and return to their various dreams.

Before noon the truck reached the company Command Post. The CP consisted of two tents, a recon jeep and three foxholes. The men dismounted and stretched while they waited for those in authority to decide where they would be positioned. In a few minutes, Sgt. McDowd came out of one of the tents and ordered his men to return to the truck. They moved down the highway to one of the blown bridges, where third squad replaced four men who had guarded the bridge the night before. At the next bridge down the highway, second squad replaced four other men.

The men guarding the engineer bridge manned two positions, one on either end of the destroyed bridge. Up by the road, the positions looked down on the lower bridge that spanned the river only three feet above the waterline.

At the east end of the old bridge a massive concrete bunker sat empty. Originally built to guard the highway bridge, the French had used the bunker like a small fort. Abandoned now as impractical, the huge block of concrete rose up eight feet above the road on the shoulder opposite the new bridge.

As the truck pulled away, Rose gave instructions to his squad. He left Perez, Minniefield and Terwilliger to man the foxhole on the west end of the bridge and he took Wilson and Perdue across the engineer bridge and up to the position at the east end, across the highway from the old French bunker.

As they dropped their gear, Daniel spoke.

"Hey, Sarge. Why don't we use the bunker?"

Rose looked at Daniel, then at the destroyed bridge.

"Besides the fact that it apparently didn't do any good," he said, "being inside that thing if charlie shows up would be suicide."

Daniel, the cherry, could not understand how the bunker would be more dangerous than an open foxhole.

"I don't see how, Sarge."

"You can't see worth a damn from inside one of those things," Rose explained, "and you can't hear worth a damn, either."

"It seems to me," Daniel argued, "that if the shooting started we'd be. . . ."

"Fuckin' deader'n shit," Wilson interrupted.

Rose laughed, "Go look for yourself, Perdue."

Daniel started across the road to the bunker.

"Perdue!" Rose called after him.

Daniel stopped and turned to face his sergeant.

"Yeah, Sarge?"

"Take your rifle with you," Rose ordered.

"Dumb fuckin' cherry," Wilson grunted.

Daniel returned to the foxhole and picked up his rifle.

Rose cautioned him, "Always, I repeat, always keep your rifle within reach." He stuck his arm straight out to the side. "If you can do this and not touch it, it's too far from you."

"Okay, Sarge," Daniel said sheepishly, embarrassed again by his peacetime mentality.

Rifle in hand, Daniel walked to the bunker.

"Dumb fuckin' cherry," Wilson repeated.

"He's okay," Rose said. "You know it takes a while for a new man to come around. If I recall, back in September you once showed up at a formation all ready to head for the boonies and you didn't have the radio. Left it in the tent, didn't you?"

"That was when I was a dumb fuckin' cherry," Wilson admitted.

"So now Perdue's a dumb cherry. Give him time. Keep an eye on him, but give him time."

Daniel stooped over and walked into the bunker. Very little light followed him through the angled entrance. The air inside was stale and damp; the concrete ceiling was just high enough for Daniel to stand erect without his head touching. He stepped over to one of the gunports and looked out.

"Sarge was right," Daniel said aloud, but to himself, "you can't see anything from here."

He stepped away from the loophole and waited for his eyes to adjust to the darkness inside. The bunker was completely empty; not even a piece of trash lay on the floor. Daniel noticed that one of the interior walls was strangely marked. He stepped up to the wall and ran his fingers across some of the marks. What he saw as marks were in fact irregular chips and small holes.

"Somebody must have spent all day with a hammer and chisel to do all this," Daniel whispered.

He stepped back to gain a better view of any pattern that the chips might form. The ceiling above the marks was also chipped. Then he realized what had caused it.

"An explosion did this!"

An eerie feeling came over him. He felt like he was in a coffin and the lid was closing. Suddenly the loopholes seemed to him to be better for shooting in than shooting out. He turned abruptly and started for the entrance.

"Like it?"

The voice startled Daniel and he jumped back. Wilson stood at the doorway.

"You scared the shit outta me, Wilson!"

"This fuckin' thing sure is spooky, all right."

"Now I know why the French lost," Daniel said as he walked to one of the gunports. "You can't see a thing from inside."

Wilson looked around as he stepped slowly up to the hole where Daniel stood.

"I sure as fuck don't never wanta hafta fight from inside this fucker," he decided.

"Me neither," Daniel agreed. "They might as well paint a bullseye on the outside."

"I wonder when this fucker was built?" Wilson asked.

"The French built it, probably in the late forties or early fifties," Daniel speculated.

"Sure is fuckin' spooky in here."

"Roger that," Daniel agreed. He started for the doorway, "I think I've seen enough."

"Wait for me, fucker," Wilson ordered as he hurriedly followed Daniel out.

They crossed the road together.

Rose greeted them, "You still want to use the bunker, Perdue?"

"No way, Sarge," Daniel answered. "No way!"

"Looks different from the inside, doesn't it?" Rose asked.

"Really different," Daniel answered.

"It's spooky as Hell in that fucker," Wilson repeated for the squad leader.

"A great place to spend the night, huh, guys?" Rose joked.

"If you like sleeping in coffins," Daniel replied.

"Didn't all that concrete make you feel safe, cherry?"

"No, Sarge. It definitely did not."

"You're learning, " the sergeant laughed.

"You oughta see the inside," Daniel advised. "I think charlie blew it up."

"Blew it up how?" Rose asked.

"One wall looks really chewed up," Daniel answered.

"I didn't see nothin'," Wilson said.

"On the wall on the left as you go in," Daniel directed, "something sure as hell gouged holes."

"That's worth looking into," Rose announced as he stood.

"I'll go with you," Wilson said.

The two veterans crossed the road and entered the bunker.

Daniel surveyed his surroundings. He looked out over the engineer bridge and into the trees beyond. He watched the clear, fast-flowing river rush under the low bridge and then disappear into a hole in the jungle. He stepped over to the edge of the fallen bridge and looked down at the destruction. The river formed small eddies as it curled around the span that lay in the water. He stood there awed by the sight of so grand a monument to war.

Rose came up beside him and spoke, "See anything?"

"No," Daniel answered, "I was just looking at the bridge. I've never seen anything like it."

"You mean they don't have blown up bridges where you come from?" Rose asked jokingly.

"Not since Sherman passed through in 1864."

"Somethin's coming," Wilson said as he pointed down the road towards An Khe.

Rose stared into the distance before speaking, "Looks like another convoy bound for Pleiku."

The three men sat down around the foxhole and waited for the trucks. Daniel watched them make the same detour his truck had travelled the day before. Roaring engines and grinding gears filled the area with noise. Several GIs waved as they rode by.

Rose spoke, "We'd better get the hooch put up!"

"Can't we eat first?" Wilson asked.

"Sure, Wilson," Rose answered. "There's no hurry."

During the afternoon Daniel discovered that highway security was considered easy duty by the veterans. The squad had little to do during daylight hours as long as one man stayed alert and kept watch. Much of the afternoon was spent napping.

After the convoy, only two vehicles passed second squad's position. Neither was U.S. Army.

The first vehicle was an army truck loaded with ARVNs. Again Daniel was disappointed by the appearance of South Vietnamese soldiers. Their uniforms were not uniform and their manner implied a lack of discipline. Their weapons were of World War II vintage. Most of the ARVNs carried old M1 rifles, but a few had small M1 carbines. Daniel saw one old .30cal. machinegun.

"Gives you a sense of security," Rose joked, "just knowing those guys are on the job."

Daniel and Wilson laughed.

Rose continued, "They're like the Keystone cops in green."

Daniel joined in the jest, "I bet their sergeants are named Larry, Curly and Moe."

Wilson fell over laughing.

Rose laughed, too, "I wouldn't be a bit surprized."

"You'd think the Viet Cong would eat those people alive," Daniel said.

"They do," Rose agreed, "every once in a while."

"What keeps the VC from killing them off every night?" Daniel asked the veteran.

"They've got guns, Perdue," Rose explained, "and even children are dangerous when they've got guns."

Daniel pondered that thought. He had not yet accepted as fact that the rifle in his hand was designed to kill people. He still had the civilian perspective: he respected guns, he even feared them, but his mind did not yet picture the violence, the horror, that happens when fully armed men exchange fire in battle.

An hour before dark a second vehicle approached.

Rose saw it first and spoke, "Get your rifles and stay alert, guys. We've got visitors." Then he called across the river to the rest of his squad, "Heads up, Perez."

Coming down the road at them from the west was a three wheeled scooterbus like the one Daniel had seen the day before.

Rose turned to Daniel, "It's nothing to worry about, usually."

"Usually?" Daniel echoed.

"Usually is the best you can hope for around here," Rose said.

"I guess nothing's definite in war," Daniel opined.

"What'd I tell you about guessing?" Rose asked.

"Sorry, Sarge."

Rose returned his attention to the approaching scooterbus.

"Charlie's been known to sneak a sapper on those things," Rose explained. "They use the civilians as cover."

Daniel was uneasy, "Are we supposed to start shooting if one of 'em throws a grenade or something?"

"I don't know," Rose answered. "It's never happened before."

"That's a big help, Sarge," Daniel replied.

"We'll just play it by ear," Rose suggested. "But remember that there's a bunch of civilians on that thing, too."

A perplexed expression appeared on Daniel's face. Rose saw it and laughed.

"Hey, guy. Nobody said war was easy."

The squad stayed at the ready as the scooterbus made its way through the detour. The mob on board smiled and waved at the American soldiers.

Rose looked at his watch as the vehicle disappeared down the road. Night would fall soon.

"That should be the last one," Rose announced. "Fortunately, there's not a whole lot of traffic."

"What about tonight?" Daniel asked.

"Traffic at night?" Rose asked rhetorically.

Wilson started laughing; Rose shook his head.

With a father's tolerance, Rose forgave Daniel for being naive.

"Perdue," he began paternalistically, "Anything that moves at night, you shoot. And I mean anything, whether it's rolling, walking or crawling."

"Okay, Sarge."

"Nothing moves at night but the VC." Rose continued, "absolutely nothing. Remember that."

"I will, Sarge."

Wilson added, "Ev'rybody in the whole fuckin' army knows that."

"He's right, Perdue," agreed Rose. "Be damn sure you don't go wandering around after dark or you'll get yourself killed."

"I won't, Sarge."

Wilson decided the cherry was too stupid even for ridicule, so he turned his attention to more important matters. He began opening a can of C rations for dinner. Rose and Daniel followed Wilson's lead and began preparing their own meals. Soon all three were eating.

While they ate, the radio squawked. Daniel did not notice the faint sounds that came from the small speaker in the handset, but Wilson did. He picked up the handset and held it against his ear like a telephone receiver. The radio squawked again and Wilson answered.

"Camel Six India, this is Camel Two India. Read you loud and clear. Over."

He put down the handset and returned to his dinner.

Made aware of the radio, Daniel listened to the faint sounds that continued to come from the handset.

"Camel Three, Camel Three. This is Camel Six India. Radio check. Over."

"Camel Six India, this is Camel Three India. Read you loud and clear. Over."

"Roger Camel Three India. Camel Six India out."

Daniel spoke to Wilson, "What was that all about?"

"Commo check," Wilson answered without looking up.

"What was all that about camels in India?" Daniel asked.

Rose looked up, "Don't you know?"

"No," Daniel replied. "Am I supposed to?"

Somewhat perturbed, Rose asked, "Didn't anybody familiarize you with radio procedure?"

"A little in AIT."

Rose shook his head. Wilson grunted, but kept eating.

"Didn't you give Sit Reps on the mountain?" Rose asked.

"I repeated what I heard the others say," Daniel answered.

"Listen up, then," Rose ordered. "I'll fill you in on some things you need to know. I don't expect you to remember it all right away, but you've gotta start sometime.

"Everybody has a call sign. The battalion commander is Quarterback. A company commander is Right Halfback; B company commander is Left Halfback; Captain Dunn is Fullback."

Daniel interrupted, "Who's Captain Dunn?"

Rose frowned, "You're kidding?"

"No."

Rose shook his head, "I don't believe it."

Wilson's comment was "Dumb fuckin' cherry."

"Didn't anybody give you the chain of command?" Rose asked.

"No."

"I'll teach it to you later," Rose decided. "For now, just remember that Captain Dunn is your company commander. His call sign is Fullback Six, Fullback being the designation for C company and Six identifying the

CO. Fullback Five is the XO and Fullback Four is the supply sergeant. You'll learn the others as you go along. Our platoon is Camel. Sgt. Stovall is Camel Six and Sgt. McDowd is Camel Five. This is second squad, so I'm Camel Two. First squad is Camel One; third squad is Camel Three."

"What does 'India' mean?" Daniel asked.

" 'India' is what you call the RTO. Wilson is Camel Two India. If you talk on the radio,, you're Camel Two India. Are you following all this?"

"I think I've got it."

Rose continued, "When you're on guard at night, Camel Six India will call around asking for Sit Reps."

Daniel started to ask, but Rose cut him off.

"Sit Rep stands for Situation Report."

"Roger," Daniel replied.

"At least the cherry knows 'Roger'," Wilson mumbled.

"When he calls for Camel Two," Rose continued, "just say 'Sit Rep negative, over'. You don't have to say anything else unless he asks you a specific question. Remember that when somebody calls Camel Two, they're calling for the squad. The RTO can relay any messages. When you acknowledge the call, they may ask for Camel Two specifically. In that case say 'wait one' and give me the handset. Have you got all that?"

"I think so," Daniel answered. "The platoon is Camel. Sgt. Stovall is Camel Six. You're Camel Two, and if I'm ever on the radio, I'm Camel Two India. Sit Reps are situation reports and, with luck, they're always negative."

"That's right," Rose said. "I tell you what." Rose picked up the handset and handed it to Daniel. "Call the CP and ask for a Tango Charlie."

"Tango Charlie," Daniel repeated. "T C. What's T C stand for?"

"Time check. Give it a shot."

Daniel took the handset from Rose, took a deep breath, and squeezed the push-to-talk button.

"Camel Six. This is Camel Two India. Tango Charlie. Over."

"Two India, this is Six India. Eighteen thirty hours. Over."

"Roger eighteen thirty hours. Camel Two India out."

"That was perfect, Perdue," Rose congratulated.

Wilson spoke up, "I think th' fucker's talked on the radio before. Haven't you, cherry?"

"Other than on the mountain, that was my first time."

"You picked it up quick," Rose said.

The squad leader remembered that Wilson had taken weeks to get used to talking on the radio and made a mental note that Perdue seemed to have a knack for it. The cherry still did stupid things, but Rose saw that he had potential.

At dark, Wilson went on guard and Rose and Daniel settled into the hooch. Daniel listened to the river churn over the rocks and around the fallen bridge. The pleasant sounds put him to sleep.

Daniel awoke easily when Wilson called his name. He crawled from the hooch and stepped over to the foxhole. The night was clear and warm. The reflection of the moon danced across the rippling water. Daniel ducked into the foxhole and lit a cigarette, making a mental joke about the Camels and wondering what they would be called on the radio. While lighting the cigarette, it dawned on him that it had not rained at all that day.

"I guess Rose was right about the monsoon being almost over," he whispered.

Keeping the cigarette cupped like a veteran, Daniel sat on the edge of the hole and watched. The minutes passed slowly, as they always would, but Daniel did not notice. To him, guard duty was as close to war as he had come, and the danger that lurked in the night was ever present. He waited with the intensity of a boxer waiting for the bell, yet a boxer knew when and what would happen. Daniel could only wait, his head wanting the moment to come, and his heart hoping it would not.

When a voice came over the radio, it startled Daniel. In the still of the night, the radio sounded much louder than it had before. He listened.

"Camel One, Sit Rep. Over."

"This is Camel One India. Sit Rep negative. Over."

"Roger, One. Out, Camel Two, Sit Rep. Over."

Daniel picked up the handset and spoke softly, "This is Camel Two India. Sit Rep negative. Over."

"Roger, two. Out. Camel Three, Sit Rep. Over."

"Sit Rep negative. Over."

"Roger, three, Out."

After the murmur of the radio ended, the night seemed deathly quiet. The soft, pleasant sound of the river covered up the normal, anxiety producing sounds of the jungle. Daniel looked out over the bridges and into the dancing shadows among the trees.

All seemed perfectly safe.

"For now, anyway," he whispered.

But Daniel knew from the movies that looks could be deceiving. Was not the war at it quietest just before the enemy attacked? He knew that at any moment VC could come charging out of the darkness from any direction. He felt empty and alone. His hand tightened on the grip of his rifle. But he was not scared, or so he thought. He worried only that he would react like a soldier, that he perform his duty properly. His fear had begun to be internalized, a mechanism for self-preservation that allowed the conscious mind to function without the distraction that every person's fear causes. The intensity of war forced each man to control his fear, for over time the fear would destroy even the bravest. The mind will not tolerate such fear day after day, night after night, so the mind subdues the outward awareness and places it deep inside. Even Daniel, so recently in the war zone, was losing that overt fear. It was changing to a controlled, permanent intensity, an alertness that was essential for survival in war. It was the lack of that intensity that identified every new man as a cherry. And a cherry he would remain, until such time as his fear was gone from his personality and replaced by an intensity that made warriors different from all other people.

Sitting alone at night, Daniel faced his fear. And it was the night that eventually made every man a veteran.

Daniel looked out over the river each night for three weeks. As Christmas neared, he and the squad learned that they would not return to base camp in time for a holiday celebration. they would reach base camp on the 26th, and as compensation they would receive a hot turkey dinner.

After dark on Christmas Eve, Daniel walked across the road to where Rose sat atop the French bunker.

"Thinking about Christmas back home?" Daniel asked.

"I'm Jewish, Perdue."

"Oh. I didn't know. Sorry."

"That's okay. I've had to live with Christmas since I was a kid. I take it in stride now."

Daniel stood by the bunker without talking. He had hoped to talk to Rose about the added loneliness of being away from home on Christmans, but he did not think that it was proper for him to discuss a religious holiday that did not apply to the squad leader. Finally, the silence was worse than saying something stupid.

"I guess this is a strange time for you, what with everybody talking about . . ."

"Christmas," Rose completed the sentence. "You can say the word. I had gentile friends and they were always talking about what they would get. It's such a cultural event that it's hard to ignore it."

"That's true," agreed Daniel. "It hadn't occurred to me that it was a religious holiday until you said you were . . ."

"Jewish. You can even call me a Jew."

"I'm not very religious myself. I never went to church and neither did my parents. To me Christmas has always seemed like a time for being in love. I guess television does that."

"I never watched much TV after Thanksgiving."

"I can understand that. How does a Jewish kid make it through all the commercials?"

"I got gifts for Hanukkah."

"That's at Christmastime, isn't it?"

"Close enough."

Daniel was quiet. He wanted to talk about his loneliness, but he was afraid that he might say something offensive. He had never talked to a Jew on Christmas Eve and he did not know how to act.

"Anything special on your mind?" Rose asked.

"I'm just lonely. I've never been away from home on Christmas before."

"Me neither."

"I never felt so alone in my life. I wish I was in love."

"Gotta girl back home?"

"No, but I really wish I did."

"It's tough to be alone, anytime. There ought to be a law that says only married men can go to war."

"I hate the thought of dying. . . ." Daniel was about to finish the sentence with "a virgin," but decided that he had enough problems in the squad just being a cherry. He saw no sense in telling them he was also a virgin.

"Nobody does," Rose said. "You're better off if you don't think about it. If it happens, it happens. If you worry about it, you'll drive yourself crazy."

"It's hard not to think about dying, given the situation."

"True. How very true."

The two were quiet, Rose sitting on the bunker and Daniel standing beside it.

"Time to turn in," Rose advised. "Guard comes quick."

The squad leader hopped down from the bunker and started across the road. Halfway there, he stopped and turned towards Daniel.

"Merry Christmas, Perdue."

"Thanks, Sarge," Daniel replied. Then, as Rose turned and continued across the road, Daniel called after him, "Happy Hanukkah."

In the afternoon of December 26, second squad was picked up and carried back to Camp Radcliff. They arrived in the company area at five o'clock and learned immediately that Bob Hope's Christmas Show had been at the camp that day from twelve-thirty to two-thirty.

The men celebrated their return to base camp as best they could. Captain Dunn arranged for water to be in the showers so that the men could clean up; Daniel took a bit longer in the shower that evening than he had during his first shower. The Enlisted Men's Club opened after supper, but its meager supply of beer and soft drinks was consumed in less than an hour. Daniel was uncomfortable among the rowdy veterans in the club, so when he was able to buy one of the last Cokes, ice cold, he took it with him back to the platoon tent, where he enjoyed it in peace and quiet.

The next morning the men's hopes for a trip to town were ended when Sgt. Stovall announced that the company was moving out again that afternoon. Wilson and Perez acted as designated complainers for second squad.

The company's mission on the operation would be outpost duty two miles from camp.

The defensive strategy for Camp Radcliff provided for layered protection around the area. The primary, and inner, defense was the base perimeter. In the area within one mile of the perimeter close-in patrols and ambushes operated; Daniel's first patrol from the small mountain was a part of this second layer of protection. Father out, small unsecured positions acted as bases for patrols and ambushes that covered the area two miles out from the perimeter; it was in this third layer that C Company would operate. The layered defenses were meant to prevent the Viet Cong from massing sufficient troop strength to attack the perimeter, and to prevent them from comfortably setting up rocket and mortar positions from which they could shell the camp. The defenses did not totally protect the base; charlie was able, on occasion, to avoid all the patrols and ambushes and lob shells onto the chopper pad. Such attacks were rare after the defensive strategy was implemented, but they still occurred.

The company moved out on trucks after lunch. The ride through base camp reminded Daniel of the difference between the infantry and the support troops. Seeing the thousands of soldiers who worked daily within the safety of base camp, Daniel began to realize only the infantry actually fought the war. The garritroopers worried about the occasional mortar attack, but they were well protected from any possible small arms fire. Cherry that he was, Daniel still felt pride in his role as an infantryman, and he felt vastly superior to the garritroopers and their mundane chores.

The trucks passed through the main gate and rolled along the drive that led to Highway 19. They turned left and headed for the village of An Khe. They passed the Special Forces camp on the right then crossed a broad river. The bridge dated from the same time period as the blown bridges Daniel had seen and was of the same style. The difference was that the bridge at An Khe was very, very long, having ten separate spans, and that it had not been destroyed. Perhaps the VC realized that the river was too deep and too wide for temporary structures, and that destroying the bridge would effectively disrupt the civilian population more than any army.

The village of An Khe passed by too quickly for Daniel to form any opinion about it. What appeared to be a main street ran at an angle from the highway and was crowded with Vietnamese and soldiers, so Daniel caught only a glimpse of the shops that edged up to the street.

Just beyond the village the small convoy turned right onto a narrow trail that the natives used and moved slowly through what appeared to Daniel to be occupied land. The terrain was a mixture of rice paddies, pastures and huts. Unusual hedge-like growths, unlike anything Daniel had ever seen, divided the paddies and pastures. Each hedge was a line of trees and bushes so thick that they served as fences. Neither water buffalo nor infantry could negotiate them easily. Although the area looked tended and used, Daniel saw no Vietnamese along the trail.

Third platoon was dropped at a site that other units had used. The men spent the afternoon improving the foxholes and familiarizing themselves with the area. The platoon's position was not surrounded by barbed wire, but Daniel was already sufficiently experienced from his time on the highway that its absence did not concern him. Except for his brief tour on the small mountain overlooking Camp Radcliff, Daniel had not manned a position that was protected by wire. It was just as well that Daniel's first month exposed him to so little set perimeter duty, for once the battalion moved out on an extended mission in the boonies, barbed wire would become an unavailable luxury.

During that first afternoon, Sgt. McDowd sent Rose out to a hedge that seemed a perfect location from which charlie could fire small arms at the platoon position. Rose took Daniel along and showed him how to set up trip flares.

The next day first and second squads were out on patrol. Second squad moved in a wide arc a thousand meters out from the platoon position. The patrol was long and tiring, but the ground was level and Daniel did not get sick. They saw no signs of VC.

Most of the patrols on the outer defenses found no enemy. The area around base camp was patrolled every day and was well within the range of every artillery piece in the camp. The VC had learned that the instant availability of massive artillery support made it all but impossible for them to attack any of the patrols with any chance of success. Even harassment attacks were too costly against well-armed infantry that could call in accurate and deadly artillery fire.

Being new to the boonies, Daniel was less aware of the power of artillery and more concerned that the area was one that the Viet Cong knew well. The novice imagined secret tunnels and paths enabled the enemy to move anywhere, anytime, and that they could magically pop up any place or time that they chose. Such was not the case and the veterans knew it, but charlie did operate in strength in the area and had for a long time.

The First Cav was assigned to this area because it had been a Viet Cong stronghold. An Khe was a small town but it was important because it was halfway between Qui Nhon, on the coast, and Pleiku, near the Cambodian border. The two cities were connected by Highway 19, the only east-west highway in the central highlands. By closing the road charlie could, and had for years, effectively cut off the entire western part of the highlands. Reopening the highway was easy for the Cav, but clearing the area of VC was taking some time; the VC had operated there for a long time and was not inclined to give it up without effort.

Two of the three squads in third platoon went on patrol every day; the other squad set up a night ambush. On the third night second squad moved out to take its turn on ambush, and Daniel experienced his first night as part of a very small unit separated by distance from any ground support.

When the squad moved out, Daniel was the only man who suffered anxiety. The veterans were relaxed, for to them any activity so close to base camp, and its artillery, was safe by comparison to the missions they had performed in areas accessible only by chopper. But for Daniel, it was the first night ambush ever, and, to the cherry, the first night ambush was an event wherever it occurred.

The cloudy sky was dark gray when Rose halted the squad at the location assigned for the ambush, a main trail at the point where it passed between a dry rice paddy and a native cemetery. Rose placed his men among the burial mounds and headstones; they provided excellent cover in all directions, not just from the trail, for an ambush, although intended to surprise an unsuspecting enemy, might itself be discovered accidentally by any group that approached from the wrong direction. To Daniel the ambush site seemed perfect; even a cherry, with common sense, could see that Rose knew what he was doing. Daniel had also seen the need for protection from all directions, for he was painfully aware that the squad was on its own.

The light faded and stars appeared through gaps in the clouds. All was ready. Rose crawled up beside Daniel.

"Ready for your first ambush?" he whispered.

"I guess so," he said, then he added quickly, "I mean yes."

"You're learning," the squad leader whispered. "There will be two men on guard tonight, but that doesn't mean you can talk. Remember," Rose warned, "an ambush works only if we catch 'em by surprise. If they hear us, then we'll be the ones in trouble."

"Not a sound," Daniel promised.

"If anything comes by while you're on watch, wake everybody up immediately. Quietly, but immediately. Don't screw up and try to pull off a one man ambush."

"I'll remember, Sarge."

"And stay alert for anything that might come up behind us," Rose warned. "Charlie might not be using the trail."

"No problem there, Sarge," Daniel replied. "I just wish my head would revolve in a circle on my neck."

"Maybe they'll be teaching that in basic training during the next war," Rose chuckled softly. "Don't be afraid to wake me if you think there's something out there. Don't take any chances. I'd rather lose a few minutes sleep if you're wrong than my life because you didn't know you were right. Keep your cool, but don't take any chances. Got it?"

"Got it."

Rose moved over to where Perez had set up the M60 and began talking in whispers to the machinegunner.

In the last few moments of dim light, Daniel studied the land around him. He wanted to be sure that he had a clear idea of where things were in case the shooting started. When he laid his rifle across the ancient grave that provided his protection, he whispered a soft "excuse me."

Rose sensed Daniel's excitement and put him on first watch with Perez. He explained his reasoning to the machinegunner.

"The cherry's so keyed up that we may as well take advantage of it,"
he explained. "He couldn't get to sleep for an hour even if he wanted
to."

"Are you sure the fucker will stay awake?" Perez asked, fully aware
that ambushes were no place for a cherry to be caught sleeping.

"Positive," Rose answered. "I trust him more than I do Minniefield."

"The preacher learned his lesson."

"I hope so, Perez. If Stovall or McDowd had caught him instead of
me, he'd have been court-martialed."

"We were all cherries then," Rose reminded Perez. "But falling asleep
here is a lot worse than back in the world. Here charlie can wake you
up."

"Minniefield will be all right, I think. You scared the hell outta the
fucker when you woke him up. He won't go to sleep again."

"He'd better not."

"I'll kick the fucker's ass if he does."

"I just hope you're alive to do it.

Rose crawled to his place within the ambush and stretched out to go
to sleep. Perez checked his M60 one final time, then settled down to
sleep with his arm across it.

Daniel lay on the grave and watched and listened. He was startled
once when Perez made a sudden noise, but other than that nothing
happened. Unlike the veterans, Daniel expected something to trigger
the ambush. During his second watch in the middle of the night, he
could not have been more alert if he had been on a landing craft
approaching the beaches at Normandy.

Daniel's anxiety about the unknown served him as the warrior's
instincts served the veterans. Excitement could serve the cherry in his
first days, but eventually the newness wore off. If the soldier's instincts
were not alive and growing before it did, then the cherry never became a
veteran, either because he did something stupid and got himself and
others killed, or because the other men would never fully trust him. Rose
was aware that Minniefield was slow to develop the veteran's instinct.
Perhaps it was Minniefield's devout belief that his God controlled all
things that prevented the preacher's son from acquiring the cold, hard
heart that every veteran has in the jungle. Whatever it was, Rose felt its
presence. He had already decided that someday Daniel would be the
better soldier of the two. What Rose saw, even if he did not know it, in
Daniel that he did not see in Minniefield was a basic belief that each man
was solely responsible for what happened to him, that the only power
which served a warrior was his own mind, and that the gods of man
might watch wars, but they rarely participated.

During those days between Christmas and New Year's, Daniel began acquiring patience. Patience, and quick reactions, kept a soldier alive. Patience was required because the men continuously searched for an unseen enemy. Day after day could pass without incident, and, without a sizable helping of patience, every infantryman would go crazy with anticipation of that which never seemed to come. But come it would, or could, and patience allowed each man to maintain the high level of intensity and alertness that would, or could, save his life.

Until the first shot was fired, or the first round fell, only patience helped the warrior. Luck got a man through the first volley; after that, quick reactions kept him alive, and the warrior's instinct to act instantly without having to think. That instinct could not be turned on and off like a water faucet. It grew slowly during each day and was nurtured each night. Eventually the soldier forgot the personality that had developed amid the safety and security of his peacetime existence. Then one day, the tightness in the cherry's stomach was gone, and, without a particular moment to mark the occasion, the young boy became a hardened veteran.

Daniel was far from being a veteran, but already the process was underway. His conscious fear lessened each day, for the warrior's instinct secretly found its foothold deep in his soul.

On New Year's Eve the platoon sent out no ambushes. All three squads remained at the platoon position and defended the small perimeter.

At ten minutes to twelve midnight, Terwilliger woke Daniel.

"You got to see this fer yerself," is how he advised Daniel that something interesting was happening.

The booms of outgoing artillery rolled overhead one after another. Daniel's first thought was that the Viet Cong were attacking and that he had been aroused to add strength to the small perimeter. But when he crawled hurriedly from the hooch, he saw everybody standing around staring into the distance. He looked, and what he saw amazed him.

Every artillery piece in base camp was firing flares. Above one hill east of An Khe, six flares burned continuously; as one flare went out it was replaced by another. Other hills received the same treatment from other batteries. Closer to camp, flares from mortars filled the night sky.

At midnight proper, the camp erupted in a celebration of 1966. Noise and light covered the camp and its environs. Tracers streaked through the sky from hundreds of machineguns; the .50 calibre guns put out slow, steady streams of lights that rose high above the camp; M60s let fly rapid, almost solid lines of orange. Never before had there been a fireworks display to equal the one put on that night by the First Cavalry Division.

Perez picked up his M60 and prepared to fire.

"What do you think you're doing?" Rose asked.

"Come on," Perez pleaded, 'cain't I fire just one burst?"

Those guys are inside the perimeter," Rose reminded him. "Unless you're dead certain you won't need those rounds later tonight, I suggest you save them."

"Just one burst?" Perez begged.

"Do what Rose says," came an order from McDowd. Perez put down the machinegun and mumbled, "Can't have no fuckin' fun at all around here."

The fireworks continued until twenty minutes after twelve. The sights and sounds had been so spectacular that none of the men returned to their bedrolls until one o'clock.

On New Year's day, second squad sat around the platoon position while first and third squads went on patrol. After a conversation on the radio, Sgt. Stovall walked over to where Rose sat.

"We'll be heading in when the patrols get back," he announced.

Wilson and Perez overheard Sgt. Stovall and immediately jumped to their feet.

"We gonna get to go to town tomorrow, Sarge?" Wilson asked.

"It looks like we're goin' to have the day off," Stovall answered without enthusiasm.

"All fuckin' right!" Wilson shouted.

"Fuckin' A," Perez cheered.

Rose turned to Daniel and spoke, "Looks like you'll get your first trip to town tomorrow, Perdue. What do you plan to do?"

Daniel did not answer; he did not even look at the squad leader. His attention was directed elsewhere.

Rose looked in the direction of Daniel's gaze and saw what held his attention. Moving slowly across the sky towards base camp was a flying crane, a giant, powerful cargo helicopter that could lift almost anything. Below the huge chopper hung a twin engine Caribou cargo plane with part of its tail section missing.

Second squad awoke in a holiday mood, as they did on any morning when they knew they were going to town. At breakfast Perez and Wilson began a running debate that lasted the rest of the morning about which establishment in town employed the prettiest ladies. In line for the showers, Wilson only once interrupted the debate to demand that those ahead exercise greater celerity. Upon returning to the platoon tent, the men shaved, except for Minniefield, who needed to shave only once a month. For reasoned never explained, payday was delayed until the second of January; it was the only occasion that the army was ever late. The men became impatient waiting for pay call and Wilson condemned the delay in his departure for An Khe with a loud "When's th' fuckin' eagle gonna shit?" By nine thirty the eagle had done as Wilson requested, and Daniel passed the time before the trucks arrived by examining the military script that the army issued instead of real money.

When someone in the company area yelled that the trucks had arrived, all the men in second squad grabbed their weapons and left the tent, except for Daniel, who had to be told by Rose to carry his rifle along. Daniel was surprised that he had to carry a weapon to town, but he did not question his squad leader's order. Before Daniel's second trip to town, the division commander decided that the area could be secured adequately by the military police during the day and that weapons carried by soldiers on pass had caused more trouble than they prevented. But that would be next time; on this trip Daniel carried his rifle and worried all the time that he was in town that he might have to use it.

The men crowded on the trucks; there was room for everyone only because the army could always make room for one more. Along the way to the main gate the trucks stopped at division finance so the men could convert some of their money into piasters, the native currency.

The ride into town provided Daniel with a surprise, and a lesson in the value of looking in all directions. When Daniel crossed the long bridge at the edge of An Khe the first time, he sat on the right side of the truck and observed the river and the activity along its banks from that side, looking south. Feeling more the tourist this morning, Daniel glanced to the left and saw a second bridge several hundred yards upstream. The newly found structure was very narrow and showed the scars of decades of traffic. Daniel was puzzled before as to why the Viet Cong had not destroyed the long highway bridge, but now that he knew there were two bridges, he really wondered why at least one of them was not blown.

The trucks stopped at the intersection of the highway and An Khe's main street. As the men dismounted, a sergeant yelled for their attention. When he got it, he spoke in a firm but quiet voice.

"The trucks will be back at 1600 hours to pick you up," he announced. "Anybody who misses the trucks will be considered AWOL. Understand?"

"That all?" someone asked.

"No," the sergeant replied. "Keep track of your weapons. Don't let somebody steal it while you're screwing some whore."

The men punctuated that statement with assorted hoots and howls.

"And use protection," the sergeant ordered. "Anybody who gets VD gets an Article 15."

The assembly did not wait for the sergeant to say more. The men scattered among the soldiers and civilians already in the street.

Daniel stood at the intersection and gazed at the carnival of sights and sounds. The visible businesses were small shops one beside the other on both sides of the street. The absence of vehicles gave the area the appearance of a pedestrian mall, one which the merchants were slowly filling in as they spread their wares on tables and on the ground in front of their shops.

Rose stepped up beside Daniel.

"What are you waiting for?" he asked. "It's party time!"

Daniel held up his rifle and replied, "I've never been to a party with a loaded rifle."

"Don't worry about that at all," Rose advised. "It's just something to keep track of. You're off 'til 1600. Enjoy."

"I'll try," Daniel said without conviction.

"Tell you what," Rose decided, "stick with me and I'll show you around."

"I'd appreciate that, Sarge," Daniel said, visibly relieved that he would not have to wander around alone.

"First stop is the barber shop," Rose stated flatly.

"I don't need a haircut."

"Who does?" Rose laughed. "Come on, you're in for a treat."

Rose led Daniel through the crowded street. One after another, the sidewalk venders called to them, urging them to buy some item of junk that was exactly the same as the junk in every other shop.

"Do all these people sell the same things?" Daniel asked.

"Yeah, they do," Rose answered, "but their prices vary. If you haggle with them you can get a better price."

Daniel followed Rose when he stepped between two sidewalk shops and into what passed for a barber shop. They entered through a doorless doorway into a room with a dirt floor and two simple, straight back chairs. Three teenage boys appeared to run the shop, but the floor was littered with small children and an old woman who watched over them. A handlettered sign listing services and prices hung from one wall. None of the natives in the shop spoke English.

"Haircut," Rose said, using his fingers to demonstrate.

"Number one GI," one of the boys replied as he motioned for Rose and Daniel to sit.

"Shampoo," Rose said, against demonstrating with his fingers.

"Number one GI," the boy repeated with another motion to sit.

"Massage," Rose continued, still demonstrating.

"Number one GI," the boy said a third time.

"Are you sure about this?" Daniel asked the veteran.

"It'll be great. Just sit back and enjoy."

Rose and Daniel sat in the two chairs as the "barbers" made their preparations.

"I don't believe this," Daniel said as he positioned his rifle comfortably in his lap.

"You'll love it," Rose insisted. "There's nothing like it in the world."

Daniel's barber spread a cloth over him, wrapped a towel around his neck, and then led him the few steps to a corner. There Daniel was directed to lean over a bucket while the young barber poured a small quantity of water over his head. As the barber washed his hair, Daniel spoke to Rose.

"I always wash my hair after a haircut," Daniel said. "How do I tell him that?"

"Unless you speak Vietnamese, you don't."

The barber finished quickly and again poured water over Daniel's head. The amount did not seem to Daniel to be sufficient for a thorough rinse, but Daniel was unwilling to bring up the question under the circumstances. The barber led him back to the chair and motioned for him to sit.

"Number one GI," the barber said.

"I wonder if Westmoreland knows I'm the number one GI?"

As Daniel's barber began drying Daniel's hair, the other barber led Rose to the corner and began the shampoo process.

Daniel's hair was still very short from the close-croppings he received in jump school, but the barber somehow managed to comb it. Then the barber picked up a hand clipper, there was no electricity in the shop, and started cutting Daniel's hair. When Rose was done with his shampoo, he sat in the chair while his barber waited for the one clipper to pass to him. The clippers pulled and pinched occasionally, but the haircut was enjoyable. When he finished, the barber handed the clippers to Rose's barber and picked up an American safety razor. Much to Daniel's surprise, the barber used the razor to trim his forehead hairline.

"Rose?" Daniel called.

Rose did not open his eyes, but answered, "Yeah?"

"How can I tell this fella that he doesn't need to shave my forehead?"

"You can't."

The barber finished with the razor and removed the towel and cloth. Daniel thought the service was complete and tried to stand, but the barber held him in the chair and began the massage. The boy rubbed Daniel's head and neck firmly, but gently, and Daniel was very quickly enraptured. The boy put his hands together, fingers spread apart, and tapped lightly on Daniel's head and shoulders; the fingers made a clicking sound as the hands worked their magic. Daniel was in heaven. The barber rubbed a while, then he clicked a while. Rub a while; click a while. Daniel was so relaxed that he very nearly went to sleep.

Without warning the barber twisted Daniel's head abruptly to the left. There was a loud "pop", and Daniel thought for a second that his neck was broken. But, to his surprise, it felt great. The barber rubbed and clicked some more, then he caught Daniel by surprise again when he twisted Daniel's head to the right. There was another loud "pop", but Daniel was unconcerned. He could have sat in the chair all day and let that barber's fingers work their wonders.

But Rose had other ideas. They paid the barbers three hundred piasters each, less than three dollars, and gave them their thanks. They left the shop amid a chorus of "Number one GI."

Many bars opened to the street between the sidewalk shops and Rose led Daniel through several of them. For reasons Daniel did not know, Rose chose one bar and suggested they sit. A Vietnamese woman of indeterminate age came up to the table.

"What you want?" she said through a toothless smile.

"What kind of beer do you have?" Rose asked.

"You want beer? We got beer."

"What kind of beer?" Rose repeated.

"You want beer?" the waitress said again.

Rose gave in, "Yes, I want beer."

"One beer," she said as she turned to Daniel. "You want beer?"

Daniel was not a beer drinker in the best of circumstances, and,

although he knew he wanted to learn, he was not going to start his
lessons with a rifle between his legs.

"I'll have a Coke," he said.

"You want Coke? We got Coke."

"I want Coke."

"One beer. One Coke." She walked away.

"Is it always like this?" Daniel asked Rose.

"No," Rose chuckled, "sometimes you get a waitress who doesn't
speak English."

As Rose surveyed the employees Daniel surveyed the room. There
was no bar. In one corner a larger cooler contained a block of ice and the
establishment's beverages; two fortyish looking Vietnamese women
stood beside it talking to the woman who had served Daniel and Rose. A
doorway covered by a thin curtain separated the cooler from four chairs,
three of them occupied by non-beverage serving female employees; two
were dumpy ladies in their twenties, the third was an obnoxious, but
pretty, woman of twenty. Eight tables were placed around a room that
could have held twice as many. On either side of the front door was a
glassless window. The two side walls were bare.

The waitress returned with the soldiers' drinks already opened.

Daniel picked up the Coke from the table and found it was ice cold.
With grand anticipation of a taste from home, he lifted the bottle to his
lips and took a swallow.

It was terrible!

The drink was completely flat and tasted like flavored water. Daniel
was certain that Coca-Cola's quality control people had not visited the
local bottling plant in years. He was almost as certain that the establishment, or someone, was making two Cokes out of one.

"God! That fucker's bad!"

"The beer's not so hot, either. But at least it's cold."

"Cold don't help this," Daniel sat as he placed the bottle on the table.
"Have you ever tried one of those things."

"No," Rose replied. "I pretty much stick to beer."

"The beer can't taste any worse than that," Daniel said with the
conviction of a man who really did not like the taste of beer.

Unbeknown to Daniel, Rose had made eye contact with the pretty
girl in the chair by the curtained doorway. When the girl walked up to
the table, Rose handed Daniel his rifle and said, "Hold this. I'll be back
in a few minutes."

Rose stood up when the girl took his hand. She led him through the
curtain.

Even one so young and naive as Daniel knew what went on behind the curtain. As he sat alone at the table holding two rifles, Daniel wondered if this was the time when he, too, should take a girl behind the curtain. His decision would be intellectual rather than emotional, for he did not miss what he had never experienced. There was no animal urgency to speed the process and mandate the result. He had always imagined his first time would be a bit more romantic, but then he thought of sex as an extension of romance. He looked again at the ladies in the bar. No romance here; not even the one who went with Rose had appealed to him. Daniel took a swallow of Coke and grimaced.

"That is bad," he said aloud.

There are other bars and other girls, Daniel thought. He would look around and maybe he would find a girl who did interest him. Maybe he would be like the star with whom the pretty native girl falls in love.

"I'm back," Rose said as he sat down.

Rose returned more quickly than Daniel expected. It did not occur to the virgin that the event took substantially less time when money took the place of foreplay.

Rose took his rifle from Daniel. "Want me to hold yours for a while?"

"I'll pass," Danield answered; then he added "for now."

"Go ahead and enjoy yourself," Rose urged.

"I don't see anything in here that I like," Daniel said truthfully.

Rose was satisfied with that answer and offered a solution, "Let's check out some other places."

"Okay," Daniel agreed.

Rose finished off his beer while Daniel took one last, unpleasant swallow from the Coke.

Rose signaled for the waitress; Daniel reached for his wallet.

"Your Coke's on me, Perdue," Rose said. "Thanks for watching my rifle."

They left the bar and walked along the crowded street. At each bar they came to, they stopped at the doorway and looked in. Daniel was pleased that Rose was being so particular and had no intention of suggesting they stop in a bar without any girl that caught his fancy.

When they stepped to the doorway of one bar, Rose saw a girl with whom he had visited before. She remembered him and ran up and hugged him. The girl was very pretty, having long black hair, oriental brown eyes and a pointed, almost occidental, nose. Before Rose could give Daniel his rifle, the girl pulled him and his rifle through a curtain covered doorway that led to the rear.

As Daniel stood in the door, another of the working girls, this one older and with crooked teeth, approached him.

"Boom boom five hundred," she said.

Daniel had no idea what she meant.

"Boom boom five hundred," the lady repeated as she took his hand and tried to pull him towards the curtain.

"No, thank you," Daniel said firmly.

The woman said something, probably insulting, in Vietnamese and immediately turned her attentions to another GI just entering the bar.

Daniel decided to wait for Rose in the street, out of range of the working girls. By the time Rose came out of the bar, Daniel had seen everything that was available at the sidewalk shops near the doorway.

"Nothing in there you like?" Rose asked.

"Not in there," Daniel answered.

"Let's keep moving. We'll find you one."

"You go on without me, Sarge. I'd like to scout around on my own for a few minutes."

"Fair enough," Rose agreed. "But keep one hand on your rifle and the other on your wallet."

"I will."

Rose vanished among the crowd.

Daniel felt fortunate that he was able to get through the bars without Rose discovering that he was a virgin. And he did it without lying; none of the girls he saw did interest him. He could imagine the hazing he would get from Wilson and Perez if they learned of his virtue.

Daniel decided to see the sights, for, although it was corrupted by the presence of the U.S. Army, An Khe was still the first town he had ever been in that was not American.

There were no sights. All the bars were the same; all the shops were the same; all the items for sale in the shops were the same.

After haggling with several different shopkeepers, Daniel purchased an elephant-hide wallet, his having deteriorated during the monsoon. He stuck the wallet in his shirt and walked on.

He was walking the street for the fourth time when one particular shop caught his eye. The shop was totally inside a building, but what Daniel noticed was the girl who worked there. She was the most beautiful female his nineteen-year-old eyes had seen. Her face was more angular than the other girls and her nose was slightly bigger. Her short black hair bounced around her neck when she moved. Her skin was clear and smooth. Green pajamas covered her lean but well curved body.

"Now that's a girl I would like to make love to," Daniel said softly, knowing full well that she was not that kind of girl and that he was not the kind of boy who would try to make her that kind of girl. His next thought exemplified his naivete, "Given half a chance, I could fall in love with her."

Daniel walked around the shop for thirty minutes hoping that somehow she would find him interesting. But she was very shy around GIs and she spoke no English at all. He bought a small leather cigarette case just so she would wait on him.

But only in the movies does the beautiful native girl fall in love with Audie Murphy, so Daniel looked at her longingly one last time and left the shop. As he walked again through the crowded street, he daydreamed of what might have been.

Frustrated in love, Daniel decided to eat. Only a few places even pretended to serve American food, and none of them looked much different from the barber shop where he got his hair cut. Finally, he chose the least of the several evils, a place with a big sign that read "Hamburgers." He ate a tough, stringy burger on an oddly shaped bun and drank another flat Coke.

After the meal Daniel walked the street again. He stopped in front of the shop with the beautiful girl, but she did not notice him. An Khe was small, and soon he was bored with seeing the same shops over and over. He asked a passing GI the time and was pleased to learn that it was fifteen minutes until four. He headed down the street towards the highway, stopping for one last look at the beautiful girl, and waited for the trucks.

Rose walked up behind him.

"Did you find yourself a lady?" the veteran asked.

"I found one that was absolutely beautiful," Daniel answered truthfully.

"All right! Good for you." Rose looked at his watch. "Chow ought to be ready when we get back to the company area. I'm starved."

"Didn't you eat?" Daniel asked.

"Noooo," Rose said, then after a thought, "Did you?"

"I had a hamburger."

"Really?" Rose asked. "How do you like dog meat?"

"It tasted like dog food."

"I didn't say 'dog food', I said 'dog meat'."

"Dog meat?"

"You didn't really expect them to have beef, did you?"

"I guess I did."

"I warned you about guessing. See what can happen?"

"You're serious about the hamburger being dog meat?"

"I sure am. Stringy, wasn't it?"

"Yes."

"Don't tell anybody else or you'll never live it down."

A crowd of soldiers gathered at the intersection and eventually the trucks arrived.

After dinner the squad sat around the tent and talked about their various liaisons. Even though the EM club was closed, the men maintained a festive attitude throughout the evening. One aspect of base camp that was always celebrated was that no one had to pull guard; a night in base camp was a night of uninterrupted sleep.

That night, however, there was an interruption. Daniel awoke for no apparent reason and sat up. Rose and some of the others were also sitting up. Before he could ask Rose what was happening, Daniel heard the distinct sounds of distant explosions. The sound was completely different from the outgoing artillery.

"Sounds like charlie's mortaring the chopper pad," Rose said calmly. "Everybody up and into the creek. Wilson, wake up Minniefield."

"Can I put my boots on?" Daniel asked.

"Sure," Rose answered as he slipped on his own boots. "Just don't lace 'em up."

Daniel followed the squad to the creekbed near the footbridge. It served as a company bunker; GIs squatted at the bottom, the creek was at a trickle, and along both banks.

"Charlie usually only shoots at the chopper pad and airstrip," Rose explained to Daniel, "but once in while a stray round lands somewhere else. It's nothing to worry about. Attacks like this are war stories for the garritroopers."

The squad sat quietly for a few minutes. Daniel listened to the rounds exploding in the distance. When one round fell significantly closer, all the men in the creekbed cheered.

"Rose?"

"Yeah, Perdue?"

"What happens if charlie mortars the place when the creek's up?"

"Don't mention that to anybody," Rose ordered. "They'll have us digging bunkers."

The brief sojourn at base camp ended the following morning when Sgt. Stovall entered the tent.

Everybody listen up," he ordered. "The battalion is moving out at 0900 hours. I want each squad to send a man to supply to pick up Cs and ammo."

"Where are we going, Sarge?" Perez asked.

"Over near Pleiku. We'll be setting up a Fire Support Base."

"Been any shit there?" asked Wilson.

"Enough to fire up your ass," Stovall replied. "Everybody be in formation at 0830." He looked at his watch. "That gives you twenty minutes. Get moving."

Stovall left the tent without further comment. Rose turned to Daniel and spoke.

"Perdue. You still need magazines?"

"Yes, Sarge."

"Then you go to the supply tent to pick up the Cs. You can ask Sgt. Canella if he's found any more magazines."

"Roger."

"And hurry back," Rose ordered.

Daniel walked across the company area to the supply tent, where he found Sgt. McDowd with two privates. McDowd pointed at Daniel and started to speak, but he did not remember the cherry's name.

"What's your name, Trooper?"

"Perdue, Sergeant."

"Perdue," McDowd repeated. "Grab that case of Cs."

"Yes, Sergeant."

McDowd and the two privates, each carrying a case of C rations, started across the company area towards third platoon's tent as Daniel ducked into the supply tent. Sgt. Dunwoody sat on his bunk opening a box of radio batteries. Sgt. Canella was in the middle of the tent with a private searching through a stack of jungle fatigue trousers.

Dunwoody looked up. "You're Perdue? Right?"

"Yes, Sergeant."

"What can I do for you?"

"Sgt. Rose sent me to ask Sgt. Canella for magazines."

"Canella's in the back. He'll be finished in a second."

"Thanks, Sergeant."

Sgt. Canella walked to the front of the tent with the private, who carried a new pair of trousers.

"If that's not the right size, bring 'em back," Canella said, then he turned to Daniel, "Whadaya need?"

"Magazines."

"Everybody needs magazines. How many?"

"As many as you can let me have, Sergeant. I've only got eight."

"Eight's not enough. I've got some somewhere." Canella searched through a crate under his cot. "Four. I can give you four." He pulled the magazines from the crate and handed them to Daniel.

"Thanks, Sergeant."

"Gimme an hour, I'll get some more."

"We're moving out in twenty minutes," Daniel said.

"Gimme an hour," Canella repeated as he walked towards the back of the tent.

Dunwoody spoke, "You might as well take one of these since you're here." He pulled from the box a large battery covered by a thick, clear plastic bag.

Daniel held out the C ration case like a tray and Dunwoody put the battery beside the magazines.

"Save that bag," the commo sergeant ordered. "You can use it to protect your wallet."

"I know. Sgt. Rose told me."

"Rose is a good soldier."

"I think so, too, Sarge. I gotta go."

Back at the platoon tent, Daniel had just enough time to load the four new magazines and still make the formation.

The company marched to the brigade chopper pad and waited with the rest of the battalion. Daniel was impressed by the largest gathering of armed men he had ever seen; more than three hundred soldiers sat around the fringes of the knoll.

The roar of approaching helicopters drowned out any attempt at conversation. An endless line of Hueys stretched back to the airstrip. Four abreast, the choppers came in and picked up their loads. For fifteen minutes foursome after foursome touched down before third platoon charged into the wind and boarded.

The choppers soared out over the division perimeter before they fell in behind the westbound formation. The mass of helicopters followed the highway for several miles, then veered slowly away from the road and out over the jungle. All signs of man disappeared from the unbroken canopy beneath the roaring rotors. At an altitude of fifteen hundred feet the formation was above the range of small arms fire, but that did not make the jungle look any less forboding to a cherry.

Daniel knew the company was going out on a major operation, but he did not know what being on a major operation meant. The jungle below was his only clue to what lay ahead.

The army controlled its bases and, in daylight, the towns, but the jungle belonged to charlie. Daniel flew over that realm with mixed emotions; he was eager to face the challenge of a unique adventure, but he also feared the danger. The farther out over the jungle he flew, the more his fear grew; it tied his stomach in knots; it made his mouth dry and his hands wet.

The force that makes war possible surely must be curiosity, curiosity to make known the unknown. Boys fly off to war not to kill, but to learn if they are men, to learn if they will hold their ground when the bullets zing by their heads. The quest for adventure and the fear of death filled each man on the chopper, but Daniel did not know it. He wondered if the others were as scared as he, but they would not reveal their fear to Daniel any more than he would reveal his fear to them.

The formation began its descent and soon the choppers were landing four at a time on a dirt runway just yesterday scraped from rice paddies and pastures. There were no soldiers anywhere around it when the first choppers landed.

Second squad jumped from the Huey as it touched down and ran for cover as it lifted up and flew away. They trotted across the runway and into the scattered shrubs, where they dropped their gear and began creating a perimeter defense.

Rose again divided the squad into two groups: he kept Wilson and Perdue with him and sent Perez, Minniefield and Terwilliger to dig their holes thirty yards to the right. Rose commented that they were lucky to be on three man positions again, and that in the jungle they would likely be on two man positions.

In less than an hour Daniel dug a one-foot-deep prone shelter, and by the end of the day he finished a waist deep foxhole. The dirt was the softest he ever encountered.

Although the dirt was soft, Daniel worked long and hard in the hot sun, so when night came he fell asleep quickly.

When Wilson woke him for guard, the wind was blowing hard and cold. Even before lighting a cigarette, Daniel returned to the hooch and got his poncho liner to wrap around him. For an hour and a half he fought the cold while trying to keep his attention directed out to where charlie might be. He decided then and there that Korea must have been a rotten place to fight a war; he had seen films about the winters there and wondered how anyone could keep his mind on the war in freezing temperatures. The cold wind blew all night, making Daniel's second shift on guard as miserable as the first.

Rose aroused the squad at first light, the time when the Viet Cong were most likely to launch a ground attack. The wind died out as the sky brightened and by 0800, when the squad went across the airstrip to breakfast, the sun had already removed the chill from the air.

The Fire Support Base was just being established and all day long men and materiel were brought in. A steady stream of Chinooks flew in with their cargo hanging beneath them, punctuated by C130 cargo planes that roared in on the short runway. Slowly the support facilities were unloaded and began to function.

The engineers were delayed in setting up a water purification unit, and by midmorning of the second day the battalion used up the little water it brought with it. The men were issued two more meals of C rations for the mess unit ran out of water and would be unable to prepare lunch; the second meal of Cs indicated to the squad that the mess hall would not prepare supper either. The squad, too, ran out of water.

The army expects privates to complain. It must be written in some field manual: all privates are required to complain about something at least once a day. Of course, the army insures that the privates have something to complain about, but occasionally it goes out of its way to demonstrate that matters can always be worse.

The sun was directly overhead and the heat was intense; the rare breeze kicked up dust that clung to sweaty bodies. In spite of the heat, Perez and Wilson decided to take advantage of empty wooden ammo crates they found and build a fire to heat their noon C rations instead of using one of their precious heat tablets.

All six members of the squad sat around the fire when the roar of an approaching Chinook caught Daniel's attention. He looked up and saw it coming in low to drop a fuel bladder on the other side of the airstrip. The huge-blade chopper was less than fifty feet above the ground and was coming straight at the squad.

"Oh, fuck!" shouted Wilson as he lunged for his Cs.

"Look out! Here it comes!" Rose warned too late.

Daniel sat motionless and stared at the roaring Chinook.

In a moment the position was engulfed in a manmade tornado of swirling dust and dirt.

"Fuckin' shithook!" shouted Wilson.

"Grab the hooch!" Rose yelled as a poncho pulled loose and blew away.

"Look out for the fire!" Perez warned as he dodged bits of burning wood that flew through the air.

Perez and Rose chased after the fire and stomped on patches of burning brush that the scattered flames ignited. Daniel held on to one poncho wile he chased after a second.

"Fuckin' sonavabitch!" Wilson screamed above the roar.

Then the air was still; The Chinook and its tornado moved across the runway. In the stillness, the men surveyed the chaos that seconds earlier had been their position.

"Fuckin' mother fucker," Perez yelled after the chopper.

"Look at this shit!" Wilson said softly. "There's a ton of fuckin' dirt in these fuckin' Cs."

Everything was blown around and covered with dirt. C rations were overturned and spilled upon the ground; the fire was gone except for a place a few yards away where Perez stomped on a burning bush. The men were covered, head to toe, with dirt blown by the blades.

"The whole fuckin' runway to come in over," Rose cursed, "and that fucker had to fly right over us." He reached and picked up his rifle, which had blown to the ground. "Look at this fuckin' mess. Shit!"

"Anybody got any fuckin' water left?" Wilson asked. "I got a mouthful of fuckin' dirt."

No one answered him.

Daniel took off his shirt and shook the dirt from it. The back of his neck was caked with mud that formed when the flying dust made contact with his sweat.

"Fuckin' shithook!" Wilson repeated.

In a few seconds Daniel learned how it got its nickname.

As Wilson and Perdue rebuilt the hooch, rain began to fall hard. Everything turned to mud instantly.

Before Wilson could curse the rain, Rose had his shirt off and was taking a pseudoshower. The rest of the squad quickly followed their leader's example.

"This is the first fuckin' time I was ever glad to see it fuckin' rain," said Wilson.

"I just don't believe it," Daniel said as an odd thought crossed his mind.

"What now?" Rose asked.

"Do you realize that in the last twenty-four hours I have been freezing cold, dying of thirst, burning hot and now soaking wet in the rain?"

"Anything's possible," Rose agreed, "in the army."

"All in twenty-four hours. Less than twenty-four hours," Daniel repeated.

"You want a fuckin' medal?" Wilson asked.

"The good Lord done looked down and taken pity on us," Min-niefield announced. "This is God's own shower."

"Gimme a break," Rose whispered to himself.

Less than ten minutes after the rain stopped the sun was out and the temperature returned to its pre-rain level. Cleaned and refreshed, Daniel sat on his helmet and watched the steam rise from his trouser leg.

Late in the afternoon Sgt. McDowd came by and informed the squad that the engineers had finally set up a water point and that Rose could send men over to fill canteens. The water made it possible for the mess unit to serve evening chow, but not until 1800.

Perez led his team across the runway just before six and did not return with them until after dark.

As Daniel walked across with Rose and Wilson, he watched an airplane flying near a mountain in the distance. He watched the faint flashing lights until suddenly they disappeared in a ball of flame. Daniel pointed.

"Look at that!" he said rapidly.

"What?" Wilson asked.

"Over by the mountain there."

"I don't see nothing," Wilson grunted.

"A plane just blew up!"

"Get serious, Perdue," Rose ordered.

"I am serious, Sarge," Daniel insisted. "It was flying along and then it just burst into flames."

"You probably saw a flare explode," Rose reasoned.

"Flares don't have blinking lights," said Daniel. "I'm sure it was a plane."

"Cherries see strange things," Rose decided. "But don't go telling that to everybody or they'll take you off to the funny farm."

The next morning, when the squad was at the mess tent for breakfast, Sergeant McDowd told Rose that a Vietnamese Air Force DC3 crashed last night. No one knew for sure, but the suspicion was that it had been hit by ground fire.

After breakfast Sergeant Stovall and Sergeant McDowd came by second squad's position with news that the company was moving out again by air.

"Listen up!" Stovall began. "Get your gear together and be ready to move by 0830."

"Where we goin', Sarge?" asked Perez.

Stovall stared briefly at the machinegunner, his look clearly indicating that if Perez had remained silent he would have been told anyway.

"The POOP is we're headed for the Cambodian border."

"Oh, shit!" said Wilson.

Stovall continued, "There's spose to be some kinda infiltration route somewhere in the area."

"Double shit!" said Wilson.

"We'll be landing on a hostile LZ," Stovall added, "so be ready when you hit th' groun'."

Wilson turned to Daniel, "Ready to die, cherry?"

"Knock it off, Wilson," Sergeant McDowd ordered.

Stovall continued, "Th' platoon will be on perimeter duty. . . ."

"All fuckin' right!" Perez interrupted.

Stovall repeated the phrase sternly, "Th' platoon will be on perimeter duty, so doublecheck your flares. If. . . ."

"I ain't got no fuckin' flares, Sarge," said Wilson.

"If," Stovall repeated, "you don't have enough flares, Rose, you send a man to th' CP to get some from Sergeant Canella. But do it quick; you don't have much time and he's already begun packin'."

"I'll go," Wilson volunteered.

"Then go," Stovall ordered. "I'm through. We move out at 0830. Be ready."

"They'll be ready, Sarge," Rose assured the platoon leader.

Stovall and McDowd moved on to third squad.

Daniel was concerned about two phrases that Stovall had used. He asked Rose about the first.

"Sarge, what exactly is a hostile LZ?"

As Rose readied his equipment, he explained to Daniel. "There are three kinds of LZs. The first is a secured LZ; that's one that has a defended perimeter around it. The second type is a hostile LZ; that's when there is no perimeter and anything can happen. The third type is a Hot LZ; that's what a hostile LZ becomes as soon as the shooting starts."

"That sounds scary."

"You better be scared," Rose warned. "Only a fool isn't scared of a hostile LZ. It's no picnic. People die."

"Any suggestions on how to stay alive?" Daniel asked.

"Move fast and stay low."

Daniel thought for a second, then said, "I was hoping for something a little more detailed, Sarge."

"There is no more detail. If the LZ's hot, you either get it or you don't. There are no 'tricks' that can get you through it. There ain't a fuckin' thing you can do if that first charlie has you in his sights."

"That's not very reassuring."

"There's nothing reassuring about a hot LZ," Rose said. Then he looked around to make certain that Perez could not overhear, "Air assaults always make my hands sweat and my mouth dry. All you can do is sit up there and wait for the chopper to get low enough so you can jump out. You're a sitting duck for those few seconds before touchdown. It scares the Hell outta me every time."

"I was scared just landing here," Daniel admitted.

"I knew when I saw the airstrip that this wasn't a real assault. But if we're heading for the Cambodian border, there's no telling what we'll run into."

"Cambodian border" was the second phrase that caused anxiety for Daniel. He conjured up images of long lines of Viet Cong moving through the jungle like army ants. He prepared his equipment with a degree of fatalism for he imagined that the expected encounter with the enemy would occur this day. He lit a cigarette and waited, more scared than he would admit, but less scared than he thought he would be. His real fear was not that he might die, but that he might somehow prove to be a coward, that he would cower in terror when the first shots rang out. He sat up straight. Whatever happened, he swore to himself that he would not freeze. If he were meant to die this day, at least he would die like a man, he would die fighting. He vowed to act quickly and properly, whatever the situation. But more importantly, he hoped that he would have the chance to react, that the gods of war would preserve him through the first volley.

"I got myself into this," he said softly, "I'll just have to see it through; and I'll be damned if I'm going to make a fool of myself."

"Say again?" Rose asked.

"Talking to myself, Sarge."

"Yeah," Rose said through a broad smile, "air assaults can make you do that."

The platoon moved out and boarded the Hueys. The flight to the Cambodian border lasted only thirty minutes. Sitting on the floor in the middle of the chopper, Daniel could not watch the jungle below, and was not interested in the actions of the pilot.

When the chopper started down, Daniel peared over Wilson's shoulder trying to see whatever he could. He could not see the ground below, only the canopy of the jungle on the horizon. Instead, Daniel watched Rose, who stood on the skid of the helicopter and leaned out, holding on to the chopper with one hand.

Rose leaned back inside and shouted, "Get ready!"

When he saw the others checking their weapons, Daniel pulled back the bolt on his rifle just enough to see the round in the chamber, then he let the bolt slide forward and he closed the dirt guard. Wilson looked over his shoulder at Daniel.

"Stay close!" he shouted.

Daniel was tense, but he was not the only one. The whole squad was keyed for action. On the verge, not even Wilson mentioned Daniel's status as a cherry. During the first few moments of an assault, there were no cherries; everybody was the same; everybody was a target. A charlie in the jungle would not look through his sights and decide, "No, I will not shoot that one; he's a veteran." Or, "Yes, that one is okay; he's only a cherry." There would be not such decisions, for during those few critical moments, there was nothing the veteran's experience enabled him to do. Like the cherry, the veteran waited and took his chances.

The LZ that second squad approached was created the night before by artillery. Shell after shell had pounded the jungle until the trees splintered and disappeared, leaving a hole in the canopy just large enough for one chopper at a time to land.

Leaning out from the skid on which he stood, Rose saw the LZ moments after the Huey began to descend. Inside the chopper, behind Wilson, Daniel sat beside Minniefield, who would exit from the other side behind Perez and Terwilliger. Daniel knew the time was at hand when he looked straight out and saw the trees at eye level.

Rose jumped before the chopper touched the ground; Perez went out the opposite side at the same time. Wilson and Terwilliger dismounted as the chopper bounced on the ground. Daniel and Minniefield leaped from the platform as the pilot started up. The chopper pilot had bounced his craft on the ground and was gone.

The LZ was covered with underbrush and broken parts of trees. The men took cover until the Huey cleared the area, then they ran for the treeline before the next chopper bounced and dropped its load. Burdened with equipment as they were, the men looked awkward stepping over branches and plowing through the brush, but they cleared the LZ and came to a stop a few yards into the treeline in seconds. Rose yelled for the men to spread out and watch for any sign of charlie. There was no gunfire, yet.

One after another, the choppers came in and bounced until the whole company was on the ground. Stovall and McDowd appeared and gave orders to follow them. McDowd led the way as the platoon moved deeper into the jungle. They struggled through the vines and thorns for fifteen minutes, until Stovall began assigning men to positions in a wide arc around the Landing Zone. The positions were thirty yards apart, isolated by the thick jungle.

Daniel was assigned a position and told to dig in and clear a field of fire. As the column moved on, he dropped his gear and pulled out his entrenching tool. He adjusted it so that it served as a pick and began to dig a hole.

Unsuccessfully. The ground was as hard as rock.

After an hour of digging and scraping, Daniel cleared a hole the size of a man laying down, but no deeper than an inch. The rocks and roots had been there undisturbed for thousands of years and saw no reason to move just because some human wanted it. A second hour of work added only another inch to the depth to what should have been a foxhole. Daniel took a break and lit a cigarette. He took a long drag from the Camel and blew the smoke out slowly.

Rose walked up with a machete in his hand.

"Are you okay, Perdue?" the squad leader asked.

"I'm exhausted."

"How's your hole coming along?"

"Entrenching tools were not designed for carving stone."

"I know," Rose laughed. "I came over when I heard the clanging stop."

"Is the ground this hard everywhere, or just here?"

"I haven't been everywhere," Rose said, emphasizing the word "everywhere." "But it's easier over on my position."

"How deep is yours?"

"It's a nice sized prone shelter."

"I'll need a jackhammer to get this thing any deeper."

Rose pointed. "Drag that log over here and put it in front of your hole. At least that will give you some cover."

"Yeah. Good idea."

With his cigarette in his mouth, Daniel stood and walked over to the fallen tree trunk. A large section of it was broken off and made manageable because a convenient limb provided a handle for pulling it. Daniel dragged the log the twenty feet to his position and placed it so it provided protection from whatever might be out front.

"Take the machete," Rose ordered, "and start clearing your field of fire. I'll see if I can make this scratch in the ground any deeper."

"God, thanks," Daniel said. "This entrenching tool was about to kill me." He gave Rose the implement.

Daniel took the machete from Rose and stepped out in front of the log, then he stopped and returned to pick up his rifle. He stepped back into the underbrush and placed the rifle nearby.

"I see you're learning," Rose said.

Daniel looked back and smiled.

The cherry hacked away at the underbrush and the vines that grew from it into the lower branches of the trees. He found a rhythm and slashed his way along without paying attention to the bits of tree, vine, leaf and twig that flew around him. As he chopped at a particularly stubborn vine, he did not notice, at first, that the material falling on him was any different.

When he saw the ants on his arm, Daniel realized that the debris falling on him was alive.

"Damn ants," he said calmly as he brushed the few critters he saw from his arm.

Then the ants he did not see began to bite.

"Fuckin' ants!" he said with great enthusiasm.

Too late Daniel realized that the ants were all over him.

"What's the matter?" Rose asked.

"I've been attacked by fuckin' ants!" Daniel shouted as he feverishly brush away ants. "And they're winning!"

As Rose arrived to help with the brushing, Daniel began to come out of his clothes. His fatigue jacket came off quickly; as he unbuckled his pants, he spoke again.

"Who the fuck ever heard of ants in trees?"

"Not in Queens."

"Th' fuckers are biting!"

"Just one of the many wonders of Nature to be experienced and enjoyed in the pristine tropical paradise."

"Paradise my ass!"

When Daniel at last freed himself of ants, he returned to clearing the area in front of his position, carefully. He made a point of checking every vine for wildlife before chopping.

Rose returned to his own position after verifying for himself that Daniel's hole would get deeper only with great effort, or a jackhammer.

By midafternoon Daniel chopped and hacked his way for twenty-five yards, to where the ground sloped down into a ravine of undeterminable depth. The jungle was so thick that the ravine could have been a gorge, or the bottomless entrance into Hell, for all Daniel could tell. He was distressed that Nature provided any potential enemy with better protection than he could provide for himself. He decided that his position should be at the edge of the ravine, rather than where it was, but he was much too new to the platoon to be questioning the sergeants.

As underbrush fell away at the hands of a tired cherry, three trees appeared. The afternoon was over before Daniel was able to cut down the two smaller trees with the machete. All that remained in his field of fire was one large tree, twelve inches in diameter, at the edge of the ravine.

"Fuck that," Daniel decided, aware that a machete was not the proper equipment for a lumberjack.

xiii

It was almost dark when Sergeant McDowd came by leading a distraught crowd.

"I've got reinforcements for you, Perdue," said he.

"I was wondering if I was going to be here all night by myself."

"These men are from the artillery battery down on the LZ," McDowd explained. "They'll be helping out with guard at night."

The platoon sergeant left a man with Daniel and moved on towards Rose's position. An eighteen year old stood awkwardly in front of Daniel, loaded down with a wide assortment of equipment of war. A trip to a jungle perimeter was for an artilleryman the equivalent of assaulting the beaches at Salerno, ergo, he carried everything that he possessed. He had more magazines than Daniel.

"My name's Perdue," Daniel said as he extended his hand.

"John Gryzwasczewski," the artilleryman said as they shook.

"Right," Daniel said. "I'll call you John."

"Everybody does. When the first sergeant is calling out names in formation, he calls me John."

"I'll bet that keeps you off KP."

"You lose. Top can't pronounce it, but he can spell it."

"When did the artillery come in?"

"Before lunch. How long have you been here?"

"Since this morning. Do you have a watch?"

"Yes."

"Great! Pulling guard without a watch isn't easy. I figure if we each pull two two hour shifts starting at dark, we'll finish right about first light."

"Whatever you say. You're the boss."

"I haven't had much experience being a boss."

"You're the infantry, I'll do whatever you say. This is my first time on the perimeter."

Daniel saw that John was scared and decided not to tell him that this was Daniel's first time in the jungle.

"All I ask is that you stay awake when you're supposed to."

"You can count on it. I may even stay awake during your watch."

Dark comes quickly on the jungle floor. The treetops intertwine to form a continuous, almost solid, layer of vegetation high above the ground. This canopy blocks out the sky and even stifles the breeze. From the floor of the jungle, the sun cannot be seen as it moves across the sky. The dancing shadows created by the little light that trickles through the leaves give no indication of the direction of the sun. Twilight is unnoticed in an environment that affords no sunsets. Without these warnings of approaching night, a soldier can be caught by surprize when the light fails rapidly and day becomes night in as few as ten minutes. When darkness falls down through the canopy, engulfing everything, the soldier's eyes become useless. The night is completely, over-whelmingly dark. No ray of light penetrates the trees, no starlight, no stray moonbeam reaches the floor. No blind man sees less than a soldier in the jungle at night.

Daniel could not see John sitting beside him, nor John's hand when it reached out and touched his face.

"What the Hell?"

"I'm sorry," John whispered, "but I couldn't see you and I wondered where you were."

"I'm right here. If I decide to go anywhere, I'll let you know."

Even in the dark, Daniel knew that the artilleryman was too nervous to sleep. Daniel was scared himself, but he accepted as true what John had said about him being the infantry. He had to be responsible; if any decisions had to be made, he would have to make them. Daniel gained confidence from John's lack of it, and he felt more like a real soldier than he had at any time since he arrived in-country. Since it was unlikely John would get to sleep anytime soon, Daniel's first decision was that John take the first watch.

"I'm exhausted," Daniel said truthfully. "You pull the first guard."

"Sure. Two hours, right?"

"Right."

That infantry outranked artillery on a jungle perimeter was a new concept for Daniel. But then, if he were ever around a cannon, he would defer to an artillery cherry.

Daniel worked hard that day, first at the hole, then clearing his field of fire. He was asleep moments after lying down.

John woke Daniel two hours later, then went to sleep himself.

The night was still pitch black, so Daniel felt for the log in front of the shallow hole to determine which direction to face.

The jungle at night was noisy only when compared to total silence. In the thick vegetation that grew undisturbed for ages, dead and dying foliage fell gently to the ground. Yet in the dark, the sounds of falling leaves, twigs and limbs all but echoed through the forest. When a leaf fell, it floated softly to the ground, making a faint sound as it brushed against other leaves, vines and branches; it was barely a sound at all, just enough to be noticed in a jungle void of activity. When a twig fell, it hit the ground with enough force to sound like a man stepping on a twig, and to make a man wonder what was out there. When several twigs fell at the same time, one after the other, they sounded just like someone walking and caused serious concern. One twig was relatively safe from attack, but multiple twigs often drew a burst of rifle fire or a grenade. On those rare occasions when a limb fell from a tree, even veteran troopers froze, and prayed that a falling limb had, in fact, caused the noise, not any of the countless dangers that can be real or imagined in the dark in the jungle.

Daniel listened to every falling leaf and twig, and he spent his two hours wondering what, if anything, was out there. At the appointed time, he gladly turned the watch and the worry over to John.

Sometime after that, Daniel was awakened by the touch of John's hand.

"Perdue?" he whispered.

"What?"

"There's something out there."

Daniel sat up and grabbed his rifle. He heard the now-familiar sounds of leaf and twig, but he listened carefully just in case the scared artilleryman had really heard something. As he was deciding that John was only jumpy, he heard the distinct sound of something moving through the jungle in the ravine. Daniel did not know what was making the noises, after all, he had never listened to anyone, or anything, sneak through the jungle, but he was positive that the noises were not made by leaves, twigs, limbs, or any other inanimate jungle phenomena. Something alive was walking in the ravine.

The scared artilleryman kept his hand on Daniel's shoulder, the touch giving him courage as well as directions.

"What are you going to do?" asked John.

As if I knew, Daniel thought.

All he knew for sure was that they were four hundred yards from the Cambodian border, and that any friendly soldiers in the area were inside the perimeter, not out walking in a ravine in the middle of the night. Thirty jungle filled yards separated him from anyone who could help him, and he could not call out without giving away his position to whatever was in the ravine.

"Think you should throw a grenade?" John whispered.

That sounded like a good idea. So much for the wisdom of the infantry.

"Okay," Daniel agreed. "Lie flat in the hole."

"What hole?"

"Just duck down behind the log."

As Daniel pulled the pin on a grenade, he wished that the ground had been soft enough for him to have dug a real hole. Using the log as a direction finder, he zeroed in on the area from whence the noise came.

"Stay down," he whispered to John. "Here goes."

Daniel threw the grenade as hard as he could, making certain that it would clear the edge of the ravine. The fuse popped as he ducked behind the log on top of John.

Then he heard the dull thud of metal striking wood.

In total darkness, Daniel hit that one big tree that stood alone at the edge of the ravine.

The grenade bounced off the tree and exploded, throwing dirt and shrapnel against the log and over the heads of the two young soldiers.

Daniel raised himself from behind the log and listened. There was no sound of any kind to be heard: no leaves, no twigs, no walking in the jungle. Daniel listened as he waited for whatever was supposed to happen next. The silence was broken by the return of the sound of the walking in the ravine.

"Who threw that grenade?" Rose shouted.

The voice was clear and very loud, startling Daniel. In the darkness, he could not tell if Rose was still on his position or if he had come all or part of the way to Daniel.

"I did!" Daniel yelled.

"What in the Hell are you throwing grenades at?" Rose yelled. The squad leader was upset because debris from the blast had landed too close to him.

The sound of the walking still came from the ravine, but now it was past Daniel's position and nearly in front of Rose's.

"The same thing that's walking in front of you right now!"

Daniel heard no more from Rose. The noise moved on and slowly faded into the night.

With the first rays of daylight, Sergeant Stovall arrived at Daniel's position. John was still asleep.

"Who threw that fuckin' grenade?" Stovall demanded to know.

"I did, Sarge."

John woke up and stretched.

"What in the Hell are you throwing fuckin' grenades at, cherry?"

"There was something walking in front of the position." Daniel could not understand why Stovall was so upset.

"Did you see anything out there?"

"It was too dark."

Rose walked up.

"Goddammit, cherry!" Stovall roared, "if you don't fuckin' see nothing', you don't fuckin' do nothing'!"

"But sergeant," Daniel pleaded, "it was pitch black. I couldn't see my hand. . . ."

"I don't give a fuck how dark it is! You coulda killed somebody, you dumb fucker!"

"I'm sorry, Sarge. I heard something. I thought I did right."

"You didn't hear shit, cherry. You fucked up is what you fuckin' did!"

"I heard it too, Sarge," said Rose. "It could have been charlie, or it could have been an animal of some kind." He looked at Daniel, sympathetic that the cherry had attacked some wild creature. "Something was definitely out there."

Stovall looked Daniel square in the eyes, bending down to do so. "I don't give a fuck if there was somethin' out there, cherry. If you don't fuckin' see it, don't throw no fuckin' grenades at it!" He turned abruptly and walked away. "Fuckin' children."

"I'd better head back," John said. He was shaken by the scene Stovall created and he could not understand its cause.

Daniel turned to John, "See you later." Daniel watched the artilleryman vanish into the jungle, then he looked at Rose. "What th' Hell is Stovall so upset about. I'll pay for the fuckin' grenade!"

"With him you never know," Rose said. "I'm the one who ought to be pissed. Your grenade threw shrapnel all the way to my hole."

"I'm sorry, Sarge. I really am."

"Where did you throw the damn thing, anyway?"

"I aimed for the ravine, where the noise was," Daniel said. "I didn't know I'd hit that fuckin' tree." He pointed.

"Are you kidding?"

"Fuck no, I'm not kidding!" Daniel picked up a rock and threw it at the tree; he was not even close. "I couldn't hit that fucker with Stone Mountain, if I was trying. But I hit the fucker in the middle of the goddamn night." He picked up another stone and threw it in anger; again he missed the tree. "What th' fuck am I supposed to do? Yell out, 'oh, sergeant? oh sergeant? Can I shoot at the charlie who's cutting my throat?"

Rose laughed, "I told you war wasn't easy."

xiv

During the nights that followed, rifle bursts and grenade explosions were heard regularly, for the dark jungle and its creatures spooked even some veterans. Two GIs on the other side of the perimeter said they actually saw some Viet Cong, but Rose speculated that their sergeant had been giving them a hard time about their firing, as Stovall had given Daniel, and they lied just to get him off their backs. Daniel followed Stovall's orders to the letter: he saw nothing and he did nothing.

Just before dark one afternoon, as Daniel sat on Rose's position with the squad leader and Wilson eating supper, something tripped a flare in front of the position. Before Rose, Wilson, or Daniel could grab a rifle, the flare went out. An eerie silence ensued as they waited for whatever would happen to happen.

"Aren't those things supposed to burn longer than that?" Daniel asked softly.

"Yes," whispered Rose.

"What could have made it go out?" Daniel asked.

Wilson whispered, "Maybe a VC cupped it."

Rose and Daniel roared laughter, for the very thought of anyone wrapping his hands around a burning flare as though it were a cigarette was more than either could take without breaking up. Since they were not killed while they were helpless laughing, Rose surmised that the flare was triggered by an act of Nature, and that it burned out too fast because it was a dud.

For ten days the men cleared their fields of fire and for ten nights they endured the anxiety of noises in the dark, but, on the eleventh day, the pattern was broken.

As Daniel worked for the third day with the ax Rose found on that lone tree which he hit with the grenade, learning the meaning of the term "jungle hardwoods", Stovall came by leading a column of artillerymen.

"Get your gear together and report to Sergeant McDowd down on the LZ," the sergeant ordered.

"What's up, Sarge?"

"You'll find out down on the LZ," Stovall replied. Then to the artillerymen, "Next man drop off here."

Daniel picked up his fully loaded harness and started to put it on, but Stovall stopped him.

"Leave your pack here," he said, "all you'll need is your rifle, ammo and canteens."

"Roger, Sarge."

Stovall moved on with his group of replacements as Daniel began removing unneeded items from his harness. Rose walked up with Wilson.

"You ready?" Rose asked.

"Almost," Daniel answered. "Do you know what's going on?"

"All Stovall told me was that we're going on a combat patrol," the squad leader replied.

Daniel had not heard the expression "combat patrol" before; it sent a chill up his spine.

Wilson spoke, "Will we have a chance to fill our canteens before we move out?"

"We should," said Rose.

Perez arrived at the position leading Minniefield and Terwilliger.

"What's this combat patrol shit?" Perez asked Rose.

"Fuck if I know," Rose replied. "Let's move out."

Second squad followed the trail along the perimeter until they reached the platoon CP, where they picked up the recently worn path to the LZ. When they stepped out into the open area, Daniel was surprised at how much the LZ had changed. All the underbrush was beaten down and mud was everywhere. Four 105mm Howitzers were set up and sandbagged. An assortment of support personnel and their tents were scattered about.

Rose led his men to the company CP, where Sargeant McDowd stood talking to Sargeants Canella and Dunwoody.

"Anybody need grenades? I got grenades," asked the supply sergeant.

Daniel took one to replace the one he had bounced off the tree that first night. Wilson and Minniefield each took one.

Rose spoke to McDowd, "What's the POOP, Sarge?"

"I have no idea," replied McDowd. "The CO and XO are in the tent now. I expect they'll tell all of us once the other squads get here. You might as well take a break."

Second squad sat down to wait. First and third squads arrived in a few minutes and they, too, were told to wait.

Daniel was nervous. Whatever was about to happen must be serious, for the veterans were unusually quiet. They checked their weapons and generally acted as if they were preparing for battle.

A chopper came in and the battalion Executive Officer, a Major Barnwell, got off. He walked directly to the company CP and entered the tent.

"Who was that?" Daniel asked Rose.

"The battalion XO."

"What's he doing here?"

"Anything he damn well pleases, Perdue," Rose said sarcastically. "Sometimes you ask the dumbest questions."

"Sorry, Sarge," Daniel apologized. "It's just that he's the first major I've seen."

The company Executive Officer, 1st Lieutenant Gerald Meade, came out of the tent with a map in his hand. He was the officer Daniel had seen in base camp reading in the latrine.

"Let me have your attention," Meade said to the three squads gathered around the CP. He pointed to some spot on the map, "Intelligence reports VC in this area."

The map meant nothing to Daniel. Although he could read an army map as well as any officer, having learned the skills in high school ROTC, he was a private, and privates were never exposed to, or required to use, maps. All he knew about his location was that it was west of Pleiku, near the Cambodian border. In the vast roadless region called the Central Highlands, all travel was done by helicopter. A private need only know the direction and distance of the nearest Landing Zone; others were responsible for getting from the LZ to civilization.

"This river is the Cambodian border," Meade continued. "The charlies were reported to be just on the other side."

"How far is that from here?" McDowd asked.

"About four hundred meters," the XO answered. "We're going to try to spot them so the artillery people can get a shot at them."

"How many VC are there?" asked some private.

"Intelligence didn't say," Meade replied. "Maybe we can find out."

Daniel wondered who "intelligence" was and how in the world they could know there were VC in any given place.

Meade addressed McDowd, "Have the men mount up, Sergeant."

"Yes, Sir! On your feet, troopers!"

The XO led the platoon across the LZ. When he reached the trees, he put first squad on the point; second squad fell in behind Meade and McDowd and the third squad brought up the rear.

Leaving the hot tropical sun, the column snaked into the steaming humidity of the jungle. They worked their way through the vines, thorns and underbrush, passing around and between the trunks of the giant trees that held the canopy high above. Thick jungle slowed the point man to a snail's pace.

Daniel remembered the punji stakes he did not see on his trip down Hong Kong Mountain's nameless little brother. He now knew that, no matter the difficulty of the terrain, the enemy was the focus of his attention. He would keep his eyes open and his mind on the business at hand, all while he negotiated almost impenetrable jungle. But men were worn out by the physical quicker than the mental, and the larger, apparently stronger, men faded first. Every man was in top shape, and the bigger men simply carried more weight: their own. No one stopped, nor requested a break, but the big men suffered more, and, veterans or not, lost that attentiveness that Daniel tried so hard to acquire. At five feet eight inches tall, and a mere hundred and thirty pounds, Daniel looked more than any of the others to be a child playing at war. Yet his size was his greatest advantage. He could carry the army's weight because he carried so little of his own.

After an hour of humping, Meade called a halt to rest. They had covered two hundred meters. All of the soldiers were soaked with perspiration. Only the silver bar on his helmet separated the officer from the privates, for the jungle played no favorites; Meade was as tired as anyone, and he was just as soaked. He relished the warm water in his canteen no less than did Daniel the warm water in his. Even under the adverse conditions, the veterans knew how to rest; the break was enjoyed, but it was enjoyed as the veterans, and Daniel, too, watched the jungle for the enemy. Daniel finished his Camel as Meade gave the order to move out.

The platoon struggled through the jungle for another hour before the point man reached the river's edge. Rose led his squad to the right along the bank, where they took cover with their weapons pointing out into the clear field of fire provided by the river. Lt. Meade called a conference of his NCOs while the men rested.

The river was fifty meters wide and rippled over the rocks as though it were not too deep. Downstream, to the left, a small stream entered on the far side. The opposite bank was jungle as thick as the men were in, only the opposite bank was Cambodia.

Again Daniel wondered how "intelligence" could possibly know there were Viet Cong over there; he knew no one could see through the canopy and that there were no men over there sending in reports. What he did not know was that the army developed heat sensing devices that could identify from the air men walking under the canopy. The heat of their bodies betrayed them, and it would do it in the dark as well as in the light.

Rose crawled back to the squad in a manner that reminded Daniel of someone in a war movie. One of the strangest aspects of war is the *déjà vu* the soldier experiences. It makes it impossible to experience war without referring occassionally to Hollywood.

"The XO is sending a squad across," reported Rose.

Wilson's eyes opened wide, "Not us, I hope."

"No, first squad's going," Rose said. "Their squad leader volunteered.

Wilson turned to Perez, "That's what I fuckin' like about Rose. The fucker don't volunteer."

"While they're over there checking things out," Rose continued, "we're supposed to provide covering fire. If necessary."

Perez patted his M60, "That I can do."

"I gotta question, Sarge," Daniel said.

"What?"

"Isn't Cambodia neutral?"

"So file a protest with the United Nations. Everybody stay alert and be careful. Don't shoot any of our guys. Okay?"

Rose moved over beside Wilson and the radio and settled down with his men to wait.

First squad moved into the water with weapons held high. The river was waist deep and the bottom was very slippery. They moved very slowly into the middle. One of the men slipped and dunked his rifle, but another man grabbed him before he disappeared into the swift current.

Daniel directed his gaze towards the far bank and only glanced at first squad in the river. Daniel worried that VC might appear over there and start shooting at the men in the water. Daniel and the others left behind would have to suppress the fire, for the members of first squad would be greatly disadvantaged. Daniel was facing a confusing inner question. He wanted to be out there in the river, out there taking the chances, and yet his was relieved that he was not out there.

Daniel smiled when the thought crossed his mind that the movies always ignored the men who were left on the fringe. Perhaps Hollywood assumed that the fringe was not exciting, not as interesting as the point of the action. That may well be true, but more people experience the fringe than are involved in the action. If being on the fringe would ensure his survival, Daniel would glad play a cameo role in the movie of his life. Then again, it was often the fringe character who got killed, so the stars could carry on until the end. Daniel offered himself a solution.

"I'll be the star now, so I won't get killed, then be a bit player at the end so I won't get killed."

"What th' fuck are you grumbling about, cherry?" asked Perez.

"Oh, nothing," he said to Perez. Then to himself, "Edit that part out."

Daniel flipped the safety switch on his rifle over to full automatic and curled his finger around the trigger. A drop of perspiration rolled down the left lens of his glasses; he quickly wiped away the smear with the sleeve of his shirt. Dirty glasses were the norm in the jungle. He returned his gaze to the far bank, where every dark space was a place for a man to hide. First squad was taking forever to get across. Daniel followed the barrel of his rifle as he moved it up and down the opposite shore, from tree to tree, from opening to opening. Back and forth the barrel moved. Daniel watched and waited.

Finally, first squad reached the other side. One by one they scrambled up the bank and disappeared into the jungle.

Daniel did not know where they were going nor when they would return. He did not want to shoot any of them accidentally, so he flipped the safety on, but kept his thumb on the switch.

War is designed so that those in the most danger are usually too busy to worry about it. Waiting and watching, on the other hand, allows a soldier to think. Daniel worried, but not for his own safety. He knew that the first squad could be in real trouble if they found VC. There were too few of them to do much good against a large VC unit, and there were too few left with Daniel to be of help if they got pinned down. Daniel wondered if the XO would lead the rest of them across in a rescue attempt. No one could make it across that river under fire, neither first squad returning nor the rest going to the rescue. The river was too wide, the footing was too slippery, and the volume of fire from an AK47 was too great. If anything did happen, all Daniel and the rest could do was hope that first squad made it back to the river and across it before any charlies following them could reach the far bank and open fire. Daniel could not understand the XO's thinking. If there really were VC over there, then first squad did not have much of a chance. Either all of them should have gone across, or none of them. First squad had been ordered to avoid contact, which was every infantryman's desire at all times, but to avoid contact, one must see the enemy before being seen by the enemy. To Daniel, as to every soldier better equipped than his adversary, that seemed much easier said than done. Paranoia dictates that the enemy is always harder to see.

A short burst of M16 fire echoed across the river.

Daniel's thumb instantly flipped the safety over to full automatic and strained his eyes peering into the jungle on the far bank. He hoped that the first people he would see were Americans hurrying back. Lt. Meade was on the radio talking to first squad's leader and Rose listened in on second squad's radio, but Daniel had no idea what was happening.

Other M16s and an M60 started firing.

"Oh, fuck!" whispered Wilson.

"First squad's made contact!" Rose advised his men. "Everybody stay alert!"

Daniel envisioned first squad leaping into the river with a thousand charlies right on their heels. Daniel opened one of his ammo pouches and placed a magazine in front of him, where it would be handiest if needed.

Moments filled with tension passed before Daniel saw movement in the trees above the river. Through the underbrush came the first of the men in the squad, with the others following right behind. They did not appear to be in a great hurry as they waded into the river. The return trip seemed quicker than the journey over and in little time the men had rejoined the platoon.

First squad saw Viet Cong, or, perhaps, North Vietnamese regulars. After reaching the far side, they moved left towards the smaller stream, which they expected would provide clear viewing of any north-south traffic. When the point man reached the stream, he saw several charlies crossing some distance upstream. Rather than wait for the rest of the squad, as he should, he opened fire alone. The other men got into firing positions as quickly as they could, but the charlies vanished into the jungle and they fired only briefly into the underbrush where they disappeared. The VC did not return fire and none of them were hit.

Meade was upset that he had not gone along with first squad. He was certain that the skirmish would have unfolded differently if he had been there. He began talking on the radio.

Daniel thought first squad was lucky. Had the VC been there in larger numbers, they might not have run without returning fire. They would easily determine how small the American force was and likely would have chosen to eliminate it. That might still be their intention, after they recover from the shock of seeing GIs in Cambodia. Yes, they were lucky.

Artillery shells sailed overhead and crashed into the jungle on the far side of the river. Daniel looked at the XO, crouched some twenty yards away, as the officer called in corrections to the gunners. More shells came over and fell into the jungle, farther to the left, nearer the stream. Another correction was called in and the guns fired in earnest into the area beyond the stream.

Shells flew overhead most of the time the platoon spent returning to the perimeter. They struggled along the trail they had blazed coming out and therefore made better time going back. The artillery stopped firing when two helicopter gunships arrived. They were still flying above the river when Meade led his men through the perimeter and into the clearing.

The officer went into the CP tent while the men collapsed around it outside. Daniel was surprised by the buzz of activity on the LZ. Everybody was talking as if the engagement were a major battle. He wondered how they would react to a real fight.

Sargeants Canella and Dunwoody poured water into canteen cups from a five-gallon can. Rose turned to Dunwoody.

"What's all the shit about, Woody," Rose asked. "We didn't do much of anything."

"We lost a man." Woody answered calmly.

"Lost a man?"

"Yes."

Rose looked at Perez, "Did I miss something?"

"Fuck if I know what he's talkin' about," Perez said.

Dunwoody spoke, "Major Barnwell was blown away while you were out chasing charlies."

"How? What happened?" asked Rose.

Woody closed the top of the water can and set it off to the side. "He came out from the rear because of the intelligence reports," he began. "He was walking around acting bossy, you know how XOs can be, and he started to step in front of a cannon as it was about to fire. Some private told him that he shouldn't be there and he told the private that privates didn't order majors around. He was about fifteen feet from the barrel when the gun went off."

"You're kidding?" McDowd said from his seat nearby.

"No I'm not," Woody argued. "It damn near blew the fucker's head off. It wasn't pretty."

"You lying fucker," Wilson said calmly.

"There's what's left of his helmet," Woody said pointing.

A section of the helmet the size of a softball was missing and the remainder was slightly out of shape.

McDowd took a long drag from his cigarette. As he spoke the smoke came from his mouth, "XOs and sergeant majors have no business being anywhere near live ammunition."

After twelve days and nights on the Cambodian border, the company was ordered to pull out. When second squad reached the LZ, the artillery was gone and all the tents were struck. The company CP and all the company support people had moved out. The LZ was being abandoned, apparently, for there was no indication that any other unit was coming in to maintain the perimeter.

The men loaded on Hueys and took off over the jungle with no idea as to their destination. Rose speculated that they were going back to the airstrip at Pleiku, which satisfied the squad because, at least, it wasn't the jungle.

As the choppers roared along, Daniel noticed Benny trying to get something from one of the pockets on his pants leg. Daniel watched with interest as the grenadier extracted a can of sliced peaches that he had saved from his C rations and began trying to locate a can opener. In full harness with all his equipment, Benny could not get into the pocket where his P38 was kept, in spite of twisting and contorting himself in every way possible. Flying at fifteen hundred feet with his feet dangling over the side, Benny was appropriately careful about how he moved, and when he could not get to his can opener with his one free hand, he considered giving up on the peaches. To help, Daniel offered to hold Benny's M79. With two hands free, Benny was able to reach his P38. Having accomplished that chore, he took his weapon from Daniel and placed it securely between his legs. Slowly the can opener worked its way around the can until, at last, the lid bent back to expose the prize. Benny put away his can opener and began searching for a spoon. Even the cherry Daniel had learned to carry a plastic C ration spoon in his shirt pocket, but, for unknown reasons, Benny's spoon was not where it was supposed to be. Watching Benny search in vain, Daniel decided to offer the use of his spoon. Before Daniel could pull his spoon from his pocket, Benny's M79 slipped. He grabbed the weapon with one hand as the can of peaches slipped out of the other. Daniel and Benny watched the peaches fall until they disappeared into the jungle. Benny sat there with his spoon, which appeared at the wrong moment, and stared down at the canopy. Daniel envisioned some Viet Cong private looking up into the sky and wondering, have the Americans begun bombing with sliced peaches?

Perez slept the entire flight, which surprised everyone.

The choppers flew directly to Camp Radcliff, which delighted everyone. They flew past Hong Kong Mountain and over the air strip, landing gently at the brigade chopper pad.

Perez felt bad. He was able to walk unaided to the company area only because Minniefield and Benny carried his machinegun and equipment. He staggered into the platoon tent and collapsed on his sagging cot. Rose sent Daniel to fetch Doc Dupre, who promptly took Perez's temperature and found it to be one hundred and five. He announced that Perez had malaria and that he was going to get a stretcher. As Dupre left the tent, Rose spoke to Perez.

"Looks like you're headed for Japan, Perez."

From misery, not knowledge, Perez moaned, "Then I'll die in Japan. If they fuckin' hurry."

"Doc says you're going to be fine. In a week or two you'll be partying with geisha girls and shopping at the Tokyo PX."

"Can I buy a new watch?" asked the ailing veteran, somewhat more delirious. He reached into his left front shirt pocket and pulled out a battered old watch. One strap was missing and the crystal was badly scratched.

"They practically give them away."

"Take this," Perez said as he held his hand out to Rose. "Give it to somebody."

"Who?"

"I don't know. The cherry. Yes, give it to the cherry. He wakes up easy."

With that, Perez closed his eyes and slept. He did not wake up again until he was comfortably in bed at the 325th Evac Hospital in Qui Nhon.

The loss of Perez forced Rose to shuffle assignments within the squad. He put Wilson, the biggest, on the machinegun and gave Daniel the squad radio. Daniel considered it a promotion; no increase in rank, but a definite increase in responsibility. Wilson gave up the radio gladly, for he was convinced that the VC shot RTOs first because they were the ones who called in choppers and artillery. Daniel was elated at becoming the RTO, for he knew it would provide him with more knowledge about what was going on, and because it meant that he would be on two man positions with Rose, who always paired off with the radio.

That evening was unusually quiet for a first night in base camp. The EM club was closed and, with Perez gone, Wilson had no one with whom to argue. Even the prospect of a trip to town did not create excitement, especially for Daniel, who was informed that he would spend the day on KP.

By the time second squad left for An Khe, Daniel had been up for six hours, hard at work cleaning pots and pans.

While the company was out on the operation, the mess hall moved from its two tents into a large, new building built by the engineers. The new mess hall could feed the entire battalion in one sitting, but it lacked certain modern conveniences, such as running water. A water trailer was parked outside, behind the kitchen, near the station where pots and pans were washed. Daniel spent the day there.

Hot water was particularly hard to come by, and copious amounts were needed to clean up the grease that the army kitchen produced by the gallon. To heat water, the army had an oil-burning apparatus that sat in a standard metal garbage can. When operating, the gadget looked like someone converted the garbage can into a space heater, but it worked. By keeping the thing supplied with oil, and by constantly skimming off grease, Daniel was able to do an acceptable job. He burned himself only twice.

Daniel was released from KP several hours after dark. The showers were empty, but Daniel was too tired to worry about how dirty he was. He collapsed on his bunk and went to sleep.

For the next few days second squad worked under the supervision of Staff Sergeant Lars Mellerud, the strangest NCO in the company. Daniel had seen Mellerud around the company area many times, always working on something, but no one had ever explained exactly what his title was. He did not serve in a line platoon because no one would serve with him; he lacked a combatant's sense of urgency and was at least one beat off reality. But he could build anything.

Mellerud's skill as a builder was envied by every commander in the battalion. C Company was the first to have a latrine with four walls and a roof. C Company's commander, Captain Dunn, was sleeping in a combination CO's office and Orderly Room when the battalion commander slept in a tent. Only the footbridge failed to meet his standard for sharp appearance, but then, he built it in two hours while the water was waist deep and it was so sturdy that no one thought to replace it.

Second squad was helping Mellerud construct a building to replace the supply tent. In a flash of creativity, one of his shortcomings within the military social order, he decided that the new supply room should be an octagon instead of a square. The concrete floor was poured and setting before Captain Dunn heard about the design, and by then it was too late to argue. Argument with Mellerud was impossible; there was no chance of winning, regardless of rank. Whenever challenged, whether by captain or corporal, his Swedish accent worsened, until he eventually spoke only Swedish. They could not put him in jail for ignoring military procedure because he had not built one yet.

Mellerud was never happy. Whenever his mind wandered away from the work in his hands, complaints resulted. He complained that someone did something wrong, either then and there, or at Fort Campbell, Kentucky, in 1957. He complained about the lack of building materials or, if he had them, their quality. He once spent ten minutes straightening a nail while a bag of new nails sat at his feet.

Mellerud never talked about himself, at least not around privates, and rarely talked about anything beyond the work of the moment, but he did let a break run long one day when he started talking about a building he put up in Korea. On Mellerud's word, it shall always be believed that the two-by-fours in Korea were straighter and better than the two by fours available in Viet Nam. He seemed to think that was important.

One morning as Daniel left the latrine, he crossed paths with First Sergeant Everett.

"Come here, trooper," he ordered.

"Yes, First Sergeant?"

"Go burn the shithouse," Everett said without explanation.

"What is 'burning the shithouse', First Sergeant?"

"I don't have time for your fuckin' around, trooper. Just do it!" He turned and walked away.

Daniel had no idea of what was meant by the order, so, rather than do something wrong, he naturally went to Rose.

"Hey, Sarge," Daniel called as he entered the platoon tent, "what does the First Sergeant mean by 'burn the shithouse'?"

"Ah, so you've got latrine duty?"

"I guess so, but just what is it that I'm supposed to do?"

Rose cleared his throat and pushed out his chest; when he spoke, he tried very hard to sound like Everett.

"Trooper," he began, "burning the shithouse is extremely important. I'm glad you came to see me." He paused. "It was back, let me think, the first week in November when a young trooper such as yourself was given the assignment, but he didn't come to his squad leader for advice. No, he was afraid of the mean old First Sergeant and did exactly what he was told."

"You don't mean. . . ."

"Yes, indeed, trooper. He poured gasoline around the latrine and burned it to the ground."

Rose dropped his imitation of Everett when he began laughing. Daniel broke into laughter also.

"You should've seen Top," Rose said between laughs. "He was irate.

He cussed and threatened and stomped and stormed. If he'd had his way, the private would have been shot by a firing squad right then and there."

"Someone really set fire to the latrine?"

"It was a sight to behold! The latrine blazing away and Top ranting and raving!"

"I don't think that I was ever that cherry."

"Come on," Rose said as he stood, "I'll show you what to do."

They walked to the latrine. On the way they stopped at the orderly room and picked up one glove. At the rear of the latrine, Rose gave the glove to Daniel.

"Pull up the panel," Rose directed, "and slide out the can."

"Give me a break."

"Somebody has to do it. They won't come out by themselves."

"This must be why we draw combat pay."

Daniel lifted the panel and pulled the first can out from under the seats. It was half full and sloshed.

"Now slide one of the empty cans under there." Daniel did. "Now the other three cans. It's a four seater, you know." Daniel pulled the remaining three cans from under the latrine and pushed three empties in their places. "Drag those cans away from the building. You don't want to burn it down, do you?"

"It's a thought."

"Patience, guy. It gets worse."

"Worse?"

"Yeah. Here comes the fun part. Grab that gas can." Daniel walked over and picked it up. "Good. It's full. When it's empty you have to go over to the motor pool and fill it with JP4."

"What's JP4?"

"Jet fuel. Now pour it in the cans."

"How much?"

"Quite a bit. It has to burn for a while." Daniel emptied the gas can evenly into the four fifty-five gallon drum halves. "Now light 'em."

Daniel tossed a match into each can. The jet fuel caught fire and slowly spread around the inside of each drum.

"That wasn't too bad," Daniel said, emphasizing the "too".

"You're not finished."

"Oh, no. What next?"

"See that stick over there?"

"Yes."

"Pick it up."

"You don't mean. . . ."

"Oh, yes. You've got to stir it around so it all burns away." Daniel looked at Rose, but said nothing. Rose pointed at the stick, "And be careful which end you pick up."

"I always thought 'the shitty end of the stick' was just an expression."

"All expressions have their origins somewhere."

As Daniel picked up the stick and began stirring, the First Sergeant walked up.

"How's he doing, Rose?" Everett said.

"He's a natural, Top."

"Put some fuckin' muscle into it, trooper. You afraid you'll strain yourself?" Daniel stirred harder. "That's better. Keep it up 'til there's nothing left but a fine powder. If you do it right, it all goes away."

"Yes, First Sergeant."

Everett turned and walked away. After a few steps, he stopped and looked over his shoulder at Daniel. "I'll be back to check on you."

"I'll be here, First Sergeant."

When Everett was well out of earshot, Rose spoke, "He takes his shit seriously."

"Literally."

"Now, if you will excuse me, I'll be splitting myself. Upwind, of course."

"Of course."

The army did not give Purple Hearts for injuries to the nose sustained in non-hostile action. Before the fires got going good, the drums smelled as would be expected, but the smoke from the fires posed an additional hardship, one more unpleasant even than the occasional splash that occurred when the drums were moved. Nothing else on Earth smells like it, and few things smell as bad. Dodging smoke became an artform to be envied by every backyard barbecuer. Daniel was the epitome of grace and agility as he ducked and sidestepped while rarely missing a stir. Ambushes by drums other than the one he stirred caused Daniel to beat hasty retreats on more than one occasion, but being blindsided was justification for taking a break.

Daniel lit a cigarette and took a drag, but he lacked the dedication to tobacco that was required to smoke under those conditions. After a few blasts of latrine smoke, all smoke tended to smell the same.

Daniel finished the duty before noon, but he skipped lunch.

xvi

Base camp began to get on Daniel's nerves after a few days. Some soldiers preferred the hassles of base camp over the dangers of the boondocks. Some preferred sordid work details over the hard marches and lonely nights of the jungle. Daniel was not one of them. Talking to rear area personnel, he learned that they feared the unknown, and the jungle, to them, was an unknown. The garritroopers knew about the jungle only through stories they heard, yet, even in base camp, they were closer to danger than ever before in their lives. They were scared within the safety of a perimeter. They were terrified of what lay beyond the barbed wire.

Even a cherry, having been there, felt otherwise about the boonies. Life in the jungle was real and exciting. Priorities were reordered. The insignificant duties of base camp were discarded. The daily routine was long and hard, but the importance of a task did not depend on the time of day; there was no clock to punch, no starting times nor quitting times. There were no hassles in the jungle, no sergeants creating busywork, no salutes nor army formalities. The privileges of rank were few; all the men in the jungle shared a common lifestyle. They all walked the same distances and took the same chances, and, when the bullets flew, they all relied on the same survival instincts. Each man had a clear purpose and knew that the job must be done right. Attention to detail was required, not by the army, but by the jungle and the enemy. Those who shirked their responsibilities or performed their duties haphazardly were punished, not by the army, but swiftly and surely by the war itself, a fair but unforgiving judge.

Salvation came and the spirit of the squad improved with every step towards the brigade chopper pad. The company marched at a fast pace, as if every step shook off the pins and needles that base camp put under the skin. Laughing and joking that was missing for days reappeared while they waited for the choppers that would whisk them away.

Walking to the chopper pad, Daniel noticed that the extra weight of the radio, about twenty pounds, would require some getting used to. Wilson gladly gave up the radio for the M60, for the machine gun

123

weighed less and, as Wilson put it, the radio was of no use once the shooting started, unless one planned to talk the enemy to death. Yet Daniel was happy with the change, for he felt differently about the radio than did Wilson. Daniel knew the radio was the link to civilization, to artillery, to airstrikes, to choppers and to chow. Carrying the squad radio, he would know more about what was happening, and, too, he felt like Rose was beginning to trust him.

The Hueys came in and the company was off. After so long in base camp, the chopper ride was a relief. As Daniel gazed out over Camp Radcliff, he wondered if doorgunners ever got used to the grand view of the world provided by a flying machine. Once the formation was out over the jungle, Daniel passed the time trying to learn how to sit comfortable with a radio on his back. He even tried to convince Benny to have some peaches.

Daniel's assumption that they were flying to another forward support base was proven wrong when the doorgunner yelled to Rose that the LZ was hot. A strange feeling came over Daniel. He could accept the unknown without problems, but he could not face a known, impending danger calmly. His rate of breathing increased noticeably.

Daniel pulled the magazine from his rifle and checked to see if there were bullets in it, knowing full well there were. He slipped the magazine back in the rifle and gave it a rap on the bottom to snap it into place. After checking to make sure the weapon was on safety, he pulled the bolt back and chambered a round.

When Daniel saw Rose do the same things, it looked like a scene in a movie, the scene in which the stars check their weapons before going out to infiltrate a division of Germans. But the men in the chopper were not actors in some movie, they were just five ordinary young men who were forced by circumstance to face real dangers.

As the chopper started down, Rose and Wilson stepped out onto the skids. The ground came up quickly, for the pilot was intent on dropping his load in the shortest possible time. Daniel noticed an unfamiliar tapping as the chopper dropped below the trees and onto a very small LZ. The noise of the chopper blocked out the sounds of gunfire.

Rose jumped before the chopper touched the gound and Daniel came out right behind him, hitting the LZ at the same time the chopper did. Minniefield followed Wilson out the other side and Terwilliger followed Daniel, Benny having to jump from the chopper as it lifted off. Rose ran to the treeline, his squad on his heels. As he ran, Daniel saw the platoon CP squad huddled in the open in the middle of the LZ. As he ducked into the jungle and knelt beside Rose, Daniel wondered, briefly, why they did not seek cover.

Daniel heard an M16 firing, then, for the first time, the high pitched crack of a Chinese-made AK47 automatic rifle. Another chopper came in and bounced. Sergeant McDowd signaled Rose by hand to move towards the firing. Rose waved for his squad to follow and led his men through the jungle around the edge of the LZ until they came up beside third squad and stopped. The gunfire was loud and steady.

The radio squawked, "Camel Two, Camel Five. Over."

Daniel handed the mike to Rose, "McDowd wants you, Sarge."

Rose took the handset, "This is Camel Two. Over." He listened for a moment, then said, "Roger, Five. Out." He looked at his men. "We're supposed to move around to the right and flank 'em."

Daniel spoke, "We're one Hell of a small flanking force."

Rose moved without commenting and the squad followed. Rose pushed through the jungle keeping the gunfire on his left. The vines and thorns were brushed aside without thought, for the jungle was not the enemy. The squad moved closer and closer to the gunfire.

Daniel saw the three VC as Rose fired. He instantly raised his own weapon and squeezed the trigger. As the three charlies bolted into the underbrush, one of them fell; the other two vanished. Rose and Daniel fired in their direction until the magazines emptied.

Rose jammed another magazine into his rifle, "Give me the radio."

Daniel reloaded his rifle before handing the mike to Rose.

Rose spoke calmly, "Camel Six, this Camel Two. Over."

"This is Five, Two. What's happening over there? Over."

"We made contact. One Victor Charlie down. Over."

"Roger, Two. Good work. Keep moving and keep me informed. Over."

"Roger, Five. Two out." Rose gave the handset to Daniel. "Let's go, guys. And be ready!"

Rose led the squad to where the charlies had been.

The charlie on the ground was dead, but blood oozed from the bullet holes in his side and back. Rose led his men on without stopping to examine the kill. Daniel looked at the body as he walked past it.

They moved through the jungle without seeing any more charlies. When the radio squawked, they stopped.

"Camel Two, this is Camel Five. Over."

"This is Two India. Over."

"Tell Two to hold what he has. Over."

"Roger, Five. Will inform Two. Over."

"Roger, Two India. Five out."

Daniel spoke to Rose, "McDowd says hold what we've got."

"Everybody down," Rose ordered. "And for God's sake, you guys keep your fuckin' eyes open."

Daniel watched the jungle, but he thought about the dead Viet Cong.

Had he killed a man? Did Rose get him alone? Daniel knew that he had the man in his sights when he fired, but he was not positive he had hit him. Perhaps both he and Rose had hit him. It was a strange circumstance, but there was no time to dwell on it.

The radio squawked again, "Camel Two, this is Camel Six India. Over."

"This is Two India. Over."

"The charlies seem to have skipped out. Fullback wants everybody to assemble on the Lima Zulu ASAP. Over."

"Roger, Six India. Over."

"Six India out."

The platoon CP squad reached the Landing Zone before second squad. Stovall and McDowd went out opposite sides of the chopper at the same time, as was their habit, but they reacted differently to the small arms fire that greeted them. The two RTOs, one with a radio on the company frequency and the other with a radio on the platoon frequency, followed the sergeants out. The RTO with the company radio always stayed with Stovall, who was more concerned with orders he might receive from above than with the men who implemented those orders. The other RTO followed McDowd. Doc Dupre, the platoon medic, chose to follow McDowd also.

As Stovall touched the ground, three rounds from an AK47 sailed close by his head. In one moment of panic, the platoon leader dropped to the ground prone. His RTO knelt beside him, expecting the sergeant to pop right up and run for the trees, but when Stovall stayed down, and the bullets kept flying, the RTO was forced to drop to the prone position himself.

From the treeline, McDowd looked back at the LZ and saw Stovall flat against the ground. He, too, had heard the bullets zing by, but he raced to the cover of the trees without hesitating. He expected Stovall to be up and moving quickly, but when Stovall did not rise, McDowd feared he had been hit. McDowd called for Doc to follow and ran out into the open, diving for the ground when he reached the platoon leader. His RTO ran after him.

McDowd pushed Stovall to turn him over, "Are you hit, James?"

Stovall looked McDowd straight in the eye, but did not speak.

Stovall's RTO acknowledged a radio call, then spoke to McDowd, "The CO wants to know what's going on down here."

"Tell him I just got here myself."

"Roger, Sarge," the RTO replied before speaking into his handset.

Doc Dupre crouched beside Stovall, "Where're you hit?"

Those words convinced Stovall that he was in a predicament. His only injury was to his pride. When a bullet passed so close to his head that he actually felt it go by his ear, he was gripped by a fear he had never imagined was inside him. At no time during his tour in Korea nor thus far in Viet Nam had he ever before come so close to being killed. For a brief moment after hitting the ground, he panicked and froze. All he heard was the gunfire, until Doc spoke. When the realization of what he had done hit him, he was embarrassed. His thoughts of danger evaporated, replaced by a question: How would he cover up his momentary indiscretion?

"I'm okay. I tripped."

"Then let's get th' fuck off the LZ!" McDowd shouted to the privates. "Move it! Move It!"

McDowd followed the RTOs into the trees without looking back to see Stovall behind him.

"Gimme the radio," McDowd ordered the company RTO. "Fullback Six, this is Camel Five. Over."

"This is Six. Over."

"We've got small arms fire coming at us from the north. Tiger's in there now. Over."

"This is Six. Move around to the right and see if your group can catch the Victor Charlies in a crossfire. Over."

"Roger, Six. I'll get around there as quick as I can. Out."

McDowd motioned to his three squad leaders to move towards the firing. He stared hard at Stovall, then motioned for the RTOs to follow before heading in the direction of the firing. After a few yards, an RTO called to him.

"The CO wants to talk to Six."

"I'll take it," McDowd replied without even looking at Stoval. "This is Camel Five. Over."

Captain Dunn had been in contact with Tiger, the call sign for first platoon and, although still in the air, he obtained a clear understanding of the locations and directions involved in the fight. To Dunn, third platoon was perfectly positioned to flank the enemy, who so far had shown no inclination to retire into the jungle. He ordered McDowd to implement a flanking action, forgetting for a second the difficulty of moving in the jungle and the many minutes that would pass before third platoon could be in position on the enemy's flank.

"Roger, fullback. Wilco. Out." McDowd reached for the other radio. "Camel Two, Camel Five. Over." He paused until Rose answered, then gave orders for Rose and second squad to lead the way around to the right. He told first and third squads to follow. Before he moved out to follow his men, he turned to Stovall, "You squared away now, James?"

"Yeah."

"You sure?"

"Yeah."

"Then let's move. The war's waiting."

Stovall followed McDowd through the jungle with Doc and the RTOs in train. They moved only a few yards before nearby gunfire forced them to the ground. McDowd knew from the direction that Rose's squad had fired at something. When the radio squawked, he grabbed the mike from the RTO.

"This is Five, Two. What's happening over there?" He paused briefly, "Roger, Two. Good work. Keep moving and keep me informed. Over."

Stovall still suffered from acute embarrassment and was unable to think of anything to say. McDowd avoided the issue when he spoke.

"Rose's squad got a charlie. If they can move fast enough, they might get some more."

Stovall knew he had to say something, "Anybody hit?"

Doc tried, unsuccessfully, to stifle a giggle, but Stovall ignored it. Both RTOs smiled the smile people smile when laughter is inappropriate.

"Not yet," McDowd answered in a tone that suggested the situation could change, for he knew his men were pushing charlies who might turn and fight. "Let's keep moving. We've got a platoon to catch."

Stovall motioned for McDowd to lead the way. They had caught sight of the trailing squad when Captain Dunn called. McDowd took the handset from the RTO.

"This is Camel Five. Over."

Dunn asked, "What's the matter with Camel Six?"

"He's okay," McDowd answered. He looked Stovall straight in the eyes, "He fell coming out of the chopper and got the breath knocked out of him. It took him a few seconds to come around."

Stovall looked at McDowd with mixed emotions. He was grateful that McDowd had covered up his actions, but angry that McDowd knew the actions needed to be covered up. His stern gaze at Doc and the RTOs failed to remove the smiles from their faces.

"This is Fullback Six. Tell your people to hold up. I don't want anybody to get lost before we can secure a perimeter. And send your medic over to first platoon ASAP. Over."

"Roger, Fullback. Wilco. Over."

"Fullback Six out."

McDowd gave the one handset to its RTO and took the other. "Camel Two, this is Camel Five. Over." He paused to listen. "Tell Two to hold what he has. Over." Another pause. "Roger, Two India. Out."

"What's up?" Stovall asked.

"Doc, they need your help in first platoon."

"Where's first platoon?" Doc asked.

McDowd raised up a bit to get a better perspective on the direction.

130

"Get back to the LZ and follow it around that way." He pointed. "Somebody'll give you directions from there."

"Roger, Sarge. Give me a call if you need me."

"Stay low," Stovall ordered the medic.

McDowd watched the medic until he reached the LZ. "Let's catch up with Rose," he said as he started moving.

"Hold it a second, Sarge," an RTO called. "It's the CO again."

McDowd took the handset, "This is Camel Five. Over." As he listened, a frown crossed his face. "Roger, out." He returned the handset to the RTO. "Well, that's that."

"Now what?" the RTO asked.

"The CO's called off the chase. Tell the squad leaders to bring their squads back to the LZ. We'll form up there."

On the edge of the clearing, McDowd and the others sat down to await the arrival of the squads. Stovall sat beside McDowd, then looked around to see if anyone listened.

"I'm sorry about what happened out there."

"Forget it."

"Thanks for what you said to Dunn."

"I said to forget it, James." After a pause, Stovall started to speak again. McDowd cut him off, "I said forget it!"

"Sure," Stovall whispered.

Too ashamed to accept the reality, Stovall's memory began to change the events. Nothing had happened, not to the company, not to the platoon, not to him. The whole thing became in Stovall's mind, just another routine helicopter ride. He never mentioned it again.

xviii

Second squad joined the rest of third platoon on the LZ just as two wounded men were brought into the clearing. A bloody bandage was wrapped around the head of the first man, who was nearly dropped when one of the four men carrying him tripped over a vine, while the second, in better shape, had a bloody bandage on his left leg. A crowd of men, all from first platoon, gathered around their injured comrades.

Doc Dupre, third platoon's Cajun medic from Louisiana, left the group and walked over to where his platoon was and sat down. He took off his helmet and lit a cigarette.

"How'd it go, Doc?" asked Rose.

"I'm glad that shit's over."

"Who got hit?"

"Three men in first platoon."

"Bad?"

Doc took a drag from his cigarette and blew the smoke out slowly. "Two of them got the million dollar wound, a guaranteed ticket back to the world. Some cherry named Jenkins bought it, though. He stepped in front of an AK47. Got it three times in the chest. He was dead when he hit the ground."

Rose turned to Daniel, seated nearby, "Was that the guy you came in with, Perdue?"

"Yeah. Jenkins and me came together."

"Too bad."

"Yeah." Daniel thought how easily it could have been him. "How did it happen, Doc?"

"The best I can figure, first platoon caught some fire when their choppers came in. . . ."

Rose interrupted, "Our chopper was peppered, too."

Daniel said aloud, "Is that what that tapping was?"

Rose did not answer the obvious.

Doc continued, "They moved into the jungle to get the snipers, but there turned out to be more than just snipers in there." He puffed on his cigarette, "They saw at least a dozen. God only knows how many were

131

hidden by the jungle. The squad leader and machinegunner from first squad got hit right away. The squad leader got it in the head. Messed him up pretty good, but I think he'll be all right. The other kid got it in the thigh. Broke the bone. Third squad was moving up to help, as I heard it, when they ran into some shit themselves. That's when the cherry got it. He never knew what hit him."

Daniel heard a chopper coming in and looked up. A Medevac Huey landed on the small LZ, its blades blowing dirt and debris over the men sitting around the edge of the clearing. Supervised by their medic, men from first platoon carried their wounded to the chopper. The men ducked away and the Huey lifted up. Daniel watched it clear the trees, then listened to the whoosh-whoosh of the blades fade away as the chopper headed for Camp Radcliff and the 2nd Surgical Hospital (MASH).

Three men emerged from the jungle carrying the limp, lifeless body of Terry Jenkins. The men of third platoon watched as the men brought him over and put him down only ten yards away.

"What a fuckin' waste," Doc said as he flipped away his cigarette. "What a fuckin' waste."

Daniel's hands began to shake as his thoughts took him back to the moment when Rose opened fire. He lit another cigarette in hopes that it would calm him down, but the shaking hands were made more noticeable by the act. What if the charlies had seen them before Rose saw the charlies? They would have fired first. Daniel stretched his shoulders in an effort to suppress the cold chill in his spine. He squeezed his fist to keep his hand from shaking.

Rose noticed, "Relax, Perdue. It's over."

Daniel pointed at Jenkins, "That could have been you or me."

Rose moved over beside Daniel and put his hand on the shoulder of the RTO. "If you're gonna survive, you've got to block out shit like that. Those who are gone, are gone. Nothing can bring 'em back. And it damn sure doesn't do anybody any good to start worrying about what might have happened. Jenkins is dead and you're alive. Forget him, that's the only way you can keep your head screwed on right."

"God, that's cold hearted."

"Yes, it is. But that's what it takes to keep your sanity. People are gonna die, there's no way to avoid it. You just can't let other people get to you. That's why none of the guys want any new friends. It hurts bad when a friend gets it. I know it sounds cruel, but you just can't worry about one of our guys getting it any more than you can worry about the dead charlie out there."

"I've been thinking about that, too."

"Don't."

"I never shot at a person before."

"And you didn't today. Charlies aren't people, they're soldiers like you and me. You forfeit your status as a human being as soon as you pick up that rifle. You gotta do what you gotta do, so don't drive yourself crazy." Rose paused for a long moment. "It was my first time, too."

"Did you get him, or did we both?"

"It really doesn't matter, Perdue. Does it?"

"I guess not, I mean, no."

Rose smiled. The cherry was no longer a cherry in the mind of the squad leader.

Another chopper came in and landed on the LZ, forcing Rose and Daniel to turn away from the blowing debris. Four men from first platoon picked up Jenkins and carried him to the chopper. He was placed aboard, then the men hurried away. The chopper lifted off. Rose and Daniel both watched the dead body until it was no longer visible.

McDowd called to his men, "Mount up, troopers. It's time to move out."

Second and third platoons moved into the jungles in single files ten yards apart. First platoon stayed to secure the perimeter.

Captain Dunn received permission from the battalion CO to persue the charlies. He forced a fast pace through the jungle in an effort to catch them, but a fast pace in the jungle was not necessarily fast enough to catch people who moved quickly and quietly under the canopy with years of practice.

"Catching them" always seemed so simple in the movies. The chase always ended in a pitched battle in some clearing. But this was different. If they caught up to the charlies at all, they would see no more than their last man, and just one rifle burst from him would stop the company and allow the rest to disappear.

Or the charlies could catch the company. They could be leading the Americans right into an ambush, a ploy they had used since the days of the French. Captain Dunn could have them chasing more than they could handle.

The more likely scenario was that Dunn had no idea where the charlies were or what direction they had taken once they were out of sight in the jungle. He might stumble on some more charlies by accident, but it was unlikely that he knew enough to be led into an ambush.

As the company moved through the jungle, Daniel struggled with the radio. Every dangling vine grabbed it and pulled Daniel back. Benny, behind Daniel, helped untangle the radio often, and Daniel was able to keep up with the fast pace. Daniel did not yet consider himself a veteran, but he did travel through the jungle while monitoring his radio and watching for the enemy. He knew that things happened suddenly, and he stayed ready.

The company moved the rest of the morning and through the afternoon without stopping for noon chow. The hard pace continued until almost dark, when they came to a clearing, a pasture that separated the jungle from a small village. Beyond the huts, a pattern of rice paddies spread out for several hundred meters.

The CO ordered his men to deploy just inside the treeline and dig in for the night. They would wait until morning to clear the village.

Rose and Daniel settled in together. Wilson, Minniefield and Terwilliger manned a position only a few yards to the right. Spread out as the company was, the men on guard had to watch both front and rear.

In the fading twilight, Daniel ate a can of cold beans and franks. He thought how easily he accepted cold C rations as the evening meal, the dinner at the close of a day at the office. He was almost totally adjusted to life in the boonies now. He accepted the constant danger and occasional excitement as normal. Whatever happened, happened. He was alive and a part of all that was real and important. For the first time in his life, he felt truly secure. He was not losing his fear of death, no sane man could, but he felt like he was equal to whatever challenge might present itself. He was confident that he could react in any situation. He stopped thinking about things that were beyond his control, things like fate and odds. How great it would be to take home his newfound confidence. He could face anything in the states calmly, without intimidation. Daniel smiled with anticipation of how good his life would be when he got home·

The next morning the sky was light and the sun nearly up when Daniel saw Captain Dunn talking on the radio.

Officers had stories. Their lives revolved around a coherent body of information. They shared in the decisions that affected their lives and they walked in the circles of power. They knew where they had been and where they were, but, more important, they knew where they were going. Perhaps a nurse waited for them back in base camp, creating for them a particular drama that gave texture to their stories. They exchanged dramatic dialogue in dramatic moments.

Privates did not have stories, yet their's was the true reality. They were the extras who stood on the fringe of the story. The extras, the followers, experienced events as the masses experienced events, the nameless, faceless crowds, the cast of thousands since the beginnings of time. The private did not know what lay ahead, rather, his life was one unexpected, unique adventure after another, without the benefit of a script. He never knew one minute where life would take him the next minute. He went where he was told to go and did what he was told to do. He did not know the plot, for the scenes changed too rapidly, the connections were too vague. There was no dramatic ending to expect, no classic reunion upon his return to safety. The lot of the extra was to survive, to be around for the next scene. The faces changed as the years went by, but still the extra stood on the fringe of some officer's story. The part went unnoticed as the cherry arrived and grew up to be a soldier. Unnoticed, the veteran was written out of the script, never having had a part. But the departing veteran was recently a cherry himself, a young man, once, who came and stood on the fringe. And changed forever.

Daniel watched Captain Dunn talk on the radio. The sun was rising, and the delay made it unlikely that the company would find anything in the village. Warnings not given the night before were surely given as the Americans huddled in the morning. Anyone not interested in meeting them was surely gone. Anyone waiting for them would be a poor host. Anyone surprised by them must be a fool and already drafted into the ARVNs.

The sun cast long shadows when the CO finally gave the signal to move on the village. It appeared deserted, but the men would take no chances. Daniel stayed beside Rose as the company, in line, crossed the open pasture and entered the village. Second squad stayed together searching huts and sheds and bomb shelters. Daniel followed Rose through courtyards and houses, and then through a narrow opening in a punji stake fence and a bamboo barricade, a traditional structure designed to protect the villagers from the occasional tiger.

Minniefield's voice pierced the air, "Aw, fuck!"

The entire squad turned to see what made the Preacher use profanity.

Minniefield had caught his pants leg on one of the punji stakes and yanked his leg quickly away, lest he be scratched by its infection causing point. But when he made the movement, he pushed his leg into a punji stake behind him. It had penetrated nearly an inch.

Wilson spoke first, "You done fucked up, Preacher."

"Damn them sticks!" Minniefield said slowly as he balanced on his good leg amid the punji stakes.

"Be careful!" Rose warned. "If you fall over, you could kill yourself!"

Wilson and Terwilliger helped Minniefield from among the stakes and sat him down. A tear trickled from his eye, but he uttered no sounds and would not admit to the others how much it hurt.

"You done got yourself a fuckin' Purple Heart," Wilson said with a grin. "You sure as fuck have."

"And a trip to the Philippines, at least," said Rose as he placed a sterile bandage over the wound. "Maybe even Japan."

"I'd just as soon I didn't," Minniefield said. "It hurts."

"Medic!" called Rose.

"Fuck, Preacher," Wilson said, "it's supposed to hurt."

Doc Dupre trotted up, followed by McDowd and Stovall.

"What's going on here?" Stovall asked.

"Minniefield caught a punji stake," Rose answered.

Doc removed the bloody bandage that Rose had held against the wound. "You'll be okay. Don't worry. It looks pretty deep. You want a shot for the pain?"

"I don't want none of that dope!" Minniefield insisted.

"It's your leg," Doc said as he pulled a fresh bandage from his kit. "Leave this loose so it'll bleed. The blood will help clean it out." Doc wrapped the bandage around the wound and tied it off loosely.

Stovall spoke, "Get your people moving, Rose. Everything's under control here."

"Take care, Preacher. You'll be fine," Rose said as he patted Minniefield's shoulder. "Okay, guys. Let's move out."

Rose stood up and motioned for the squad to follow. As they walked away, McDowd called the CO on the radio to report and request a Medevac chopper.

Second squad was now down to four men. When Rose had told Daniel to expect two-man positions in the boonies, the squad leader had not anticipated that two of his men would be missing.

Captain Dunn decided to set up the company perimeter on the far side of the village. The dry paddies were a better, a bigger, LZ than was the jungle clearing where they landed the day before. The men spent the afternoon digging foxholes in the soft dirt of the paddies. A chopper brought in hot chow, but too early for first platoon and the company CP section; they did not make it to the new perimeter until after dark.

xix

When morning came, the company began what would become the standard pattern of operations. Two platoons moved out every day on search and clear missions while the third stayed to secure the perimeter. Each night the platoon that remained behind sent out squad ambushes. The duties rotated, day after day, night after night. Patrol, ambush, move to a new perimeter.

The privates lost tract of days and dates. Yesterday was gone and tomorrow belonged to those who controlled events.The privates knew only today, from firstlight to twilight, and tonight, from twilight to firstlight. Each day was like the day before. There were no Sundays or Wednesdays, no weekdays or weekends. There was only today. And the day was filled with individual moments, each as distinct as the day was blurred.

Each day dawned with intensity, for firstlight always brought with it the possibility of an attack. A breakfast of C rations began another day of walking and searching. When change came, it came without warning. Choppers arrived and the infantry rode for a few minutes. Then they landed in a clearing that looked just like the clearing they left. The trees were the same, but in different places. The rice paddies were the same, but in different shapes. The form varied with movement, but the substance, the image, the feel remained the same. The memory of a Landing Zone blurred into a memory of all Landing Zones. The memory of a field of fire blurred into a memory of all fields of fire. The privates remembered a mound of dirt in front of a hole, but not the hole nor its field of fire. The days ran together, yesterday the same as the day before, tomorrow the same as today. Was it yesterday? Or the day before? Three days? A week? This operation or the last one? A familiar image, but of what? Of where? They were there once. Somewhere. Sometime. They were there.

One day second squad boarded the choppers and landed at the brigade chopper pad.

That evening after chow, Daniel and Rose sat on their bunks in the platoon tent.

Rose spoke, "Top said we could go to town tomorrow."

"I'm really looking forward to that barber's chair."

"Me, too," Rose agreed, "and to being with a lady of pleasure again. I'd hate to buy the farm without at least one more piece of ass."

"No shit," said Daniel, knowing his next "piece" would be his first.

"I'm gonna turn in early. I'm just not up to that crowd at the NCO club."

"At least it's open," Daniel said. The EM club was not.

Rose stretched and yawned, "A whole night's sleep without interruption. It's like heaven." He fell back in his bunk.

Daniel settled back on his cot, "I'll probably wake up in an hour and a half out of habit."

"Not me. I'm gonna rest up for tomorrow. Goodnight."

"Goodnight, Sarge."

As Daniel lay on his bunk and listened to the sounds of base camp, his mind replayed Rose's comment about being with a girl one more time before dying. The phrase troubled him. He had believed that, if he wanted the girl he married to be a virgin, he should require the same of himself. But war changed that, for next week he could walk in front of an AK47. Daniel did not want to die, but especially he did not want to die a virgin. Here, all objections to sex vanished into the great unknown called tomorrow. And what if the girl he eventually fell in love with turned out not to be a virgin? How would he feel if she knew more than he did? He remembered that pretty girl in the shop in An Khe. No, he would never have her; he would not even try. But there were other pretty girls in town he could have simply by paying the money. And if he could not find one that aroused him, he could always wait.

Daniel Perdue decided. Tomorrow he would do it. Tomorrow he would see to it he never worried again about Wilson and the others discovering his virginity. He thought about the beautiful Vietnamese girl in the shop. He dozed off with an erection. Out in the company area, a C ration can exploded in the burning trash and, for an instant, Daniel saw the dead charlie lying in the jungle at his feet. But the image of the beautiful girl returned and he went to sleep.

The morning came and Daniel awoke as excited as a kid on Christmas morning. He tried not to grin too much, lest the others discover his plan. He expected Wilson to blurt out at any moment, "Perdue's gonna get laid today."

The morning passed too slowly for Daniel, but the trucks eventually arrived and the men headed for town.

Changes had occurred. They no longer carried their weapons to town, and town itself had moved. The division commander tired of GIs getting drunk and shooting up the place, so he decided that MPs would guard everyone. To make that possible, a new native compound was built, completely enclosed by barbed wire and guard bunkers. Establishments in the village that catered to Americans moved into the new "Sin City". In one large horseshoe pattern, all the shops and barbers, bars and brothels, spread out for business. As the truck pulled up to this new recreation area, Daniel realized that he would never again see that beautiful girl in the shop on the main street.

After a refreshing stop in the barber's chair, Daniel and Rose walked out into the compound.

"Let's get away from the gate," Rose suggested. "Maybe the bars won't be so crowded farther back."

"I'm with you, Sarge."

Rose and Daniel passed many crowded bars and a number of shops that sold the same trinkets as before. Along the bottom of the horseshoe, Rose found a less crowded bar to his liking and led Daniel in. A waitress walked up to their table.

"Beer and boom boom," said Rose.

"No boom boom," the lady replied. "You want beer?"

"Does anybody here boom boom?" Rose asked.

The lady pointed to three girls in a corner, one of which was quite pretty. "Boom boom."

"Then bring me a beer," Rose said.

"Me, too!" said Daniel, intent on continuing his effort to acquire a taste for beer. Anyway, the Cokes were not worth drinking.

"Two beer," the waitress acknowledged as she walked away.

"And send boom boom!" Rose called after her.

His call got the attention of the three girls who did "boom boom". They walked over to the table. The first to reach the GIs was old, perhaps forty, and had lost her attractiveness with her youth. The second was young, but large and still eating. The third was thin and pretty, although not beautiful.

"You boom boom me?" the old one asked Rose.

The fat one put her chubby hand on Daniel's shoulder and smiled. "You boom boom?"

Rose parried the advance of the old woman and grabbed the hand of the pretty girl. "You boom boom?" he asked as he pulled her into his lap.

Daniel looked up at the fat girl, "No, thank you."

"Git it while you can, Perdue," Rose joked.

"Not 'til something better comes along."

The old woman stepped up where the fat one had been and spoke to Daniel, "You boom boom me, GI?"

"Not a chance in Hell, lady," Daniel said through a smile.

"You boom boom me?" the woman repeated.

"No!" Daniel said forcefully.

"That's right, Perdue. Stick to your standards."

"I'm just not that horny."

"Something better will come along. We've got all day."

"Right," Daniel said. He truely hoped something better would, indeed, come along.

The waitress returned with two beers of unknown origin. They were cool, but not cold. Rose turned his up and downed a third of it without stopping. Daniel turned up his bottle and took a swallow. He grimaced at its foul taste and feared he had given himself away as a novice drinker.

"Lord, that's bad," Rose said as he put the bottle on the table. "I wonder whose latrine they brew that in?"

"I don't know, but that's one shithouse that really ought to be burned."

Rose turned his bottle up again. Daniel did the same.

"Lord, that's bad," Rose repeated. "At least it beats water."

"Just barely," lied Daniel. Water would have been much better.

"Are you ready to go, fair lady?" Rose asked the girl seated in his lap.

"Number one GI," the girl replied.

"Let me make that easier for you. Boom boom?"

The girl stood and pulled at Rose's hand.

Daniel spoke, "I see you've mastered the language barrier."

"Roger that." Rose took a long swallow of beer, then stood up. "Keep an eye on my beer, will you?"

"Sure."

"Keep looking around. Maybe you'll see something you like." He turned to the girl and motioned towards the curtain covered doorway that led to the rooms. "After you, my dear."

"Have fun."

As Rose followed his girl through the curtain, he bumped into a really pretty girl who was coming out. He looked back at Daniel and pointed at the girl. He winked, then disappeared. When the girl looked in Daniel's direction, he waved at her. She walked over to the table where Daniel sat.

"Boom boom, GI?" she asked.

That was exactly what Daniel hoped she would say.

The girl was perhaps twenty, maybe younger. Her hair was shorter than that of the other girls and it bounced around her ears. Her complexion was flawless and her nose slightly pointed. She wore thin black pajama pants and a thin pink shirt that buttoned in front. Her breasts were just large enough to press against the shirt and cause sexy gaps between the buttons. She definitely aroused Daniel's interest.

"Number one pretty girl," Daniel said, motioning for her to sit down.

To his surprise, she sat in his lap and put her right arm around his shoulder.

"Number one GI. You boom boom me?"

"As soon as I can, pretty girl," Daniel said.

She looked at him without understanding. "You boom boom me?"

"Yes. yes. yes." He rubbed her back with his left hand.

The girl leaned over and kissed his neck, then started to get up. Daniel stopped her.

He pointed at Rose's beer and said, "GI boom boom now. He come back, we go boom boom."

He felt like a fool. He did not know if she knew what he said. He felt silly for having spoken as she spoke, as if talking the way she talked would make it easier for her to understand him.

"GI come back. We boom boom?" the girl said.

"Yes!" Daniel said, surprized that she understood.

Maybe the girl spoke more English than he thought. Maybe not. She knew little of the American's language, but was well experienced in the activities that led up to her earning her living.

"What's your name?" Daniel asked.

"GI number one," she said as she kissed his neck.

"So much for conversation."

Between her kissing his neck and her presence in his lap, Daniel began to get aroused. The girl felt him grow and reached between her legs to stroke him. At the moment her hand touched his trousers, he felt a sensation that he had never felt before.

"Oh, boy," he said softly, but to himself. "Hurry up, Rose."

Daniel tried as hard as he could to appear casual, but the girl's hand made the task futile. Daniel was in no position to care, and no other American noticed, but the grin on his face was that of a child. He was delighted beyond his expectations and he had yet to go behind the curtain. Each movement of her hand brought new excitement and joy. Daniel closed his eyes and let his mind go where his body took it. He had experienced such feelings only in his wet dreams.

"Oh, boy!" he repeated, louder than before. "Lady, you're gonna hafta stop that or I'll fuck you right here, right now."

She knew the effect she was having on him, but she did not know he was a virgin. She thought of her actions as part of her job, a part that invariably made the man so excited that he would climax quickly, saving her time behind the curtain.

But to Daniel, all her attention was totally new. The girl's hand was an experience unto itself, one that he would have let continue until a conclusion were they in private. Each gentle stroke of her hand caused him to shudder. When she squeezed, he almost gurgled out loud.

Daniel knew he could take it no longer. He took another swallow of his beer; that would bring him back to the real world. It did. He grimaced.

The girl laughed, "Beer number ten thou."

"Beer number ten thou," Daniel echoed. The girl's hand squeezed him again. "Oh, boy," he said again.

"GI number one," the girl said, stroking him again and again.

Daniel spoke softly, "You better hurry your ass up, Rose, or your beer's gonna hafta fend for itself."

"GI number one," the girl repeated.

Daniel could take no more without being embarrassed right then and there. He grabbed her hand and pulled it away from him.

"You're number one," he said to her. She tried to put her hand on him again, but he held it tight.

When she realized his condition, she laughed.

"Laugh if you will, lady. Just don't touch me."

As the girl giggled, Daniel unbuttoned the button directly between her breasts. The gap in her shirt widened because of the pressure of body against the tight shirt. Daniel slipped his hand under her shirt and stroked her. He was no longer in unexplored territory. The girl began to get impatient.

"Number one," he said, in reference to her anatomy.

"GI number one," she replied without emotion.

Rose walked through the curtain and over to the table. As he sat down, he spoke, "I see you got her attention."

"I thought you'd never get back."

The girl asked, "You boom boom now?"

"You better believe it, lady."

She stood and took Daniel's hand, pulling him from his seat and through the curtain. As they crossed the threshhold, she dropped his hand.

"Boom boom five hundred."

Daniel reached in his pocket and withdrew a five dollar note of military script. The girl took it and gave it to an old woman who sat in the hallway. She turned and walked past several doorways before turning in to one. Daniel followed. As he entered her chosen compartment, he realized that there was no door, just a thin cloth that stopped a foot above the floor. He immediately wished there was a real, closeable door. The room was completely bare except for a piece of plywood covered with a straw mat; it posed as the bed.

The girl quickly slipped out of her shirt and dropped her pants. Before Daniel knew it, she was naked on the bed, waiting for him impatiently. When he sat on the bed to remove his boot, the girl said something in Vietnamese. A girl's voice answered in Vietnamese. It sounded like both were in the same room.

They were. The cloth that Daniel thought hung on the wall was, in fact, the wall itself. Daniel became ill at ease when he realized that only a cloth separated his girl's "bed" from that of another girl. The two girls talked in Vietnamese as Daniel undressed.

The event was not unfolding as expected. It was definitely not what he expected his first sexual encounter to be like. He was becoming embarrassed and uncomfortable, and he began to lose his erection even as he lay down beside the girl. When he rolled over on top of her, she pulled out and opened a small foil package. She removed the prophylactic and began putting it on him.

Daniel had given no thought to the possibility of disease. When he saw the object in her hand, he decided it was probably best. He rose up to his knees and watched her put it on him. Her touch reversed the decline he was experiencing.

She finished and laid back. As Daniel followed her down, she took him in her hand and guided him into her. He entered easily.

The touch of her body was exciting. He had never before been quite this close to a woman. Her breasts felt good against his chest; her stomach against his own caused him to tingle. The setting did not matter. Even though he felt almost nothing by being inside her, the touching of their bodies was sex enough. She said something in Vietnamese. It did not matter.

The girl on the other side of the cloth, likewise engaged, answered. That mattered. The apathy of his girl killed his excitement. As they carried on a conversation, his erection failed.

His lady stopped talking, but she continued to act as if he were not there. He kept trying, but he knew he was losing the battle. When the girl next door said "Fini? Fini?" he almost gave up. When that girl's GI said "Yep", it was over. He could not go on. His mind was so discouraged that it ignored what his body was doing. His erection was gone. Everything was wrong. He stopped moving.

"Fini?" the girl asked instantly.

"Yes," Daniel said as he raised himself from her.

He was finished, indeed, but he had not come close to a climax. He dressed quickly and joined Rose out front.

"That didn't take long," the squad leader said.

"Long enough," Daniel said as he sat at the table. He picked up the beer that he left there and turned it up. It was hot and flat and worse than before.

"Let's check out another place," Rose suggested.

The girl who was with Daniel came out through the curtain, looked around and walked over to some GIs on the other side of the room.

"Yeah. Let's."

xx

Wilson walked into the platoon tent leading two new troopers.

"I been pickin' cherries," he grinned.

"Are they ours?" asked Rose.

"Yep. The first sergeant just gave 'em to me," replied Wilson. "Can I keep 'em?"

Rose jumped to his feet, "Great! Welcome to second squad." He offered his hand, "I'm Bill Rose."

"Sonny Morgan," said the first of the cherries, a five foot eight inch Japanese-American from Burbank, California

"I'm Terrel McGee," said the other as he shook Rose's hand. McGee was a tall, lean black from Louisville, Kentucky. Like Morgan, McGee was eighteen years old.

Rose pointed to Daniel, "That's Perdue."

"Hi there," said Daniel.

Rose continued, "That's Terwilliger over there."

Benny looked up for the first time when he heard his name. "Howdy, fellers."

"You've already met Wilson," Rose concluded

"Can I keep 'em, Sarge?" joked Wilson. "Please?"

"We're glad to get you guys," said the squad leader. "We were starting to run out of people." He pointed to Perez' bunk, "You can take this bunk, Morgan." He pointed to Minnifield's cot, "And you can have that one, McGee."

"I didn't want th' fuckers, no way," said Wilson as he sat on his bunk. "They're too fuckin' clean."

Rose laughed, "In a week they'll be as dirty as you are."

"Dirtier," said Wilson smugly. "I'm goin' on R&R tomorrow."

"Really?" asked Rose.

"Sure as shit," grinned Wilson

"That's terrific!" Rose said. "Where?"

"Bangkok, wherever that is."

"Thailand," Daniel said from the edge of the conversation.

144

"I don't give a fuck where it is, as long as they got pretty women."

"You're leaving tomorrow?" asked Rose.

"First fuckin' thing in the morning."

Rose turned his attention to the new squad members, "Where are you guys from?"

"Kentucky," answered McGee.

"Southern California," said Morgan.

Benny interrupted, "He looks like a VC to me."

"I don't have a prayer," Morgan said, collapsing on his new bunk. "My own squad thinks I'm the enemy."

Daniel tried not to laugh.

"Don't pay any attention to Benny," Rose said. "He's just kidding. Aren't you, Benny?"

"Fuck no," insisted Benny. "He does look like a VC."

Morgan cringed, "I think I'll cry."

"Don't worry, Morgan," consoled Rose. "Benny's just giving you a hard time because you're a cherry."

Morgan turned to Benny, "My mother is from Japan, but I swear I never left California 'til I joined the army."

Benny just looked at him.

"I'm as American as you are," pleaded Morgan. "Really. Elvis Presley? Sandy Koufax?" He paused, expecting some sign of acceptance from Benny. When it did not come, he added, "Johnny Cash?"

"I guess you're okay," Benny conceded.

Daniel offered advice, "Just be damn sure you stay in uniform."

"Thank you, I will," said Morgan.

The possibility of being mistaken for a Vietnamese had not occurred to Sonny Morgan until Benny mentioned it. His life in and around Los Angeles was almost totally free of bigotry. He was accepted as just another one of the boys, and his expertise on a surfboard made him very popular with the women; he had two different girlfriends back at home, one a blonde and the other a redhead. He now faced a new situation. In addition to the normal dangers associated with the infantry, he ran the added risk of his own men mistaking him for the enemy. But neither worry nor depression was part of his personality. He was basically happy and self-confident, and, although he would always keep the inconvenience fresh in his mind, he could never concern himself with any unpleasantness for longer than a few minutes.

Rose turned to the other new man, "Where in Kentucky are you from, McGee?"

"Louisville."

Daniel spoke, "Is he all right, Benny?"

"Aw, sure."

"Is there any water in the fuckin' showers?" Wilson asked no one in particular. "I don't wanna get on that plane smellin' like shit."

"Not the last I heard," said Rose.

"Fuck!" Wilson replied. "Them fuckin' showers ain't never got no fuckin' water." He sniffed at himself. "Do I smell bad?"

"How would I know," Daniel answered. "I don't even smell me anymore."

A GI stuck his head in the tent, "Sergeant Rose?"

"That's me."

"Sergeant Stovall wants to see you."

"Be right there," said Rose. He turned to his veterans, "You guys square away the cherries. I'll be back as soon as I can."

Rose returned in fifteen minutes with word that the company would move out first thing in the morning to begin two weeks on division perimeter duty.

With Wilson to be gone for a week and two new men to break in, Rose reorganized the squad. He gave the M60 to McGee, who was big enough to handle it easily. How the five of them would break down depended on how many positions the squad would have to man.

After breakfast in the battalion mess hall, the company formed up and marched to the perimeter. Wilson left by jeep for the airstrip and Bangkok.

The squad was assigned two positions. One was a guard tower, the other a simple covered bunker for riflemen. The squad leader and the machinegun were required to be in the tower, so Rose kept McGee and the M60 with him, along with Benny, whose M79 Grenade Launcher would be more effective from the tower. Rose also kept the radio, but he put Daniel in charge of the other position and Morgan.

Daniel dropped his gear behind the bunker and went inside to check it out. The hole was deep enough and wide enough so that four men could stand and fire through the two three-foot-by-one-foot openings which faced the barbed wire. The inside was lined with sandbags and contained two well-positioned grenade sumps, into which any live grenade that entered the bunker could be kicked; the grenade would explode in the sump, if not harmlessly, at least without killing the bunker's occupants. The roof was solid enough to withstand most small to medium explosions.

Thirty yards to the left of the bunker was the guard tower and Rose. An equal distance to the right was a 106mm recoilless rifle position and two crewmen from D Company. They had been working in the jungle as infantrymen without their big gun and were delighted to be manning it again, if only for a while.

No man's land was in front of the bunker. The jungle was stripped bare for a hundred yards out; not even grass grew. Two parallel barbed wire fences ran all the way around the perimeter. Each was ten feet high with a dozen strands of barbed wire running between the long engineer stakes. Six rolls of barbed concertina wire were stacked in front of each fence. Beyond the forward fence, in-ground mines were planted. Electrically fired Claymore Anti-Personnel Mines filled the thirty yards between the fences; six wires ran back to the bunker. A series of light poles stood even with the bunkers and towers and held sufficient lights to change midnight to midday at and in front of the fences.

To Daniel, the position was impregnable. A fight from the bunker would be more like Hollywood pictured war. He almost wanted charlie to attack.

This would be like a vacation, compared to the jungle. No one hassled them. The army considered them to be on station even in the daytime and gave them no other duties.

To make life even easier, the army sent out reinforcements at night. Every evening just before dark, a truck came by and dropped off two garrison soldiers to augment the infantry. Perimeter guard was assigned duty for them, like KP, that came up once a month. To the garritroopers, the duty was a night away from their regular shifts on regular jobs, a night away from their comfortable bunks in cozy tent corners, a night away from the countless personal items, unknown to the infantry, collected to make their lives more bearable. For them, perimeter guard duty was a trip to the front lines and the war, a night of danger and hardship. Two of the once-a-month warriors arrived each night, always two new ones, never any repeats. Daniel was the only soldier on the position who appreciated having four, count them, four, people pulling guard every night. To Daniel, this was truly a vacation.

Daniel was also the only veteran on the position. He believed that to be proof that Rose now trusted him. Daniel's status as a veteran gave him command of the small force. The clerks, who were often Specialists Fourth Class, a grade higher than Daniel, assumed that the senior infantryman was in charge, which was just as well, since Daniel assumed that, too.

Daniel was responsible for setting up nightly guard duty. He knew enough to take certain things into consideration. First, the least competent garritrooper always took first watch, since he would proably be the most scared and would therefore be likely to stay awake through the first watch. The second watch went to the other garritrooper, in hopes that he could stay awake if he could do it early enough. Daniel put Morgan on third watch so he would get used to getting up in the middle of the night; Daniel considered having everyone pull two, shorter shifts just so

Morgan would get the practice, but he decided not to spoil the vacation. Daniel took the last watch himself; he wanted to be sure that he was awake at firstlight, less out of concern for a dawn attack than because firstlight was when officers usually came around checking on the troops.

One morning as Daniel and Morgan played rummy in the shade behind the bunker, a small reptilian head appeared under Daniel's leg. Morgan saw it first.

"Hey, Danny! Look at the lizard."

"Never, ever, call me that again. Either call me Perdue or call me Daniel."

"Hey, whatever makes you happy."

"The lizard's cute. Discard."

"You're mighty casual about having a lizard under your knee."

"It really doesn't matter much."

The little head moved forward, followed by a snake's body. It slithered towards Morgan

"It's a snake!" the cherry shouted, immediately realizing that he was in the wrong place. Somehow, without dropping his cards or using his hands, he sprang from his prone position and landed on his feet three yards away. As he moved, his hand unintentionally hit the snake under the chin and flipped it, like a somersault, through the air.

Daniel chose to give the snake as much room as possible in which to land and quickly moved his person to a safer distance.

The snake hit the ground on the dead slither and raced into the tall grass nearby. The two men searched for it, cautiously, but were unable to find it.

When telling the story to Rose and describing the snake, Daniel learned that it was a particularly deadly variety of coral snake found in southeast Asia. Americans referred to it as the Viet Nam Two Step snake; if it bit you, you took two steps, then dropped dead. Daniel's own experience revealed that, in addition to any other characteristics, the first two inches of its head looked just like a lizard.

Perimeter guard was easy duty and the days passed pleasantly and quickly, but the nights were still lonely, if not so intimidating. The fence, the lights, and the close proximity of visible support did not change the purpose of guard duty. The enemy believed that the random assault on the perimeter was a necessary part of their political strategy, and it could happen on any night. And there was always the possibility, though a slim one, that charlie might somehow slip through the outer defenses in large enough numbers to mount a serious ground attack. The garritroopers were somewhat justified in their fear, and even Daniel preferred guard here only by comparison to guard in the jungle.

Wilson returned from R&R. Rose let the cherry, McGee, keep the machinegun and sent Wilson with an M16 to take charge of the bunker. Wilson kept Daniel and Morgan entertained for a week with stories of his adventures and misadventures in Bangkok. He was particularly impressed by the number of beautiful women that were available for only ten dollars a day.

With Wilson joining Daniel and Morgan, only one garritrooper was added each evening, and it was during the clerk's watch one night that Daniel awoke at the sounds of incoming rockets. Explosions rumbled softly from the airstrip and division chopper pad. Daniel got up and walked over to the bunker.

"You better go wake up Wilson and Morgan," he told a clerk from division finance.

"I'm already up," said Wilson as he walked up.

"What's the matter?" asked the clerk.

"Charlie's throwing some 122s at the airstrip," Daniel replied. "Go get Morgan."

"I don't hear anything," the clerk said.

"Just go, fucker," Wilson ordered.

The clerk walked away.

"Fuck charlie," Wilson said angrily. "I was having' a great fuckin' dream." He paused, expecting Daniel to ask about it. When Daniel did not, Wilson went on anyway. "I was in bed with two beautiful Thai girls."

"Working on a wet dream?"

"It was fuckin' gettin' there."

The clerk returned with Morgan.

"The man here says we're being attacked," Morgan said in a manner that indicated he thought someone was pulling a joke. "I don't hear any attack."

"It's fuckin' stopped now, cherry," said Wilson.

"It sounded like outgoing to me," the clerk volunteered.

"And an AK47 sounds like firecrackers on the Fourth of July," Daniel countered.

"I've never heard an AK47," the clerk admitted.

"Well, fucker," said Wilson, "now you can say you've heard fuckin' 122 rockets."

A voice said "Wilson" and the four men looked around to see Terwilliger approaching.

"Whatcha need, Benny?" asked Wilson.

"Rose just got word on th' radio that ev'rybody's on full alert," Benny announced. "He told me to come over here and git ev'rybody up."

"What? The fucker don't trust us?" Wilson said indignantly. "Go tell th' fucker we was already up."

"Okay," Benny said without emotion. He turned and walked away.

"Do you think they're going to attack?" the clerk asked any of the infantry who might know.

"Fuck, no!" said Wilson.

"How can you be so sure?" the clerk asked.

"Yeah?" agreed Morgan.

Wilson looked Morgan straight in the eye, "You is a cherry and best oughta keep your fuckin' mouth shut." He turned to the clerk, "You is a fuckin' clerk and don't know no better, so I'll tell you."

Daniel was unsuccessful in an attempt to stifle a giggle.

Wilson continued, "Ain't gonna be no fuckin' attack cause charlie's done fired his fuckin' rockets and gone home. Charlie'll be in fuckin' bed a fuckin' sleep before I finish this fuckin' cigarette." He turned to Daniel, "You got a light?" Daniel tossed Wilson a book of matches. He looked at Morgan and the clerk, "Now I'm gonna duck down and light this here cigarette, if you fuckers is scared why don't you both jump down in the hole and watch the wire all fuckin' night."

"And keep your fuckin' rifles pointed that way," Daniel ordered as he pointed to the wire. "We don't want you two shooting each other."

Morgan and the clerk stepped into the trench that led into the bunker.

As they settled in, Wilson spoke, "Garritroopers and cherries is stupid fuckin' fuckers."

"Might as well get comfortable," Daniel said as he leaned back against the sandbags. "We'll probably hafta stay up all night."

"Prob'ly," agreed Wilson, "you know how them fuckin' officers git when some fucker shoots at the fuckin' choppers."

An unexpected crash inside the bunker startled both Wilson and Daniel.

"What th' fuck?" said Wilson. "What are you two fuckers doin' in there?"

Morgan's voice answered, "Everything's cool. I just dropped my rifle."

Wilson looked at Daniel, "Did I hear that fucker right, Perdue?"

"I think so."

"Did he really say he dropped his fuckin' rifle?"

"That's what it sounded like."

Wilson moaned, "Gee-sus fuckin' christ. And he's gonna go to th' fuckin' field with us?"

"I'm afraid so."

"I can't be fuckin' around with no fuckin' cherry. I'm too fuckin' short."

Rose walked up one morning while Wilson, Morgan and Daniel were eating C rations.

"I've got some POOP, guys."

"What's up?" asked Wilson.

"We're heading back to the company area at 1500 hours."

"Are we gonna get some time off?" Morgan asked.

"It doesn't look like it," said Rose. "The word is the company's going out on an operation tomorrow morning."

"Just my fuckin' luck," Wilson complained. "We get two weeks of easy fuckin' duty and I gotta spend fuckin' half of it on fuckin' R&R."

"That's the breaks," Rose said. "Cheer up. You're gonna be squad leader for a while."

"Where you gonna be?"

"Hong Kong, the day after tomorrow." Hong Kong was another of the exotic places that hosted Americans on R&R. Like Bangkok and Singapore, Tokyo and Taiwan, the name conjured up the mixed images of ancient cultures and modern conveniences. Unfortunately, the ancient cultures and their fascinations were lost on men too young to appreciate them. Rather, the soldiers who spent long periods in the jungle were more likely enraptured of electric lights and flush toilets, hot showers and hotter women. Whatever else might be offered by the assorted jewels of the Orient, the veterans of the jungle sought those things which reminded them of home. They wanted to get as far away from the inconveniences of war as they could. Even pleasures of the flesh, to which many GIs declared their dedication, would have finished a poor second if the choice were made between vice and technology. Sin was available to the jungle warrior, if not often, regularly, but soft beds, hot showers and steaks medium rare were available only on R&R. The anticipation of sinful pursuits received the most verbiage, for a young man in quest of maturity could not easily explain to his peers that what he missed most about America was the crowds and the lights, cold beverages of any kind, and water that flowed endlessly hot and cold. Such things were not manly in the eyes of the children at war, so the secret longings remained secret, hidden from the others by bold talk of sex and alcohol.

When the company left for the boonies, Rose stayed behind, leaving Wilson and Daniel to watch over the cherries. Benny was a good soldier and took orders as well as anyone, but his hill country personality and poor education forced him to echew responsibility and rarely offer his opinions, even when asked. Thus Daniel, so recently a cherry himself, was now, in the eyes of the new arrivals, a hardened veteran whose advice was valued and whose suggestions carried the weight of law.

Except in matters of personal property.

In spite of warnings from Wilson and Daniel, the cherries took everything with them to the field. McGee carried his own razor and blades, for he was unwilling to use the one shared by the squad. He carried a can of shaving cream, two extra pairs of socks, pens, paper, envelops, and a small portable radio. Morgan carried many of the same items plus an extra set of fatigues and a small pocket camera. Wilson's exhortations that none of those things were necessary fell on deaf cherry ears.

"Them fuckers'll have to learn the hard way," he told Daniel.

And learn the hard way they did. What the jungle did not destroy was eventually discarded as unnecessary extra weight. McGee's radio and Morgan's camera corroded and became inoperative long before either could be used. In two days the humidity ruined the writing paper and envelops and caused the fatigues and socks to mildew in the packs. During one particularly long march through the jungle, McGee tossed the can of shaving cream into the brush with the comment "That fucker's too heavy."

Any items not absolutely essential for survival in the jungle were "too heavy." The infantry carried a heavy load without the added weight of useless luxuries. Morgan's curiosity led to his estimating the total weight each man carried. The average was one hundred and ten pounds. Daniel, who weighed only one hundred and twenty-five pounds, carried one hundred and thirty pounds, including the radio and an extra battery.

Arranging that much weight so that it could be carried long distances required experience. Loaded ammo pouches were placed properly on the pistol belt or they cut into the hipbone. If the harness were adjusted incorrectly, it either provided no support or cut off circulation to the arms and shoulders. Ponchos and poncho liners were rolled properly and secured to the harness correctly or they came unraveled and were dragged through the jungle. The two canteens, some men carried three, were put in the right place on the pistol belt or they made it impossible to sit without removing the harness, an impossibility on short breaks.

The cherries began the slow process of learning many things.

They learned to wrap their wallets in the plastic bags that radio batteries came in.They learned that it did no good, for the humidity would ruin a wallet and its contents in time no matter what the soldier did.

The cherries learned quickly about C rations. They learned to carry the cans in a sock tied to their harnesses and to convert the three daily meals into meals and a day's supply of snacks. They learned to balance cans on rocks over heat tablets and how much C4 plastic explosive to use to heat a can of beans and franks when heat tablets were not available. The learned how to take apart a Claymore mine to get the C4. They learned that every case of C rations contained the same twelve meals and that the veterans knew the contents of each meal and where it was located in the case, even when the case was opened from the bottom, hiding the names. Eventually the cherries learned which fruit was in which meal, which meals had peanut butter and which had jam, which had cookies and which had cake. They learned to save a spoon and a roll or two of toilet paper, and where to carry them.

But only slowly did the cherries learn about war.

The veterans simply could not trust the cherries. Their reactions were the slow reactions of children. Instead of reacting when they heard a sound, they looked. They did not hear sounds that foretold danger and heard sounds that were harmless. They fired at tree limbs and raindrops. They were the last ones to get up and last ones to get down. They lacked survival instincts.

Some adapted to the mentality of war more quickly than others, but they all adapted.

Morgan and McGee were children learning to surive as adults. Their reactions, reflexes, minds and values were changing in an environment alien to the American lifestyle. They would become warriors or die in the attempt. The survival instincts that were nurtured in war would not vanish in peace, but how those instincts would affect the warriors when they went home was not of concern to young men trying to stay alive; that is another story.

McGee's civilian innocence was demonstrated in a village far from any road. As the platoon searched for Viet Cong or VC suspects, McGee glimpsed an adult male, a suspect, ducking into a hut across an open field.

"There's somebody over there!" he called.

McDowd reacted quickly, "Everybody down!" He moved over beside McGee, "What did you see?"

"Some fucker went in that hut," McGee answered as he pointed.

"Did he have a gun?" asked McDowd.

154

"I couldn't tell."

McDowd motioned to the platoon, "Spread out and stay down." He took the handset from his RTO and called Captain Dunn.

While McDowd reported, his men waited. The village was deserted up to that point and the men wondered if the presence of an adult male, a rarity in isolated villages, presaged enemy activity. Wilson moved over to where McGee lay beside Daniel.

The cherry spoke, "Why don't we charge over there and check the fucker out?"

Wilson looked at Daniel. Both were prevented from laughing only by the circumstances.

Daniel spoke first, "Charging is something the cavalry does in old movies. Real people do not charge, unless, of course, they're marines."

"Marines ain't real people," insisted Wilson. "Them fuckers is crazy."

"Why don't you charge over there, McGee," Daniel suggested. "If you don't get killed, we'll know it's safe for the rest of us."

"I ain't going over there by myself. There could be a whole fuckin' regiment of Cong over there."

"Fuckin' right!" agreed Wilson. "That's why we ain't doing no fuckin' charging." He looked at Daniel, "Stupid fucker, ain't he?"

Late one afternoon, after the company had formed a small perimeter for the night, small printed cards were given to the men as they went through the hot chow line. The cards were reminders that if captured the men were required to give the enemy only their names, ranks, and service numbers.

During basic training, and beyond for infantry, the army emphasized the Geneva Convention. The private had it drilled into him what he could and could not reveal to the enemy if captured. The drills were serious, with the private being led to believe that the war would be won if only he did not break under the pressure of questioning by some gestopo captain. The private was made to think that he would possess information vital to the battle and to the war effort. His honor, and the safety of the nation, depended on him keeping the military's secrets. No matter the pressure, no matter the torture, all that could be revealed was name, rank, and service number. Nothing more. God bless John Wayne.

The reality of war in the jungle was that the private need not have worried about his honor, or the success of a battle. His name, rank, and service number were all he knew. He knew nothing about the location of his company or battalion; he knew where he was only in relation to the last place the choppers landed, and he did not know where that was on a map. The private had no information at all beyond his own platoon.

The army could have saved time and money if it had taught the private just to be honest. "I don't know" would come naturally from the soldier, and it would not antagonize an interrogator as would "according to the Geneva Convention. . . ."

What little the private did know about what he was doing filtered down to him as catchy words and phrases. The strategy was simply the type of operation that day: search and clear, search and destroy. The tactics were the things to be done: patrol, ambush, look inside that hut. The private merely did what he was told at the time he was told to do it. But occasionally a phrase was heard that caused anxiety. Such a phrase was "blocking force". To the private, it meant that the officers expected the enemy to be pushed right into him.

The operation was outlined on a map in some Command Post somewhere. Thick, bold lines depicted the expected action. A red circle identified the suspected location of an enemy unit. Big blue arrows indicated an American unit would advance against the enemy unit. On the other side of the circle, straight blue lines showed the position of the blocking force, the place at which the enemy would be trapped. On the map it all looked very clear, very effective, very military.

On the ground, the blocking force merely waited. Long hours were spent watching the jungle and wondering what would happen and when. It meant staying on one position for as long as was necessary, knowing all the time that the enemy would appear if all went as planned. It meant sitting alone in the jungle, separated by yards of vision-restricting undergrowth from the men on either side who would help, if they could, when any number of enemy soldiers stepped from the jungle.

Rose returned from R&R and was in charge of second squad when it landed in the small clearing nearest to the site chosen for the blocking force. The entire company was landing in the tiny LZ one chopper at a time. They moved into the jungle and humped for three hours through rough terrain, thorns and vines. They climbed hills and slid into narrow valleys. The heat and humidity wore them down as they struggled through the shadows under the canopy.

At the bottom of one valley, the column found a small creek and followed it upstream to the assigned position. Where the valley widened out into a jungle covered ridge, the CO halted the company and the platoon sergeants began assigning men to positions.

Sergeant McDowd gave second squad two positions. Rose kept Daniel and Morgan with him and put Wilson on the right, out of sight through the jungle, with Benny and McGee. Blocking force or not, the thick undergrowth isolated each small group of men.

Daniel dropped to the ground, leaned back and slowly unbuckled his harness. He slipped out of it and stretched, then leaned back for a moment of rest.

Morgan spoke, "How come he gets to take a break and we don't?"

"Because he's carrying the radio," Rose explained.

"So what?"

"If and when you carry that extra weight, you can take breaks, too. Now grab your entrenching tool and start digging us a hole. I'll use the machete and start clearing our field of fire."

Rose and Morgan had only just started working when Sergeant Stovall appeared.

"You fuckers are making too goddamn much noise," he growled. "I can hear you all the way over on my position."

"Sorry, Sarge," Rose answered, "we'll try to be quieter."

"You goddamn well better," barked Stovall. He looked at Daniel, who rested with his rifle in his hands. "Get up off your dead ass, Perdue. This ain't no fuckin' picnic."

"Right, Sergeant!" Daniel replied as he scrambled to his feet.

"I want one man on the position to keep his rifle in his hands at all times," Stovall ordered. "No telling when them fuckin' charlies will show up."

"Yes, Sergeant," acknowledged Rose.

"And no goddamn heat tabs at chow," Stovall warned. "Charlie can smell them fuckers for a mile." He stormed off to Wilson's position and began bitching at them.

Morgan asked, "What's Stovall so pissed off about?"

"Beats me," replied Rose. "He's been that way for weeks."

Morgan shook his head, "If the fucker can't handle it, he ought to ask for a desk job." He swung his entrenching tool hard at the ground, hitting a rock that caused a clang sounding like a church bell.

"Be careful!" ordered Rose.

"Sorry. I'm just trying to dig this hole."

"Do it quietly."

"How the Hell can I dig 'quietly'?"

Daniel spoke up, "I imagine Stovall can show you. You want me to call him?"

"Fuck no!" answered Morgan.

"Then hold down the noise," Rose ordered.

"Is it okay if I fart?" Morgan asked.

"Not loud," replied Rose quickly.

"And not if you're upwind," added Daniel.

"Right," conceded Morgan. "We don't want the Cong smelling us."

As Rose and Morgan worked, Daniel watched for the enemy. They were positioned where a small opening in the canopy created the illusion of a clearing, but the hot tropical sun brought life to the jungle floor, causing a waist-high growth of tangled brush, grasses and vines. The ground on the left rose up gently, while on the right, it disappeared into the jungle on a barely noticeable downhill grade.

Rose, Morgan and Daniel worked the rest of the day in shifts enlarging the foxhole and clearing their field of fire. By the time they stopped for evening chow, the ground was clear for twenty yards in front of a three foot deep hole.

For supper, Daniel pulled out a can of chicken and noodles, a favorite meal of his and one easy to eat cold. He and Rose ate with their rifles in their laps, but Morgan struggled through a can of ham and lima beans without paying any attention to the world around him.

As the light began to fade, the last sounds of hacking against the jungle stopped. The primordial stillness returned to claim its own. Rose, Morgan and Daniel would each face the silent blackness of the night in his turn.

xxii

Sunset was not visible under the jungle canopy. The thick vegetation high in the trees blocked out the sun the entire day. As if hidden behind an overcast sky, the sun could not penetrate to the jungle floor. The first warning of approaching night was the slow, subtle fading of the indirect light. The cavern under the canopy began to lose its clarity. A colorless gray filled the gaps in the foliage and began to darken almost perceptably. Night started on the ground, turning black all but the very tops of the grass. It rose quickly, engulfing the bushes and the spaces between them. Ever rising, it blackened the void between brush and trees, grabbing first the lowest branches, then racing into the trees as if pulling itself higher limb by limb. Long before dusk ended for the open world, the jungle was cloaked in darkness, a cold, empty darkness devoid of sound. No birds sang, no creatures of the night made noise, the sound of no living thing was heard in the jungle night. The cooling breezes in the canopy drifted down to the floor only as whispers of mystery.

In the final seconds before total darkness, Daniel imprinted in his mind the field of fire. In one brief moment, he memorized the trees and the bushes, the openings and the hiding places, in preparation for the fight that could come any night. He would know the area from which the enemy fired, seeing with his mind what he could not see in the dark with his eyes.

Caught again by the suddenness of nightfall, Daniel and Rose rested quietly, smoking cigarettes, unready to turn in or begin guard. Morgan fell asleep with his feet dangling in the hole, and might have been allowed to remain there until his guard had he not started snoring.

Rose and Daniel sat and waited, for what and for how long, they did not know. They were on their position, serving their purpose. They knew all they needed to know until someone came up in front of them. They would not be told if the companies sweeping towards them made contact with the enemy. They simply waited. Their world was no larger than the field of fire, and, for now, there were no VC in their world. If or when there might be, they did not know. Tonight, maybe. Or at firstlight. Or the very moment when they relaxed and dropped their guard. They waited.

Night watch was particularly lonely for Daniel that night, even with Rose and Morgan sleeping just feet away. They would face their thoughts alone when their turns came. Now was Daniel's time, just him and his thoughts and the black where the jungle had been. Night watch required a thousand decisions, each to be made with too little information. That brief sound! Was it a man stepping on a twig, or just a natural part of the jungle cycle of growth and decay? Every sound, no matter how faint, was weighed. Did it mean danger? Should the others be awakened? No, it was just the jungle. More sounds! Some new! Was it charlie? Had the blocking force plan worked? If only one could be home in bed, perhaps watching TV and drinking an ice cold Coke. That sound again! A breath of a breeze floated by. Maybe the leaves were making noises. What if he were wrong? What if it were a charlie sneaking up on the position? Was the charlie this scared? That sound! No, just the jungle. But that one? Maybe he should wake Rose and ask him to listen. No. Daniel was no cherry now; he knew the sounds as well as Rose. He would make his own decisions. Nothing out there now, not a sound. How nice it would be to have someone to talk to, maybe a girl to sit with at McDonald's, just listening to her talk. Daniel missed the sound of a girl's voice. And hamburgers. And lights at night. That sound! No, just another twig. And later another twig. And still later another. Again and again. Until this watch was over.

"Morgan," Daniel whispered. "Wake up." Morgan did not move. Daniel shook him gently. "Morgan. Wake up."

Morgan did not move, but mumbled, "I'm awake."

"Get up. It's your guard." Morgan did not move, so Daniel shook him harder. "Dammit, Morgan! Get up."

Morgan spoke much too loudly, 'I'm awake."

"Tell the world," Daniel whispered.

Morgan sat up, but was slow to shake the sleep from his eyes.

"Are you awake?" whispered Daniel.

"Yeah. I'm awake."

"Wiggle around some so I'll know for sure."

Morgan crawled out of the hooch, "I'm up."

"Stay awake. And stay alert."

"I'm awake," whispered Morgan, sounding as if he were not.

"There are supposed to be charlies out there," Daniel whispered, "so stay alert. Do you understand? Stay alert."

"I will."

Daniel crawled into the vacated space in the hooch and took off his helmet. He placed his glasses in it and lay down. He put his hand on his rifle and in seconds was asleep. Only a limited amount of time was alloted for sleep, and the veteran did not waste it.

"Perdue?" said Rose.

Daniel opened his eyes. It was still night. "My guard?"

"No. We're moving out."

"What time is it?"

"0300."

"Why so early? What's up?"

"We're going to get into position to attack a village."

Daniel was surprized by the word, "Attack?"

"That's what Stovall said on the radio."

"For a second there, you had me worried."

"Get Morgan up. I'm going over to tell Wilson."

In less than ten minutes, in the dark, the squad struck the hooches, packed their gear and was ready to move. At Stovall's position, the squad joined up with the rest of the platoon and moved to a location near the company CP. They waited there for twenty minutes more. At three-thirty in the morning the company began a slow, difficult march through the jungle at night.

The jungle floor was pitch black, and only by touching the man in front could any of them keep track of the others. Daniel kept his left hand on one of Rose's canteens, and he felt the tug of Morgan's hand as the cherry tried to keep up in the dark. They played a sort of blindman's follow the leader as they moved steadily through the jungle.

When they reached a large drainage ditch, the starlight revealed a large clearing, and beyond it the faint outline of a few huts. Captain Dunn directed everyone into the ditch. Second squad moved along for thirty yards, then everybody stopped.

They waited in the ditch, which was part of the irrigation system for a large area of rice paddies. Behind the men was the jungle, in front of them a dry paddy.

As the predawn gray creeped in upon the black of night, the few huts appeared as a village. As the gray sky lightened, the village grew in size and the scope of the paddies surrounding it became clearer. The village sat fifty yards from them, like an island amid a vast sea of open fields and paddies. They were closer to "civilization" than Daniel thought.

Captain Dunn came down the ditch giving his version of the encouraging word to his men.

"Everybody do their job right," he said, "and take care of the men on either side of you. Remember you're a unit."

Rose looked at Daniel, who shrugged his shoulders.

The CO continued, "We'll move out in five minutes. Watch for the signal. Do what your NCOs tell you. Good luck and good hunting."

Dunn moved down the ditch and began repeating his brief speech.

"Do you suppose he thinks we're in the RAF?" Daniel asked Rose.

"Damned if I know."

"The way he was talking, you'd think there was charlies in that village."

"Could be."

"Do you think he knows what he's talking about?"

"We'll find out in five minutes, won't we?"

Rose moved over to talk with Wilson. Morgan slid over beside Daniel.

"Perdue?" whispered Morgan.

"Yeah?"

"I've got this funny feeling inside."

"Cold ham and lima beans can do that to you."

"It's not that. It's like I know we're gonna run into some Cong in that village."

"You don't know shit, cherry."

"I mean it. I just got this feeling."

"That feeling is called fear. We've all got it."

"I know I'm gonna die."

"Everybody does."

"I mean today."

Daniel did not know what to say. He was certain that Morgan felt nothing more than the same fear he felt, but he did not know how to convince the cherry.

"There ain't no fuckin' way you could know that. Now stop thinking about it."

"I can't help it. I know it's gonna happen today."

"If you were any fuller of shit, you'd leak. Now cut that bullshit and I mean it!"

"But. . . ."

"No fuckin' buts. I don't want to hear you say another goddamn word about that or I'll kill you myself. You're gonna be right beside me, fucker, and the bullet you're so fuckin' sure's gonna kill you will probably hit me instead. Now shut the fuck up!"

Rose returned, "What's all the talking about?"

"The fuckin' cherry has a 'funny feeling'."

Rose looked at Morgan, "It's too late for that now. You should have gone to the bathroom before we got on the freeway."

Morgan hoped Rose would be more sympathetic, "I've got the feeling that I'm gonna get it today."

Rose looked at the cherry in disbelief, "What?"

"The fucker thinks this is a movie," Daniel said angrily.

"Are you serious, Morgan?"

"I sure am."

"I don't fuckin' believe it," Rose said softly. "Look, cherry, I've been here a lot fuckin' longer than you have, and you can believe me when I tell you there's no such thing as 'feelings'."

"But. . . ."

"Not another word. You say one more thing about that and I'll kick your butt so hard you won't sit down for a fuckin' week."

"Not another word, Sarge. I promise."

McDowd came up. "What in the Hell are you people doing over here? keep it down. What's going on?"

Daniel turned towards the village, "Not again, Lord."

Rose explained, "The cherry here thinks he's gonna die today."

"Bullshit," said McDowd.

"That's what I told him," agreed Rose.

"Keep it quiet here. We'll be moving out soon."

"Cherries," Daniel said softly.

Daniel grinned at the cherry's behavior. Now that the moment to speak was past, he could more fully understand Morgan's thoughts. The cherry was no more scared than the others, he just reacted to the fear differently. It was not easy to face the prospect of death for the first time, and the sudden activities in the night and Captain Dunn's little speech most certainly convinced Morgan that danger was imminent. He could not yet accept that fate and random change controlled his life as long as he was in the field. The unknown was more easily handled by the cherry if he removed it by accepting death. This gave substance to the void of the unknown, and to Morgan, even morbid fatalism was better than not knowing. His mistake was to announce his fatalism; he should have kept quiet and allowed it to pass.

Daniel's perceptions of the immediate future were now the perceptions of a veteran. He had been through many villages and he knew what to do and how to react. He was not even afraid that the CO was right, that charlie did hold the village. If the shooting started, no one, nothing, would have control over where the first bullets flew, and there was no value in being scared of things which could not be controlled. Daniel would attend to the business at hand, whatever it might be or become, and do the things he now knew were necessary to increase his chance for survival. When the order came, he would get up and move across the rice paddy. If shooting started, he would deal with it. Wondering about what could happen, or might happen, was counterproductive.

The sky changed from dark gray to light gray, then to morning blue.

The first rays of the sun appeared on the horizon and cast long shadows across the paddies.

"Let's go!" called McDowd.

Rose and Daniel scrambled from the ditch. The company rising together gave the brief, but definite vision of World War One doughboys charging from their trenches. The company moved forward in one long single rank, something like the forward skirmish line in a civil war battle. Daniel had seen nothing quite like it: the whole company advancing in line towards the village. The large number of soldiers visible gave Daniel a feeling of security. Whatever was in that village, there were enough of them to handle it.

Daniel's feet moved through the dry rice paddy, but his eyes and mind focused on the village. He saw every corner, every hedgerow, every doorway, every opening where a charlie might hide. He watched for any sign of movement.

On the far left, the line reached the first huts that jutted out to meet them. Second squad continued in the open, still some twenty yards from cover. Daniel's eyes moved back and forth across the part of the village still before him, from the hut on the left to a hedgerow, across a path and into a doorway, past the corner of a hut and over low bushes at the edge of the rice paddies on the right.

The squad reached the edge of the village and stepped out of the paddy. Now there was cover if anything happened.

McDowd called out, "Check every hut. If there's so much as a slingshot around here, I want you to find it."

Rose and Daniel approached a hut with Morgan tagging along behind. To the left, Wilson and Benny reached a hut with McGee trailing them.

Rose and Daniel stepped quickly to either side of the doorway, Rose having to grab Morgan and pull him to the side. The squad leader and his RTO stood with their backs against the straw wall. They stood there for the longest second, just looking at each other. Rose took a deep breath and nodded. He stepped through the doorway and into the darkness; Daniel dropped to one knee in the doorway, prepared to fire, if necessary.

The room was empty. Sparse funishings bordered the walls. A small cabinet sat in one corner and several straw mats were rolled up in another corner. A single saucer sat on a small table against the back wall. There was no back door and no windows. Rose checked the cabinet quickly, then he walked back into the light. Morgan stuck his head in the hut and looked around.

Rose made eye contact with Wilson and directed his group to check the huts on the far side of the path as his group checked the huts on this side.

Rose and Daniel moved to the next hut. Their process of entry was repeated and the search of the interior was quick. Again Morgan followed up. As far as second squad could determine, the village was deserted.

Daniel's radio squawked.

"This is Camel Two India," Daniel answered.

"This is Camel Six," Stovall's voice said. "Fullback reports Victor Charlie suspects on the left flank. Acknowledge. Over."

"Roger, Six. Acknowledge Victor Charlie suspects on the left flank. Over."

"This is Six. Out."

Rose watched Daniel, "What's up?"

"VC suspects on the left flank."

"So this place isn't deserted after all." Rose turned and called Wilson. "Watch out over there, guys. There are VC suspects in the village."

Viet Cong suspects were any Vietnamese males between the ages of thirteen and very old. Among the women and children that first platoon encountered were two boys who were almost old enough and one little man who was too old.

Captain Dunn was disappointed that the information given him during the night by battalion was turning out to be false. VC were no where to be found, and were it not for the three suspects, he would have nothing at all to show for the effort.

For the privates, the presence of civilians complicated matters. In an empty village, anything that moved could be considered the enemy, but with women and children around, the soldiers were forced to make quick decisions. Was that an old lady in the corner, or a VC with an AK47? Daniel wondered if John Wayne ever faced that problem.

Second squad continued to search huts, but, in spite of the warning from the CO, they found no people at all.

Their backs pressed against the wall of the next hut, Rose and Daniel nodded. Rose spun through the doorway and Daniel followed. There was an immediate scream.

"Don't move!" Rose ordered.

Daniel froze where he stood, not knowing if Rose were talking to him or to someone inside the hut. Then he saw the old woman in the corner huddled with two small children. Rose walked over to a doorway that led to a second room and looked inside. Daniel smiled at the old lady and the children.

When Morgan entered the hut, the old lady stood and began chattering in Vietnamese. As Daniel walked over to the doorway where Rose stood, the old woman walked up to Morgan and continued her alien diatribe. Morgan, of course, had no idea what she was saying. She could have been explaining that she was not a Viet Cong sympathizer, or that she was Ho Chi Minh's mother.

"No comprende, Senora," Morgan said, using of habit the phrase that applied in southern California.

The woman talked until Morgan finally silenced her with a loud "No!"

"Let's get outside and take a break," Rose ordered.

The squad settled down around a well. Two GIs walked by escorting new VC suspects, three young men. They saw Morgan and began talking rapidly in Vietnamese.

Morgan was helpless, "Is this gonna happen ev'ry time?"

Daniel felt sorry for him, "Probably."

"Gimme a break, God."

McGee spoke up, "These folks sure are friendly. Every one I've seen is smiling."

"You'd smile, too," Daniel said, "if you were at home and a bunch of men showed up with guns." He paused for a moment, then added, "They smile at the VC the same way."

Rose looked at Daniel, but said nothing.

"Come on Sarge. I thought that was right clever."

Rose looked down at the ground between his boots.

"Something wrong?" Daniel asked.

"I almost shot that old lady."

XXIII

Military Intelligence again was proven wrong or late, for there was no sign of Viet Cong in the village. The company searched the area around the village for a week, but no charlies were found. Again the men were keyed for action, only to be let down. No one complained.

The morning was still cool when Rose interrupted his breakfast to respond to the radio. A short communication ensued in which Rose mainly listened. After a last "roger", he put down the handset and returned to his meal. Between bites of Boned Chicken, Rose spoke.

"The company's moving out by chopper this morning, guys."

"I could use a fuckin' ride," acknowledged Wilson. "I'm tired of walking."

"Where are we going?" asked Morgan.

"That's anybody's guess," answered Rose. On the radio, McDowd had said he thought they were heading back to base camp, but he was not sure. Until official word came, Rose was advised to refrain from raising his men's hopes. The possibility existed that the company would land on another LZ with another village.

Daniel asked, "When are the choppers due?"

"About 0900," replied Rose. "You guys go ahead and get your gear together after you finish chow."

By nine o'clock the company had pulled in the perimeter around the rice paddy that served as the LZ. Along with the others, second squad lounged around the edge of the paddy, but the relaxed manner of the group did not prevent the veterans from watching the distant tree line. The cherries, Morgan and McGee, slept, still unaware of the need to stay alert whenever there was no barbed wire.

The morning passed slowly, but the choppers did not come. Lunchtime came without an issue of C rations.

"When are we gonna eat?" McGee asked Wilson.

"Any fuckin' time you want to, cherry."

"Are they gonna give us Cs?"

"Fuckin' no. They probably thought we was gonna eat noon chow in

166

the fuckin' mess hall. If we was going anywhere else the fuckin' army would have fed us."

"You sure we're going back to base camp?"

"Fuck, yes. We gotta be. If we was going anyplace important, the choppers woulda already been here."

"I wish they'd hurry up. I'm starving."

"Break into your fuckin' sock, cherry," advised Wilson. "This operation is as good as fuckin' over."

The veterans were already dipping into their strategic reserve, those extra cans of fruit, cookies, or a favorite meal acquired judiciously from the unused parts of the meals they were issued. The reserve was now expendable, for they would be eating in the mess hall. A new reserve would be built up on the next operation. Even so, few socks were emptied completely; the veteran always prepared for the unexpected, and a snack came in handy even in base camp.

The choppers arrived in midafternoon and the company moved out in a noisy, but routine, exercise in air mobility. The squad was happy and playful, for the holiday atmosphere began when the veterans surmised by the delay that they were heading home. Still, they had not been told officially that they were, in fact, bound for Camp Radcliff. Daniel wondered what would happen if they landed on a hot LZ instead of the brigade chopper pad; what a surprise that would be.

When the long flight passed over the barren perimeter of base camp, Daniel knew he had worried needlessly. The choppers descended towards the familiar grassy knoll and landed, actually coming to rest on the ground long enough for the men to dismount casually. The company formed a loose column and marched to the company area at an informal route step.

The first order of business upon reaching the company area was that the men take their gear down to the muddy creek and wash it.

"This is stupid," Morgan decided. "This creek is dirtier than my equipment."

"Just do it, cherry," ordered Wilson.

"It don't make sense," argued Morgan.

Daniel spoke, "If you wanted things to make sense, you should've joined the Air Force."

First Sergeant Everett walked up, "Who's in charge here?"

"I am, Top," answered Rose.

"Yeah, Rose," said the first sergeant, remembering the squad leader's face and name. "Get your men down to the supply sergeant and have them turn in their ammo."

Wilson perked up, "Turn in our ammo?"

"You heard me, Trooper."

Rose asked, "What brought this on, Top?"

"First of the Twelfth and Second of the Twelfth had a firefight last week. It seems you fuckers ain't got sense enough not to try to kill each other."

Wilson was not pleased, "What the fuck are we sposed to do if charlie shows up?"

"The troops on the perimeter can take care of charlie."

Wilson was unconvinced, "What if the fuckers break through the perimeter?"

"They won't."

Wilson turned away, "I don't fuckin' like it."

"Tough shit," Everett responded. "Times are changing." He walked away without another word.

Wilson shook the water from his canteen carrier, "This fuckin' place is gettin' too fuckin' civilized."

Rose gathered the squad's munitions: M16 bullets, belts of M60 ammo, assorted grenades. He and Daniel carried it to the conex container behind the supply tent in which it would be locked by Sergeant Canella. As they waited for the supply sergeant to conclude some matter, Daniel voiced his concern about the situation.

"I really don't like having a lock between my rifle and its bullets."

"Neither do I," agreed Rose, "but it seems like garritroopers see the world different from you and me."

Canella exited the supply tent, "I heard that. I heard that."

"You're not a garritrooper, Sarge," said Rose. "You're in the field when we are."

"Damn right!" insisted Canella. He knew the importance of supply, and he kept in touch with the needs of the soldier by setting up shop at the company CP when in the field. Were it not necessary that he work in base camp to acquire the things his men needed, he would spend all of his time out with the company. "All garritroopers do is count!"

"Somebody has to, Sarge."

"Don't I know. They want me to spend all my time counting. What do they think I do with this stuff? It gets used, that's what. It gets used."

Sergeant Canella was constantly at odds with the staff at battalion supply. For those who never left the security of base camp, the war was one of numbers and balances, and they were happy only when the numbers balanced. Their goal was to issue as little as possible, and, towards that end, they required precise explanations for every item being replaced. Canella learned quickly that the column marked "combat loss" explained it all; anything the soldier in the jungle needed to replace was "combat loss" regardless. He used that justification to order whatever was needed. Canella was not responsible if things wore out more quickly in the jungle than they did in the office of the battalion supply staff. Let it be understood: Canella took care of the military's materiel as well as did anyone, and better than most. This attribute was noted and appreciated by Canella's superiors throughout the supply hierarchy, and it was his primary defense when attacked for excessive "combat loss."

"You two need clean socks? I got clean socks."

"Always," replied Rose.

"DX them right now. Let me have them."

Rose and Daniel sat on the ground and pulled off their boots.

Canella dropped a bayonet beside Rose, "You can't DX socks unless they got holes." He turned toward conex container and began counting nothing.

Direct Exchange was the combat soldier's only method of acquiring clean clothes. Garritroopers could take advantage of native laundries, but combat soldiers were in camp too briefly and too irregularly. Their uniforms and socks were often too dirty to be cleaned; after two or three weeks in the tropical jungle, a uniform usually was a "combat loss." The practice was not as wasteful as it may appear, and Sergeant Canella's system was anything but unique.

Rose and Daniel punched holes in their socks with the bayonet, then tossed them into a corner pile. They put their boots on their bare feet, for the new socks would wait for clean feet. From supply, Rose and Daniel were going straight to the showers.

The two soldiers crossed the foot bridge and fell into line for the showers. The original shower had been replaced by a new, larger facility, but the plumbing worked exactly the same and was just as subject to running out of water.

Rose encountered an old friend. Donnie Herwig was leaving the showers as Rose and Daniel got in line. Herwig was of medium height with a lean build. His blond hair was short, but clearly visible under his cap. Herwig had been a squad leader in third platoon back at Fort Benning before the division moved by ship to the Orient. Herwig was in an auto accident on his last pass before embarkation and did not make it back. He was in the hospital when the company moved out. When his minor injuries healed, he was flown over, but was assigned to A Company, not C Company.

Rose saw Herwig first, "Hey, Donnie!"

Herwig looked, "Bill! How you doing, man?" He walked up and the two embraced. "I never thought I'd see you again. How you been, man?"

"I'm all right, but what the fuck happened to you?"

"Car wreck."

"Good."

"Good? I coulda been killed."

"I thought you'd deserted."

"Deserted? Me? The Army is my life!"

Rose and Herwig both roared with laughter at a private joke. Rose had heard Herwig use the expression many times. It became his pet phrase on a field training exercise at Fort Benning when, while lying in the mud with Rose, Herwig was asked by Sergeant Stovall if it bothered him to get so dirty; the phrase was his response.

"How is old Stovall these days?"

"The same, only worse since we got here. Why didn't you show up for shipment?"

"I broke my leg in the wreck and spent two days in a civilian hospital. By the time the Army came and got me, you were already gone. I tried to hang around Benning as long as I could, but the army doctors finally decided my leg was well enough to hump the boonies. They shipped me out the week before Christmas, the bastards."

"Don't you get out soon?"

"Sixty-two days."

"I've got less time than that."

"But you're just getting out of the country, man. I'm getting out of the whole fuckin' Army."

"I thought you got out sooner than that?"

"The Army docked me for the time I was layed up."

"The fuckers! Why?"

"I was kinda in the prison hospital."

"What for?"

"I was kinda drunk when I had the wreck."

"That was stupid."

"I know that now, man."

"I'm really glad you're all right. I was worried about you. When you missed shipment, I just knew you had skipped out."

"I thought you knew me better."

"I do. That's why I thought you skipped."

Herwig looked at his watch, "Look at the time! I gotta go, Bill. Can I meet you tonight at the NCO club?"

"You bet!"

"I hope I can find it. I've never been to it."

"You're kidding?"

"No, man. I haven't had a drink since the wreck.

"They serve sodas, too."

"Great. Meet you there at seven."

"Seven it is." They shook hands, a long four-handed grasp, "Damn, it's good to see you, Donnie."

"You, too, Bill. I'll see you tonight."

Herwig waved as he walked away. After a few steps, he broke into a trot.

Daniel spoke, "Nice fellow."

"And I forgot to introduce you. Fuck!"

"That's okay. I could tell you were busy."

"I haven't seen Donnie Herwig since I left the States. I'm looking forward to tonight. It'll be nice to have a friend to talk to at the club."

"Don't you usually have people to talk to?"

"Not often. And never a friend like Donnie. I don't have many friends here."

Daniel could not understand why. Rose came with all the others; it was only the new arrivals who were excluded. He could do nothing but ask.

"Why?"

"Let's just say that most NCOs are conservative."

"What's that got to do with anything?"

Rose looked at Daniel, but said nothing.

Daniel was perplexed, "You haven't done something screwy that I don't know about?"

"No, Perdue. I'm not a pervert. I'm a Jew."

"What's being Jewish got to do with it?"

"Beats me."

Rose stepped into the shower as a warning was given that the water was running low. Another man exited and Daniel stepped in. Some of the men still in line would have to wait for the next time the water trailer came, and some of those already in the shower might find themselves soaped up with no water to rinse off.

Daniel nursed the water as best he could and left it to the more aggressive types to remind the cherries to use as little water as possible. He was lucky; as he rinsed the last of the soap from his body, the water slowed to a trickle and stopped.

Rose and Daniel returned to the platoon tent and put on their clean socks. So little was needed to create pleasure for an infantryman. The soft wool tickled Daniel's toes and gave him a feeling of comfort that civilians, and garritroopers, would never understand.

Cleaned and refreshed, the members of second squad followed the movement to the battalion mess hall. They ate slowly, enjoying the table and benches; after weeks of C rations eaten sitting on the ground, the seating facilities were appreciated. Mess hall food was given the respect due a Thanksgiving feast. The dessert that evening was a square of plain white cake with some kind of sweet orange sauce poured over it; it was delicious, and Daniel would remember it as long as he lived. On returning to the company area, Daniel stopped off for a leisurely sojourn in the latrine, a pleasure in itself after squatting over holes just dug.

The EM club was packed with people that evening. Daniel stood alone in a corner and watched the soldiers begin the process that led to inebriation. He wished the Army were less picky about the separation of sergeants and enlisted men, for he would have been much happier with Rose, either at the NCO club or here. Rose was the only person in the country that he could call a friend, and he was not completely sure that Rose felt a similar friendship. All the veterans avoided new friends, just as Daniel wished to avoid friendship with Morgan and McGee. This was, indeed, a strange war. There really should be someone to talk to. Other wars might have had more killing, but at least the soldiers had friends. This war was too lonely.

The noise level rose in response to some drunken activity. The noise seemed to emphasize the loneliness. Daniel walked to the bar and bought one last Coke, ice cold. He sipped it slowly as he walked back to the platoon tent.

He lay back on his cot and relaxed, pleased with the knowledge that there was no guard to pull tonight. He finished the Coke and closed his eyes. Through his mind floated thoughts of home and American girls. He drifted through fantasies of city streets bright with lights and peaceful lawn-covered parks smelling of fresh mown grass. At his side was some unknown female who held his hand. Daniel was happy in his fantasy, with someone who loved him, away from the intensity of war. Too soon, the feeling became sleep.

Morning came with all the preparations for a trip to Sin City. Wilson talked endlessly to McGee about the pleasures that awaited them.

After the compulsory stop at the barber shop, Daniel followed Rose through a few bars, even trying to drink a beer at one, but when Rose found a girl and prepared to enter the back room, Daniel excused himself with the pretense that he was going to find a lady in some other bar.

As Daniel walked, he considered trying sex again. He wanted to have sex, he had made that decision, but he was just as sure that he did not want a partner who talked to someone else. Sex was supposed to come naturally, and Daniel worried a little that something might be wrong with him. Another disaster like last time and he could really develop a case of self-doubt. He decided to wait for R&R. Then he could have a girl in a less hurried, more private setting, even if she were a professional.

"Maybe I'm just too romantic," he said aloud. "Or maybe I'm just stupid."

He stepped into a bar and ordered a Coke. As he expected, it was terrible.

xxiv

That evening after chow, Rose entered the tent with news. "Vacation's over, guys."

"What's up?" asked Daniel.

"We're moving out tomorrow."

Wilson was disappointed, "Fuck! Ain't we ever gonna get to go to town two fuckin' days in a row?"

"It doesn't look that way."

"Where are we going?" asked Daniel.

"Sergeant Stovall didn't say."

"It's just as fuckin' well," Daniel said. "With my luck, I'd get KP tomorrow, anyway."

Wilson pointed at the cherries, "When's these fuckers gonna get to burn the shithouse?"

"Burn what shithouse?" asked McGee.

Daniel joked, "That's the best duty you can get."

"Don't tell the fuckers nuthin'," insisted Wilson. "Let 'em learn the hard fuckin' way."

Rose continued, "We move out at 0800, guys, so get your shit together tonight."

"When do we get our ammo?" asked Daniel.

"In the morning."

Second squad expected to fly out, such was the routine, so they were surprised the next morning when trucks pulled into the company area. Stovall announced they were to man security positions along Highway 19 around An Khe.

The roads were getting better and the ride through Camp Radlciff seemed shorter. The little convoy followed yesterday's path to Sin City, out the main gate, along the drive, turning left at the highway, past the Special Forces Camp on the right; then they passed Sin City and continued on towards the village.

At the large bridge just before town, the trucks stopped and first squad was ordered off. The trucks crossed the bridge and stopped again. Second squad dismounted and watched the trucks drive into the village.

173

Daniel examined the area as a military position, having developed the habit of determining the best way to defend against attack wherever he was. From the edge of the bridge, a steep bank fell away to the river's edge, some forty feet below. He measured the distances to the nearest houses and noted every window, corner and ditch, every place from which an enemy might fire. He sought and found the best place along the bank for cover if he were unable to reach either of the two foxholes. The survey took less than fifteen seconds. Daniel acquired the habit slowly in the jungle, where he was constantly moving and establishing new positions. He noticed his surroundings from a perspective unimagined by civilians, or even, perhaps, by a soldier whose duty allowed him to become accustomed to places. The combat veteran sees every ground as a battlefield, and always will. It will go unnoticed by those around him, for it is done without visible effort, but it happens. Every time.

Daniel carried the radio and his harness around the concrete railing and down below the abutment, and dropped it in the dirt beside the concrete slab that ran the width of the bridge right below the roadway and supported the beams which stretched to the first tower support rising from the water's edge. The spaces between the beams were used as two man hooches by the soldiers on duty there. Daniel looked at the river and the towers which supported the bridge, each of which was surrounded by barbed wired to deter sappers. The wire caught the flotsam of the river, giving it the appearance of age and neglect.

Rose called for the squad to assemble up on the road, so Daniel picked up his rifle and climbed up. Rose stood with an MP sergeant, whose cleaned, starched and pressed, Jungle fatigues clashed with the humble attire of the infantry.

"Listen up, guys. The MPs will watch the bridge during the daytime. You want to tell them about that, Sarge?"

"There'll be one MP stationed at each end of the bridge from 0600 hours to 2000 hours. We will be supervising traffic and watching for daylight attacks, which aren't likely."

"The fucker sure is clean," Wilson said dryly.

"You people can take it easy during the day," continued the MP, "but if anything does happen, we'll expect you to save our asses on the double."

McGee patted the machinegun, "Can do."

"Can do?" repeated Wilson. "Where'd you pick up that 'can do' shit? 'Can do' my fuckin' ass."

"At 2000 hours, we go home. She's all yours then."

Rose spoke, "The only traffic on the bridge at night is an occassional recon jeep. Keep your eyes open for them and don't fire up any of our guys."

"What about people on foot?" asked Morgan.

"Nobody crosses the bridge on foot at night," Rose warned.

Wilson looked at Morgan, "Stupid fuckin' cherry."

"And I mean nobody crosses at night, and that includes us. You walk down to the other end and first squad will blow you away."

"What about civilians in the area?" asked Daniel.

The MP answered, "There's a dusk to dawn curfew for the villagers. They all know it and they all abide by it. They don't want to get killed by a trigger happy American."

"Then can we assume that anybody around on foot is a charlie?" asked Rose.

"Yes," answered the MP. "But that doesn't give you permission to shoot up the place. Remember that those folks live there. Some fool could always be stepping out to take a piss."

McGee grinned, "I'll shoot his fuckin' dick off!"

Wilson barked, "Shut up, fucker!"

"I was only kiddin'."

"Fucker, you don't joke about shootin' people." Wilson turned to Daniel, "Right, Perdue?

"Right."

"Right," agreed Rose. "Guard starts at eight. One man up on the road and one man underneath watching the river. Everybody pulls two ninety minute shifts. Everybody gets up at five."

"Why so fuckin' early?" asked Wilson.

"Orders. They assume that sooner or later charlie's gonna take a shot at the bridge. Firstlight and all that shit."

Second squad spent the morning up on the road watching civilian traffic. The adults smiled and waved and the children were outright playful. Wilson drew a crowd of kids quickly when he began growling like a bear. None of the civilians spoke English and none of the Americans spoke Vietnamese, so there was no conversation. They all mostly looked at each other.

In the heat of the tropical afternoon, the infantry retreated to the shelter of the cool concrete below the road, leaving the MP alone.

One afternoon as Daniel watched the traffic, an older boy rode up on a bicycle and stopped.

To Daniel, he said, "Hello. What is your name?"

Daniel was surprised to hear a Vietnamese speak English so well. The people in Sin City used only disjointed phrases.

"My name is Perdue. What's your name?"

"I am Nguyen (pronounced 'Win')."

"Hello, Nguyen. You speak English very well."

"No, no. My English is poor."

"No, it's not. You speak English a lot better than I speak Vietnamese."

"Do you speak Vietnamese?"

"No. Just a few phrases."

"What are they?"

This was Daniel's chance to find out if the phrases the GIs used in the villages meant anything.

"*De de*, for one."

"It means 'go go'."

"The children sure don't pay much attention to it."

"All the Americans say '*de de*', Perdue. The children hear it too much. They laugh."

"I know. How can I tell them to go away?"

"Say *de loon*. It means go away."

"*De loon*."

"Yes."

"I'll try it next time."

"What else can you say?"

"*Dung li* means 'stop'."

"Yes. *Dung li* very good to say 'stop'."

"And I know *li di*."

"It means 'come here'."

"That's what I thought."

"What else can you say?"

"Nothing. That's all."

"That is not much."

"I know. That's why I said you should be proud of how well you speak English."

"Do you like the army, Perdue?"

"It's okay, sometimes."

"I go in the army someday."

"When?"

"When I am nineteen years. I am fifteen years now."

"How long will you have to stay in the army?"

"I do not understand?"

"I am in the Army for three years. In two more years I will get out. How many years will you stay in the army?"

"When I am in the army, I will fight Viet Cong."

Daniel did not know it, but the problem was not one of language. The very concept of limited military service was alien.

"How long will you be in the army?"

"Until there are no more Viet Cong."

"You must stay in the army as long as the war lasts?"

"Yes. Until there are no more Viet Cong."

Nguyen would serve for the duration. Daniel began to understand why the ARVNs were so casual about things. For them, the military was not a tour of service for their country, it was their lives. War had ravaged the country for so many years that the youth came to think of it as a permanent aspect of life.

"Will you be an interpreter?"

"That is my hope. I want to be with the Americans."

"I wish you good luck."

"Thank you. I must go now. I will see you tomorrow?"

"I think so." The infantry never knew.

"Good bye, Perdue."

"Good bye, Nguyen."

The boy hopped on his bicycle and pedalled away. He looked back over his shoulder and waved.

The next afternoon Daniel was up on the bridge talking to the MP. He hoped Nguyen would come by, but he did not count on it. His life in the infantry all but prohibited future plans, and he had begun to assume that the rest of the world functioned the same way.

Nguyen rode up on his bicycle, "Hello, Perdue."

"Hello, Nguyen."

He stopped and jumped from the bike, "How are you today?"

"I am well, Nguyen. How are you?" Daniel spoke more slowly than usual. During the night he came to appreciate his first ever conversation with a person not American. He also began to realize that rapid or slurred speech, and slang, could be difficult to understand for someone who was just learning the language. He wanted to make it as easy as possible for Nguyen to communicate.

"I am well, also." They walked to the shoulder of the road. "Will you tell me about America today?"

"Sure. What do you want to know?"

"Do you have a bicycle at home in America?"

"No, I do not. But I will buy a car when I get home."

"A car? You must be very rich?"

"Me, rich? No."

"How can you buy a car if you are not rich?"

"I send home most of my army pay every month. I am saving my money."

"You must be rich?"

"No. In fact, GIs are poor. The army does not pay much."

"All GIs have much money. All Americans are rich."

"No. GIs have money to spend in town because the army provides them with food to eat and a place to sleep. They spend all the money the army gives them because they do not have to pay to live. They may spend a lot of money during one visit to town, but they go to town only once each month."

"GIs spend much money."

"We have nothing to pay for. You do not see the married men in town. They send money to their families in America. Family men do not have much money."

"Married GIs do not come to town?"

"They might come. They just do not spend much money. The GIs that spend a lot of money have no one to take care of."

"Cars and motorcycles cost very much money. Americans must be rich to buy such things."

"Americans buy those things on credit."

"What is 'credit'?"

"Credit is when you pay a little of the money when you buy the thing, then a little more every month until it's paid for."

"I do not understand."

"In America, you do not have to pay for expensive things all at one time. I'll give you an example. To buy a car, you give the dealer a little part of the cost when you buy it; that's called the downpayment. And you promise to pay them the same amount of money every month until the car is paid for. You may pay every month for three years or more. If you do not pay each month, they can come and take away the car."

"That is wonderful."

Wonder truly filled the eyes of the Vietnamese youth. He lived in a country at war since long before he was born, and with no end in the foreseeable future. Credit for the consumer was unheard of. The risks involved in daily life in a war zone precluded credit. No guarantee could be given that the buyer would survive the three years or so needed to pay for things like cars and motorcycles. In Nguyen's culture, a man's word was his bond only as long as he was alive to secure it. The word "credit" meant no more to the youth than would have the phrase "hockey face-off".

"A person can buy expensive things and promise to pay a little every month because America is a safe place to live. There is no war in America. There hasn't been for one hundred years."

"Do all merchants give this 'credit'?"

"Yes, for many expensive things."

"In America the merchants are generous, yes?"

"Not exactly. They charge interest."

"What is 'interest'?"

What is interest? Daniel had always taken the system for granted, even if he had never used it. How to explain it?

"When you buy something on credit, the person you owe the money to charges you a small percentage of the money you owe as interest. You actually pay back more than you owe."

"I do not understand."

"Because you can not pay all the money when you buy the car, the person loans you the money to pay for it. Then you pay back the person who loaned you the money a little each month. The person charges a fee each month on the unpaid debt. The extra money is profit for the person who loaned you the money."

Daniel ran out of explanations.

"I think I understand a little. America is a wonderful country."

America was, indeed, a wonderful country. Daniel had never thought of it quite that way, but explaining to Nguyen taught Daniel some things as well. He appreciated his homeland much more than he had just a few moments before.

Daniel took Perez's old watch from his shirt pocket and looked at the time.

"Your watch is broken."

"Only the band."

"I will have it fixed for you."

"Can you?"

"Yes. I will take to a man I know who fixes watches. I will bring it back to you tomorrow."

Daniel could hear Wilson shout, "You gave that fucker your watch?" It would seem quite stupid if Nguyen kept the watch. But he was such a nice kid.

"It's okay the way it is."

"But you must keep it in your pocket. You will lose it."

Nguyen looked at Daniel with the sincerity of the native awed by the rich American. Perhaps he really did want to help.

"Well."

"I will bring it back tomorrow. I must go now. My mother is not well."

"Okay. Here." Daniel gave the watch to Nguyen.

"I will bring it to you tomorrow. Good bye, Perdue."

"Good bye, Nguyen."

Daniel watched the boy mount his bike and pedal away. He decided not to say anything to the others in the squad about Nguyen and the watch. If he never saw the watch again, he could tell them that he had lost it. He preferred not to admit how stupid he had been.

Daniel turned his attention to the children that played around the bridge every evening. They lived in the nearest houses and were playing in their own yards. The GIs on duty always tried to send them home at dark, but they rarely left before their mothers called them in.

Wilson was involved with the kids. Each of the half dozen kids would run up and try to touch the "bear" without being caught. The "bear's" victims suffered a full minute of tickling before being allowed to escape. The kids were having a delightful time, and Wilson's growls revealed the fun he was having.

As the light faded, artillery batteries in base camp fired flares to set their guns for the night. When each shell exploded high in the sky, the flare was ignited and a metal casing blown loose from the bottom. The casing streamed to earth with a distinct whistling sound, a sound familiar to the veteran soldiers and to the children. Daniel noticed that the flares were coming closer and the whistling growing louder. The children paid no attention to the noisy routine of the evening. A flare ignited directly overhead and the metal casing screamed down.

Daniel and Wilson froze. Morgan looked up. There was no place to hide, no time to run away. The children were oblivious to the danger falling from the sky.

The casing crashed to the ground in the middle of the group, three yards from where Daniel stood. It gouged the pavement, then ricoheted across the street and into some weeds. The children screamed and scattered. In seconds, Daniel, Wilson and Morgan were alone, standing motionless, in awe of what had happened.

Wilson spoke slowly, "Gee-sus fuckin' Christ."

"Did it hit any of the kids?" asked Daniel.

"That goddamn thing hit right there," Morgan said, pointing at the scuff mark on the pavement. "Don't those fuckin' artillery people know what they're doing?"

"Gee-sus fuckin' Christ," Wilson repeated slowly.

Morgan was angry, "That thing could have killed us!"

"Were any of the kids hurt?" Daniel searched the nearby houses with his eyes. Not a person was visible.

"I don't think so, but they scattered so fast I'm not sure."

"I don't see how it missed them."

"Or us!" Morgan added. "In fuckin' credible."

"Gee-sus fuckin' Christ," repeated Wilson the third time. He had allowed himself to forget about the war for a moment, playing with the children. He was surprized and shaken.

"We are lucky as shit," decided Daniel.

Another flare popped near by, and the casing whistled down, unseen in the growing twilight. The children began returning, each running over and touching Wilson's leg, ready to resume the game. To them, nothing had happened, but the "bear" was no longer in the mood for play.

"Gee-sus fuckin' Christ."

Daniel looked at the children. Soon the soldiers would start guard. It was time for the children to go home. Daniel remembered what Nguyen had told him.

"*De loon.*"

The children stopped playing and looked at Daniel.

"*De loon,*" he repeated, motioning with his hand.

The children walked away toward their homes. The three soldiers stood next to the concrete abutment in silence. Rose came up from below the bridge.

"Time for guard."

In some ways, the position was safer at night. The darkness brought with it the emptiness of the jungle. The natives vanished and all movement stopped. The attentiveness of the combat veteran was suited to the stillness of the jungle, where sounds and movements were few. The crush of people during the daylight filled the veteran's mind with too many stimuli. Too many sounds, too much movement, too many people. Most of the veterans stayed below during the day, coming up to the road only in the evening, when the traffic lessened.

The night was clear and the starlight reflected in the ripples of the river. The structure of the bridge was visible in the eerie glow. Up on the road, the moon was visible rising above the eastern horizon, its bright round form a backdrop for the silhouettes of the village houses.

Daniel noted the serenity, but kept one hand on his rifle. The bridge seemed safe compared to the jungle, but Daniel had become a warrior. He was not disarmed by illusions of safety.

Morning at the bridge was a cautious time. A comfortable chill was greeted in the eastern sky by a slowly brightening gray. The first vehicle of the early morning was the noisy recon jeep. The sky turned from dark gray to a deep, rich blue. Pedestrians appeared before the rays of the sun. The first traveler was always the same old man. The soldiers watched him carefully as he made his way from the village to his fields somewhere, as he had done for sixty-three years.

As the sun peaked over the horizon, a three-quarter-ton truck drove across the bridge, dropping off an MP with a rifle in one hand and a box of C rations in the other. Slowly the traffic picked up, and then, at some point, there were too many to worry about individually. The day's routine had started.

Two days passed without Daniel seeing Nguyen and Daniel was certain the boy was gone for good. Then one afternoon as he napped below the bridge, Benny woke him and said that the MP wanted him. He climbed up and saw Nguyen standing beside his bicycle.

"Hello, Perdue."

"Hello, Nguyen. Where have you been?"

"My mother is ill. I stay with my brother and sisters."

"I am sorry. I hope she feels better soon."

"Thank you, Perdue. She is feeling better." He unstrapped the watch from his wrist. "I have your watch."

"Thank you."

"The man put on a new strap and a new. . . ."

"Crystal."

"Yes. Crystal."

"How much money do I owe you?"

"You owe nothing."

"It must have cost you something to have it fixed."

"It cost nothing. My . . . how do you say the brother of my father?"

"Uncle."

"Yes, uncle. My uncle fixed the watch for me."

"Thank you, Nguyen. And thank your uncle for me. I really appreciate this."

"You are welcome."

"Isn't there anything I can give you?"

"I like what you call 'C rations' very much."

"Wait here. I'll get you some."

"It is not necessary."

"It's my pleasure."

Daniel hurried below and emptied his sock into a C ration case that still held a few unwanted cans.

"Anybody got any extra Cs? It's for the kid on the bicycle."

"I left some in the box," replied Morgan.

"There's some ham in there, too," said Rose.

"Thanks."

Daniel carried the box up to the road.

"This is all I have."

"You will be hungry?"

"No. The army feeds me enough."

"Thank you very much."

"I'm sorry I can't give you more."

As the boy looked through the box excitedly, Daniel was touched at how little pleased the people of this culture. He wanted to repay Nguyen's kindness in some memorable way. He remembered the seven cents in his pocket, the nickel and two pennies he had carried from the United States.

"Here, Nguyen. I brought this from America."

"It is money?"

"Just a little. About seven piasters. But it is real American money, not the paper the Army uses."

"It is from America?"

"Yes. I've had it in my pocket since I got on the airplane in San Francisco."

"Thank you very much. It is good to have something from America."

"I wish I could give you more."

"No. This is enough. I will keep it to remember you."

Daniel never saw Nguyen again. The next morning the squad returned to base camp.

Rose entered the platoon tent and walked past the bunk on which Wilson, McGee, Morgan and Perdue played cards, stopping where Benny lay dozing on his cot.

"Are you awake, Benny?"

"Yep."

"You'll be staying behind when we pull out tomorrow."

"How come?"

"You're scheduled to start R&R on the thirtieth. You're going to Singapore."

"Where's Singapore?"

Wilson spoke without interrupting the play of the cards, "Ask Perdue. That fucker knows where everyplace is." Wilson was impressed when Daniel told him the whereabouts of Bangkok.

Daniel was embarrassed, for, although he was a good student in high school, he was not as informed as Wilson thought. He merely remembered his geography. He answered only when he realized that the squad expected it.

"It's south of here. It's a little island at the southern tip of Malaysia. The British have a big navy base there."

"I told you," Wilson said dryly.

"Does it cost much?" asked Benny.

Rose answered, "No more than the other places."

"I ain't got but a hundred dollars."

Rose spoke from experience, "Tell the first sergeant you want a partial pay."

Wilson agreed, "That's what I did."

"Can I go ask him now, Sarge?"

"Roger. I'm going to give the POOP on the operation. You don't need to hear it."

"Thanks, Sarge." Benny left the tent.

"Where the fuck we going this fuckin' time?" asked Wilson.

"Southeast of here somewhere. We're going to clear an area that's supposed to have a lot of charlies."

"Aw, them fuckers say that ev'ry fuckin' time."

"Let's hope they're wrong again," said Daniel.

"Don't count on it," warned Rose, "They've got to be right sooner or later. It's the law of averages."

"Don't you fuckin' know it. The law gets me ev'ry fuckin' time."

The company began a period of truly mobile war, for the First Air Cav was learning how to use its helicopters most effectively. The company was flown to a new area every day, where it searched the surrounding villages or jungle until late afternoon. As night approached, a hasty perimeter was formed, and ambushes were spread around it. The next morning the company continued to search, until, at some prearranged time and place, choppers arrived and carried the men to a new area. The process repeated every day with Daniel and the other's digging new holes each night. The only constant was the repetition of events and the daily long marches. Often four thousand meters or more were covered between dawn and the rendezvous with the choppers, followed by another few kilometers after the daily air assault.

As the body adjusted to the constant exertion, the mind adjusted to haphazard sleep. Night watch on two man positions meant half a night's sleep: two hours of guard, two hours of sleep, two more hours on, and then two off. The infantry never slept more than two hours at a time, but sleep came quickly when there was time for it. Even on a ten minute break during a march, sleep came to those who needed it most, catching eight minute naps while the others kept watch. The sleepers were awakened quietly when the break ended and they rose to their feet with the others. Neither discussion nor argument determined who slept, rather it occurred spontaneously that whoever needed to sleep was allowed the nap. The rest watched the war and waited for the time when, without order, they would sleep.

The only time of day when the soldiers relaxed was the hour that followed setting up the perimeter in the afternoon. In the minutes before dark, the men dug prone shelters before assembling at Rose's position to enjoy the one restful time of the day. Sometimes a card game started up, other times the men cleaned up as best they could. The time was often used to dig one's cathole without being hurried.

The jungle soldier carried with him everything he owned, for anything left at base camp was stolen or ruined by the climate. The infantry had no creature comforts in their base camp since it was occupied too infrequently to be maintained as cozy living quarters. The infantry lacked the advantages acquired by those whose work allowed them to spend every night in the same place. Items of convenience or comfort were never carried to the field by the infantry, who carried only those things which were needed. A soldier carried his weapon and ammunition, his bedroll of poncho and liner, a sock full of C rations, and canteens of water. Such were the essentials for survival. Hygiene was limited in the jungle. Each man carried his own toothbrush, but other articles were spread among the squad: one man carried the toothpaste, another the bar of soap, a third the razor and a fourth the blades, a fifth man carried the washrag and the sixth man the towel. The only non-essential item in the squad was the tattered deck of cards that Wilson carried everywhere.

Almost every day, America was visited through daydreams or stories. The remembered little irritations of life became humorous misadventures to be enjoyed upon returning to the States. The challenge of the vending machine that did not work brought smiles, as did thoughts of not having correct change for the Coke machine. Cokes sparked memories of favorite foods and favorite places. All dreamed of hamburgers, dressed according to hometown preference, served at some teenage eatery described in detail, always with the teller accompanied by a pretty girl.

Girls were the preferred fantasy, always related in crude language. Profanity spread among the soldiers because no one was present who might be offended, and because young men often use vulgarity as a symbol of maturity. For some, the foul language concealed the inner desire for a simpler, more innocent relationship, a thing too personal to be shared among real men.

Daniel's dreams were of benches in landscaped gardens where he sat and held hands with beautiful girls. He dreamed not of sex, but of peace and love, and a place where he could close his eyes and know the war would not encroach. Girls were symbols of Daniel's ideal, for they were as far removed from the anxieties of war as were the scenes in his dreams in which they appeared. His imaginary companion was always different, partly because he left no one girl behind to be remembered, but also because, unknown to Daniel, the war was beginning to change him. Somewhere in the inner recesses of his subconscious, his mind was building barriers against pain, barriers that prevented friends or loved ones from dying by eliminating friends and loved ones. The lonely war was creating warriors who would avoid love to avoid pain.

None of the men in second squad were married, although Benny had dated the same girl for four years and Minniefield had been engaged. The squad did not share the special worries and extra rewards experienced by husbands and fathers away from their wives and children. They never saw the steady stream of letters from America that nurtured the married man, that buffered him from the stresses of war and protected him from the personality changes experienced by boys becoming men.

The mail from America that most interested second squad was the random letters from American girls addressed simply "To a Soldier in Viet Nam." Impossible circumstances did not prevent the young men from hoping that some lonely girl in America might become that one special person to go home to.

Two letters caught Daniel's attention.

The first letter was from a Jewish girl in high school near Boston.

"This one's for you, Rose," Daniel said without indicating to the others a reason.

The second was written by a girl named Karen who was a high school junior in Hamilton, Ohio. Her letter implied more need than the others, as if the girl really wanted to find a boy. Daniel knew she was too young; she would still be in high school when he returned home. His fantasy ran more towards a girl just out of high school, but Karen's letter revealed a hunger that no lonely boy could help but want to satisfy.

Daniel wrote Karen, from Ohio, and thanked her for caring enough to write. He wrote about his duties and suggested that, if she were to write directly to him, she include an envelope and a sheet of clean paper that he could use to write back. The letter went out on the next day's supply chopper.

Two weeks later, a letter from Karen arrived that changed Daniel's fantasy. She wrote that she was delighted that he was the one to receive her letter and that she would love to write to a nice boy like him. Moreover, she included with the letter a snapshot of herself in a swimsuit.

Daniel was not desperate for love, but he could not resist the pretty little girl in the picture who had so much American skin. He was confident that no relationship could develop with her safe at home twelve thousand miles from his lust. Wilson and Morgan decided from their readings of the letter that Daniel had latched on to a hot property. He wrote to her that he thought she was beautiful and that he definitely wanted to visit her when he returned to America. He admitted that he dreamed about her and apologized that the dreams were erotic.

Karen's next letter was a surprise. She admitted that she, too, dreamed about Daniel and that her dreams were also erotic. She wrote that she knew it was silly, but she thought she was falling in love with him.

With much encouragement from Wilson and Morgan, Daniel wrote a description, politely, but in detail, of exactly what he would most enjoy doing with her when he came to Hamilton. He began to give serious thought as to how they might get around her parents if he really did go visit her. Daniel was letting himself become wrapped up in a symbol, if not the reality, of the lover waiting longingly at home.

Karen's third letter written directly to Daniel brought him back to reality and provided the squad with more humor than Daniel wanted. She wrote that she was sorry, she could not write to him any more. She was pregnant and getting married.

The First Air Cav covered more territory than other units because it had more helicopters than other units. The division spread its squads over vast areas to search for the enemy. If any squad encountered opposition, reinforcements were flown in quickly. The squads were the strands of the spider's web; touch any one strand and the spider closed in.

As the operation moved into its third week, the areas covered contained more and more villages that held Viet Cong suspects. The villages were so remote that the ARVNs were unable to draft the males of military age. No one could know why the Viet Cong had not pressed into service the males of the villages. Young women were never seen in the areas of the Cav's operations, and their seemingly permanent absence puzzled the American privates.

The increasing numbers of suspects created a problem that worried Morgan and amused others in the squad.

In one nameless village, second squad was assigned to guard the assembly area where all the suspects found in the village were brought. When the first group was escorted in and directed to sit in the open where the squad could watch them, three of them walked straight to Morgan and began talking. They thought he was the interpreter.

Morgan held up one hand to stop them, "Hold it. I got no idea what you people are talking about."

The suspects chattered away.

"Give me a break, people. I'm an American. You know: hot dogs, apple pie and all that shit."

The locals were unaffected by Morgan's protestations and continued talking.

"Help, somebody."

"What fuckin' for?" joked Wilson. "You're doin' all fuckin' right by yourself."

"Sergeant Rose?" Morgan pleaded weakly. "Please help."

· Rose intervened, "Benny, move those guys over there and sit them down."

Terwilliger stepped between Morgan and the suspects, "I don't blame the fuckers none. You do look like a charlie."

Morgan looked to the sky in prayer, "God, please help me get through this shit alive."

The suspects were confused. They accepted that American soldiers were black and white, but they knew nothing about oriental Americans.

Morgan faced the same problem with each new group of suspects brought in. The locals' reactions to Morgan amused Wilson, McGee and Terwilliger, but Morgan himself was rapidly becoming distraught.

"I don't have a fuckin' chance. If they think I'm Vietnamese in broad daylight, what's some GI gonna think in the dark?"

Wilson grabbed Morgan around the neck with his strong right arm, "Stay close to me, fucker. Ain't no fuckin' body gonna mess wi' you if I'm around."

Morgan, six inches shorter than Wilson, did not enjoy being held like a sack of groceries, "I gotta find something better than this."

Wilson loosened his grip, "I know! I know! When I get you back to base camp, I'm gonna rub you up wi' fuckin' Kiwi. You'll be lookin' like a bro in no fuckin' time."

Daniel spoke, "I've got an idea, cherry. Every time they come at you, start singing surfer songs. They aren't many Vietnamese that know about the Beach Boys."

When the next group was brought in, Morgan turned his back to them and began singing "Little Surfer Girl". The suspects did ignore him, but because they did not see his face.

Rose began to give serious thought to Morgan's problem. He could see that it would not go away on its own.

Daniel was curious about the disposition of the "suspects", "Rose, what happens to these poor fuckers?"

"They'll be flown to the rear on a shithook and be questioned by people who are supposed to know how."

"Then what?"

"If they're not charlies, they'll be let go."

"How will they get back here?"

"I never thought about it."

"Are they flown back home?"

"Could be, but I doubt it."

"Somebody ought to give the fuckers a ride, if they're not charlies. How the fuck are they supposed to get home?"

"For all I know, they have to walk."

The squad ate supper early that day, for the consequence of having easy duty during the day was having to go out on ambush that night.

As Rose ate, he thought about Morgan's problem. He hit upon a solution and moved over beside Daniel.

"Morgan's really got a problem, Perdue. I've got to do something about it, if I can."

"I know."

"I think I've got an answer, but it's up to you."

"Me?"

"Roger. If he were carrying the radio, he would look more like one of us and less like an interpreter. Wouldn't he?"

Daniel gave the idea a moment's thought, "I guess he would. I've never seen any ARVNs with prick 25s."

"Would you give it up?"

"I don't really have a choice, do I? Morgan's no good to us scared to death."

"And there's another benefit, at least for me. I've been walking point myself because I've had to put Wilson in the rear. Now I can put you back there and let Wilson take the point."

"What about Benny?"

"He won't give up his M79, and that thing's not designed for the point or the rear."

"And there's no fuckin' way a cherry could do either."

"Roger."

"I guess that settles it. Send Morgan over and I'll show him the radio ropes before we move out."

"Thanks, Perdue. You were damn good on the radio and I really fuckin' appreciate your giving it up."

"I'll miss it, that's for fuckin' sure."

The ambush site for that night was a small collection of huts eight hundred meters across open rice paddies from the perimeter, which was fifty yards from the edge of the large village the company cleared that day.

The squad moved out from the perimeter before dusk. The plan was to move across the paddies while there was still daylight and set up the ambush just at dark.

Three hundred meters out from the perimeter, the squad reached flooded paddies. Rose directed Wilson to walk on the dikes, for, in the open as they were, the squad would be no more exposed on the small dikes than in the paddies, but walking in the ankle deep water and its mud would slow down the progress of the squad so much that they would not reach the treeline until well after night was upon them. The flooded paddies posed an additional problem. They acted as a barrier between the squad and the rest of the company. The squad would be unable to return to the perimeter quickly in case of emergency and the company would be unable to move quickly to the squad's aid were that to become necessary. Flooded rice paddies were always an inconvenience.

Bringing up the rear was a new experience for Daniel. The last man was responsible for insuring that nothing surprized the squad from the rear. That task was considerably easier in open paddies than it would be in the jungle, and it pleased Daniel that he was given the chance to practice walking in circles in easy terrain. On dikes sometimes less than a foot wide, Daniel walked in circles. One step forward, one step sideways, one step backwards, another step sideways. Over and over, around and around, Daniel walked in circles.

Daniel was a veteran now, though only nineteen years old and in the army barely more than a year. He could keep his eyes and mind focused on the distant treelines while his feet negotiated whatever ground was beneath them. The danger in the distance held his attention, yet every step was taken consciously and cautiously. The Viet Cong had a dozen tricks with which to harm the unwary, but they were of primary concern to the man on the point, the spot that required the greatest awareness. Only a veteran could walk point, for only a veteran could watch both where he stepped and the distant treeline. Daniel's turn on the point would come, but, for now, he walked in circles.

They reached the treeline and the scattered huts in the deepening twilight. Rose ordered Wilson to turn left and move along still in the paddies until an appropriate ambush site was found; Rose had no intention of walking his men through the small village in the dark.

The huts appeared to be deserted, but people lived there earlier, perhaps yesterday. Daniel wondered why so many of the villages were deserted. Did the people flee when the Americans approached? Had they left at the arrival of Viet Cong? Were all the people carried off by the charlies? Daniel would never understand how a place could look so inhabited, yet not be.

The squad moved along the edge of the paddies for nearly a hundred meters before Rose saw an ambush site to his liking. He moved the men into the village and dispersed them in a large ditch that parallelled what appeared to be a main trail.

As the squad settled into position, Daniel noticed McGee pulling at something under the barrel of his machinegun.

Daniel whispered, "What are you doing, cherry?"

"Trying to get this piece of wire out from under my gun."

"Freeze!" ordered Daniel.

"What for?"

"Don't move a muscle, cherry. Don't let go of nothing and don't pull nothing. Whatever you've got, hold it."

"What's up?" asked Rose.

"McGee's found some wire."

Rose and Daniel converged on the barrel of the M60. A thin wire led away from the weapon in each direction.

Rose spoke softly, "I think you've got hold of a boobytrap, McGee. Don't move a fuckin' muscle."

The cherry was suddenly quite scared, "Oh, shit."

Rose spoke softly to Daniel, "You go that way and I'll go this way."

Daniel followed the wire to a patch of tall grass a few feet away, "I found it."

In the grass, taped to a stake in the ground, was a hand grenade. The wire was connected to the pin, which only partially held the handle in place. McGee had almost set it off, for another fraction of an inch movement would release the handle, causing the "pop" that began the five second count before the grenade exploded. If McGee had pulled one more time, the boobytrap would have worked.

Rose came up beside Daniel, "The other end's tied off."

"Good. At least it wasn't set with grenades at both ends."

"Do you want me to secure that thing?"

"No, I'm already here. I'll do it."

"Be careful." Rose turned to the rest of the squad, "Wilson, take the guys over to that hut and keep 'em down."

"Roger, Sarge."

The others moved quickly and quietly to a safer distance.

"You better move out, too, Sarge," advised Daniel. "No sense in both of us getting killed if I fuck up."

"I'll check the ditch and see if charlie has left any more fuckin' surprises." Rose crawled down to the other end of the ditch and began feeling for wires.

Daniel took a deep breath, "Here goes."

He gently moved the grass from around the grenade, then carefully curled his thumb around the fat body of the explosive and the stake to which it was taped. He placed his fingers against the handle and slowly applied pressure; the tension from the wire pulled the pin from its slot and the small piece of metal fell to the ground. As long as Daniel held the handle against the grenade, all was safe.

With his free hand, he tried to remove the wire from the pin, but he was unsuccessful.

"Rose, could you give me a hand here?"

"Sure." Rose crawled to Daniel from his safer position.

"Get the wire off this thing, will you?"

While Daniel held the grenade, Rose unwound the wire from the pin.

Rose smiled, "I imagine you want this."

"I can find a use for it, yeah."

Daniel took the pin from Rose and carefully inserted it into its proper place. He examined the grenade carefully to make certain that the pin was, in fact, holding the handle in place the way it was meant to.

Daniel reached for his pocket knife, but changed his mind, "Can I borrow your knife?"

Rose pulled his pocket knife from his pants and opened the sharpest blade.

Daniel used the knife to cut slowly the tape that held the grenade to the stake. He would not let go of the handle until he could toss away the grenade if things did not work out as he intended. The tape cut, Daniel lifted the grenade from the stake and looked at it from every direction. The pin was serving its purpose. The grenade was now safe, but Daniel took the added precaution of bending over one prong of the pin so that it could not fall out accidentally. Slowly, he released the pressure he had kept on the handle.

"Just like it came from the factory. Anybody want a grenade?"

McGee and Morgan, the cherries, offered congratulations, but Rose stopped them.

"Quiet!" he ordered. "We're still on a fuckin' ambush." he moved to the radio, "Camel Six, this is Camel Two. Over."

"This is Six India. Over."

"This is Two. Tell Six we are in position. Over."

"Roger, Two. He heard. Over."

"Also tell Six we found a boodytrap. Over."

There was a brief pause.

"Camel Two, this is Camel Five. Roger that boobytrap. What kind is it? Over."

"This is Two. It was a trip wire attached to the pin of a grenade. Over."

"Roger. Be careful with it. Do you need help disarming it? Over."

"It's already disarmed. Over."

"Good work, Two. I'll pass the info on to Fullback. Anything else? Over."

"Negative, Five. This is Camel Two, out."

Daniel crawled over to McGee, "The next time you see a piece of wire, fucker, will you please not play with it?"

"I won't."

"Thank you."

Rose whispered to the squad, "Listen up, guys. We all don't need to be up. We'll go ahead and start watch. Two guys will be up all the time, one watching each way. If anybody sees anything coming, wake up everybody else before you start shooting. Ambushes work best when we all get to fire." He looked directly at the cherries, "Understand?"

Morgan and McGee nodded.

"Perdue, you and Morgan take the first watch. Wilson and Benny, you take the second. I'll take the third with McGee." He loooked at his wristwatch. "Let's go ahead and pull two and a half hours at one stretch. That way there'll be less moving around."

The squad quietly settled down for the night.

Daniel sat and stared down the trail, still tense from his experience with the boobytrap grenade. He ducked low and lit a cigarette. At least when guard was over, he would be able to sleep for five full hours.

Small arms fire crackled in the distance. Daniel recognized instantly the sounds of M16s and an M60, but he heard no AK47 fire. Perhaps some cherry on the company perimeter was jumpy and started shooting at shadows. Or maybe another ambush had opened fire on some charlies. The firing stopped in a few seconds and did not start up again.

Daniel sat with his rifle in his hands and watched the trail. One hundred and twenty-three days remained in his tour.

Just how night watch affected America's too young warriors may never be known. The loneliness, the uncertainty, and the intensity of guard at night might not have altered the personalities of grown men, even when repeated night after night, but teenage boys were vulnerable. Unable because of their youth to distinguish the conduct of war from conduct in general, the teenagers acquired personality characteristics they would carry home to the streets as part of their adult consciousnesses, characteristics not so much inappropriate to the civilian world as misunderstood by it. The veterans of World War II came home to a society that knew of their challenges and was prepared to accept the limitations imposed on them by wartime experiences; they came home to a society that understood that men who endured war were forever different from those who stayed behind, and society was prepared to allow for certain irregularities in their behavior. But the men who fought World War II were grown men, mostly, a full seven years older on average than the teenagers who went to Viet Nam. Those grown men knew who and what they were, their adult personalities were fully formed, and they could keep their war experiences in perspective. The nineteen year olds who traversed the jungles of Indo-China became men in those jungles, not because war matured them, but because their age required changes that would occur anywhere; nineteen year olds in American factories and on American campuses were becoming men also. So a task that required grown men was assigned to teenage boys, and those boys accomplished the task as well as grown men could have. Only the grown men would not have learned war quite so well, or quite so permanently.

Night watch taught its lessons, and young students of war, like Daniel Perdue, slowly learned to fear the coming of night. At night, the soldier sat and waited alone, sealed in a world often no larger than the reach of an arm, a world of darkness, of sound, and of anxiety. No matter the hardship and danger that might come with the dawn, anything was better than the loneliness of the night, when Daniel Perdue and all the others waited and worried, and grew to manhood one lonely minute at a time.

Yet the end of night was in itself an awkward time for soldiers, for firstlight always brought with it the possibility of the dawn attack. From the beginnings of warfare, battles have begun with the sunrise. The first gray shades of morning ended the anxiety of the night, but they provided no relief, because the first moments of daylight were themselves filled with anxiety. Not until some indefinite time after dawn did the soldier's day begin, when the dangers were faced as a group.

Second squad prepared to return to the company perimeter while dew still covered the grass. They assembled at the treeline and stared out over eight hundred meters of open rice paddies.

Rose walked up to Daniel, "Perdue, you take the point."

"Me, Sarge? I've never been on point."

"You've got to start sometime."

Rose knew this was a good place for Daniel to take point for the first time. In open terrain, with the company perimeter visible in the distance, the point man would have an easy time. The rear would be more important, and Wilson had the rear.

Walking point was, and remains, the most daring of the duties experienced by the citizen soldier. In the continuous one year war called Viet Nam, no hardened professional soldier led the way, no grizzled old veteran blazed the trail. The point devolved to the most able of the inexperienced citizen soldiers, a boy who little more than a year before worried only about girls, football scores and English tests. Qualified only when compared to even newer arrivals at war, the point man led his unit through the unknown, ever vigilant for danger underfoot and in the distance. The point man must not fail to see the punji stakes in the tall grass or the trip wire of the boobytrap, yet his eyes and attention must be directed outward, to the treeline, or through the tangled vegetation of the jungle, where armed men could lay in ambush. On the shoulders of nineteen-year-old soldiers, so recently schoolboys, rested the responsibility for life and death decisions.

Daniel stepped out into the dry paddy, gazed for a moment at the company perimeter barely visible in the distance, and moved forward. For the first time, no soldier walked in front of him. The paddies spread out before him unbroken and unobstructed.

Rifle in hand, the selector switch set to full automatic, Daniel walked quickly and carefully. He glanced down to clear the ground in front of his feet even though the short grass in the paddies afforded no concealment for punji stakes. He scanned every dike for the glint of a rifle even though no enemy could hide in the paddies. Daniel walked and watched and blazed the most efficient trail. The trip back seemed longer than the trip out.

The squad reached the perimeter and moved through it to the platoon CP. Rose directed his men to break for breakfast while he reported to Sergeant Stovall. Although still in sight of the perimeter positions, the veterans in the squad relaxed and enjoyed the relative security.

Rose joined the squad and dropped his gear, "I found out what the shooting last night was about."

"Some fuckin' cherry firin' up a fuckin' water buffalo?" asked Wilson without looking up from his Cs.

McGee turned to Morgan, "I didn't hear no shooting."

Morgan explained, "It was during first watch. You were asleep."

"Dumber than that," answered Rose to Wilson's question. "Two squads out on ambush had a firefight with each other."

Wilson looked up, "You're shittin' me?"

"A squad from first platoon got off track and walked up in front of a squad from second platoon."

"Stupid fuckers," said Wilson.

"No shit," agreed Rose. "A cherry was walking point for the squad that walked up on the ambush. He was the only one hurt."

"The rest of them fuckers musta been fuckin' lucky," decided Wilson.

"They didn't have to be. It was a cherry on the ambush who opened up without telling the rest of his squad. He was the only one to fire."

"Didja hear that, cherries?" asked Wilson.

"It was the ambush that was lucky," continued Rose. "After the cherry got hit, the machinegunner in this squad opened up on the ambush. It was amazing nobody was killed."

Daniel asked, "Was the cherry hurt bad?"

"He got hit seven times."

"Musta blowed that fucker away," said Wilson.

"No. The guy doing the shooting walked his sixteen up the fucker's left side. Hit him three times in the leg, three times in the arm, and creased his head with one."

"Lucky fucker," said Wilson.

"They were all minor wounds. The medic gave him a shot of morphine and he smoked a cigarette and joked about the whole thing. They flew him out when it was light enough for a chopper to come in."

"That fucker really was lucky," repeated Wilson. "He could have gone home in a fuckin' body bag."

"I've got some other news. First, we've got the whole day off. The company's just gonna sit here."

"All fuckin' right!" roared Wilson.

"And second, Perdue goes back to the rear for R&R today."

"Really?"

"Really. Hell, you've been here eight months."

Wilson spoke up. "Perdue's gonna get hisself a whole fuckin' week of pussy."

Every member of the squad perked up at the news of Daniel's R&R. For the cherries, it sparked fantasies of the future, and, for the veterans, it brought back pleasant memories.

"Where's he going, Sarge?" asked Morgan.

"Japan."

"You oughta go to Bangkok," suggested Wilson. Then, just realizing it, "I banged my cock for a whole fuckin' week!"

As Daniel packed his equipment for the ride to base camp, a broad grin spread across his face. At last he would have the chance to have a girl who would not be in a hurry, a girl who would not be talking to another girl on the other side of a curtain.

For Daniel, a week of R&R meant even more than his first chance for sex. It meant hot baths and cold Cokes, real food and soft beds. It meant a chance to get drunk for the first time in his brief life, the age old remedy for men on leave who want to forget about war.

Daniel reached Camp Radcliff late in the afternoon and walked from the brigade chopper pad to the company area. He ate supper in the battalion mess hall, then spent the evening alone in the empty platoon tent. With the battalion in the field, the EM club was closed and the company area virtually deserted. Daniel went to bed soon after dark, but lay awake for hours thinking about the coming week, too excited to sleep.

Daniel thought mostly about sex and alcohol, the two truely manly pleasures. Too young to appreciate the ancient culture of Japan and without a friend with whom to share the experience, Daniel dreamed of those things which men enjoyed, or so he believed. Sex and alcohol could fill his senses and rid his mind of thoughts of war, or so he believed.

R&R could not be planned. Boys who lived their lives in urban ghettos returned to the jungle talking about beaches and pagodas. Farmboys returned with tales about bustling cities and crowded streets. The sons of preachers bragged about whiskey and women, while the sons of sinners spoke of some old man who carved tigers of ivory. Teenage boys rarely had the maturity to take advantage of the situation as it happened, whatever the advantage was.

xxviii

Daniel awoke at sunrise and put on the wrinkled, mildewed khaki uniform that he salvaged from his dufflebag. Unneeded by Daniel and unwanted by thieves, the pants and shirt grew foul through the months. Only a jungle soldier could have worn them, for only to a jungle soldier were they an improvement.

Daniel rode to the airstrip and caught a C130 transport plane to Qui Nhon. From the airbase there, he would fly by chartered commercial jetliner to Japan.

At Qui Nhon, a sergeant put Daniel's name on the manifest with clerks and infantry, truck drivers and artillerymen from all over the central highlands, but most were also from the First Cav. Every one of them was as excited as Daniel, for whatever their jobs, the jobs were in Viet Nam.

The sergeant announced that the flight did not take off until the next morning and that they would be billeted in a nearby compound for the night.

As Daniel lay on a cot fantasizing about the future, a GI walked up.

"You want to walk over to the EM club?"

"Do you know where it is?"

"I think so. According to the directions I got, it's quite close."

"Why not? I'm on vacation."

"You look like a grunt. What unit are you with?"

"First Cav. Second of the Eighth."

"First of the Seventh. My name's Tom Badger."

"Daniel Perdue. How did you know I was infantry?"

"First, your Class As look as bad as mine."

"It's the best I could do."

"I know. Mine look like shit, too."

"You said there were two ways."

"You've got grunts' eyes."

"What the fuck are 'grunts' eyes'?"

"I never noticed it myself until a chaplain told me about it. There's something about an infantryman's eyes. They are alert. I'll show you."

Tom looked around at the other GIs walking in the compound. "See that dude over there? Look at his eyes. See the way they move? I guaran-fuckin'-tee you he's a grunt. Want to go ask him?"

"No, I see what you mean. I never noticed it before."

"How could you? Everybody you see is a grunt."

"That's true. Do I look like that?"

"Your eyes do. The rest of you looks like a clerk."

"Thank's a fuckin' lot."

"No offense. How many people do you see who look like John Wayne?"

"My platoon sergeant really looks like a soldier."

"The exception proves the rule, right?"

Daniel looked at the eyes of those who passed. Most of them appeared happy enough. Then he saw one whose eyes darted from side to side. He could tell that the soldier was aware of everything going on around him. He nodded to Daniel.

Daniel nodded, then turned to Tom Badger. "You're right. I can tell just by looking at their eyes."

"That chaplain was no dummy. Where are you from?"

"Atlanta."

"That's a pretty town. I passed through there on my way to Fort Jackson."

"I went through processing at Fort Jackson."

"I had Basic there, too."

"I went through Basic and AIT at Fort Gordon."

"That's where I had AIT. Here's the EM club."

They entered the building and walked up to the bar. The club was bigger than Daniel expected, and less crowded.

Tom Badger addressed the bartender, "What kind of beer do you have?"

The bartender was a twenty-four year old Staff Sergeant on his third enlistment, "What kind do you want?"

"PBR."

"You got it. What about you?"

Daniel was honest, "To tell the truth, I'd really like an ice cold stateside Coke."

"You got it."

The bartender reached into the cooler directly in front of him and pulled out a can of Pabst Blue Ribbon, then turned around and pulled a can of Coke from a cooler behind him. He opened both cans with a big churchkey tied to a cord.

Tom reached for his wallet, "This one's on me, Perdue."

"Thanks. I don't have a lot of money."

"I'm not loaded, but I've got enough."

"I hope I do. I was hoping to go to Bangkok. I heard you could get by there on two hundred and fifty dollars."

"Is that what you've got?"

"About two sixty. That's how much I've saved."

"I started putting money back three months ago."

"I send home two hundred bucks every month. I'm going to buy a car when I get back to the world."

"That's not for me. Fuck, I could get killed next week. I'll start saving money when there's a guarantee I'll be alive to spend it."

"I plan on living through this. And I'm going to celebrate in a new car."

"Compared to you, I'm rich. Tonight is my treat."

"Thanks, but it won't cost you much. I still can't drink beer without making a face."

"Beer is sacred."

"So are Cokes."

"You won't get high on Cokes."

"I'm not looking to get drunk. I drank once in high school and got sick as a dog."

"The trick is not to get drunk. Try to catch a nice buzz and keep it."

"That would be great."

"Now you're talking."

"But that can wait until Japan. As long as I'm in this fuckin' country, I want to stay straight."

"Not me." Tom turned up his beer.

"Where are you from, Badger?"

"Cleveland. Ever been there?"

"No."

"If you ever get there, stop in and see me. I'll show you the grave of Great-great-great-great Uncle George E. Badger."

"Sounds really exciting."

"Old Uncle George is the family hero."

"No doubt."

"Oh, yes. He was Secretary of the Navy under William Henry Harrison in 1841."

"Terrific."

"What make's him neat is that he had the job for only a month. Harrison caught pneumonia on Inauguration Day and died after a month. John Tyler replaced Uncle George with someone else."

"Fascinating."

"Until I got drafted, old Uncle George was the only Badger ever to work for the government."

Daniel and Tom sat in the EM club all afternoon. They ate supper together, then returned to the club. Tom eventually convinced Daniel to drink a beer. Daniel did, and immediately got drowsy. He went back to his billet alone and went to sleep.

At daybreak the two infantrymen were up and on their way to the airfield. As they stood outside the terminal and watched the activity, Tom pointed to a silver speck above the horizon.

"I'll bet that's our plane."

"I hope so."

As they watched the jetliner approach, a sergeant stuck his head out of the door, "Get your gear together. Your plane's here."

The plane rolled to a stop near where Daniel, Tom and the others waited. As the ground crew pushed the steps into place, a stewardess opened the plane's door. Daniel watched her as she stood in the doorway and said goodbye to the soldiers exiting the plane. They were returning from R&R.

The sergeant who spoke earlier appeared again, this time with a clipboard in his hand.

"When I call your name, move onto the aircraft."

He did not need to repeat the instructions. The men whose names were on the list were exceedingly attentive.

Daniel's name was called before Tom's, and Tom called to him as he started for the plane.

"Save me a seat."

Daniel had not taken his eyes off the stewardess since she opened the door. He watched her as he walked to and up the steps. She was the first American female he had seen in eight months.

As he reached the top of the steps, he spoke to her, "Hello."

"Hello, soldier," she answered. "Welcome aboard. Have a seat anywhere."

Daniel would have stayed there, but the stewardess began greeting the man behind him, so he walked on. Inside the plane were three more stewardesses. The one at the door was a redhead; inside were two blonds and a brunette. By the time Daniel took a seat, he decided that he loved all four of them, but that one of the blonds, the smallest, was the prettiest.

Tom walked up the aisle and sat down beside Daniel, "I'd like to spend a week with that redhead. She's built like a brick shithouse."

"Not a chance. You can bet real money that she's heard every line ever tried. Twice."

"No doubt you're right, but I can dream, can't I?"

"If this were a movie, you know, two of them would fall in love with us."

"I'll keep smiling and praying. What about this real money? I'd almost forgotten what it looked like."

They had exchanged their military script for American greenbacks in the terminal.

"It is nice to see Andrew Jackson again."

"And Lincoln, and Washington, and the fucker on the ten."

"Hamilton," said Daniel.

"Whatever. All of them are beautiful."

A few seats in front of Tom and Daniel, a GI got very loud in his efforts to get the attention of the stewardesses.

"Come on over here, Honey. Come sit in my lap."

The brunette walked up to him, "If you'd really rather stay here, I can arrange it."

The soldier's attitude changed instantly, "Sorry."

A GI across the aisle roared with laughter, "She done shot you down, fucker!"

The stewardess turned toward the front of the plane, "Hey, Sally. Break out the mouthbelt for the gorilla in thirty-one."

The loud comments stopped. Throughout the flight, many of the soldiers approached the ladies in hopes that each might be the one who was lucky, but none of them did it loud enough for the other passengers to hear him being rebuffed.

After the plane was airborne, the brunette came by Tom and Daniel with a serving cart. "Can I serve you anything?"

Tom smiled, "How about the redhead?"

"You'll have to get her husband's approval. He's a Marine Colonel."

"How about a beer?"

"No beer. The Department of Defense doesn't trust you fellows with alcohol."

Tom turned to Daniel, "Can you believe that?"

"That's the breaks. Ma'am, could I have a Coke?"

"Sure, soldier." She opened a can of Coke and handed it to Daniel, then she looked at Tom. "Coke, orange, tea or coffee. What will it be?"

"Coke, I guess. But I really want a beer."

"I could use one myself. I guess we'll both have to suffer."

"I like a woman with a sense of humor."

"And I like men with laryngitis."

Daniel drank his Coke and watched the ladies as long as they moved up and down the aisle. Soon after the ladies stopped moving, the hum of the engines and the vibration of the plane put him to sleep. He awoke for the refueling stop in Taiwan, then slept the rest of the way to Japan.

Tom woke Daniel when the stewardess announced that they were flying over Japan.

Daniel looked through the window. Night had come and the countryside below twinkled with lights like a terrestrial heaven. Daniel had never seen a city from the sky and he stared in awe at the Christmas tree of lights on the ground below him.

The jetliner landed smoothly, quite different from the rough C130 landings to which he was accustomed. The jet taxied to a stop and the passengers stepped into sounds and sights that reminded Daniel of the times he had taken girls on dates to the Atlanta airport.

The line of soldiers entered the terminal building at Camp Zama and were processed through with a rapidity that surprised Daniel, Tom and all the others.

As he waited for Tom to finish, Daniel saw a display for a hotel in the resort city of Atamishi. The display advertised five nights, meals in the restaurant, drinks and other amenities, all for one hundred and seventy-five American dollars.

Were Daniel older, more worldly, he would not have considered a package deal. All of Japan was open to him and he had five full days in which to experience it, but he could not. Although he could endure the hardships of war, and its dangers, without difficulty, Daniel was afraid to expose himself to the unknowns of a vacation in Tokyo. His youth prepared him not at all for the enjoyment that he could have derived, were he older, tasting the ancient Nipponese culture. Instead, Daniel sought a refuge from excitement and adventure, and further anxiety. The hotel in Atamshi, whatever else it provided, would eliminate his worries about money.

When Tom walked up, Daniel pointed to the display, "What do you think about that?"

Tom read the advertisement, "What do you think?"

"It fits my budget. I'd hate to run out of money in Tokyo and have to spend the last days of my R&R here at the Camp Zama 'Hilton'."

"Inside I heard a dude say he actually wanted to stay on base. Can you believe that?"

"He must be even poorer than me."

"This place in, Atamishi, sounds all right to me. I'm not real fuckin' excited about spending a week in any place as crowded as Tokyo is."

"At least there we'd be sure to have a place to sleep and something to eat."

"I like that about the free drinks. It's okay with me."

"Then let's do it."

"How do we get to the place, anyway?"

"There's a pad on the display that has the directions."

Tom looked at the small pad, "That's in Japanese."

"I know. They're for the taxi driver."

Daniel ripped a sheet containing directions from the pad on the display, "It even gives the price of the taxi."

"How much?"

"Thirteen hundred yen."

"Thirteen hundred! Isn't that a fuckin' lot of money?"

"Let's see. The sign over there says you get three hundred and twenty yen to the dollar. Three twenty into thirteen hundred. That's right at four dollars."

"Is that all?"

"That's what I figure."

"Fuck, dude. That ain't shit."

"I wonder how much money we should exchange?"

"Fuck if I know."

The soldier in the nearby currency exchange cage overheard them and offered advice, "Any reputable hotel will exchange money without gypping you. Exchange as little as you can every time. Any yen you have left over can't be converted back into dollars. It becomes very expensive toilet paper."

"Thanks," said Tom. "How about fifty bucks' worth for starters?"

Tom and Daniel each exchanged fifty dollars. In return, each received sixteen thousand yen.

Tom thumbed through the stack of bills, "Damn, that's a lot of money. I feel rich."

"Let's wait and see what things cost around here. They could want five hundred of these for a beer."

They left the building and walked to the street where several taxis waited by the curb. As they walked up, the driver of the first taxi in line jumped out and ran around to open the door for them. The driver was all smiles. Daniel gave him the printed instructions and climbed in the back seat with Tom. The driver closed the door, ran around the car and slid behind the steering wheel. He had the taxi moving before Tom could speak.

"He's sitting on the wrong side!"

The taxi sped away from the curb and moved rapidly into the modest flow of traffic.

"And he's driving on the wrong side of the road!" shouted Tom.

"So is everybody else. I guess they drive here on the left side like they do in England."

"Son of a bitch!"

The driver looked over his shoulder, "Gah damn sunny beech!"

"You said it, driver," agreed Tom.

"Gah dam sunny beech!" repeated the driver.

"That must be all the English he knows," surmised Daniel.

"It seems like enough. Hey! Watchout!"

The taxi raced through the streets and every passing vehicle caused the Americans to wince. Neither could adjust quickly to riding at high speed on the wrong side of the road. Tom ducked as the taxi swerved around a car.

"The fucker must be late for a date in Yokohama!"

"Slow down!" shouted Daniel, hoping volume would suffice where a translation was unavailable.

Tom shouted even louder, "Slow down, goddammit!"

"Gad dam sunny beech."

"Just hang on and pray," said Daniel.

"I damn sure don't want to die before we get to the fuckin' hotel. I'd like to get drunk first, at least."

The taxi sped through the streets and onto a freeway. The passengers began to relax, then Daniel saw the speedometer.

"The fucker's driving eighty-five miles an hour!"

"Can't be."

"Look for yourself."

"Those aren't miles per hour. They're kilometers."

"That's a relief. I wonder how fast he's really going."

"Fuck if I know."

The taxi left the freeway and raced through the narrow streets of an old town. The vehicle screeched to a stop and the driver said something in Japanese as he pointed to the hotel.

"I guess this is it," said Daniel.

Tom handed the driver a thousand yen note and a five hundred yen note, "Gah dam sunny beech."

The driver smiled, "Gah dam sunny beech."

The hotel was large and modern, only three blocks from the massive seawall that protected the old buildings facing the Pacific Ocean.

Atamishi was a resort town for Japanese tourists and it differed from American resorts only in the age of the small buildings that crowded against the narrow streets. No other Americans were staying at the hotel and, as a rule, the employees did not speak English.

Tom and Daniel walked up to the registration desk and were greeted in Japanese by a small man behind the counter.

Tom spoke. "We saw a sign at Camp Zama about a special deal."

The clerk said something in Japanese, then bowed and walked into an office behind him. In a moment, he returned with another, younger, Japanese man.

The younger man spoke with a heavy accent, "May I hep you?"

"Yes," replied Tom. "We saw a sign at Camp Zama that advertised a special rate for a week."

"Ah, yes." He reached under the counter and produced two registration cards and two small booklets. "One hun-dled seventy-five dharels."

"That's right," said Tom.

"Ah, yes. Prease comprete these."

Tom and Daniel filled out the registration cards then counted out their money. The young Japanese flipped through the booklets explaining what each coupon represented, then took the money and gave Tom and Daniel each a room key.

The man bowed, "Prease enjoy."

"I'm going to do my best," assured Tom.

As they walked through the lobby to the elevator, Daniel thumbed through the various coupons.

"With all the drinks this thing includes, I'm damn sure gonna get that buzz you were talking about."

"You want to start on it now? I can meet you in the bar in five minutes."

Daniel looked at his watch, its new crystal already scratched from service in the jungle, "It's past midnight. I'm just gonna go up and spend an hour in the shower, then go to bed on a real bed."

"Not me. If the bar's willing to stay open this late, I damn sure can drink this late. See you in the morning."

XXX

Daniel awoke at noon, but he lay in the soft bed and enjoyed its comfort for an hour before getting up. He dressed in his khakis and went down to the hotel gift shop, where he bought a pair of cheap slacks, a plain cotton shirt, a razor, blades, shaving cream, a toothbrush and toothpaste. He returned to his room and brushed his teeth. He took a hot shower for the pleasure and then shaved with hot water. He put on his new clothes and laced up his jungle boots, which did not, in Daniel's mind, disturb his enjoyment at wearing civilian attire for the first time in eight months.

Daniel walked across the hall and knocked on Tom's door. A full minute passed before the door opened. Tom was still half asleep, and totally hung over.

"Good afternoon, Tom."

"What time is it?"

"One-thirty. When did you turn in?"

"Half past dawn. Give me a minute to get my shit together, will you?"

"I'll wait for you in the bar."

"I won't be long. I definitely need a hair of the dog that bit me."

Daniel went down to the bar and ordered the first of what would be many, many bourbon and Cokes he would consume during the week. The drink was not very strong, but that served Daniel's purposes better than a regular strength drink would. Daniel was not a drinker, and the weak drinks were far more palatable. He downed the drink quickly and ordered a second. He was sipping the second drink when Tom arrived at the bar looking much better than he had in his room.

Daniel raised his glass, "Welcome to paradise."

"I need a drink, bad."

"After you get it, let's check out the hotel."

"Barkeep! One gin and tonic." The drink was placed in front of him and he downed half of it in one gulp. "Lord, I needed that."

The exploration of the hotel ended quickly when they found the indoor swimming pool and the bar beside it. They ordered more drinks and sat down to watch two Japanese girls in bikinis.

After watching for a minute, Tom turned to Daniel, "If those girls weren't with men I'd hit on them, for sure."

"Assuming they speak English."

"It doesn't matter. Sex is the international language."

"I'd like a job as translator."

"Wouldn't we all?" Tom grew impatient watching the girls. "I'm going to check around and see if any ladies of the evening work here."

"Let me know what you find out."

"If I don't come back, you'll know I lucked out."

Daniel felt the effects of his drinks. "I'm just going to sit right here."

"I'll meet you at six. We can have dinner somewhere."

"Good luck in your search."

"Hell! It's the oldest profession. It shouldn't take luck to find a working girl."

Tom left Daniel sitting by the pool. Daniel was satisfied just sitting and watching the people play in the pool. Never in his life had he felt the alcohol buzz he presently enjoyed. He was wise enough to slow down his drinking; he enjoyed the buzz, but he did not want to get sick.

Tom returned in less than an hour.

"Back so soon?" asked Daniel.

"This is a 'nice' hotel."

"No ladies?"

"Not one."

"Cheer up. Something's bound to turn up."

"I fuckin' hope so. I need a drink."

Tom had envisioned an R&R in which he spent considerable time in bed with females. His discovery that the hotel contained no ladies of pleasure disappointed him; but, when he learned that the hotel did not approve of such ladies being brought into the hotel, he was totally discouraged.

Tom downed his drink quickly, "Let's eat."

"They serve hamburgers here at the bar."

"Honest-to-God cow?"

Daniel remembered his dogburger, "I sure hope so."

"After we eat, let's check out the town. There's got to be some hookers around here somewhere."

The two jungle soldiers reveled in the joy of real beef, eating two hamburgers each, and paid with coupons.

As they walked the streets of Atamishi, Daniel made a discovery, "You know, Tom, there are middle aged people here."

"So?"

"I never realized it before, but I don't remember seeing middle aged people in Viet Nam."

Tom thought a second, "You're right. They're all either young or old. I wonder why."

"Who knows? Strange, the things you notice."

Tom stopped, "I hear music."

Daniel listened. American rock and roll music was playing somewhere nearby.

Tom pointed, "It's that way."

Several doors down a side street they found a local disco. The music came from a stereo system. The lounge was dark and almost empty. A couple danced in the small area provided and a couple sat at a small table near the even smaller bar. Two young men were drinking at a table near the door. Tom and Daniel were the only Americans. They sat at a table and ordered drinks from a cute waitress who spoke no English. The drinks were stronger than those served at the hotel, which pleased Tom. He finished his second as Daniel finished his first.

"Damn it!" said Tom, "I've been here a whole fuckin' day and I haven't been laid yet! I'm going to find some pussy if I have to walk all the way to Tokyo. You want to come?"

"I'm too drunk to go anywhere. I'll be lucky to make it back to my room."

"You seem a little high, but not drunk."

"I'm sorry. I've never been drunk before and I don't know how to act."

"This is your first drunk?"

"Affirmative."

"My apologies. For a cherry, you're doing great."

"One more drink and I'm heading back to the hotel."

"I'm off, then. And I won't be back 'til I find what I'm looking for."

"Give me a full report tomorrow, okay?"

"Roger."

Tom left the club to begin his crusade. Daniel sat alone at the table and drank one more drink. He flirted with the waitress and enjoyed his alcohol high until nine o'clock, at which time he realized that he was too drunk for his own good. Fearing he might become nauseous, he left the club and walked back to the hotel. There he fell on his bed and went to sleep without removing his clothes.

xxxi

· Daniel and Tom met at the poolside bar in the morning of their second day of R&R, but Tom left after eating breakfast to continue his quest of the night before. Daniel still had not decided definitely that he wanted to engage a prostitute. His sexual fantasies tended towards the romantic and he knew he could not buy romance. Daniel turned his attention instead to a teenage Japanese girl who played in the pool with her family. She had smiled at him once before Tom arrived and Daniel decided to try to talk to her if the situation arose.

Daniel sat at the poolside bar and drank bourbon and Coke as he waited for the best moment to attempt conversation with the girl who did not speak English. The opportunity never arose, for she left the pool with her parents before lunch time.

Daniel sat around the pool and watched the modest activity until after three o'clock. Soon after he ate a hamburger, the pool emptied and the area became deserted except for Daniel and the bartender. Bored, he returned to his room and slept.

He awoke in the early evening and went to the nicest restaurant in the hotel for dinner. He ate a steak that was not as good as he hoped it would be and paid with a coupon. After eating, he went back to the plush hotel bar and began drinking.

As Daniel sat at the bar, he watched the bartender serve a drink to a Japanese customer that looked good to his novice's eye. Later, when the drink was served to another customer, Daniel decided to vary from his bourbon and Coke.

He waved to the bartender, a tall Japanese man who spoke some English.

"What's the name of that drink?" Daniel asked as he pointed.

"It is a pink rady."

"Pink rady," Daniel repeated, naively unaware of the bartender's inability to correctly pronounce Ls. "I'll have one of those."

The bartender made the drink and Daniel sipped it.

"Hey, that's good. I'll have to remember pink radies."

Daniel drank several pink ladies, each tasting as good as the first, but his system was not accustomed to alcohol and he got too drunk, too quickly. He was already sick when he left the bar hurriedly, making it to his room just in time to throw up.

The morning of the third day of R&R Daniel found Tom sitting at the poolside bar.

"Tom! How'd it go yesterday?"

"What a bummer. It costs six thousand yen a throw and the women looked like shit."

"You passed?"

"Fuck, no! Would I have known it was a bummer if I had passed? But I won't go back unless I have to. There's just got to be some decent pussy in this town somewhere."

"So you'd think."

"Have you been around town?"

"Only to that disco."

"You want to go back there?"

"It's okay with me."

"At least the drinks there are stronger."

As they entered the disco, someone called out in English.

"Over here, fellas!"

In one corner an American sat with three Japanese girls. His short hair suggested that he was a soldier, but he was a bit overweight, suggesting that he was not stationed in Viet Nam.

"My name's Ricky. Have a seat." Daniel and Tom walked to the table.

"I'm Tom Badger," Tom said as he offered a hand to shake.

"Daniel Perdue."

"Sit! As you can see, I've got more than I can handle."

Tom smiled, "Reinforcements have arrived."

Ricky introduced the two girls who he considered excess, but not the girl he had his arm around.

"Tom, Daniel, meet Yoko and Kyoke. Kyoke speaks no English at all, but Yoko can get by."

Tom sat beside Yoko, deciding that his best chance would be with a girl he could talk to. Daniel sat beside Kyoke, who was in Daniel's mind the prettiest of the three.

As Ricky and Tom wooed the girls who spoke English, Daniel sat and smiled at Kyoke. She looked at him and smiled, and occasionally said something in Japanese. Daniel and Kyoke sat together looking like junior high school lovers until a slow song came over the stereo. Daniel motioned with his hand that they should dance and Kyoke nodded agreement.

When Daniel took Kyoke in his arms on the dance floor, he melted. She wrapped herself around him and laid her head on his shoulder as only a virgin would do, for only a virgin would not know the effect it had on Daniel. His embarrassment grew as rapidly as the bulge in his pants and he feared he would offend the girl. Daniel tried not to touch her below the waist, believing that she would break away from him if he did. They stopped when the music stopped, but a second slow song followed and they kept on dancing. Daniel almost giggled when she pressed herself full against his body and he began to believe that she might be the girl with whom he could have sex and romance.

Daniel and Kyoke danced as close together as honeymooners, stopping only when loud rock and roll blared through the speakers.

As they sat down, Yoko spoke to Daniel, "You enjoy dancing?"

"Yes. Very, very much. I like Kyoke."

Yoko said something to Kyoke in Japanese and Kyoke grinned. Her reply caused Yoko to laugh.

"Kyoke say she like you."

"I am glad."

"She say she like the way you dance."

"Tell her I like the way she dances."

The two girls exchanged comments in Japanese, then Yoko said in English, "Kyoke asks if you have a girlfriend in America?"

"No, I do not."

Again the two girls talked in Japanese.

"Kyoke says you are a gentleman."

"Where I grew up, men were expected to be gentlemen."

Yoko translated.

"She asks where you live in America?"

"Atlanta, Georgia. But I would rather you told me about Kyoke."

The girls talked, then Yoko spoke, "Kyoke is eighteen years old and has just finished school."

"Do you live here or are you visiting?"

"We live in Atamishi, but soon we will go away to find work. There is only tourist industry in Atamishi."

Another slow song began on the stereo. Daniel looked into Kyoke's eyes and motioned that they dance. Kyoke pushed Daniel out of his chair and pulled him to the dance floor. They curled together as if they had been lovers forever and moved slowly to the beat of the music. Whoever in the shadows determined the music to be played must have noticed the two as they danced, for slow music continued for some time. Daniel was delighted with the soft, affectionate girl in his arms and was completely aroused. He was no longer embarrassed, for Kyoke took pleasure in rubbing against him.

Daniel and Kyoke would have danced all night, but eventually Yoko tapped Kyoke on the shoulder.

"It is late. We must go home now."

Daniel gazed at Kyoke, "Can I see you tomorrow?"

Kyoke looked at Yoko, who then translated. Kyoke nodded her head rapidly.

"Where can we pick you up?"

"No, no! Kyoke's parents would not approve of her going with American soldier."

"Do you swim? Our hotel has an indoor pool."

"Yes. We will bring our swimsuits tomorrow afternoon."

"We'll meet you at the pool. What time?"

"One o'clock after noon."

Daniel squeezed Kyoke's hands, "Good bye, pretty lady."

"Good bye," Kyoke replied in halting English.

"See you tomorrow."

Daniel and Tom watched the girls leave. Daniel finished his drink and turned to Tom.

"You ready to head back?"

"I have not yet begun to drink."

"I've had about all I can handle. I'm going back to my room. Will you be all right?"

"Absolutely."

Daniel was euphoric as he walked to the hotel. Meeting Kyoke was like a dream come true. Between the alcohol and the physical contact, Daniel was as horny as he had ever been in his life. To be a virgin like Daniel, the tactile pleasure he derived dancing with Kyoke was the high point of his life.

When Daniel reached his room, he decided to take a shower. He sat on the bed to undress and enjoyed its softness so much that he stretched out to let the bed envelop his naked skin. In a few minutes, the alcohol overtook him and he slept.

XXXII

Daniel spent a full hour in the shower after he awoke. He was still high from yesterday's alcohol and the warm water flowing over his body gave him pleasure. He soaped and rinsed repeatedly until the last of Viet Nam's dirt was removed from his body. Daniel's naivete was demonstrated when he discovered that washing himself could arouse him. The new sensation pleased him, but he was unfamiliar with the art of masturbation and left the shower unfulfilled.

When Daniel arrived at the poolside bar, Tom was already on his third drink of the morning. Daniel ordered a bourbon and Coke and a hamburger at the bar, then joined Tom at his table.

They talked about the girls as Daniel ate, with Tom being adamant that he and Yoko would have sex before he left town. Daniel hoped for the same with Kyoke, but was too well-mannered to assume it.

When Daniel finished eating, they took their drinks and stepped to the poolside gift shop, a smaller version of the one in the lobby and specializing in pool items. They found a display and Tom picked up one of the dark blue, thin Japanese swimming trunks for men.

"Damn, these things are flimsy," said Tom. "You can damn near see through the fuckers."

"And they're small, too."

Tom glanced towards the pool. An elderly Japanese man walked near the pool wearing a swimsuit identical to the one Tom held in his hand.

"It's what the natives wear."

Daniel was less satisfied, "You'd think they'd be embarrassed."

"When in Rome and all that shit."

They bought the swim trunks and entered the dressing room to change. Daniel was embarrassed when he looked at himself in the full length mirror at the entrance. The trunks did nothing to hide his shape, and to Daniel that was almost obscene.

Daniel was embarrassed standing and waiting on Tom. Feeling as though every eye in the area was on his trunks, he walked to the bar, got a drink quickly, and hurried to the table where he hoped to hide himself.

216

Tom emerged from the dressing room in a minute, "I feel naked."

"Me, too."

"Fuck it! It's what the locals wear."

Tom and Daniel drank and joked until the girls arrived. After a brief greeting, Yoko and Kyoke went in the dressing room and came out a few minutes later wearing modest bikinis.

Daniel stood as Kyoke approached him, "You look terrific, really terrific."

Kyoke said something in Japanese, then took his hand and led him into the water. In minutes they were splashing and playing like newlyweds.

Daniel did not know that his inability to speak Kyoke's language had been the most significant factor in her deciding that she liked him. He was in the enviable position of being totally unable to say anything stupid, simply because Kyoke did not understand anything he said, stupid or not. Kyoke judged Daniel by his manners alone, and was put at ease by his embarrassment on the dance floor the night before. She judged correctly that boys who are embarrassed are not likely to pose a threat. She, too, considered having sex, but she did not want to have sex with other than a Japanese boy. She worried that Daniel might father her Amerasian child, and pregnancy would be awful enough without them having a mixed baby. For some reason she did not herself understand, Daniel's being embarrassed at having an erection convinced her that she could play with him, touch and be touched by him, and still stop short of intercourse. Had she known he was a combat soldier in Viet Nam, Kyoke would not have chosen to tease Daniel so, not because she feared he could not then be trusted, but because she would never knowingly hurt someone who could soon face death.

The inexperienced Daniel was satisfied merely touching Kyoke in the pool and the thin swimsuit did nothing to conceal his excitement. At first he was careful not to let their bodies touch in any way that might suggest to her that he wanted to have sex. He did, of course, but he assumed that she did not. He was afraid that she might run away from him if she felt his fully prepared sex organ.

So Kyoke was the aggresser. She led him into the deep end of the pool and held on to him as he held on to the edge. She wrapped herself around him as closely as she could and did not draw away when she rubbed against him. Daniel tried unsuccessfully to keep her from touching him, an innocence that actually excited Kyoke, for he had never been quite so exposed to a girl.

Kyoke forced a situation where Daniel could not turn away, and when she rubbed against Daniel, he realized unmistakably that she did it intentionally. He was not convinced that she wanted sex, but he was convinced that she would allow and enjoy foreplay. His attitude changed. No longer did he fight Kyoke off, but instead joined with her in creating new experiences for their youthful bodies. When he built up the courage to take her fanny in his hands, she giggled, squeezed herself tight against him with a pelvic thrust, then pushed herself away and swam across the pool. Daniel followed and grabbed hold of her, whereupon she forced them both underwater where she could kiss him with passion and privacy. They surfaced and she pushed away and climbed from the pool.

Daniel realized that he needed a break if he were to avoid having an orgasm in the pool. He reached the side of the pool and lifted himself out. When he saw the clearly formed bulge in his trunks, he fell back into the pool in embarrassment. He waded in the water several minutes before he felt comfortable leaving the pool and joining the others at a table.

Daniel and Kyoke passed the afternoon sitting at the table holding hands between intense sessions in the pool. After they ate supper, Daniel gathered the nerve to suggest, as best he could without language, that they go up to his room. She motioned that she could not go up, and then squeezed his hand affectionately. Daniel was ready for more contact, even if not in his room, and suggested that they return to the pool. No sooner than their bodies were under water, Kyoke wrapped herself around him.

Herself a virgin, she found more pleasure than most in feeling Daniel grow against her. Her pelvic motion sped up the procedure and Daniel was soon lost in physical pleasure as intense as a virgin can attain.

Again Daniel reached the point of action where something had to be done. He pushed Kyoke away from him and held her at arms length. He missed her touch so much that he quickly pulled her closed to him. She made a sensuous pelvic move and Daniel was forced to push her away again.

"Kyoke, I love your body, but I've got to take a break."

He motioned with his hand that they should have another drink.

Daniel envied Kyoke's ability to jump out of the pool so quickly. Again Daniel was forced to remain in the water until his excitement abated. When he felt he could walk around without embarrassment, he jumped from the pool and hurried to the table.

Tom smiled a knowing smile, "What kept you?"

"I was about to come out of these trunks. Don't Japanese men ever get hard?"

Tom laughed.

Yoko asked, "What is funny?"

Tom leaned over and whispered in her ear. A grin spread across her face and she spoke to Kyoke in Japanese. Yoko laughed, but Kyoke blushed. Daniel blushed, too.

The four of them drank and talked as best they could until well after dark. Without warning. Yoko announced that it was time for them to go home. They changed in the dressing room, then returned to the table. Daniel and Tom stood to greet them.

"We must go home now," said Yoko.

Daniel spoke quickly, "Will we see you tomorrow?"

"Tom and I have date tomorrow evening."

"Will Kyoke go out with me?"

Yoko spoke to Kyoke, whose answer was quite long.

"Kyoke says she will meet you here tomorrow at two o'clock. Is that time good?"

"Yes. Two o'clock. I can't wait."

"We must go now. Good bye."

As the girls left the pool area, Tom turned to Daniel, "I'm about to spend six thousand yen. Care to join me?"

"Six thousand yen for how long?"

"Half an hour."

"That's too expensive for me. I think I'll wait for Kyoke to come around."

"Yoko said they were both virgins."

"I suspected it, but I think she might just change her mind."

"She's been all over you, that's for sure."

"She's definitely not shy."

"What are you two going to do tomorrow without a translator?"

"I guess we'll just play in the pool."

"How can you stand that much teasing?"

"Airborne. We're trained to endure hardship."

"Maybe so, but not me. I'm off to get laid."

Tom changed in the dressing room and headed for a rendezvous with professionals. Daniel sat at the pool in his trunks and contemplated an amateur. He began to get hard again just thinking about her.

Daniel was drunk when he decided to go straight to his room without changing in the dressing room. He held a towel in front of him and ignored the world.

In his room, Daniel slipped out of his trunks and into the shower. As the spray washed over him, his erection began to return. When he washed himself, he felt sensations he had never experienced before. His knees weakened. The shower was as much a tease as Kyoke had been. He rinsed off and stepped from the shower stall. He could feel the blood pounding in him as he dried himself. His mind was subservient to its newfound pleasures, and too clouded by alcohol to consider restraint.

When he fell face down on the bed, he did not have any plans. His body moved involuntarily, slowly at first. As the movement increased, Daniel found himself making love to the bed, and completely unable to stop. His close contact with Kyoke and the constant alcohol aroused him beyond anything he had ever known before.

The orgasm came in a blast of sensation that shook Daniel down to his toes.

xxxiii

By noon, Daniel was at the poolside bar reinforcing the pleasant buzz that bourbon and Coke had provided since the first day. Although Tom's date with Yoko was not until evening, he did not appear at the pool. Daniel assumed that Tom was spending the afternoon, and six thousand yen, elsewhere.

Kyoke arrived at the pool at one-thirty, a full half hour early. They left the hotel and walked out into the street, alone together for the first time.

Daniel and Kyoke walked hand in hand all around the small resort town, doing what Daniel had dreamed of so many nights in Viet Nam. They strolled along like innocent young lovers, communicating only with their eyes and their hands. Whenever they passed a secluded doorway, they ducked out of sight and embraced. They kissed until someone saw them, then stepped back onto the sidewalk and continued their stroll as before. Daniel was very satisfied with his R&R, even if he were not in Bangkok.

As they walked along one crowded stretch of sidewalk, a passing truck backfired with sufficient force to startle all the pedestrians. The locals recovered quickly and gazed with curiosity at Daniel, who had spun towards the sound and dropped to his knees in one smooth motion. Daniel looked up at Kyoke, then down at his hands, which held the phantom rifle present only, and forever, in his mind.

Daniel and Kyoke stopped in the club where they met. The place was almost empty in the late afternoon and they played in a corner, cuddling as if they were the only two people in all of east Asia. They smiled and acted casual for the waitress, but under the table they touched each other as only honeymooners might. As they played, both grew bolder. No one in the disco could see Kyoke rubbing the bulge in Daniel's trousers. His excitement grew until he was forced to move her hand away. He put her hand in her own lap and picked up his drink. Kyoke rested her head on his shoulder and waited for their play to resume.

"You're so beautiful that I can't take much more of this. If we're going to touch like that, we'll have to go to my room."

Kyoke looked up at him, "Loom, hai."

Daniel was certain that she meant "room, yes", but he could not believe that she felt the same way he did.

"You'll come to my room?"

"Loom, hai," she repeated.

"Let's go, then."

Daniel was not the least bit embarrassed by the bulge in his pants as he and Kyoke walked across the dance floor to the door. Hand in hand, they walked straight to the hotel, through the lobby, and to Daniel's room.

As soon as they entered the room, they embraced passionately. They dropped to the bed and Daniel began unbuttoning Kyoke's blouse, with her helping, rather than inhibiting, his actions. When her blouse was off, she began unbuttoning his shirt as he tried desperately to unsnap her bra. When Daniel's inexperienced fingers were unable to achieve success, Kyoke reached behind her, awkwardly, and undid the hook herself. By the time Daniel had removed his shirt, she had tossed the bra to the floor.

Daniel lowered himself slowly into her outstretched arms. The touch of her bare skin against his chest fulfilled a dream he had nurtured for years. For each virtuous youth, the embrace was a new high in tactile pleasure.

Kyoke cried in pain, a modest sound as sensual as their embrace, and reached between them to remove Daniel's beltbuckle. When Daniel rose up to remove the belt, her hands fondled him. He could not prevent the soft moans that he uttered as she stroked his trousers. As Daniel balanced on his arms above her, she unbuttoned his trousers and unzipped them.

When her fingers touched his naked skin, he knew that his wish for R&R had been granted. To the youthful Daniel, the moment was as emotionally satisfying as intercourse itself. Even if she would not consummate their relationship, Kyoke was touching him where he had never been touched before, and he was pleased that she cared that much. 'Tis strange how some boys retain their innocence even as their bodies experience manhood. He removed his trousers as she held him, not in the assumption that intercourse would follow, but simply to eliminate an encumbrance to their play.

Daniel was naked but for his socks when he took her in his arms and began to unsnap her slacks. She offered no resistance as he unzipped them and pulled them down, even raising herself slightly so he could remove them more easily. He pulled the slacks over her feet and tossed them on the floor, then dropped down to her in an embrace closer than any he had ever known.

Almost unconsciously, his hands moved down her back and into her panties. As his hands squeezed her cheeks, she lifted herself and pushed her panties as far down as she could. Daniel rolled to one side and pulled them down her legs and off, then rolled back on top of her.

The sensual pleasure of their embrace was a first for both. Kyoke was lost in sensations she had not expected, sensations that she could not resist. Should Daniel try to enter her, she could only say no, for her body was saying yes and she could do nothing but be the slave of the pleasure she had thought she would control.

Then Daniel began to kiss her in places she had never been kissed before. When he caressed and kissed her breasts, she was the one who moaned with pleasure. He held her breasts gently in his hands as he kissed her navel. Then lower and lower. The pleasure Daniel gave Kyoke was a first for both.

Daniel caressed her with his tongue and she rose up against his face. She bowed her back as she tried to force his tongue deeper and deeper. Unable to control her emotions or her body, Kyoke jerked three times and uttered a cry of ecstacy before collapsing on the bed.

Daniel continued until she took his head in her hands and guided his lips to hers. She kissed him, softly, lovingly, thanking him for the pleasure he had given her.

The two young lovers wrapped themselves in each other, touching and tingling as if they were one body. Their bodies moved together, each pressing hard against the other.

Daniel could resist no longer and prepared to enter her. The sensations were all new as he slowly pushed himself against her. Just as he entered, she froze.

"No," she said softly.

She wanted him inside her more than anything she had ever wanted in her life. But the moment, when it came, scared her badly, and her involuntary reaction was the product of ancient oriental principles of self-control. No matter how much she wanted him, she could not give herself to him.

Kyoke's protestation would have meant nothing to Daniel in the condition he was in if her body continued to be willing, but she reacted almost out of fear. Her rigid body and tensed muscles were clear indications of her wants. Daniel could not and would not force himself on her, regardless of his urges. She had given him too much emotional satisfaction, too much physical pleasure, for him to do anything that could hurt her.

He pushed himself away from her, but she followed, keeping herself against him even as he yielded to her command. The farther away he pushed, the more she came after him. As Daniel's extended arms reached their full length, Kyoke clung beneath him, unwilling to end the pleasure she could not complete.

Slowly Daniel started back down. She squeezed him tight as they reached the bed and he gently began to enter her.

"No," she said softly, but now her body said "yes".

Daniel entered slowly, gently.

As her body melted around him, she softly whispered, "No."

Daniel would have lost himself in her pleasures, but he saw a single tear flow from her eye and trickle down her cheek.

Daniel's mind raced. Perhaps she really wanted to have intercourse with him, but her culture required at least verbal resistance. He knew that if he did enter her, she would ignore morality and consume him in her passion. Yet, he could not ignore that tiny tear, that single word. Daniel, the warrior, would never allow his emotions, his desires, to rule his mind.

Daniel rose to his knees, then bent down and kissed her breasts. He looked longingly at her beneath him, then fell on top of her and hugged her as tightly as he could. Her body responded to his presence and pressed hard against him. The temptation was too great even for one who's iron will was forged in the jungle. He pushed away from her and rose to his knees, then sat back on his haunches.

"I wouldn't do anything in the world to hurt you, little girl. But I cannot touch you like that and be expected to stop."

Daniel crawled from the bed and stepped over to the dresser. He lit a Camel and took a long, slow drag. They looked at each other. Daniel wanted to remember every curve of her body. He watched her as she picked her panties up from the floor and took a step towards the bathroom. He reached out and touched her arm. She stopped and turned to face him.

"May I hold you one more time? Tomorrow I leave for the war and I may never have this chance again."

Kyoke did not understand Daniel's words, but she understood the look in his eyes. She reached out to him and they embraced, a long, gentle, loving embrace. Eventually Daniel was forced to push her away, but she knew his reason and understood.

Daniel dressed while Kyoke was in the bathroom. He lit another cigarette and sat on the bed to wait for her. When she emerged from the bathroom wearing only her panties, Daniel stood and took her in his arms. They kissed passionately.

When Daniel stepped back, not trusting himself to continue, he bumped against the bed and fell backwards. By the time he stopped bouncing, Kyoke was laughing.

Daniel watched Kyoke dress with the excitement of a new groom, for she was his woman, if not completely, and if only for the next few hours.

When Kyoke finished buttoning her blouse, she motioned with her hands to indicate eating. Daniel nodded agreement and the two lovers left the room. They kissed as they waited for the elevator and as they rode it alone to the lobby. They walked the dark streets of Atamishi as much in love as two people could be without ever having talked.

Kyoke led Daniel into a small noodle shop patronized by the locals. The shop was no more than twelve feet wide and a low counter extended from near the door to the back wall. Small stools ran the length of the counter and behind it two men dressed in white cooked and served the few customers, each of whom looked up when Daniel and Kyoke entered.

Like young lovers oblivious to their surroundings, they sat at the counter and fed noodles to each other. Kyoke laughed with each success Daniel achieved with the chopsticks, and soon the customers and the men in white cheered each time he reached her mouth without dropping the noodles. When they finished their meal, the owner of the establishment laughed and refused to accept Daniel's money.

Kyoke led Daniel down to the ocean, where waves made large by a distant typhoon crashed against the giant boulders in front of the sea wall. All night they sat and watched the waves pound against the wall, paying no attention to the seaspray that soaked them. They watched the sun rise up from the Pacific, then, with one last, long kiss, they parted forever.

xxxiv

Daniel stood in the shower for a long time, saying goodbye to hot water. He dried himself off, and, still naked, packed his few belongings. He wrapped his new toilet articles in his mildewed khakis and stuffed everything into the paper sack in which the toiletries came. Unable to resist, he fell on the bed and enjoyed its softness for one last moment, savoring its feel the way one might savor a fine wine. He hopped up from the bed and dressed quickly, then left the room. He wanted to make a clean break from the place that had afforded him so much pleasure.

Daniel found Tom at poolside. He ordered a bourbon and Coke from the bar, then joined his friend at a table.

Tom spoke first, "I can tell by the smile on your face that you got lucky last night. Right?"

"A gentleman doesn't talk about it."

"So you pulled it off. Was Kyoke as hot in the sack as she was in the pool?"

"I'm not going to say," replied Daniel, but he began to blush.

"She was, wasn't she?"

Daniel sipped his drink and smiled.

"You lucky fucker. I got nowhere with Yoko. Copped a feel, but that's all."

"Maybe you just don't know how to talk to a girl."

"Bullshit. Hey, what are you talking about? Kyoke didn't understand a fuckin' word you said."

"Believe me, I think that helped."

"You lucky fucker."

Daniel did feel lucky, even if he was still, technically, a virgin. His R&R did not go as he expected, but he was satisfied.

Tom looked at his watch, "How long was that taxi ride from Camp Zama?"

"Forty-five minutes or so, wasn't it?"

"The dude said report back before noon, so we better leave here no later than eleven."

226

"That gives us time for one last hamburger."

Tom and Daniel ate their burgers leisurely, then strolled down to the hotel lobby and caught a taxi. The ride on the wrong side of the road was exciting, but uneventful. They arrived at Camp Zama on time, then waited eight hours for the plane to take off.

When the No Smoking light went out, Daniel lit a cigarette, let the seat back and closed his eyes. R&R now seemed like only a dream. The anticipation had been so great for so long that there was a sadness in its ending, something like the letdown the day after Christmas.

All the passengers were quiet. They did not laugh and joke as they had on the flight to Japan. Pensive men, they were going back to, not coming from, the war. Now each one of them was within himself, facing the uncertain future that awaited at the end of the flight.

The jetliner was delayed in Taiwan for four hours due to a minor mechanical problem, which was significant because it meant they arrived in Qui Nhon too late in the morning to catch the scheduled C130 to Camp Radcliff. The added delay was welcome to men who were in no hurry to return to the war, and it became downright appreciated when they learned they could spend the afternoon in town.

Daniel and Tom ate lunch in the base mess hall, then headed for the streets of Qui Nhon.

The city was alive with activity. Military personnel and vehicles blended with civilian traffic to create an urban environment Daniel did not know existed in Viet Nam. The streets were more crowded than those of Atamishi.

Tom was intent on finding female companionship and Daniel tagged along. Since the stories told in the jungle were about R&Rs spent entirely in the sack, Tom felt shortchanged. He meant to find ladies of pleasure if he had to walk every street in town. Unable to learn the whereabouts of Qui Nhon's version of Sin City, it took him longer than he wished to find a place to spend his money.

Daniel would have been satisfied just having an extra day before returning to the boonies, but Tom's persistent comments aboout his past and future interludes convinced Daniel to consider the possibility of trying again with a Vietnamese prostitute. He had hoped to lose his virginity on R&R, and he had assumed that experience would make an apathetic partner tolerable. He knew that in his present state, he would never risk failure with an unattractive or apathetic lady. He decided to try again only if he found a girl who really turned him on.

From somewhere, Tom got directions to a house where he was assured he could get laid. He led Daniel through back streets and alleyways to a house that looked like a private residence rather than a business.

Three women and four children occupied the main room. A curtain covered a doorway that led to a second room, a kitchen, and a set of stairs led to a second floor. The room was sparsely furnished, having only some straw mats on the floor and against the wall, and a single chest of drawers in one corner. The women were of three different generations. The grandmother was grayhaired and elderly; the mother looked well over forty or plain worn out; the daughter was beautiful, but still a teenager.

Tom strolled through the open doorway with a boldness that embarrassed Daniel.

"Boom boom five hundred?" he asked loudly.

The mother walked up to him and grabbed his arm.

Tom pointed to the daughter, "What about her? She's a beauty. You boom boom?"

"No! No!" said the mother, who then reinforced her point by stroking Tom's pants.

"No offense, lady. But she's the one I want."

"No, no. Number ten," the mother said as she pointed at the girl. She pointed to herself, "Number one!" She squeezed Tom and tried to guide him to the stairs.

Daniel stifled a laugh, for the scene was as funny as it was obscene.

Tom was aroused by the woman's hand in spite of himself, "Okay, lady, if you want it that bad."

"Number one GI," she said, but she kept him in her hand. She knew her business well.

"Wait on me, Perdue?"

"Sure. Have fun."

As Tom followed the mother up the stairs, Daniel shook his head, "There's no way in hell that I'd fuck that."

The grandmother said something in Vietnamese, then walked through the curtain to the kitchen. The daughter spread a large straw mat on the floor and the children placed dining utensils around.

Daniel watched, realizing that the family was about to eat dinner. He had no idea what he should do while they ate and began to feel foolish standing in their home.

The grandmother returned from the kitchen carrying a large straw basket, from which she placed on the mat a large bowl of rice, a small bowl containing parts of fish, and a third bowl of substance unknown. She spoke and the children and daughter picked up small individual bowls, used as plates, and began serving themselves. The grandmother spoke again and one of the children picked up a bowl and handed it to Daniel.

Daniel had no desire to eat with them, being concerned about sanitation. He knew things which were of no harm to them might play havoc on his insides, but he was in the wrong place at the wrong time.

He took the bowl and sat down with the family around the straw mat. The grandmother served him some rice, which he hoped would be the least hazardous to his system. He stopped her before she could fill the bowl, for he was not hungry and saw no reason to take more than a token amount. He politely refused the fish and the unknown.

The grandmother passed out chopsticks to the family, but ordered one of the children to retrieve a spoon from the kitchen for Daniel.

When the child handed Daniel the spoon, Daniel said, "No. Chopsticks," and wiggled his fingers. He felt like he had become proficient with them at the noodle shop in Atamishi.

All the children laughed when the grandmother gave him a set of chopsticks. They ate and laughed as they watched Daniel work the sticks.

As much as Daniel politely could, he watched the daughter. She was a very pretty girl, almost as pretty as the girl in the shop in An Khe. He began to get aroused just thinking about being with her, so he turned his attention fully to the rice he ate.

Tom came down the stairs with the mother.

"Dinner time! Were you that hungry?"

"No. I had to do something to pass the time while I waited."

"There's another place around here somewhere. I'm going to try to find it. I'll be back in a minute."

As Tom started for the doorway, Daniel called after him, "Hey, wait! Give me a second to excuse myself and I'll come with you."

"I'll be back before you could finish."

With that, Tom was gone and Daniel was left alone.

He looked at his hosts, "I don't even know where I am."

Daniel ate his rice slowly, hoping to stretch out his one excuse for being in those people's home. He was upset with Tom for leaving him in the lurch, but he did not show his anger.

The children began leaving the mat and the room, and soon the daughter cleared away the dishes.

Daniel felt like a fool as he stood in the corner and smiled.

"I'm waiting for the other GI," he said in explanation of his presence, even though he knew they did not understand.

The daughter returned from the kitchen with a straightback chair and offered it to Daniel. He felt only slightly less like a fool sitting down than he had standing.

After a long, awkward moment, the mother decided she might as well do some business. She walked over and put her hand on Daniel's shoulder.

"Boom boom five hundred?"

"No, thank you."

The mother would not accept his answer and took it upon herself to convince him. She sat in his lap.

"Boom boom?" she whispered in his ear.

Daniel wanted no part of her and tried to think of some way to get the message across. He decided that the best way to discourage the mother was by preferring the daughter. That might even make the mother mad enough to leave him alone. Of course, if she got too upset, he would have to wait for Tom outside.

He pointed at the pretty girl, "Boom boom five hundred."

"No! No! No!" said the mother emphatically. She pointed to herself, "Boom boom five hundred."

Again Daniel pointed to the daughter.

"No!" repeated the mother, who now added some new tricks to her arsenal. She unbuttoned his shirt and rubbed his chest.

Daniel would not go upstairs with the mother under any circumstances, but he could not help if her attention aroused him.

She felt the bulge grow in his pants and knew she was making progress. She believed that if she excited Daniel enough, he would fall under her spell. She wiggled her bottom to rub against him and spoke. "Ah, boom boom?"

Again Daniel pointed at the daughter.

The mother reached between her legs and stroked Daniel.

He began to weaken. If the mother were just a little younger, or prettier, he might have yielded to her touch. But he remembered that the girl in An Khe had been persuasive, too, until they went behind the curtain. And he had just tested his self-control in Japan and found it strong. He was sure that he would not go upstairs with the mother, but his pelvic muscles flexed involuntarily in reaction to the movement of her hand.

"Boom boom?" she whispered in his ear, gently biting the lobe as she finished the words.

Daniel pointed again, "No, her."

The daughter said something in Vietnamese and laughed. The mother said something in harsh tones and the girl responded. The women stood up and walked over to the girl. They engaged in an animated dialogue for several minutes, then the mother went into the kitchen. She returned with the grandmother and the three of them talked some more. Daniel watched the whole episode with amusement, glad the mother no longer pestered him.

After several minutes, the mother walked over to Daniel, pointed at the daughter and spoke, "Boom boom one thou."

Daniel's mouth fell open and both the daughter and grandmother laughed. He could not have been more surprised had he walked into a rival high school's dance and been asked out by the captain of their cheerleaders. He had not even remotely considered the possibility that the girl would be allowed to have sex with him.

He pointed back and forth between himself and the girl, "Boom boom one thou?"

The mother agreed, but she was not happy about it. She muttered to herself as she took Daniel and the girl by the hand and led them upstairs to a large room with four sleeping mats set up off the floor like beds. A curtain drew across each bed providing privacy for the sleepers at night.

The mother led them to one of the mats, held out her hand, and angrily demanded one thousand piasters.

Daniel pulled out his wallet and gave her ten dollars in military script.

The mother mumbled again, then stepped back and closed the curtain. Daniel could hear her stomp down the stairs.

As Daniel turned to look at the girl, she unbuttoned her pajama top and slipped it off. Her breasts were large by Vietnamese standards and were perfectly shaped by any standard. Daniel knew she was beautiful, but he had not expected her to be so well constructed. He was thrilled.

She laid back on the mat and slipped off her pajama bottoms, revealing a body that was better than Kyoke's. As Daniel gazed upon supple torso and smooth, clear skin, he knew that he would need professional counseling if he could not make it with her in the privacy of that upstairs room.

His right hand stroked the girl's stomach and breasts as his left hand undressed him as fast as it could. His jungle boots took forever to unlace enough so that they could be pulled off. He took off his shirt and dropped his pants to the floor.

When Daniel moved onto the mat and onto the girl, she took him in her hands to guide him in.

"Not yet," Daniel said softly as he moved her hand away.

He held himself just above her and kissed her lips. She did not reciprocate, but she did not turn away. He kissed her neck, then kissed her breasts, biting each nipple gently. He lowered himself against her, but made no effort to enter. Instead, he cuddled with her and enjoyed the thrill of her exquisite body touching his skin.

Daniel knew this was to be his moment. The girl was so beautiful that he would love her even if she did not share his enthusiasm or his pleasure. They were alone together and naked, and every cell in his body tingled with excitement.

Slowly he entered her. She was no virgin, yet her warmth was tight around him. Engulfed in her, he felt sensations totally new to him. Her smooth tummy against his and her firm breasts against his chest joined their pleasures together to thrill him beyond his wildest imagining. He moved up and down slowly, his mind focused on their coupling, yet lost in joy. He moved faster and faster as everything left his mind but the feel of her beneath and around him.

The orgasm came quickly with a burst of pleasure that tingled his body from the top of his head to the tip of his toes, but he could not stop. Up and down, he continued the rhythm throughout the orgasm and its afterglow. She felt so good in his arms that stopping never entered his mind.

The girl lay beneath him uninvolved, but willing to let him run his course. Up and down, in and out, she waited patiently.

Daniel was lost in the emotional pleasure of so beautiful a body against his own and her remarkable warmth around him. He lost track of time and the world, for all that existed in his mind was her and him and pleasure.

Daniel's isolation was interrupted by the voice of the mother, who had pulled back the curtain and was staring down at them. Daniel refused to break his rhythm.

"Fini? Fini?"

"No," Daniel answered softly without looking up.

"Fini! fini!" the mother said firmly.

"No," repeated Daniel with some emphasis.

The girl said something to the mother and the mother replied. The girl spoke again and the mother dropped the curtain.

The disturbance over, Daniel's movements grew more intense, yet his physical needs were now subservient to the emotional joy that being intertwined with the beautiful girl gave him. Being with her, a part of her, was pleasure in itself.

Then the girl moved!

Barely noticeable at first, she moved. Ever so little, she was coming to meet him.

The effect on Daniel was almost startling. Her involvement caught him by surprise and reignited his passion. With growing pleasure of his own, he tried with what little knowledge he possessed to give back to her the joy she was giving him.

More and more, she moved. He felt her hands clutch his back for the first time as she held him in her arms, pulling him to her as she pushed to meet him. No longer was Daniel merely using a prostitute, for, in his innocence, he maintained the relationship long enough, and gently enough, to arouse her passion. Daniel did not know that this was but her second encounter, and that she, too, was experiencing sensations she had never known. She melted around him amid waves of desire.

In his wildest fantasies, Daniel never expected to share such passion with a prostitute. He could feel his insides build towards a new eruption, but he would try to last as long as he could and give her as much pleasure as he could. He fought against the urge to explode, holding it back, controlling himself with all his will so that she might share in his joy.

The girl pressed against him with all her strength, as if she wanted to take him in body and soul. Soft, sharp moans of delight melted Daniel's ears. She pushed hard, up, up, up. She tried to lift him from the mat, higher and higher. Then with a squeal of ecstasy that was heard downstairs, she fell to the mat.

Daniel exploded with pleasure, then collapsed on top of her.

They lay together for what seemed like an eternity to both of them, his arms holding her, her arms holding him. Every few seconds she rotated her pelvic muscles and moaned. Daniel would love her again and again, and again, but he was exhausted. Even if she were willing and he had the money, he knew he was drained and could do no more. He gave her one more gentle push and she moaned with affection.

"Thank you. Thank you very much. You'll never know how much this means to me."

She smiled, understanding his tone, if not his words.

Daniel withdrew from her, causing another moan, and then rose to his knees. He kissed each nipple one last time.

"Thank you, beautiful girl. Thank you very, very much."

The girl lay on the bed while Daniel dressed, every few moments freeing a hand to stroke her breasts. As he laced up his boots, she put on her pajamas.

They stood up and the girl pushed open the curtain, but Daniel caught her hand and closed it.

"Not yet," he said, repeating the words that began their encounter.

He took her gently in his arms and kissed her softly. Her arms wrapped around him and she kissed him passionately.

They walked down the stairs holding hands. When they entered the main room, Tom looked up at Daniel.

"You lucky fucker, I didn't know you were up there with her. How did you pull that off?"

"I have no idea."

"You took long enough. What the fuck were you doing up there all that time?"

"We were busy."

234

Daniel could feel his face turning red. Sex was brand new to him, still something to be embarrassed about, and not something to talk about like a baseball game.

"I can't believe how fuckin' lucky you were to git the old lady to let you go upstairs with that beauty. If we had the time, I'd try for it myself."

"No!" Daniel said sharply, protectively. Then, to cover his jealousy, "We better head back now if we don't want to get locked out of the compound."

"I'm not sure I could get a nut, anyway. Let's go."

Daniel walked to the doorway and stopped. He looked back at the beautiful girl who had made him a man and winked. She smiled and waved slightly, afraid that her family might see.

That evening at the EM club in the compound, Tom begged Daniel to tell him how he convinced the girl to go upstairs, but Daniel refused. He sipped his Coke and smiled.

"At least wipe that shit eatin' grin off your face."

Tom never knew that it was the first time Daniel had ever had that grin.

The following morning the C130 landed at Camp Radcliff amid a downpour. A sergeant directed Daniel to one truck and Tom to another. As they drove away, the two men waved goodbye.

XXXV

Rain in the morning was a sure sign that the monsoon was about to begin, and rain would make even less tolerable the days Daniel expected to spend on work details before being sent out to the field.

The truck dropped Daniel at the company area and he walked straight to the orderly room.

Wilkerson, the company clerk, looked up from his typewriter as Daniel walked in, "Welcome back, Perdue. How was R&R?"

"Terrific."

"We've got to get you out of those civies and into some jungle fatigues." He glanced at the paper in the typewriter, "This can wait. Come on, I'll walk with you to the supply room."

"All good things must end."

As Daniel and Wilkerson walked to the supply room, First Sergeant Everett entered the company area, saw Daniel and called out, "Perdue!"

Daniel looked around, "Yes, Top?"

"Get your shit together. You're going out to the field as soon as I can get you on a fuckin' chopper."

"Not that I mind, but why so soon, Top?"

"They need you out there ASAP."

Wilkerson spoke, "I'll get him squared away, Top."

"Do that," Everett said as he turned and walked towards the orderly room.

"I'm glad as Hell not to have to hang around here and pull shit details, but what's the fuckin' rush?"

Wilkerson refused to look Daniel in the eyes, "They're short handed out there."

"How come?"

Still Wilkerson would not look straight at Daniel, "The company's had a few casualties."

As they entered the new supply building, Daniel asked, "Anybody I know?"

Wilkerson ignored the question on purpose and called out to the supply sergeant. "Sergeant Canella? I've got some business for you."

From a back room came Canella's voice, "Whadaya need? Whadaya need?"

"Perdue's back from R&R," called the clerk, "and he needs everything."

"Perdue? Oh, yeah. I'll be right there."

Daniel thought it peculiar that Canella remembered him without seeing him. He was accustomed to people ignoring him, and he could not imagine why the supply sergeant would recognize his name. Daniel did not know that he had been talked about at some length during his absence.

Canella entered the front room, "I'll have you outta here in no time at all."

Wilkerson spoke to Daniel, "Report to the orderly room as soon as you get your gear."

"Roger." Daniel had not expected such priority treatment. He wondered if every man returning from R&R was rushed through and out to the field. But that could not be, for Daniel had heard the stories that Wilson and others had told about staying in camp for days working on various details. "I guess I'll find out sooner or later."

"Say again?" asked Canella.

"Just talking to myself, Sarge."

Within an hour, Daniel was decked out in combat gear and waiting in the orderly room for transportation. When the rain eased up, Wilkerson drove him to the brigade chopper pad and put him on board the supply chopper. Daniel and the chopper waited for twenty more minutes until a bag of mail was brought from battalion.

Daniel rejoined the company on a small LZ somewhere in the jungle. He slipped in some mud near the company CP and lost any semblance of clean that he brought with him from R&R.

Daniel walked up to the CP and spoke to Sergeant Dunwoody, "Hello, Sarge. I'm back. Where's third platoon?"

Woody pointed to a water can, "Have a seat. I'll call and have them send somebody for you."

"Thanks, Sarge."

The commo sergeant called the platoon and in a few minutes Sergeant McDowd emerged from the jungle and walked across the LZ.

"Welcome back, Perdue."

"Hello, Sarge."

"How was it?"

"Terrific."

"Let's head back and I'll fill you in on how it happened."

"How what happened?"

"Nobody told you in base camp?"

"Told me what?"

"Rose is dead."

Daniel stopped in the middle of the LZ. When he spoke, his words were slow, "Aw, fuck. No."

"I'm afraid so. It happened three days ago."

"Aw, fuck," Daniel said again softly.

"I'm sorry, Perdue. I know he was your friend."

"He was the only one who would talk to me when I first got here."

"I know. As your squad leader, he had to. But he liked you. Said you were a good soldier."

Daniel tried to accept what his heart wanted to deny, "Damn. Not Rose. Not Rose."

"I know it hurts, but you've got to keep your shit together."

"I'm okay, Sarge. It's just so fuckin' wrong."

"There is no right or wrong in war. What happens, happens."

"I know. Rose taught me. But why him?"

"Why anybody, Perdue. In war, people die."

"How did it happen?"

"He was walking point and tripped a bouncing betty. The shrapnel killed him instantly. There was no pain."

Daniel pushed aside a vine and spoke more to himself than to McDowd, "It just ain't fuckin' fair."

"You can't take it personally. Nothing about war is personal. He was just in the wrong place at the wrong time. It could have been you, or me, or anybody. I know it hurts, but you've got to be cold hearted about it. You know Rose would've shrugged if off if it had been you."

"Yeah. He told me about being cold. He said veterans didn't make new friends because it hurt when friends died. If you don't make friends, you can't get hurt."

"He was right. I haven't had a real friend since high school." McDowd thought about his life, his lack of friends. "Yes sir, Rose was right."

"As many rotten fuckers as there are around here, it just don't seem fair that Rose would get it. What was God thinking?"

"God doesn't pay any attention to soldiers. Man creates the events of war and random chance selects the losers. Some people call it fate."

Somewhere deep inside Daniel, a shell formed. The war supplies the material and Rose's death constructed it. He might never consciously know of its existence, but Daniel would spend the remainder of his life in that shell, protected from the pain of death, and the joy of friendship. He did not know why, but he suddenly felt in control. Rose was gone and would not be back.

"I understand now why Rose was so cold about things like that. Everybody dies, some sooner than others."

McDowd spoke from personal experience, "That's the way a soldier has to look at it." He glanced at Daniel and shook his head slightly. He was surprised at how one as young as Daniel looked could feel the warrior's feelings. Appearances did not matter in war. The bullets cared not the age or maturity of whom they struck. "You still don't look it, Perdue, but you're turning out to be a damn good soldier."

"Thanks, Sarge. That means alot, especially coming from you."

"Keep your chin up. Before long you'll be the one taking care of the cherries."

"Sometimes I still feel like a cherry myself."

"In most any other war, you still would be."

"How's that, Sarge?"

"This is the only war I ever saw where the veterans were sent home. Pretty soon, they'll all be gone."

"My God. That's true."

"So you'll be the veteran, even if you are still wet behind the ears."

"Forces you to grow up fast, doesn't it?"

"Yes sir, it does. Second squad is over that way." Daniel started off through the jungle. McDowd called after him, "If you need to talk, come see me."

"Thanks, Sarge, but I guess I'll just suck it in."

"That's all a good soldier can do."

Daniel pushed his way through the brush and vines. He was surprised to see Perez sitting with Wilson.

"Buenos dias, Perez. What are you doing back in the jungle?"

"Buenos dias, Perdue."

Wilson spoke up, "Did you fuck your dick off?"

"Not quite. When did you get here, Perez?"

"Man, I stay in the hospital in the Philippines as long as I could, but they say I am well and send me back. The day I get to the company area, they send me out to take Rose's place."

"McDowd told me about Rose."

"Too bad. He was a good man."

Daniel looked at Wilson, "Why was Rose on point?"

"You know that as well as me, fucker."

Daniel remembered the explanation Rose gave when the squad leader assigned him to take the rear. If Daniel had been with the squad, instead of on R&R, Wilson would have been walking point instead of Rose.

"Yeah, I guess I do."

"Morgan was right behind him," said Wilson. "He caught some shrapnel in the chest and arm, but he'll be okay. The lucky fucker will prob'ly get sent back to the fuckin' world."

Wilson paused, expecting Daniel to comment. But Daniel did not care about Morgan. From now on, he would not care about any cherry.

Wilson continued, "It was fuckin' weird. One tiny piece of fuckin' shrapnel caught him in the back of the head. Didn't make a fuckin' hole no bigger than a fuckin' pin. It took Doc forever to find where he'd been fuckin' hit."

Daniel spoke softly, "Shit."

"And the fucker had only twenty-six days."

"Twenty-six fuckin' days," Daniel echoed softly.

"It don't seem fuckin' fair, do it?" asked Wilson, hoping that someone felt the loss as much as he did.

"It sure don't," agreed Daniel. "I see you've got the radio now." He wanted to change the subject; he wanted to get his thought about Rose out of his mind.

"That's right, " replied Wilson.

"Who's squad leader?'

Perez answered, "I am."

Wilson gave Perez a playful shove, "The fucker extended and they made him a sergeant."

"I don't know if I should congratulate you or not," said Daniel. "What the fuck did you extend for?"

"Six months."

"I mean why, fucker."

"When I go home, they will let me out early."

Wilson laughed, "If the fucker don't become a fuckin' lifer."

"No fuckin' way, man."

"Things sure changed while I was gone."

Wilson spoke, "You made Spec Four."

"Me? When?"

Perez answered, "The orders came down while I was in base camp. There were more than a hundred in the battalion who made it on the same orders."

Promotion to Specialist Fourth Class meant only an increase in pay. Spec Fours pulled KP, latrine duty, and all the other nasty chores reserved for privates.

Perez changed the subject, "I want you take over the other position."

"Take over?"

"Be in charge."

"Me? What about Wilson or Benny?"

"I'm too fuckin' short," said Wilson. "I can't be bothered with none of that shit."

"And you know how Benny is," said Perez.

Daniel could understand how Benny's personality excused him, but he could not understand why Wilson would not assume any authority. What Daniel did not know was that Perez wanted Wilson to take over the other position, but Wilson refused. Those two had been friends since before they arrived in country, and Wilson was inclined to take orders from Perez just about as much as Perez was inclined to issue orders to Wilson. Wilson decided that he stood a better chance of surviving his last few days if he was free to watch after only himself.

Perez walked with Daniel to the squad's other position, leaving Wilson and McGee, who had been digging a cat hole, alone. The second position was only thirty yards away, but it was completely hidden by the thick jungle.

• As they walked up, Benny saw them and spoke, " 'Lo, Perdue. Did you have fun?"

"Yeah, but I'd rather be short like you."

Benny smiled, "Ain't I though."

Perez spoke to a new man, a thin black eighteen-year-old, who sat beside Benny, "Andrews, this is Perdue. He'll be in charge of the position. Do what he say."

"Right, Sarge," replied the cherry.

"Adios," said Perez as he turned and walked back towards his own position.

Benny spoke, "The cherry's from Mayberry."

"Sport, I keep telling you I'm from Raleigh. I ain't never heard of no Mayberry."

Daniel corrected Benny, "He can't be from Mayberry, Benny."

"Why not?"

"There ain't no blacks in Mayberry."

"What in the Hell is Mayberry?" asked Andrews.

Daniel smiled, "It's a town in North Carolina on television."

Andrews looked at Benny, "You been fuckin' with me, sport?"

Benny did not look up, "Cherries is cherries."

"I'll cherry your ass," threatened Andrews.

Benny looked up and gazed at the new man with an intensity that took the cherry by surprise. Andrews had never seen that look in anyone, and he chose not to press the issue.

He turned, instead, to Daniel, "Where'd you go on R&R, sport?"

Daniel began adjusting his harness, "Japan."

"What did you do?"

"Got drunk."

Andrews did not understand Daniel's reluctance to talk. He had no way of knowing that Daniel was heeding Rose's words.

The cherry kept trying, "Have a bad time, sport?"

When Daniel looked up at him, Andrews saw the same intensity that he saw in Benny's eyes. Not knowing that the look was common among jungle veterans, he took it personally.

"Take it easy, sport. I'm just trying to be friends."

Daniel spoke slowly, "I don't want any friends."

"Well, be that way fucker. I don't give a shit!"

"What's your name again?"

"Andrews. What's it to you?"

"I'm sorry, Andrews. Not twenty minutes ago I learned that the only friend I had in this hellhole was KIA. That's not going to happen to me again. I'll take care of you and do my fuckin' best to keep you alive, but I can't be friends with you. You're new and stupid and more likely to fuck up and die. I will feel no pain if that happens."

"I don't understand, sport."

"You will someday. And don't call me sport."

xxxvi

High clouds, white and fluffy, drifted unnoticed above the jungle canopy, seen by the men on the ground only when they were in villages, on LZs, or elsewhere that a gap appeared in the trees. Unnoticed, the clouds increased in size and number until they dominated the sky with dark, billowing thunderheads that rolled ominously overhead. Afternoon thunderstorms buffeted the treetops, but dripped down to the men on the ground as large drops; the thunder merely punctuated the steady din created by rain hitting high in the trees. The afternoon showers did not prepare the men for the day the rain did not stop. It greeted them one morning as a soft drizzle, changed at times to a hard rain, and occassionally fell in a deluge harder than the hardest Georgia thunderstorm. Thus began the monsoon, a true bane to the infantry.

The jungle was a product of the monsoon and changed because of it. The lush, green vegetation thrived in the moisture, at times growing almost visibly as some forlorn soldier rested and watched. Foot trails, cut through the jungle to link positions, disappeared within hours if not used, as water and heat fed growth that eliminated paths almost as fast as the soldiers could blaze them. Mud existed only around prone shelters and foxholes, for everywhere else the jungle grew back and reclaimed ground beaten bare by army boots.

The war did not stop because of the monsoon, for the duties and dangers remained the same. Even in the rain, every step was taken with caution, every tree viewed with suspicion. Patrols went out every day and ambushes every night, and always there was guard in the dark. The men cursed the constant drone of rain high in the canopy, for it stole from them their best defense at night. The sound of the rain drowned out any and all soft noises, making detection of an enemy by sound impossible. The men walked in the rain, ate in the rain, and slept in the rain, until they grew accustomed to being wet all the time. Adjusting constantly to the demands of war, the men tired of condemning that which they could not control. Monsoon or no monsoon, the real inconvenience remained the enemy.

Living in the rain added to the woes of the infantry.

On a break in a patrol, Daniel lit a cigarette in the rain with the practiced skill of a veteran, then watched the cherry, Andrews, attempt the same. Andrews tossed away one soggy cigarette after another until, at last, with his head tilted down so his helmet protected his efforts, he successfully lit one and took a puff. Pleased with himself, as cherries often were when some new challenge was met, he raised his head to see if anyone else had displayed his skill. Daniel watched the single drop of water fall from the front of the cherry's helmet and hit the end of the cigarette, extinguishing the fire with a short hissing sound.

"Fuck it!" said Andrews in disgust.

Daniel laughed too soon, for his motion changed the angle at which he held his own helmet. Drops of water fell like a series of bombs, one scoring a direct hit on his cigarette and dousing the fire with the same brief hiss.

In addition, the monsoon indirectly attacked the men's feet. On dry afternoons prior to the monsoon, the men took off their boots to air their feet, but the practice seemed pointless in the rain.

After one long patrol, Daniel's feet began to hurt in a fashion he had not experienced before. He removed his boots in spite of the rain and, after pulling off his socks, was shocked by what he saw. From the middle of his calves to the tip of his toes, wet scabs covered the skin. He hobbled to the platoon CP to see Doc Dupre.

Doc was treating another man for the same condition when Daniel limped up. He looked up from his patient, "Have a seat, Perdue. I'll get to you when I finish here."

As Daniel waited, yet another soldier walked up in bare feet covered with scabs.

"Get in line," said Doc.

Dupre coated his patient's feet with white ointment, then pointed to the fire McDowd had started using C4.

"Get over there and dry your feet and socks, then come back. Next!"

Daniel limped over and sat on the tree trunk Doc used as his office.

Dupre looked at Daniel's feet, "You're the fourth case of jungle rot I've had today."

"Jungle rot?"

"That's what it is," Doc said as he began applying ointment.

"Sounds terrible. What causes it?"

"Some tropical fungus, probably. They didn't cover this in Medic school. The only thing that will really cure it is for this fuckin' rain to stop." He looked up into the canopy, "Fuckin' rain."

"No shit," agreed Daniel.

"We're gonna get Canella out here with some new socks, but, until he gets here, all you can do is go over to the fire and try to dry those things." He pointed to Daniel's rancid socks.

"That won't be easy in this rain."

"I know. Do the best you can. It's more important that you get your feet dry, at least this once. Come back when they're dry and I'll bandage them."

"Thanks, Doc."

As Daniel stepped over to the fire, another man walked up barefoot.

"Come on," Doc said, "I've got plenty of ointment."

Daniel sat by the fire with the others and held his feet as close to the flames as he could. Steam rose from the scabs.

Doc Dupre did his best for all the men, but what really saved their feet was the ending of the worst of the monsoon. The downpours continued every afternoon, but the rain fell less often in the mornings and evenings. The men were able to dry their feet before morning patrol or late in the afternoon, during chow. When the sun reappeared briefly after a two week absence, the jungle became a suffocating steambath, but the men's feet were dried.

Wilson and Terwilliger dried their feet in the States.

The company set up a perimeter early one afternoon and the men relaxed on their positions and waited for hot chow to be flown in by chopper.

Wearing a broad grin, unusual for him, Stovall walked over to the second squad, "Perez, you got two short timers here?"

Wilson answered, "Fuckin' right we do."

"Have 'em get their shit together and report to the LZ."

Perez asked, "What for, Sarge?"

"They're going home."

Wilson jumped to his feet and screamed, "All fuckin' right!"

"Keep it down, Wilson," ordered Stovall. "You ain't left yet."

Perez turned to McGee, "Go tell Benny."

McGee stood up and walked five steps to the edge of the jungle, "Hey, Benny! You're going home!"

"Shut up, fucker!" ordered Stovall. "You want the whole fuckin' North Vietnamese army down on us?" Stovall cleared his throat and spit, "Fuckin' children! I'll be damn glad when it's my time to leave."

"How much longer for you, Sarge?" asked Perez.

"Any day now."

"McDowd too?"

"Naw. He extended."

Perez said nothing, but in his heart he was glad McDowd was staying. Now, no matter who the new platoon leader was, McDowd would still be around to take care of the platoon.

Benny emerged from the jungle, "I got nine days to go."

Wilson laughed, "You gonna argue with the fuckers? It's time to go now."

Benny looked at Stovall, "You sure, Sarge?"

"They want you to go back on the supply chopper. It should be here soon."

Benny began to smile, "If'n you say so, Sarge."

Wilson roared, "Hot damn, Benny, we're going home! I'm gonna buy me a steak this fuckin' thick!"

Perez shook Wilson's hand, "Goodbye, amigo."

"You'd be going home, too, if you hadn't extended."

Wilson picked up his gear and followed Stovall and Benny to the other position.

Benny spoke to Daniel, "We're going home."

"That's great!"

"Great?" said Wilson. "It's fuckin' fantastic!"

"Hurry up," ordered Stovall, "or you'll miss the chopper."

"Come on, Benny," urged Wilson. "Let's get to fuck outta here."

Benny picked up his harness, "So long, Perdue."

"So long, Benny. Take care, Wilson."

Daniel watched them vanish into the jungle and was happy. He had counted Wilson's days just as he counted his own and he was delighted that people really did get to go home when their tour was over.

The chopper that took away Wilson and Benny brought to the field a new man for second squad.

Stovall led the cherry to Perez's position, where the four remaining members of the squad were gathered, "Here's a new man for you, Perez. His name's Stinky."

"Stentor," said the cherry with a voice as loud as a peanut vendor at a baseball game.

"Stentor, then," said Stovall. "Take care of him."

"I will, Sarge," replied Perez.

Jerry Stentor was a tall, husky white boy from a farm in rural Wisconsin. He was eighteen years old, but had a voice as loud as a jet engine.

Daniel felt a sudden sense of fear when he looked around the squad and saw only cherries. McGee, who now carried the radio, could not talk on it properly. Andrews, who was given Benny's M79, still displayed the childish naivete that was so deadly in the boonies. Stentor, the newest cherry, was given the M60. And then there was Perez, a cherry squad leader who achieved the position because of his time in service, rather than because of his ability.

No longer was Daniel surrounded by soldiers who knew what to do, no longer did he have the security of knowing that the men he served with would do the right things. The cherries knew nothing, and were therefore a threat to Daniel until they learned how to act in the jungle, if they learned. And Perez preferred to make mistakes rather than admit to his shortcomings.

In any other American war, Daniel would still be considered a cherry himself, but in the craziness of Viet Nam, circumstances beyond his control pushed him into the position of grizzled old veteran.

Perhaps if Daniel had looked more like a soldier, Perez and the cherries would have respected him more. But they saw only his small size and youthful face.

When darkness began to fall, Perez kept McGee and Andrews with him and sent Daniel and Stentor to the other position. Daniel did not worry about only two of them pulling guard, for he was more concerned with the cherry with the loud voice. He spent most of their first evening together trying to convince Stentor that his voice could be heard for miles.

No infantry soldier ever adjusted to crossing wide open areas. He always felt naked, exposed as he was to any enemy that might be hiding in the distant treelines. But open areas are there, and they must be crossed. Time and again, they must be crossed.

Third platoon struggled through the jungle for an hour before reaching the rice paddies that surrounded the village they were assigned to clear that morning. McDowd called for a break at the treeline and the men settled among the brush to rest and to gaze out into the sea of flooded rice paddies. Two hundred meters from the treeline stood a small village, isolated like an island in the rice paddy sea.

When McDowd gave the order to move out, Daniel tossed away his unfinished cigarette and moved with the others into the ankle deep water of the flooded paddies. The platoon spread out, forming one rank nearly one hundred meters wide, and marched slowly towards the village. Water splashed around twenty pairs of boots as the men made their way towards the one large dike, perhaps two feet high and three feet wide, that cut across their path halfway to the village.

The familiar crack of an AK47 sent the platoon splashing into the paddies. Daniel raised his head ever so little to gain a view of the village. Water splashed beside him as an AK47 fired a burst. Far to the left, M16s opened fire and were answered by rapid bursts from many AK47s. Bullets splashed around the squad when Stentor, the cherry, rose to his knees to get a better look at what was happening to the left.

Daniel grabbed the cherry's sleeve and yanked him to the ground, "Stay down, fucker!"

Bullets zinged by as AK47 rifles and ChiCom machineguns opened up on the platoon from all along the village treeline. Daniel fired a magazine into the village, then snapped a fresh magazine into place.

Stentor looked at him, "What are you shooting at? I don't see nothing."

"Keep low and fire into the village."

"But I don't see no Cong."

"Just keep firing in their direction. They've got to be in there somewhere."

As bullets zinged around them, Stentor opened fire with his machinegun, cutting loose with short, three-round bursts just like he was on a training range.

Daniel emptied a second magazine into the village, then, as he reloaded, he noticed Andrews lying flat in the water, his head barely high enough to breathe.

"Andrews! Are you hit?"

The cherry did not move.

"Andrews! Are you hit?" repeated Daniel, somewhat louder.

The cherry turned his head towards Daniel, "We can't stay here."

Daniel spoke angrily, "Have you been hit?"

"We can't stay here," repeated the cherry.

"Where the fuck do you suggest we go? Fire your fuckin' grenade launcher!"

"We can't stay here."

Daniel slid through the water until he came up beside Andrews. He kicked the scared cherry with his boot, "Shoot, goddammit, or I'll. . ."

Bullets zinged by Daniel's head as Andrews lifted his M79 and fired a grenade into the village.

Daniel fired another magazine into the village, then looked past Stentor to the squad leader, "Hey, Perez!"

Perez fired his rifle without aiming, but stopped when he heard his name called, "Si?"

Daniel pointed to the large dike some fifteen yards in front of them, "Let's move up to the dike!"

"Si," agreed Perez.

Daniel motioned for Stentor to move forward, then grabbed Andrews' jacket sleeve and pulled him to the dike. As second squad settled in behind the dike, McDowd moved the rest of the platoon forward to take advantage of the cover.

The dike provided enough cover so that the men could be more selective in returning fire. No one in second squad had yet seen any charlies, but they were all firing into the village, the proper thing to do if the enemy's fire was to be suppressed. Bullets sailed past their heads with the distinct "zing" that was imprinted forever in the minds of those who heard it.

To the left, someone called for the medic.

As Daniel fired, his mind pondered his situation. If this were a "battle", then battles were nothing like he pictured them. He had assumed that John Wayne and he would be in some foxhole firing into human waves of attacking enemy and facing the fear of seeing men fall in front of his rifle. Instead, Daniel saw no enemy, yet they fired constantly, invisible marksmen sending out death.

Daniel heard the radio squawk, but he could not hear the conversation.

"Camel Two, this is Camel Five. Over."

McGee had to punch Perez to get his attention, then handed him the handset.

Perez was too scared to remember proper radio procedure. He spoke into the handset, "Si?"

"Can you provide cover while we move the wounded back to the treeline? Over."

"No."

After a pause in which McDowd cursed the squad leader, the radio squawked again, "Two, this is Five. Is anybody hit in your group?"

"No."

"Okay, Two. Stay calm and keep your people down. Fullback is bringing up reinforcements. Keep firing, but stay low. Over."

"Si."

"Five out."

The firefight with the hidden enemy continued unabated, with Daniel and the others firing regularly, if not accurately.

Sometime later, the radio squawked again, "Two, this is Five. Over."

Perez had calmed enough to use the radio properly, "This is Two. Over."

McDowd was glad to hear Perez speak English. He considered moving over to second squad unless Perez regained his composure.

"This is Five. Fullback is in place behind us, but he's afraid to fire over our heads. He's calling in air strikes, so when you see the planes, pop red smoke to mark your position. Over."

"Roger. Over."

"If any of your people get hit, yell out and I'll send the medic your way. Over."

"Roger. Over."

"Five out."

When Daniel saw Perez give the handset to McGee, he called out, "What's up?"

"The CO's called for air strikes."

Daniel turned to Stentor, "We may be here for a while, Stinky. Save your ammo. Keep firing, but slow down." He turned to the other side, "Andrews! Save your grenades."

"I got a bunch left."

"Save 'em," Daniel ordered, knowing that Andrews had not raised his head enough to have any idea where the grenades he fired were landing.

Daniel flipped the selector switch on his M16 from automatic to semi-automatic and fired single shots at the village.

The platoon lay against the dike, half in the water, and waited for the Air Force. The AK47 fire continued sporadically, increasing on those occasions when a soldier raised himself high enough to provide a better target.

Stentor provided such an occasion. Over-confident because the enemy's fire slackened, as only a cherry would be, he rose to his knees to fire his few rounds with greater accuracy.

Again Daniel grabbed the big farm boy and yanked him down, "Goddammit! Stinky! Stay down!"

Stentor was surprized that someone as small as Daniel could move him around so easily, but he was grateful when bullets dug into the dike right where he had been.

"But I can't see them," explained the cherry.

"Nobody can, fucker," Daniel said as more bullets hit the dike. "But they can damn sure see you!"

Daniel compared the cherries on either side of him. Andrews was scared, but responded to Daniel's prodding and fired whenever he was told to. Stentor might be stupid, but at least, he was not scared.

When the first of many Phantom jets roared overhead, smoke popped on the left, reminding Perez to do the same.

Daniel watched the two jets circle the sky above the village until the first one veered off and screamed down towards the target. He saw a bomb drop from each wing of the plane as the pilot pulled his craft from its dive and roared into the sky. The two bombs sailed through the trees and struck the village. The two simultaneous explosions threw dirt and smoke into the air and shook the ground where third platoon lay.

The second Phantom made its run, and again two bombs dropped and sailed into the village. When the ground shook, Daniel noticed the water around him ripple with the vibration.

The platoon was still in the flooded paddy watching the bombs explode in the village when the afternoon rain began, but it posed no problem to men already wet and otherwise concerned.

The lower rain clouds forced the planes to alter their runs on the village. One Phantom after another appeared on the horizon and streaked towards the village at low altitude, their ordinance dropping from their wings and falling less than one hundred feet before hitting the village.

When Daniel saw close up his first napalm bomb explosion, he was awed by the mass of flames that engulfed the target. Again and again, the Phantoms dropped flaming death, yet the enemy small arms fire continued to zing overhead and kick up dirt along the dike whenever a target appeared. Daniel was amazed that people could live through the attacks, but he could not see the size of the village, nor how much of it remained untouched by the aerial bombardment.

During the day more troops joined the company in the treeline behind third platoon. The jungle surrounding the village was rapidly filling with men, as the battalion commander flew overhead in his Huey. Third platoon's contact became the focal point for the whole battalion as the battalion CO directed his companies through the jungle to surround the village.

The Air Force retired for the night just before dark, but in spite of their efforts, AK47 fire still came from the village.

Captain Dunn wanted very badly for his third platoon to pull back and rejoin the company, but every time they tried to move the enemy fire increased dramatically. Far to Daniel's left, another man was hit.

When darkness engulfed the rice paddies and the village, the small spot behind the dike that had been Daniel's position all day became his position for the night. Another effort to pull back, this one under cover of darkness, was abandoned when enemy fire blanketed the dike. The men tried to sleep in shifts, in the water, and ate cold C rations. Many times during the night, a stray shot triggered a minor firefight, forcing all the men to return to their positions and exchange fire with the muzzleflashes in the village.

When the sky to the far right began to lighten, the whole platoon was awake and in position. A deep, rich blue appeared above the eastern horizon and dimmed the stars.

When the sky turned the milky gray of morning, Daniel heard movement behind him and turned around to see, what seemed to him to be, the entire United States Army coming out of the trees. Two full companies, less third platoon, splashed through the rice paddies towards him and the village.

Stentor thought he recognized the sight, "That looks just like the movies."

Daniel agreed, but said, "People don't die in the movies."

The wave of soldiers reached the platoon and was joined by its men. The distance to the village decreased rapidly, but there was no enemy fire to oppose the advance. The formation reached the edge of the village and climbed onto the shattered island.

The surviving Viet Cong escaped in the night, leaving behind only destruction and parts of bodies.

xxxviii

The company was rewarded for its "success" in the village by being assigned to the perimeter of the Fire Support Base from which the battalion then operated. The men had been in the boonies for quite some time and they all looked forward to a few days on more or less fixed positions.

The Fire Support Base began four weeks earlier as a battalion Landing Zone cut from virgin jungle, but as the operation went on, the strategic value of the LZ's location became more apparent. It sat within artillery range of what was believed by the command structure to be a major enemy infiltration route. As the battalion expanded its operational area around the LZ, the small clearing grew into a support base. The engineers cut a road through the jungle to the base so that the heavier artillery could be brought in. Four self-propelled 175mm Howitzers drove in with an infantry escort to reinforce the four-gun 105mm battery that was flown in. The initial LZ became the chopper pad for the base, which expanded up and over a low hill. Twenty yards beyond the perimeter near the pad was a clear, fast-flowing mountain stream that was used regularly for bathing by the troops assigned to the base. Just inside the perimeter, near the stream, the engineers established a water purification point, and later cut a short road from the heavy artillery at the bottom of the hill to the light artillery on the side of the hill, and on to the Command Post at the hill's summit. The chopper pad stayed active as Hueys and Chinooks flew in with supplies, munitions, and equipment. Perimeter positions were improved continuously; foxholes were deep and lined with sandbags; a fifty meter wide field of fire and three roles of concertina wire separated the infantry from the jungle.

To those accustomed to base camps and airbases, the Fire Support Base seemed small and rugged, little more than a muddy spot in the jungle, but to those just in from the boonies, the four-acre clearing seemed like a rest area.

From Daniel's position on the hill, he could look back and see almost the entire base, giving him a sense of security, a safety-in-numbers complex, usually unknown in the jungle, where vision was restricted and missions were carried out by small groups. On the base perimeter Daniel did not worry about being overrun by hordes of North Vietnamese regulars, for he could see with his own eyes that he was not alone. Privates feel safest when there are lots of other privates around them.

But when the first incoming rockets of the day exploded just outside the perimeter, Daniel stop relaxing. From that first moment when he stepped from the plane more than nine months earlier, Daniel, like every new arrival, worried about rocket or mortar rounds landing on him. Soldiers were helpless against death that fell unannounced from the sky, and that helplessness made incoming the source of terror for garritroopers. But for Daniel and the infantry, other dangers were more immediate, and more controllable,making incoming less terrifying and more a nuisance. Even with rockets crashing in the area daily, Daniel's job was to watch for what might come through the perimeter. He would let God worry about what came over it.

The squad's second day at the base brought a change. Perez returned from the company CP with, what to him was, a new man for the squad.

McGee objected, "That fucker ain't new. That's Morgan. He came in with me."

Daniel greeted him, "I thought you were long gone for the States. What the fuck happened?"

"I've been in the hospital in Saigon. I did lots of partying before they sent me back."

"I heard you were hit bad."

"I'm okay. I was lucky."

"You'd have been luckier if you'd been sent fuckin' home."

"You can't win 'em all."

"I'm glad you're back. It'll be good to have a sixth man again."

Morgan remembered well his earlier problem in the boonies, "Who's got the radio?"

"Me," answered McGee, "but you can have it."

Perez knew nothing of Morgan's dilemma, "You're too small to carry the radio."

"Bullshit! I carried it before I was hit." Morgan looked to McGee for help, then he turned to Daniel.

"Every villager we saw thought he was Vietnamese."

Perez was unconvinced, "So?"

McGee spoke, "You gotta let him carry the radio, else they'll think he's a Cong."

"I don't have to do nothing," argued Perez, feeling threatened by the actions of the squad.

"Gimme a break, Sarge," pleaded Morgan. "It ain't the fuckin' Vietnamese I'm worried about. I don't want no trigger happy GI thinking I'm a charlie."

"I don't know," said Perez.

"Please?" begged Morgan.

Daniel spoke, "The fucker ain't no good to us scared to death, Perez. Rose gave him the radio because he was pretty fuckin' useless without it."

Morgan saw in Daniel's words both the argument and the insult, "Thanks a fuckin' lot, Perdue."

Daniel smiled at him, "You're welcome."

Perez gave in, willing to concede to Rose's precedent, "We'll try it, but I still think you're too small."

"I wasn't before."

Added Daniel, "Neither was I."

Morgan taking over the radio forced Perez to move either McGee or Andrews over to join Daniel and Stinky. Andrews volunteered, for, since the day in the flooded rice paddy, he obeyed every word Daniel said like it came from Moses on the mount.

The afternoon monsoon rains continued and kept most of the base covered in mud, so it was no surprise that the men on the perimeter slowly turned red. When a ranking visitor, he could have been anyone from a general to the battalion sergeant major, was upset by the unmilitary appearance, read mud, of the troopers guarding the barbed wire, the order was given for all the men to go down to the stream and wash themselves.

Daniel and Andrews were the last two men in the squad to take a turn in the stream. As they walked down the road past the artillery, Daniel saw, and was jealous of, the creature comforts enjoyed by artillerymen. Since the guns always moved by truck or chopper, they were able to carry with them the assortment of personal items that men can accumulate when they stay in one place for long periods of time.

At the end of the road, Daniel led Andrews through the opening in the barbed wire and along the twenty yard trail which snaked through the jungle that separated the stream from the perimeter. The mass of vegetation opened around a beautiful, clear, cold mountain stream, some thirty feet wide and two feet deep, that rippled over a bed of stones worn smooth through the millenia. Where the stream curved, a rock beach provided a place out of the jungle and out of the water.

Daniel placed his rifle and wallet on the rocks, then walked right into the stream and sat down, fully dressed, boots and all. He sat in the water, cool and refreshing, and undressed, washing each article he wore before throwing it up on the beach. Even without soap, his fatigues, socks and boots came clean, if only by comparison to how they were.

Daniel was pleased to see that the jungle rot which once covered his feet was gone completely, having left only a few permanent scars. He left the water briefly to spread his uniform out to dry in the sun before returning to the stream to wash away the layer of dirt that covered every infantryman's body. With that attempt completed, if unsuccessful, he lay in the water and enjoyed the pleasure of the cold water around him.

Daniel tarried at the stream for as long as he thought he could get away with it before moving onto the beach, drying in the sun, and heading back. Dressed and refreshed, he led Andrews back through the jungle and the barbed wire. They looked like garritroopers, they were so clean.

As they passed the water point, Andrews called out to someone he recognized, "Hey Matthews!"

Matthews, who sat in a jeep, looked around, "Andrews! I didn't know you were out here."

"I came in from the boonies yesterday."

"The boonies? What the fuck were you doing in the boonies?"

"I'm a fuckin' grunt."

"Really? Have you seen any shit?"

"Too fuckin' much."

"I'm lucky. I hang around the artillery CP and try to stay out of ev'rybody's way."

Daniel, listening politely, commented. "That beats work."

Andrews spoke, "This is Perdue. He's in my squad."

"Nice to meet you, Perdue."

"Matthews and me were in basic together."

"Where are you two headed?"

"Up the hill," said Andrews. "We're on the other side of the perimeter."

"I can give you a lift to the top of the hill. I'm carrying these water cans up to the CP at the top."

"Thanks."

Andrews and Daniel jumped in the jeep and found seats among the full water cans. Matthews drove up the hill, quickly passing the artillery positions beside the road. When the jeep stopped, Daniel and Andrews hopped off.

"Thanks for the ride, Matthews," said Andrews.

"Glad to do it. Stop by and see me if you can. I'm usually around the CP somewhere."

"I'll try. See ya."

Daniel and Andrews took only five steps before an incoming rocket screamed over the perimeter and slammed into the hill. Daniel raised himself from the mud and looked down the slope towards where the rocket hit, but he dropped to the ground again when a second rocket screamed overhead and crashed into the jungle just outside the perimeter. Daniel rose to his feet and looked down at the activity around one artillery position.

The first rocket scored a direct hit on the gun nearest the road, upending the gun, killing one soldier and wounding six others.

Daniel looked past the gun to the bottom of the hill where he and Andrews caught their ride. When he saw two men walk up the road to the destroyed gun position, he realized that the time and distance were about right: Had the two of them not caught a ride, had they walked up the hill, they would have been very close, if not actually right beside, the gun where the rocket hit when the rocket hit. A cold shiver ran up Daniel's back.

Daniel did not mention the possibility to Andrews, choosing instead not to consider the peculiarities of random chance. He preferred to use what good luck he had out in the boonies, where it really counted. Expending valuable luck to defend against incoming was, to the infantry, almost a waste.

In the jungle an infantryman's luck protected him from being hit by the first volley from people who saw him. Rockets came from people who could not see him, and so were governed by pure random chance, fate if you prefer.

In the jungle an infantryman survived by identifying sounds. Out there, knowing the difference between incoming and outgoing was more a matter of saving energy than saving life.

But on a fixed position, the sound of incoming was not a warning of approaching danger, it was a statement that danger had passed. Even if the sound was identified, and it always was, the ordinance exploded before anyone could react. The sound of the rocket screaming overhead was simultaneous with the explosion. Reaction was instinctive, but always too late. If that first round hit too close, it was just the chances of war. Even if the first round missed, it provided no warning or protection against subsequent incoming, for a foxhole provided no protection against a direct hit. All the men could do was stay near their holes and pray that the incoming landed somewhere, anywhere, other than in that hole.

For the infantry on the perimeter, night guard remained the time of greatest danger, if only because the darkness hid the base from the man on the perimeter, and because it afforded him the most time to think. Alone in the night, the soldier on guard on the perimeter sat and watched and listened for whatever might be in front of him, and, as always, wondered if this night was the night charlie would at last launch the ground assault.

Daniel sat on the edge of his foxhole and was grateful for the few coils of barbed wire between him and whatever might be in the jungle. Since charlie obviously knew where they were, Daniel hoped the enemy would be content with just firing rockets. Daniel did not want his guard to be disrupted by countless hordes of Viet Cong pouring out of the dark jungle.

Daniel listened to the artillery on the base fire all night and he wondered if they were firing at something in particular, or merely harassing areas where charlie might be. He also wondered if there were charlies out in the jungle somewhere who, like him, awaited the safety of the dawn.

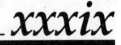

xxxix

The sun was just beginning to rise above the trees, casting long shadows across the Fire Support Base, when Sergeants Stovall and McDowd left first squad and walked up to Perez's position.

Stovall, who was more nervous than McDowd had ever seen him, spoke first, "Perez, call your people together."

Perez stood and shouted towards Daniel's position thirty yards away, "Perdue! Bring your people over here."

As Daniel picked up his rifle, he spoke to Andrews and Stentor, "Something's up, I can tell. Let's go." He led his team to Perez's position and squatted in the mud.

Stovall was as jumpy as a professional soldier could be. He knew he would be leaving soon and was terrified that his platoon of cherries would get him killed before he could rotate back to the States. He did not want to go on the mission he was about to announce to the squad and had tried his best to convince Captain Dunn to let some other platoon go instead, but Dunn knew that McDowd was the best soldier in the company and ignored Stovall's subtle pleas. Even though scared, Stovall was prevented by the unwritten, but understood, soldier's code from asking outright that he be excused.

He began, "The CO wants us to try to find the rocket position charlie's using to hit the perimeter. We'll be heading out as soon as the replacements get here to take over your holes. When they show up, report to the company CP. And for God's sake, don't fuck up out there."

Daniel tried unsuccessfully to stifle a laugh that occurred by reflex, for he believed, rightly, that Stovall was the one who made mistakes, that, were it not for McDowd, Stovall would have killed off the whole platoon months ago.

When Stovall heard the sound Daniel made and saw his efforts to hide it, he gave Daniel a hard, mean look that before the war would have terrified the boy.

"What's so fuckin' funny, Perdue?"

"Nothing, Sarge."

Stovall let the issue drop, but he made a mental note to get even with Daniel when he had the chance.

258

McDowd was sharp enough to understand the exchange and he decided to stop by and talk to Daniel after he and Stovall finished with third squad.

Daniel watched him walk up, "What's up, Sarge?"

"Step over here and have a cigarette."

"Sure, Sarge."

Away from Andrews and Stentor, McDowd spoke softly to Daniel, "How are the cherries doing?"

"As well as can be expected, for cherries."

"You weren't real smart a few minutes ago."

Daniel knew that McDowd was talking about his ill-timed laugh, "Yeah. It was pretty fuckin' stupid, but it slipped out before I could stop it."

"You know Stovall's pissed at you now."

"I wish he wasn't, but there ain't much I can do about it. Fuck, Sarge, you've been running this platoon ever since I got here, covering up for that incompetent fucker. When he told us not to fuck up, it just hit me as funny."

"He's short. He'll be rotating back to the States any day now."

"We'll be better off without him."

"That depends on who takes his place."

"Not to me. He never has liked me, not since the beginning. What did I do to him?"

"You remind him he has no education."

"How do I do that?"

"By being polite, well-mannered, and by using three syllable words. Fuck, Perdue, you look like a schoolboy."

"Because I wear glasses, right?"

"Partly. He once told me you were the smallest paratrooper he ever saw. He doesn't think boys as small as you should go airborne."

"Fuck him! I can do anything he can do."

"I know, but he doesn't. I had doubts about you myself, but Rose stuck by you and showed me I was wrong."

"I owe Rose alot. He was a helluva squad leader."

McDowd saw the chance to get Daniel's opinion of Rose's replacement, "Speaking of which, how is Perez doing?"

Daniel looked at the sergeant, unsure if he should say what he really felt, "The truth?"

"As you see it."

Daniel checked to be certain that no one else could hear him, "The fucker scares me to death."

"How?"

Daniel was hesitant to criticize, given the Army's nature.

McDowd put him at ease, "Just between you and me."

"He's not any good at making decisions. Back at the village the other day, he was too scared to think right. I don't get paid to run this squad, he does, but when the shit started flying, he just sat there."

"I figured that out myself."

"Who made him a squad leader, anyway?"

"The CO. Perez came back from the hospital with sergeant's stripes just when Rose went down. He filled the empty slot."

"The slot is still empty. I wouldn't mind it if he didn't get bent outta shape when I try to help him."

"I know the feeling. I sometimes had trouble with Stovall, but I've been in the army longer, so he finally took my 'advice'."

"Advice, Hell. You run the platoon."

"I only step in when it's important. You did the same thing in the flooded paddies."

"I had to."

"I know. But maybe you should limit your advice to those occasions when it's really important. If Perez screws up the little things, it doesn't matter. And I have a feeling that when it's really important, Perez wont't give you any trouble."

"Even when he fucks up guard assignments?"

"My advice to you is to let everything slide unless the bullets are flying."

"Thanks, Sarge. I'll take it. It won't be easy, but I'll try to keep my mouth shut unless there's bullets flying."

McDowd saw the replacements approaching, "It's time to head for the CP."

"I need to get my shit together and make sure the cherries are ready."

"You know, Perdue. If you were four sixes taller, you'd be a helluva soldier."

"I'm a helluva soldier now, Sarge. I'm a small target and big enough to pull a trigger."

"Be careful with Perez. I can't stop him from whipping your ass if you piss him off, but I can head off any bullshit he wants to make of your 'advice'."

"Thanks, Sarge. I've been avoiding getting my ass whipped since I was a kid."

"I imagine you have."

The platoon assembled at the company CP and waited for word to move out. When Stovall and McDowd finished with Captain Dunn, McDowd told Perez that his squad would be on point. That meant Daniel would, for the first time, walk point for the whole platoon. Daniel was proud that McDowd trusted him on point.

McDowd gave Daniel instructions, "We're heading that way. You keep your eyes peeled, Perdue. I'll keep you on course."

"Right, Sarge."

Daniel led second squad towards the barbed wire.

As they started walking, Stovall asked McDowd about Perdue, "Why do you have that little fucker on point?"

"Look around at all the cherries, James. He's the best we've got. We're better off with him out front than anybody else in this outfit."

"The smart-ass little fucker will prob'ly get us all killed."

"Ease up on him. He's doing the best he can with what he's got. Trust me on this one, James. The kid is a good soldier."

Stovall did not like to be told that Daniel was the platoon's best soldier. He could not accept that small men could be good soldiers, but then small men are often judged by their size rather than their ability.

As the platoon reached the barbed wire, Daniel turned to Stentor, who followed behind him with the machinegun, "Keep your eyes open, Stinky, and if I start shooting, you start shooting. Got it?"

"Got it."

Daniel remembered from his own experience that the jungle could distract cherries, "And remember to keep your mind on charlie. The jungle may be rough, but the jungle won't kill you. That goes for you, too, Andrews."

"My eyes are wide open."

Daniel led the platoon into the jungle and followed a course directed by McDowd. The terrain was rugged and the jungle dense, allowing the platoon to cover less than a thousand meters in two hours.

When an AK47 cracked, Daniel dropped to one knee and spun towards the sound of the gun. The zing of a bullet went by as he heard the AK47 fire again, so Daniel dropped to the prone position. Within seconds, McDowd was on the ground beside him.

"Can you spot him, Perdue?

"He's off that way somewhere, Sarge."

The enemy rifle cracked a third time and Morgan yelled.

McDowd shouted back, "Are you hit?"

Daniel kept looking for the sniper.

"No," called Morgan, "the fucker grazed my helmet. Scared the shit outta me."

"Stay low," ordered McDowd. "He might shoot straighter next time."

"Won't be nothing between me and the ground but buttons."

McDowd turned to Perdue, "I guess you and me have to find that sniper."

"I appreciate your confidence in me, Sarge, but how about asking for volunteers?"

McDowd laughed, "Now I know why Rose liked you. Let's go."

McDowd crawled forward and Daniel followed, willing to do what must be done and hoping to live through it.

They had crawled only fifteen yards when Morgan called out, "Sergeant McDowd! Sergeant Stovall wants you on the radio."

McDowd stopped and looked back, then spoke to Daniel, "What the fuck does he want?" He waved to Morgan that he was coming.

McDowd and Daniel crawled back to where Morgan lay flat against the ground. Morgan gave McDowd the handset.

"Camel Six, this is Camel Five. Over."

"This is Six. Pull back, I've called for airstrikes. Over."

A frown crossed McDowd's face, "Roger. Five out."

Daniel asked, "What's up?"

McDowd spoke to Perez, who lay on the ground behind Morgan, "Take your squad back and join up with Sergeant Stovall. I'll stay here with Perdue and cover you."

"Roger, Sarge." Perez crawled away and the squad followed.

McDowd spoke softly to Daniel, "Stovall called in airstrikes, of all things. Here we are less than a click from all the artillery in Viet Nam, and he calls for airstrikes. I had a feeling Captain Dunn never should have mentioned it. Let's get out of here."

Daniel followed McDowd to where Stovall huddled with his RTOs, then crawled on to rejoin his squad. McDowd kept the platoon in position in hopes of holding the attention of the sniper until the air force arrived. When the sniper did not fire for five full minutes, McDowd moved forward alone until the sniper fired at him, then returned to comparative safety.

After what seemed like an exceptionally long wait, a small single engine spotter plane flew over.

It's pilot called on the company frequency, "Camel Six, Camel Six. This is Eyepopper. Over."

McDowd answered, "This is Camel Five, Eyepopper. Over."

"Hello, Camel Five. Where are you and where are the hostiles? I've got two big birds loaded with eggs right behind me. Over."

"This is Camel Five. I'll pop yellow smoke to mark my position and throw red smoke towards the sniper. Add about five zero to the red and you'll be right on him. Over."

"Roger, Camel Five. I've got my eyes open. Go for it. Over."

"Here it comes, Eyepopper. Wait."

McDowd tossed a yellow smoke grenade a few yards in front of him, then hurled a red smoke grenade as far as he could towards the last known area where the sniper was. As the second grenade began billowing red smoke, two propeller-driven Skyraider bombers from the South Vietnamese Air Force flew over. The spotter plane circled around and fired signal rockets into the jungle close to where McDowd advised. Soon afterwards, the first of the Skyraiders dived towards the ground and dropped a bomb from each wing. The explosions rumbled through the trees, shaking the leaves on the bushes where the platoon waited.

"Eyepopper, this is Camel Five. Over."

"Go, Camel Five."

"The first run was right on the money. Keep dropping them in there and you've got him. Over."

"Roger, Camel Five. These fellows up here are Vietnamese and they don't speak American very well, but I'll keep them on target. Stand by."

Daniel and the others on the ground caught only fleeting glimpses of the planes as they passed over small gaps in the canopy, but the roar of their engines held the platoon's attention. When the second Skyradier made its run, its bombs were off target and came uncomfortabley close to the platoon.

"Eyepopper, this is Camel Five. Over."

"Go, Camel Five."

"This is Camel Five. Your boys came too close on that last run. I've got yellow smoke burning here, what else do I need? Over."

"This is Eyepopper. As best I can understand them, one of them says he's spootted the hostiles and they're going after them. Keep me advised. Over."

"You can count on that. Out."

The third bombing run of the first plane changed the platoon's situation completely. The bombs fell less than fifty yards from the platoon and threw shrapnal and shattered pieces of jungle onto the men. McDowd popped more smoke and ordered the platoon to move back, but the second plane dropped its bombs even closer.

"Eyepopper, this is Camel Five. Over."

"Go, Camel Five."

"What are those fools doing up there? If they come any closer to us, we'll be in big trouble here. Over."

"I roger that, Camel Five. I'm doing my best. Every time I tell them they're wrong, one of them repeats that he sees the target. Over."

What neither Eyepopper nor McDowd knew was that the target the Skyraider pilots saw was third platoon.

"Don't they know yellow smoke when they see it? Over."

"They're supposed to. Stand by."

When the next two bombs exploded so close that sheer luck prevented casualties, McDowd ordered a full and rapid retreat.

As Daniel hurried by McDowd, he spoke, "Hey, Sarge. I didn't sign up to shag bombs."

McDowd laughed, "If this keeps up, you may have to. Keep it moving, people."

Quite by accident, the retreating platoon came to a rare opening in the jungle, a long abandoned field used once by the *Montgnards* in their slash and burn agriculture. The men popped smoke all around the clearing and waited.

Daniel looked up and saw one of the Skyraiders diving straight at him. The image was frozen in his mind forever. He watched the bombs drop from the wings and followed them with his eyes until they sailed over his head. He hugged the ground as the double explosions shook the ground mightily and threw shrapnel and debris that tapped on his helmet.

"Eyepopper, this is Camel Five. Over."

"Go, Camel Five."

"You better figure out how to stop those flyboys or my men will open fire on them. It's at that point, Eyepopper. Do you understand that I will fire on them if they try that again? Over."

"I roger that, Camel Five, but it's unnecessary. They have expended their ordinance and are heading home. Over."

"We're lucky they didn't kill any of us. Are they always like that? Over."

"Beats me, Camel Five. This is the first time I've had to work with them."

McDowd rolled his eyes, his words were not directed to the radio, "My God."

Eyepopper continued, "I'm heading home myself. I'm glad I was able to help. Eyepopper out."

The platoon returned to the Fire Support Base without searching for the sniper. Or the rocket positions.

The company remained on the perimeter for two more days, then mounted choppers and flew back to Camp Radcliff. When Daniel flew over the base camp perimeter, he had seventy-two days left in his tour of duty.

Although the routine remained the same, many changes had occurred in the company area. All the tents were replaced by buildings of the common type; the upper half of every wall was screened. The layout of the company area was still the same, with the minor addition of rocks lining the walkways.

More important changes were among personnel. Captain Dunn, the CO, was gone, replaced by twenty-eight year old Captain Norman Alexander, who looked like a college professor. Lt. Meade, the XO, had been replaced by a capable young black First Lieutenant, Monte Jones. First Sergeant Everett went home, his job taken by 1Sgt Richard Greer, a lean, small black man. Wilkerson, the company clerk, was replaced by Dickie Memminger, heir to a plantation in Mississippi. Canella and Dunwoody rotated home, turning their positions over to Eldrique Madison, black, the new supply sergeant, and Robert "Never call me Bobby" Watson, a career commo sergeant who as a young man flunked out of the Massachusetts Institute of Technology. The only persons still in the company from the time when Daniel arrived were Sergeant McDowd, Perez, and two soldiers in first platoon who extended and were made sergeants.

The first order of business for the company when it reached its area was to turn in its ammunition. The exercise was supervised by Sergeant Madison, who was thirty-two years old and had thirteen years of army service. As the men dropped their ammo at the conex container behind the new supply building, Madison advised each in turn that a line to DX equipment would form as soon as the last bullet was safely locked away.

Daniel hurried back to the platoon barracks building and took off his boots and socks. He punched holes in the socks before turning the bayonet on his jungle fatigues, into which he made holes in the elbows and knees. He put his feet into his unlaced boots and walked back to the supply room with his socks in his hand. He was third in line.

When Daniel's turn came, Madison asked, "Just socks?"

"I need new fatigues, too, but I can't give them to you until I have some new ones to put on."

Madison looked at Daniel with the practiced eye of a career supply sergeant and pulled from nearby stacks trousers and a jacket that were the correct size for him.

"Here. You can change in the supply room."

"Thanks, Sarge, but I was hoping you'd give me time to take a shower and bring you the old ones afterwards."

Madison pondered the suggestion. Direct Exchange meant just that; delays were not in the regulations. He looked again at the soiled, malodorous fatigues that Daniel wore. No one could possibly want to steal those things.

"How long?" asked Madison.

"That depends on how long the shower line is, but I'll get them to you just as soon as I can. I promise."

"Get them back here ASAP."

Thus, after Daniel's cold water shower, he was able to dress in new fatigues and socks, a particular pleasure he learned from Rose, one to be enjoyed whenever the company came in from a long operation.

After weeks in the field, eating in the battalion mess hall was also a pleasure for Daniel. He enjoyed the atmosphere of a place designed for the consumption of food, following as it did countless meals from cans as he sat on the ground. He smiled as he watched Stentor, he of the enormous appetite, eat like he had not been fed in weeks. Stentor was still new enough to think the best thing about the mess hall was food. Neither he nor Andrews yet appreciated the table and benches, nor the tray upon which the food was served, things which were to Daniel much more enjoyable than the bland, if varied, A ration meals.

At 1800 hours the EM club opened. Daniel presided over a table that included Stentor, Andrews and Morgan, all of whom drank beer while Daniel savored his ice-cold stateside Coke. The conversation centered around girls and sex, highlighted by Stentor's admission that he was a virgin. Daniel was thankful he had kept his condition a secret when he heard the attempts at humor directed at the big farmboy. Stentor even came to approve of the nickname "Stinky" that Daniel had given him, when he realized that the alternative was "Virge", suggested by Morgan.

By the time Daniel finished his second Coke, the cherries were becoming inebriated, so he excused himself from the table, bought a third Coke at the bar, and returned to the peace and quiet of the platoon barracks building.

Only nineteen years old, Daniel could not know the reason why he was uncomfortable in the crowded, noisy club. He did not know that his senses, honed sharp on war's grindstone, were overtaxed by the confusion of sound and movement that characterizes large gatherings. Not yet having acquired a taste for beer, Daniel was without the numbing effects of alcohol, which dulled the senses and placated the killer instinct of those who could and did consume it, thereby allowing them to tolerate, even enjoy, the crowds in the EM club. Yet those who sought relief through alcohol while still so young, planted the seeds of alcoholism, which would flourish in the future among those warriors whose personalities found no place amid the tranquility of post-war America.

So Daniel was alone in the quiet, darkened platoon barracks. He sipped his Coke and reveled in the lack of stimuli, the absence of night guard duty, and the knowledge that any sniper outside the perimeter could not see him. At ease and comfortable on his cot, he thought about the next day's trip to town and about the working girl with whom he would visit. He fell asleep aroused and dreamed all night of naked girls.

The squad rode to Sin City together on the truck, but split up when only Stentor accepted Daniel's advice that every trip to town should begin at the barber shop. They formed an odd looking pair, what with the tall, muscular farmboy following wherever the diminutive Daniel led.

In the third bar they visited, Daniel found a girl who he hoped was cute enough to hold his interest even if she engaged in conversation with a co-worker while she was with him. Stentor waited patiently outside at a table, just as Daniel once waited for Rose.

The order had been given for all the soldiers to use protection when engaging the services of a business lady, and said protection was given to the men free of charge before they left for town.

When the girl pulled the curtain across the doorway, Daniel tossed the small foil package on the straw mat before sitting and removing his boots. He undressed rapidly, even though his attention was directed to the naked girl who lay beside him. Nudity itself excited Daniel, causing him to climb on top of the girl without remembering the foil package. The girl, interested in business, remembered, but the touch of her hands as she put in place the contents of the package excited Daniel so much that the numbing effects of the protection mattered to him not at all.

That evening Daniel stopped by the EM club only long enough to learn that it sold out of Cokes the night before. He bought a beer just to have something cold to drink and took it back to the barracks. For another evening, Daniel lay on his cot in an empty building, enjoying the serenity and the cold beverage, even though each sip tasted bad and caused him to frown. The beer affected him just enough to relax him and he fell asleep before the first man returned from the club. Daniel had seventy-one days left.

Morning came and with it word that Sergeant Stovall was going home. Unfortunately for Daniel, Stovall's last order was to assign him to latrine duty.

When Daniel walked around behind the latrine, a cherry from second platoon stood waiting, having been assigned to the duty without explanation. He was delighted when he saw a veteran arrive.

Having first stopped at the orderly room, Daniel tossed the one glove to the cherry before lifting the panel to expose the full drums under the latrine.

"You want to set up the cans or stir them?"

The cherry looked at the full cans and became slightly nauseous. He did not want to pull them out, but he did not know what stirring would be like. He gambled.

"I'll stir."

"Fine. Is that gas can full?"

The cherry walked over and picked it up, "No. It's almost empty." He looked around for another can.

"You'll have to take that over to the motor pool and fill it up with JP4. I'll have the drums set out before you get back."

"Where's the motor pool?"

Daniel pointed, "That way."

As the cherry wandered in search of the motor pool, Daniel replaced each of the drums under the latrine with an empty from the last burning. He finished long before the cherry returned and was waiting when Sergeant McDowd walked up with a young, chubby lieutenant.

"Lt. Hastings, this is Perdue. He's in second squad."

"Good morning, Perdue."

"Good morning, sir."

"The lieutenant is our new platoon leader."

Second Lieutenant Andy Hastings was a June graduate of the University of Iowa, where he was vice president of his fraternity and a cadet captain in ROTC. Andy was more comfortable as a frat officer than he was as an army officer, primarily because he was clumsy. He bumped into and tripped over things, having personally destroyed two lamps at the fraternity house and all the glasses that were on the dinner table the day he turned that over. Andy was clumsy because he was overweight, less so after some time in the army than when he was in school, and had been so from childhood. His reputation in the fraternity was sealed when he was a sophomore on the day a frat brother saw him trip and fall while walking across an empty basketball court. Andy knew he was the least agile officer in the army and he tried to make up for it with enthusiasm.

"Welcome aboard, sir," greeted Daniel.

The lieutenant was new, "What duty are you pulling here?"

"It's called 'burning the shithouse,' sir," answered Daniel.

Andy stepped forward and gazed into the nearest full drum, "I see." The breeze changed direction slightly and the officer's nose caught the smell full force. "Ooooh," came the sound from his mouth as he abruptly stepped back. "Carry on, soldier."

Daniel grinned, "Yes, sir."

"What's next, sergeant?"

"This way, sir. By the way, Perdue, we're moving out in the morning."

"You're not taking me away from all this, are you?" Daniel said as he waved a hand over the latrine drums.

McDowd smiled, shook his head at Daniel's humor, and led the officer away.

Daniel rested on the grassy knoll, the brigade chopper pad, and watched the cherries in the squad as he waited for the choppers that would take them on the operation. Even though baptized by fire in the flooded paddy, the new men still acted more like cherries than veterans. Enemy fire tested courage, but the instincts of a veteran developed slowly over weeks and months. McGee had begun to display the calm intensity of a veteran, and, to a lesser extent, so had Morgan, but Andrews and Stentor, especially Stentor, still lacked the awareness of one's surroundings needed to function in a combat zone. That lack of awareness was what made cherries dangerous, even ones who had faced hostile fire.

The Hueys came in four at a time and picked up the company. The formation flew eastward for a long time, heading into the morning sun, bound for the South China Sea. The choppers descended a mile inland over a vast area of sand, not jungle. As far as could be seen, everything was sand. Odd bushes and trees were scattered about, but everywhere there should have been dirt or grass, there was sand. Small villages, some only a few huts, were isolated one from another and all from the nearby sea by endless acres of roadless sand. One large fishing village, ten miles to the north, was located on a small bay, the far end of which was marked by a preeminent point jutting into the sea, at its top a four foot wide mesa fifty feet above the waves that crashed against its rocky base on three sides.

As the choppers approached the ground, Daniel reminded Andrews and Stentor to get off rapidly before he himself stepped out onto the skid. The Huey was still six feet above the sand when Daniel jumped, followed immediately by Stentor then Andrews.

The squad assembled by some bushes and waited for the platoon and company to get organized. A group gathered around Captain Alexander, the new CO, and studied a map. After a few minutes, Captain Alexander pointed north and the group split up.

Lt. Hastings returned from the meeting, shouted "Follow me," then started walking off in the direction of the march his platoon was to lead.

McDowd stopped him, "Sir! Usually one of the men takes the point."

"Oh? Very well."

"Perez, your squad leads."

Daniel asked, "Which way, Sarge?"

"Head towards that distant clump of trees."

"Roger, Sarge." Daniel turned to Stentor and Andrews, "You guys keep your eyes open."

Attending to his business, Daniel did not consider the significance of him leading the entire company through the sand. He was so young, so small, and so recently a cherry, yet now McDowd trusted him the same way the new company commander trusted McDowd.

Daniel scanned the horizon constantly, paying no attention to the difficulty posed by the sand. Walking in the soft sand was strenuous, for with each step the boot sank down and to the rear. Loaded with equipment, the cherries struggled from one ten minute break to the next.

The company marched in the sand until 1500 hours, covering only eight thousand meters, when they stopped and established a perimeter for the night.

The company had marched in column, making no effort to scout the area along the route, a situation that caused Daniel to wonder why the company had not landed at the new location in the first place.

McDowd placed the platoon in their positions on the perimeter and the men began to dig foxholes in the sand. The soft sand did not cooperate, for it fell into the holes, making them shallow depressions rather than straight-sided foxholes.

Lt. Hastings walked up, "Get that hole deeper, and straighten up those sides. That hole looks like Hell."

"Yes, sir," Daniel answered militarily, knowing the officer was ignorant of the situation.

Hastings walked on to the next position.

Stentor asked Daniel, "How in the Hell are we supposed to keep the sides from falling in?"

"Don't worry about what the fucker said. He hasn't started digging his own hole yet."

Stentor mumbled out loud, "Stupid officer."

"Being a cherry don't make a fucker stupid, it just makes him a cherry. Although I will admit he might be a cherry and stupid."

Lt. Hastings finished his "inspection" and returned to the platoon CP, where McDowd waited with orders.

"Sir, we've got orders to send out an ambush tonight."

"Send second squad. They're good."

"Whatever you say, sir."

McDowd walked to Perez's position. Perez left the foxhole digging to

Morgan and McGee while he rested and ate supper. Lt. Hastings had come by just as he finished his C rations, so Perez guessed that he was through with authority for the night and lay back to take a nap. He was asleep when McDowd walked up.

Morgan looked up from the hole, "Que passa, Sarge?"

"Ambush," replied McDowd, who then kicked gently the bottom of Perez's left boot.

"Hey, man!" said Perez before he saw McDowd. After, "Oh, Sarge. You want something?"

"Come along, Perez."

Perez picked up his rifle and followed McDowd to Daniel's position, where the platoon sergeant stopped and spread a map on the sand.

"What's up, Sarge?" asked Daniel.

"Ambush tonight. I'll show you where."

McDowd hovered over the map with Perez and Daniel on either side. Andrews and Stentor stood and looked over their shoulders.

"The perimeter is here," said McDowd as he pointed. "There's a village about five hundred meters west of here: there, the other side of this sand ridge. Set up the ambush so that you can spot anybody coming or going from this direction."

Perez looked at the map, but he did not know how to read it.

Daniel asked, "Do I get a compass, Sarge?"

"You won't need one. This village should be visible once you top that ridge."

"It'll take us a while to get there."

Leave about 1800, that should put you there about dark."

At six o'clock, Daniel led the squad from the perimeter and up the broad, low ridge. From the top Daniel could see the village. He chose the small cemetery in front of the village as the best ambush site, one that afforded cover behind the burial mounds and tombstones, and one that covered both major entrances to the village on this side.

Daniel led the squad straight to the cemetery, reaching it just before dark, as McDowd had predicted.

Perez asked, "Why are you stopping here?"

"This is the best ambush site."

Perez absolutely refused to spend a night in a cemetery, "No! No! Not here!" Perez thought quickly, seeking some way to direct Daniel's attention from his necrophobia. "There is a better place over there."

Perez quickly walked away from the graves in the direction that led him farthest away most rapidly, thinking not at all about a site for an ambush.

Daniel called after him, "Where are we going, Perez?"

Perez led them farther to the left, stopping after the cemetery and the entrance to the village on the right were both well out of sight.

"We set up here," Perez said as he pointed to a row of low bushes.

Daniel opened his mouth to speak, but he remembered the advice McDowd had given him about letting Perez have his way unless the bullets were flying. He closed his mouth and said a private prayer asking that nothing happen that night. Even when Perez announced a guard set up that kept only one man awake on guard, Daniel said nothing. He knew that the ambush now had no chance of success and disliked being outside of the perimeter for no reason, but he said nothing. Seventy more days to go.

Morning broke without incident and the squad returned to the company perimeter. The day was spent with the platoon on patrol searching a nearby village, then the company assembled at the end of the day at a new perimeter farther north.

That pattern continued for more than three weeks: platoon patrols every day, an ambush every third night, and a new perimeter every night. The infantry adapted to the sand but never liked it. Every day the footing wore down the men; every night the foxhole was but a shallow depression. Morgan's surfer songs, sung to discourage villagers, became repetitious.

The pattern remained unbroken until the company reached the large village on the small bay. For three consecutive days the company en masse searched the seaside houses, but on the fourth day third platoon was given the afternoon off to go swimming in the South China Sea.

Perez and some others who chose not to enter the water pulled guard on the dunes overlooking the beach while Daniel and the rest of second squad played in the water naked. Morgan taught them all how to bodysurf, and Daniel felt really clean for the first time since R&R.

When warm beer and Cokes were flown in with hot chow, the afternoon took on a holiday flavor. McGee and Andrews started a card game that eventually involved the whole squad, and the late afternoon was passed pleasantly drinking one beer and one Coke each, except for Daniel, who swapped his beer with Morgan for an extra Coke.

During the afternoon festivities, the company was visited by the brigade commander. Second squad never knew of his arrival nor departure, but the colonel's visit directly affected Daniel and the others.

While flying in, the colonel saw the sheer wall of the point at the north end of the bay, and on his flight out he decided that the First Cavalry Division should leave its mark on the area. He ordered that a volunteer who could paint be assigned to create on the cliff a six foot high unit patch, and he sent out the yellow and black paint needed for the job.

A qualified volunteer was found, a young black private who had studied art before being drafted, and second squad was detailed to provide security for the project.

Lt. Hastings was placed in charge, and early the following morning the small command marched the half mile, passing the village, to the point. The group stopped at the base and looked up at the cliff.

The artist, nicknamed Detro because he was from Detroit, turned to Hastings, "Sir, how am I supposed to get up there?"

Hastings had been briefed, even if he did not hear the question correctly, "You'll hang down from the top on a rope tied to your harness."

"How are we going to get up there to tie the rope?"

Hastings looked again at the cliff, which offered no obvious method of ascent, "I guess you'll have to climb up."

Detro was adamant, "Not me! Not without a rope!"

Hastings turned to the squad, "Can any of you climb the cliff?"

Daniel thought it might be fun, "I'll try, sir."

"Good! Now be careful."

"I'm always careful, sir."

Daniel dropped his equipment and slung his rifle over his head and shoulder. With his hands free, he stepped up to the sheer rock face and began climbing, using small finger grips and narrow edges for his toes, tiny steps not visible from a distance. Slowly he scaled higher and higher. About thirty feet up, still well short of the summit, Daniel reached a point where the one possible place for his next step was beyond his reach. He clung to the cliff and searched for another way, but there was none.

He called down to the lieutenant, "It's a dead end, sir."

"Come on down. We'll try another way."

Daniel started down, but his last step up was impossible going down. If he stretched for the narrow edge and missed it, he knew he would fall.

He called down again, "Well, sir. It looks like I'll have to go up. I can't get down."

"Be careful!" called Hastings.

Daniel gauged the distance to the next toe step, took a deep breath, and lunged up for it. He teetered on the edge, found a finger grip higher up, and steadied himself. From there on up, the steep cliff provided enough cracks and tiny ledges to enable Daniel to reach the top without much additional trouble.

When his hand reached the flat summit, Daniel turned to call down to Hastings. What he saw surprised him.

Just below him, hugging the cliff, was Lt. Andy Hastings, the army's clumsiest second lieutenant, with a huge coil of rope slung over his shoulder. Daniel scrambled to the top and reached a hand down to assist the officer.

"You shouldn't have tried this, sir. You coulda been killed."

Hastings struggled to the top, "I won't send my men anywhere I wouldn't go myself."

"Excuse me, sir, but that's movie shit. You could have gotten hurt bad. I barely made it myself."

"It was easy for me. I just followed the trail you blazed. Some of those steps were easier for me because my legs are longer. Wherever you put a foot, I put a foot."

"I'm proud of you, sir."

The compliment surprised Hastings, for officer training had led him to believe he would be the one doing the complimenting.

"Thank you, Perdue. You did a good job yourself."

"Thanks, sir. Now let's get that rope down and get my ammunition and your rifle up here."

"Good point."

Daniel took the rope from the officer and tied one end securely around one of the several boulders along the top of the mesa, then Hastings dropped the rope down to Morgan at the bottom.

The painting of the patch lasted all day and into the next. Daniel spent the work time with Detro at the top, eventually hanging down himself to paint solid color where the artist had outlined. Near midafternoon, the task was finished and the men descended to the ground.

As the detail packed up to head back to the company perimeter, Detro, Hastings and Daniel stood together and looked up at their accomplishment.

Hastings spoke, "You did a fine job, Detro."

"Thank you, sir."

"Yeah," agreed Daniel, "They'll be looking at that patch for years to come."

With the painting of the patch completed, the company resumed its previous pattern of spreading out on platoon patrols each morning and reassembling at a new perimeter each afternoon. The area of sand seemed to the infantry to stretch on endlessly, mile after mile, day after day, but the sand also was the base upon which some interesting geologically formations sat.

Third platoon encountered such a formation one day on its patrol. From a distance, a huge rock outcropping appeared to rise up from the sand behind the trees and bushes and reach up into the sky like a smaller version of Georgia's Stone Mountain. With the trees hiding its base, only the solid body of the giant rock mountain was visible, making it appear to be a domed monolith the shape of a loaf of bread.

When the men neared the formation, they saw that its base was surrounded by piles of giant stones, stacked on top of one another like gravel pushed against a curbstone, yet each individual stone was immense, some as much as twenty feet in diameter. Great gaps occurred between the rounded rocks, forming passageways and enclaves large enough for men, not only at ground level, but also up among the stones.

McDowd and Lt. Hastings stood together pondering the geological oddity.

Hastings spoke first, "It looks like Cong could hide in there, doesn't it, Sarge?"

"Yes, sir. I'll take a squad and check it out."

"Good. I'll spread out the other two to provide security."

McDowd called, "Perez! Bring your people over here."

Perez and his squad walked over to where McDowd and Hastings stood looking at the rocks.

"What do you want, Sarge?" asked Perez.

"We've got to clear those rocks. There could be charlies in there. And we'll have to check out the cracks up there, too. Who have you got that's a good climber?"

Hastings interrupted, "Perdue."

Perez agreed, "Yes, sir. Perdue."

McDowd looked at Daniel, "Can you climb those rocks, Perdue?"

Daniel studied the rocks for a moment, "I don't see why not, Sarge. Can I drop my gear?"

"Over there," ordered Hastings. "I'll keep an eye on it."

"Thank you, sir."

McDowd turned to Perez, "You and your people follow me."

As Daniel began climbing, McDowd led the rest of the squad into the groundlevel gaps in the rocks. McGee was the first to find evidence of people, the ashes of a small fire.

McDowd stepped back into the sunlight and called up to Daniel, "Perdue!"

"Yes, Sarge?" shouted Daniel.

"There's an old campfire down here. That means there have been people using this place. Watch out up there."

"Roger!"

Daniel leaped from rock to rock, looking into every crack and crevice big enough for a man, but he found no signs that humans occupied the area above the sand floor. He enjoyed climbing on the rocks and continued his search long after he was certain nothing was there.

When he began to tire, Daniel called down to McDowd, "There's nothing up here, Sarge!"

"Roger! Come on down!"

Daniel scrambled down from the rocks and walked over to McDowd.

"I appreciate that, Perdue," said the sergeant. "Those rocks could be treacherous in jungle boots."

"Not really, Sarge. I had fun."

McDowd smiled, "You would."

The company continued its daily trek north, eventually leaving the soft sand and entering an area where the sandy soil held together enough for grass to grow. Rice paddies and grassy trails surrounded the villages. The sandy soil also was firm enough to permit the natives to maintain bunkers, the entrances to which loomed as black holes in the Earth that led to the unknown.

Second squad was the first to encounter the ominous holes.

Daniel called to Perez, "Hey, Carlos. Come look at this."

Perez walked over and gazed into the void, "Is it a tunnel?"

Every soldier in the country had heard of the tunnels charlie had dug around Saigon, tunnels supposedly large enough to drive trucks through and containing enemy troops by the battalion.

"I don't know," answered Daniel.

"Check it out," ordered Perez.

"Me?"

Benny, having been in the coal mines of West Virginia with his father, had always been the man in the squad who investigated holes. Daniel had never done it, but he knew from watching Benny that the holes in villages were almost always bunkers used by the villagers for protection against the war's explosive intrusions.

Perez waved his hand towards the remainder of the squad, "Who else?"

Daniel looked at the cherries and realized that he was, indeed, the one to do it. He answered fatalistically, "Okay."

Perez breathed a private sigh of relief. He was not at all sure what he would have done if Daniel had refused.

Daniel spoke to Stentor, "Give me your forty-five."

The machinegunner pulled his handgun from its holster and handed it to Daniel, who pulled back the bolt and chambered a round.

"Be careful," offered Morgan.

Daniel looked at Perez, "If I'm not back in five minutes, send three naked nurses to look for me."

Perez began, "Where would I find. . . ."

Daniel interrupted, "It was a joke, Perez. A joke."

Perez did not laugh, but Morgan did.

Daniel spoke again, "You know I'm too fuckin' short to be crawling in holes?"

Perez shrugged his shoulders.

Daniel dropped to his knees and flipped off the weapon's safety, knowing he had no intention of starting a firefight underground. If he ran into anything, he planned to scramble out as fast as he could and suggest grenades.

On his hands and knees, Daniel slowly entered. A few feet in from the entrance, he paused to allow his eyes to adjust to the reduced light. The tunnel remained dark and foreboding and he wished that someone in the squad still had a flashlight. He could see that the tunnel curved to the right a few feet in front of him, but he did not know whether the tunnel continued beyond the curve or opened into a bunker.

"With any luck   at all," Daniel said to himself, "this thing is empty. Please be empty."

With his handgun at the ready, he crawled towards the curve and hoped that no one heard him coming. He peered around the corner and saw only the absence of light. Daniel knew he would need light to go any further, so he reached with his free hand and pulled his plastic cigarette case from his shirt pocket. He stuck the case in his mouth and pulled it apart, then tapped the matches out onto the dirt. He pushed the case together before removing it from his mouth and putting it back in his pocket. With his one free hand, he bent down one match, closed the cover and struck the match.

Someone spoke in Vietnamese!

Daniel tossed the matches forward as he dropped to his stomach, both hands clasping his gun.

The voice spoke again and a figure moved forward.

"*Dung li!*" shouted Daniel.

The person stopped, barely visible in the faint light of the one match. It was a six year old child.

Daniel breathed an audible sigh of relief and backed out, calling to the child, "*Li di.*"

Daniel appeared at the entrance fanny first, crawled out backwards and sat on his knees.

Perez asked, "What's going on?"

And Morgan, "Are there Cong in there?"

"See for yourself," said Daniel. Then to the child, "*Li di.*"

The child that came out of the hole was a girl, followed by a boy about the same age and a toothless old woman.

"Is that all?" asked Perez.

"How should I know. I only saw the first one of them."

"Check it out," ordered Perez.

"Whatever you say."

The old woman squatted near the hole and smiled warily at the Americans, while the two kids huddled with her at her insistence, more for them to comfort her than for her to comfort them.

"Anybody got matches?" asked Daniel. "I left mine in there."

Andrews pulled out a book of matches and gave them to Daniel, who opened it and bent back the cover before folding down one match. Now prepared, Daniel crawled into the hole for the second time. When he reached the dark passageway beyond the curve, he struck the match and bent it up against the others. As the book started to blaze up, Daniel tossed it ahead as far as he could. The fire lit up a small bunker, four feet wide, six feet deep and four feet high. It was empty.

Daniel backed out. At the entrance, he spoke to Perez, "That's all of them."

Perez looked at the three Vietnamese, "What do we do with them?"

The pleasant, if toothless, smile of the old woman was a product of fear, but the kids smiled out of genuine interest in the newcomers to their isolated village.

"Leave 'em alone," advised Daniel.

Stentor reacted to their smiles, "They must be glad to see us."

"Why?" asked Morgan.

"Look at them smile at us."

Daniel corrected the cherry, "They're not smiling at us, Stinky. They're smiling at our guns."

"At our guns?"

"If strange men loaded down with guns showed up at your house, wouldn't you smile?"

"Probably," agreed Stentor.

"They smile at charlie the same way."

xliii

The company spent the next three weeks searching villages in the area. Daniel spent those three weeks crawling in holes.

During that time, Daniel passed the magic Thirty, less than a month left in country. He remembered Wilson's comment when he reached that number, "I'm so short I can sit on a dime and swing my legs."

When the company at last returned to Camp Radcliff, only twenty days remained in Daniel's tour.

Base camp barely resembled the primitive facility that it was when Daniel first saw it. All the tents were gone, and the roads were all paved or so oiled and packed that they appeared to be paved. All the barracks had dependable electric lights, lights that stayed on too late every night.

As Camp Radcliff became more and more civilized, the garritroopers who worked there knew less and less about the war itself. When they saw infantry coming or going, they were awed by the appearance and weapons. Only then were they reminded that there was, indeed, a war out there, somewhere out there beyond the barbed wire.

The conveniences of base camp made the time pass quickly for Daniel, who hoped that the company would remain in base camp until it was time for him to leave. Perhaps he would be lucky and the company would be put on base camp perimeter duty for the remainder of his days. With the caution of a true short-timer, he even declined an opportunity to go to Sin City, for he did not wish to be outside the perimeter without his rifle.

The company stayed in camp only three days before moving out again and returning to the same sandy area along the coast in which they operated before. With only seventeen days left, Daniel did not mind the sand, just as he would not have minded the jungle, or even flooded rice paddies. The nature of the terrain no longer mattered to him, for physical exertion no longer mattered to him. His mind had adapted; he was comfortable in the boonies. The learning process had been slow, but now he was the elder veteran, accustomed to the unique lifestyle of the combat soldier. He was not consciously aware that his eyes saw every movement, or that his ears heard every sound, or that his mind instantly analyzed every sitmulus. All he knew was that he was a veteran, comfortable with a loaded rifle in his hands, comfortable in an environment where his controlled intensity was of use. He did not know that at age nineteen, he was as old as McDowd, old long before his time.

As a veteran, Daniel took no chances, but he did what had to be done without fear, for now only bad luck was his enemy. He could do the things necessary to protect himself, but, in the end, fate controlled his destiny, just as it controlled the destinies of all warriors. Daniel could exercise caution, but random chance would determine where the sniper fired and where the incoming fell. War was the act of challenging the odds, and having to let it ride every time.

When the company flew out of base camp, Daniel made a conscious effort not to think about home. With only seventeen days left, he was growing more excited, but he did not want to get killed because he was thinking about going home when he should have been thinking about charlie.

The third evening of the operation, second squad was assigned an ambush along the beach only four hundred meters from the company perimeter. Daniel paid close attention when Lt. Hastings informed Perez that the company had with it an artillery Forward Observer and that artillery support was available for the asking.

At dark Daniel led the squad across the sand into the dunes near the beach. He selected a site atop a dune that was perfect for the ambush, even to the point of having a natural depression at the top which would serve as squad foxhole. The dune was forty meters from the high water mark and twenty feet above it. There was no moon, but the starlight reflected off the white sand and made the beach visible. As the squad settled in, Perez called the company and gave the exact location of the ambush.

Then Perez addressed the squad, "Perdue, you take the first watch, Stinky the second, Andrews third, McGee, Morgan, and me last. Each man will watch for an hour and a half."

Daniel again faced a situation where Perez ignored the basic principles of the ambush in favor of the convenience of all six squad members being on the same position.

Daniel cautioned Perez, "There ought to be two of us on guard at the time."

"You worry too much because you are short."

"Whatever you say, Perez."

Daniel got into position and studied the beach while the rest of the squad went to sleep. He listened to the waves break on the beach, watched up and down the shore, and thought about going home. He

smiled in anticipation: only fourteen days to go; two weeks; one fort-
night. Having such pleasant thoughts, his ninety minutes passed
quickly. He woke Stentor, then stretched out on the sand, using his
bedroll as a pillow. He looked at the stars and thought about how
different his life back in the world would be now that he has a man. But
he thought mostly about being away from the war, as far as possible
away from the war. He fell asleep with a smile on his face, and the
thought "only fourteen days to go" on his mind.

Suddenly, he was wide awake! Even in his sleep, his mind reacted to
the hollow thump of McGee's grenade launcher. He was up and beside
McGee before the grenade exploded on the beach.

"Where are they, McGee?"

McGee pointed far to the right, beyond where the explosion was,
"They were there!"

Everyone was up!

Perez asked, "What are you shooting at?"

Daniel pointed, "You'll have to ask McGee."

Perez stared at McGee, "What?"

McGee's voice was higher because of his excitement, "There was a
bunch of gooks walking on the beach."

Perez was angry, "Why didn't you wake us?"

McGee answered weakly, "I saw 'em and just started shooting."

Perez now feared he might be in trouble for not establishing guard
properly, "Fucker, we're all supposed to shoot together. Goddamn
cherry!"

Daniel added, "That's why they call it an ambush."

Morgan spoke, "Perez, the CO wants you on the radio."

Daniel smiled, glad that it was not he who must explain why a six
man ambush failed to stop any of a group of people walking exposed on
the beach.

Perez took the handset from Morgan, "This is Camel Two. Over."

"This is Fullback Six. What's going on out there? Over."

"We made contact. Over."

"Describe the action. Over."

"A group of charlies walked by in front of us. Over."

"Any hostile KIAs? Over."

Perez looked at Daniel, "He wants to know if there were any charlies
killed."

McGee spoke up, "I saw one of them fall when the grenade exploded,
but two of them grabbed him and drug him away."

Perez now had an answer, "Fullback Six, this is Camel Two. We can't
say. Charlie took the ones we hit with him. We hit some of them,
though. Over."

"Good work, Camel Two. Do you know which way they went? Over."

"He wants to know where they went."

Daniel offered an answer, "If they were headed that way, they're probably in those rocks down there." He pointed to the rocks at the base of a hill a thousand meters to the south.

"This is Camel Two. We think they might be in the rocks south of us. Over."

"Can you spot artillery? Over."

"I haven't seen any. Over."

Perez did not hear the company commander laugh, "No, Camel Two. I mean can you direct artillery fire on the location? Over."

"He wants to know if we can direct artillery."

"I can," said Daniel.

"Roger, Fullback Six. I have a man here who can do it. Over."

"Roger, Two. Is it Two India? Over."

"Negative. He used to be India, but ain't now. Over."

"Roger, Two. He will be identified as Two Xray. Artillery Foxtrot Oscar will be Bird dog. Do you roger? Over."

"Roger. Over."

"Wait one for Bird dog."

Perez spoke to Daniel, "The artillery FO is Bird dog. You're Camel Two Xray. Here." He held the handset out for Daniel to take.

Daniel took it and spoke softly to Morgan, "Listen carefully to how this is done. When I'm gone, it'll be up to you."

"Have you directed artillery before?"

"Negative. But I've heard how it's done."

"Camel Two Xray, this is Bird dog. Over."

"This is Two Xray. Go Bird dog."

"This is Bird dog. I have a map and I know your location. Where do you want the spotter round? Over."

"This is Two Xray. South of my position about one zero zero zero you should see a hill. Over."

"Roger, Two Xray. I have the hill. Over."

"They should be in there somewhere. Drop your spotter round on the hill and I will adjust. Over."

There was a long pause.

"Roger, Two Xray. Wait."

Daniel watched the rocks at the base of the hill and waited. In little more than a minute, the radio squawked again.

"Camel Two Xray, this is Bird dog. Spotter round on the way. Over."

"On the way. Wait."

Daniel stared at the hill far to the south and saw the flash of the exploding artillery shell.

"Bird dog, this is Camel Two Xray. Over."

"Go Xray."

"Right one zero zero. Add five zero. Over."

"Roger. Wait."

A few more seconds passed.

"Two Xray, this is Bird dog. On the way. Over."

"On the way. Wait."

Another flash indicated the gun was on target.

"Right on the money, Bird dog. Fire for effect. Over."

"Roger, fire for effect. Wait."

In a few seconds, the side of the hill facing the squad lit up with the flashes of explosions and shook under their bombardment, the sounds of which rumbled up the beach. Daniel watched the shells explode and felt strange, for he knew that he had directed that particular bombardment, that he had brought down death on whoever might be in that area. Daniel was sobered by the thought that he could cause so much destruction while in no danger himself, and he wondered if artillerymen ever got used to it.

The bombardment continued for several minutes. Soon after it stopped, the radio squawked.

"Camel Two Xray, this is Bird dog. Over."

"Go Bird dog."

"How did we do? Over."

"I wouldn't want to have been down there. Over."

"Roger, Two Xray. You did good. If anything else happens out there, remember I'm here. Over."

"Roger, Bird dog. I'll remember. Over."

"Bird dog out."

Daniel gave the handset to Morgan, then turned to Perez, "That's the end of that. Can I go back to sleep now?"

As he crawled to his bedroll, Daniel heard Morgan on the radio.

"This is Two India, Five. Wait."

Daniel looked at Morgan, but it was Perez who asked, "What does Sergeant McDowd want?"

"He wants to talk to Two Xray."

Daniel crawled to the radio, "Camel Five, this is Camel Two Xray. Over."

"Congratulions, Xray. You performed admirably. Over."

"Why thank you, Five. I do my best. Over."

"I appreciate it. This is Five. Out."

Daniel returned the handset to Morgan, "That was nice of McDowd."

Morgan asked, "What was?"

"He called just to congratulate me on doing a good job."

"You sure sounded like you knew what you were doing."

"Just keep your cool and attend to business, Morgan. It's not magic or anything."

Daniel crawled to his bedroll and stretched out. He looked at his watch: one thirty in the morning.

"Thirteen days."

xliv

The last few days in the boonies were days of mixed emotions for Daniel. The feeling of happiness that grew inside him as each day passed was tempered by the fear that death, which he had eluded for almost a year, would now take him at the very end of his tour. A conflict arose within him, the veteran soldier feeling confident and capable, while the short-timer was cautious and afraid. Daniel had made the mental and emotional adjustments needed to survive in war and he used his experience for the benefit of the squad, but that same experience required that he assume the most dangerous tasks. Daniel walked point, not because he wanted to, but because his skills on point most benefited the squad; he searched the holes, not because he wanted to, but because he was most likely to avoid harm should something be found.

Daniel took no chances. Anything that was not army green was a potential danger. He was extra wary of Veitnamese civilians in the villages, whether adults or children, for he could not know which were innocent pawns of war and which were dedicated Viet Cong. He was just too short to gamble, yet he challenged the odds every day that he remained in the boonies. Each day that he survived lessened the odds against him, and each day brought him that much closer to beating those odds.

During daylight hours, Daniel concentrated on the duties and dangers, but on guard at night, in the silence, his thoughts took him home, back to the America he had grown to appreciate during his year away. He thought about the little pleasures: streetlights, flush toilets, milk shakes and hamburgers. And he thought about peace, that idyllic realm where snipers did not exist, where rockets never fell, where a watchful eye and a wary mind were unnecessary. Only nine days to go.

Daniel's reverie was interrupted by unusual sounds out in the darkness in front of his position.

"Oh, shit," he said softly as he reached back to shove Andrews and Stentor.

Mortar rounds whistled overhead! Two, three, four shells exploded inside the small perimeter!

Both cherries were awakened by the explosions, but only the quicker Andrews made it to the shallow hole before the muzzle flashes of enemy weapons lit up the sand in front of the position.

Daniel opened fire on the muzzle flashes, ignoring the constant zing of bullets passing near him. He emptied his magazine and jammed in a fresh one as Andrews' M16 and Stentor's machinegun opened fire. More bullets zinged by! Daniel fired at the flashes in front of him as other weapons around the perimeter echoed through the night. He emptied a second magazine and reloaded as the enemy fire kicked up sand around him. Daniel emptied a third magazine as more explosions rumbled around the Americans. More bullets zinged by and more sand was kicked up.

Daniel kept firing, one magazine after another, oblivious to all that occurred around him, until the muzzle flashes in front of his position ceased.

Then all was quiet. A moment of stillness hung over the sand. Every soldier waited and listened, and hoped that it was over.

When voices behind him broke the silence, Daniel looked away from the area from which the enemy fire had come and checked on his two cherries. On his left, Andrews lay flat, his finger still on the trigger of his rifle, trembling with the warrior's fear of danger passed. On Daniel's right, Stentor lay motionless, his face in the sand.

Daniel reached and put his hand on Stentor's shoulder, "Stinky?"

Stentor did not move.

Andrews asked, "Is Stinky okay?"

In the dim starlight, Daniel saw that Stentor's helmet was in the sand behind the motionless cherry. His hand felt the warm fluid spread across Stentor's shoulders and his eyes focused on the back of the big farmboy's head.

"Andrews, call the medic. He's dead."

"Dead?"

"Yeah. Hey, Perez! We've got a casualty over here!"

Andrews could not accept it, "Stinky's dead?"

Daniel calmly pulled the magazine from his rifle and replaced it with one he knew was full, "Yeah."

Andrews began to shake violently, a combined reaction to the intensity just passed and the awareness that he, instead of Stentor, could have died.

Daniel remained calm, "At ease, Andrews. Everybody dies sooner or later."

Daniel, the veteran, was learning his last lesson from war. Reinforced were the feelings of cold, harsh fatalism he first felt when he heard about Rose. His mind was numbing to the death that affected his life. The war taught him that people die, no matter how much you like them, no matter how unfair the circumstances. Daniel was now immune to pain, cold, heartless, almost sadistically indifferent.

Perez scrambled over to the position, "Morgan's calling for the medic. Who was hit?"

"Stinky," replied Daniel.

"How bad?"

"He's dead."

"Are you sure?"

"The back of his head is gone."

Daniel, Perez and Andrews sat in silence until the medic finished tending the wounded and came to see Stentor.

"There's nothing I can do for him," said the medic unemotionally as he pulled a tag and pen from his bag. He took a small flashlight from the bag and looked carefully at Stentor's dogtags, then wrote something on the tag and hooked it around a button on the dead man's shirt. "Two of you want to carry him to the LZ?"

"I will," said Andrews.

"Me, too," volunteered Perez.

As Stentor's body was carried away, Daniel was left alone to watch the black of night become the gray of morning. He would never understand the mysteries of war, how random chance spared him, but not the man right beside him. Another emotion worn ragged by overuse was pushed firmly out of Daniel's consciousness, ever to fester quietly in his soul, hidden not only from those who might someday meet him, but also from his own awareness.

Activity picked up around the LZ when the first chopper came in to carry away the wounded. As the officers moved about and heard the individual stories about the firefight, the totals came in: two KIAs, Stentor and one of the men in first platoon who had extended; five WIAs, mostly from first platoon.

Soon the company would be organized and the search for slain enemy would begin.

Perez returned from the LZ with Andrews, "Perdue, they want you at the CP."

"What for?"

"They didn't say."

Daniel assumed it had something to do with Stentor, "Watch my shit. I'll be right back."

He picked up an extra magazine and walked through the sand to the company Command Post. The LZ was filled with people and activity. The battalion commander flew in on one of the first choppers, along with his entourage. The usual CP people were reinforced by the crowd from battalion, and even a few from brigade, but few of them had anything to do other than to stand around and look important. Everyone was subdued because of the two KIAs.

Daniel approached one of the new company RTOs, "My squad leader said I was wanted here."

"Are you Perdue?"

"Roger."

"You're rotating out this morning."

Daniel's lower jaw fell open. He could not believe his ears, "Say again?"

"You're going home. Get your gear and report back here."

"You're not kidding?"

"No. Now move out."

Daniel walked back to his position in a daze. The year had lasted a lifetime, the months had crawled by, the days had seemed endless, but now it was over. All that was left for Daniel was to get out of the country alive.

At the position, Perez asked, "What did they want?"

"I'm going home."

Andrews perked up, "You lucky fucker."

"I'm supposed to get my gear and report back to the CP."

"You don't seem too happy about it."

"It hasn't sunk in yet."

Daniel knelt down to gather his equipment, but when he saw the bloody remains of Stentor's brain lying in the blood stained sand, he stopped and casually covered them with sand.

Andrews brought him back to reality, "Can I have your magazines, Perdue?"

"Sure."

Daniel dropped the spare magazine in the side pocket of his trousers and gave all the rest to Andrews. Then he picked up his gear and walked away.

There was no dramatic scene when Daniel parted from the squad that had been his family for a year. None of them thought about going home, for all their thoughts were about the big, friendly farmboy who had died in the sand.

The moment Daniel walked away, he stopped being a part of their war. It was over for Daniel, no less than if peace were declared and all the armies disbanded and sent home. He was no longer a part of their world, and the void he left behind would be filled by some new cherry, who would come and grow to manhood just as Daniel had. The squad would continue as before, the patrols and ambushes would continue as before, night guard would continue as before.

Only for Daniel was the war over.

He walked back to the CP and sat down to wait for the chopper that would start him on his journey home. He waited patiently, for the minutes meant nothing after a year of anticipation.

Not far from where he sat lay the bodies of the two men killed before dawn. They were wrapped in ponchos, but Daniel knew that the larger of the two was Stentor. He gave the cherry one final hand salute, knowing it could so easily have been him lying there in the sand.

Daniel heard a chopper in the distance as the RTO came up to him. "That's your chopper," he said. "Get your shit together."

"Roger."

The chopper flew in low over the trees and settled in the clearing. As four cherries jumped off and ducked under the whirling blades, Daniel ran into the blowing sand for the last time. He climbed aboard and leaned back, wondering if Stentor and the other KIA would be put on the same chopper. Someone on the LZ signaled the pilot and the chopper's engine roared. The Huey lifted off the ground with Daniel as its only passenger.

Daniel could hardly believe that he was really going home. He looked down and saw the wind from the chopper blow the poncho off Stentor.

The Huey flew straight to Camp Radcliff. Daniel gazed down upon the elaborate perimeter and the surroundings that were once so new and strange, but now familiar. He knew he would leave a part of his life here.

The chopper sat down at the brigade pad and Daniel walked alone to the company area. He crossed the footbridge and entered the Orderly Room.

"Here I am."

The new company clerk looked up from his typewriter, "Who are you?"

"Perdue."

"Right," said the clerk, recognizing the name. "You're going home tomorrow."

"Those are beautiful words."

"Let me have your rifle and ammo."

Daniel gave the clerk his M16 and the two magazines.

"Is this it?" asked the clerk.

"Roger."

"No grenades and stuff?"

"I left that 'stuff' in the boonies."

"Your plane leaves for Pleiku at 0800. You're free 'till then, but I suggest you hide."

"Thanks, I will. See you in the morning."

Daniel took a cold shower before noon chow at the battalion mess hall, then spent the afternoon hiding from the new first sergeant. In the evening he watched a movie at the new outdoor theater near brigade headquarters. On the way back to the barracks, he stopped by the EM club, but it was closed.

When Daniel returned to the platoon barracks, he tried to sleep, but his was too excited. His thoughts jumped back and forth between home and the fight last night. He thought about girls, and hamburgers, and muzzle flashes in the dark. Eventually, he fell asleep, only to toss and turn and dream all night.

Awake before dawn, Daniel dressed and went to the Orderly Room. The clerk was busy typing the morning report and did not look up.

Daniel asked, "What time is chow?"

The clerk spoke as he glanced up, "They start serving at seven." He saw Daniel's ragged jungle fatigues. "You can't go home dressed like that. Don't you have khakis?"

"All my uniforms rotted away long ago."

"Do you have any civvies?"

"I've got a shirt and a pair of trousers I wore back from R&R. But they've been wadded up in my duffle bag since August."

"You'll have to wear them."

"They look like shit."

"You can't wear jungle fatigues. Regulations."

Daniel had not worried about his appearance for almost a year, and he was too excited about going home to start caring.

"Is after chow okay?"

"I don't care. As long as you're out of those jungle fatigues before we leave."

Daniel left the Orderly Room and walked across the footbridge towards the battalion mess hall. His grin was so wide that it caught the cook's attention.

As he served Daniel's breakfast, he said, "You must be going on R&R."

"Better."

"Better than R&R?"

"I'm going home today."

"You lucky fucker."

After chow, Daniel went back to the platoon barracks and put on the wrinkled, mildewed civilian clothes. He carried his empty dufflebag to the Orderly Room. The clerk looked up.

Daniel tossed the dufflebag on the desk, "You want this?"

"Don't you need it?"

"I'm wearing everything I own."

"You don't have anything?"

"Nope."

"Was your stuff stolen?"

"These civvies are all I had."

The clerk found that hard to believe, but saw no reason to worry about it. "Let's go, then."

"I'm with you."

Daniel follow the clerk to a jeep and rode with him to the airstrip. A crowd of garritroopers stood around a sergeant with a clipboard. Daniel stepped from the jeep, said goodbye to the clerk, and walked over to the sergeant.

"Is this the place, Sarge?"

"What's your name?"

"Perdue, Daniel."

The sergeant searched the manifest, "Right. Perdue. This is the place."

"Thanks."

All the others in the manifest were garritroopers with whom Daniel had nothing in common but going home. His war had been different than theirs.

Only a few minutes passed before a C130 landed and taxied to a stop. The rear ramp lowered and the men walked on the plane. The ramp closed up behind them and the C130 taxied around and took off. The ride was rough and bumpy, causing several of the garritroopers to get sick. The ride was sheer joy for Daniel, for he was going home.

The plane landed at Pleiku and the rear ramp lowered. As the passengers deplaned, a sergeant with a clipboard called to them.

"Wait over there by the building. The next C141 that lands is yours."

A C141 was a large jet cargo plane that, when fitted for passengers, had seats facing the rear.

Daniel walked to the building, sat down and leaned against the wall. He closed his eyes to savor the unparalleled joy of the moment, but his mind's eye saw Stentor lying in the sand. Daniel opened his eyes and stood.

The garritroopers with Daniel on the C130 were joined by clerks, truck drivers and one infantryman. He walked over to Daniel.

"Got a match?"

"Sorry. I used my last one waiting for the plane at An Khe."

"Those garritroopers are too much. I just had to get away from them."

"I heard some of their shit on the plane ride here."

"Three of them are convinced they won the war all by themselves.

What a crock a shit. I'm fucking desperate for a cigarette. I gotta find a match. See you later."

The soldier walked away and again Daniel was alone. His eyes gazed at the eastern horizon, the direction from which the C141 would come. He wanted to see it as soon as possible, so he would have more time to enjoy this dramatic moment in his life's story. He wanted to say something profound, something befitting the situation, but no one was there to hear him, no one was there to listen to the perfect phrase that never came to his mind. Daniel stood alone, in silence, and waited. The dramatic phrase did not come. The plane did.

Daniel saw the tiny speck of silver far in the distance and his heart throbbed. The speck moved slowly, always coming closer, always growing larger. The speck became a plane. The plane became a C141.

At last one of the garritroopers saw it, "There it is!"

The group cheered.

That was Daniel's plane, his ride home. He still could not believe this was really happening. His chest knotted up and butterflies flew in his stomach. An uncontrolable grin spread across his face. There is no greater happiness.

The C141 flew closer and Daniel could hear its engines.

Everything began happening too fast, too fast for those who wished to enjoy the grandness of the event.

The plane touched the runway and sped by. It slowed down at the far end of the runway and turned around. It taxied to the building and, with one last roar of its engines, came to a stop.

The high-pitched whine of idling jet engines filled the area near the plane. A side door opened and the crew chief hopped out. Behind him came a stream of cherries just arriving to began their tours.

The sergeant with the clipboard yelled, "Let's move it!" and led the veterans towards the C141. When his line met the line of cherries heading toward the building, he turned around and led the new men away from the plane.

Last in his line, Daniel watched the cherries pass. Their eyes were wide with excitement, just as Daniel's eyes had been those many months before. The year was just beginning for the cherries. The war went on.

Daniel reached the door and hopped on, but he stopped in the doorway and looked back.

"Get on in and find a seat, soldier. You're holding us up."

Daniel smiled at the crew chief, "Roger."

He found a seat, buckled the seatbelt and waited. Endless minutes passed before the crew chief finally closed the door.

When the engines revved and the aircraft began to move a tremendous cheer filled the huge cabin.

Daniel sat quietly and smiled as the plane taxied down the runway, turned around, and stopped.

There were no windows in the C141 and the passenger seat faced the rear. A captive of sounds, Daniel would fly home backwards, unable to see the country fade in the distance as he had once watched it rise to meet him.

The words came involuntarily from Daniel's mouth, "Dear God, please make charlie leave this fucker alone."

The engines roared and the great white silver bird shook and strained. The pilot released the break and the plane lurched forward. The giant aircraft bounced and jerked as it roared down the runway. When the bumping stopped, the plane was in the air.

The passengers, including Daniel, cheered the moment so loudly that their noise briefly drowned out the sound of the engines.

Daniel spoke to himself, "Snipers could still hit this thing."

The plane climbed higher and higher.

"I'm going home!"

Up and up.

Daniel had made it. The war was over at last.

He was going home, November 18, 1966, to a new and better life. Or so he hoped.